The Three Graces

Michele Wolfe

Published by 4Word Press, LLC.

Published in the USA by:
4Word Press an Imprint of
4Word Press LLC.
4Word Publishing, 15130 Dickens Street, Suite
105Sherman Oaks, CA 91304 USA

4Word Press Is a legal imprint of 4Word Press LLC. any
and all printed, electronic work, designs pertaining to
4Word Press are property of 4Word Press LLC.

The Three Graces
Copyright © 2014 Michele Wolfe
Cover Art Designed by Najla Qamers Designs

Print: 978-1-941668-02-3
Digital: 978-1-941668-09-2

Acknowledgements

First, without a doubt, my love and thanks go to my husband, Cesar. He's been with me every step of the way and I couldn't ask for a better partner in life. Second, my sons, who are my biggest fans. As I am theirs. Each of my family members, everyone I call friend, that has supported me, encouraged me and loved me over the years has a part in this novel. You all have "graced" my life. A profound and deep thank you from my heart.

Special shout outs go to Lara, who got me started on this writing path, Marcia, who led me in the right direction, and Sara who helped me get *The Three Graces* out into the world.

xo
Michele

*"Then Eurynome, ocean's fair daughter, bore to Zeus
the three Graces, all fair-cheeked, Agalia, Euphrosyne,
shapely Thalia; their alluring eyes glance from under their
brows, and from their eyelids drips desire that unstrings the
limbs."*
- Hesiod

Prologue

The Three Graces

Rome 1814

For the three sister goddesses the night's work proved easier than expected. Invisible to humans, they moved through the Duke's private party, the echoes of their touch causing even the strongest of patrons to tremble. The youngest sister, Brilliance, floated among the revelers, heightening dress color or softening a wrinkle here or a bulging waist there. Joy, the middle sister, whispered clever remarks into the ears of the tongue-tied and more often than not turned looks of boredom to ones of fascination. Their eldest sister, Bloom, touched the food and wine, inducing heady delight in all who partook.

Their duty complete for the moment, the goddesses of beauty, charm and creativity came together to admire their handiwork. Being summoned to gatherings such as this always held appeal. When humans let down their guard, with a little help from the drinks, genuine need became visible. It pleased the Graces to help along the discovery of true happiness to those it eluded. When the Graces returned to their home in Elysium, they considered it a good night's work if they were able to touch or deeply change, even just one.

They noted one handsome merrymaker leaving the crowd. He made his way down a hallway to a half-open door. Being infinitely curious, and desirous of spreading good cheer throughout the whole house, the Graces followed him and entered without another thought.

Three men occupied the room. Invisible and silent, each goddess glided over to rest a hand upon one of the gentlemen's arms to get further acquainted. Standing in the middle, arms crossed, was Falier, a nobleman's son. He lived a life of leisure and riches but fought bonds of listlessness, desperate to find some meaning to his life. To the left, seated on a small stool, sat Sartori. He was a penniless young man with talent of his own, yet making his life in the shadow of his half-brother Antonio, who stood leaning against the fireplace mantle. Antonio Canova was as fine to look at as the other two, yet possessed of the humblest character. The goddesses saw in him the ghost of an intense and unrequited love. And an artist of great merit.

The men gazed in appreciation at the only other object of interest. A lifelike creation in marble of three women adorned the center of the room. They exhibited such a likeness to the goddesses themselves that The Graces were momentarily paralyzed at the sight. Shapely arms, hips and thighs crafted to perfection. Intensely beautiful, the intimate nature of their relationship evident in every feature.

After a few stunned moments, each sister smiled, immensely pleased to see the gentlemen's adoration of such an exquisite work of art.

The Graces tuned in to the conversation.

"When is the duke taking it?" Falier asked.

"Tonight, immediately following the ceremony," Canova replied.

"He's anxious to begin," added Sartori. "That's why he sent me to find you."

"I hope you charged the old man enough," Falier said, still mesmerized by the statue. "They're exquisite."

"High praise, indeed, coming from you," Canova said, with a laugh. "Yes, he paid handsomely." He lifted his glass. "Let us have a toast."

Falier took the cue and reached for the remaining glasses on a nearby table. The three moved in close, the sisters following, still touching each one, happy with the obvious camaraderie between the men.

As one, flutes of champagne were raised in tribute.

"A La Trez Grazie!" The men exclaimed in unison.

A gust of wind through the open patio doors caused the candlelight to flicker madly and their shadows to dance.

Canova continued, "May all who look upon them know... 'their alluring eyes glance from under their brows, and from their eyelids drips desire that unstrings the limbs.'"

Exhilarated beyond measure, the sisters recognized the ancient song commemorating their beauty. So involved in their own spiraling emotions and those of the three gentlemen, they were caught unaware when a trembling force shook the room. Within moments they were coiled and ensnared completely within the marble likeness.

Shocked to the core they cried out as one and were met with silence. They watched in horror as the men went on as if nothing had happened.

The Graces were trapped, not knowing how to undo what had been done. The stone image and their spirits one, housed together, their fates intertwined.

"you will remember
for we in our youth
did these things
yes many and beautiful things"
- Sappho

One

Jessie

Autumn   Present Day
Boulder, Colorado

Jessie Marie McIntyre heard the opening notes of music and knew it meant trouble. She was familiar with trouble, but not like this.

In disbelief, she looked around and realized the other students in her humanities class at Stone College were oblivious to it. They chatted on, unaware.

"I'll do the research."

"Okay, and I'll put together the visual presentation."

The two classmates in her group for the project Professor Saunders just assigned didn't hear it either. Their voices were a murmured accompaniment to the haunting instrumental sounds that, despite the warm classroom, made her shiver.

The music came from every corner of the room, building in intensity. Long ago memories, still snapshot moments of her and her father flickered on the walls, floors, faces of the room.

Where the hell was it coming from? Why couldn't anyone else hear it? What did it mean?

When the music ended abruptly, she was off balance. Like she'd gotten up too quickly, a head rush of stars exploding in her eyes. Something shifted inside her then, a brutal, almost physical twist that turned her inside out. Exposed.

Jessie took a long drink from her water bottle, struggled to focus, push the pounding in her head away.

"Jessie?"

"You okay?"

Watchful eyes got her attention. Isabel Cordova's gaze was sharp; Sara Caldwell's showed concern.

"Ah…Sure. I'll present it."

"See, she was listening," Sara said to Isabel.

What a lucky guess.

"Okay, it's settled then." Isabel went back to writing in her notebook.

Jessie felt completely wiped. Glancing at her phone, she saw there were only fifteen minutes left and decided to stick it out. She'd once enjoyed classes like this but no longer. She had trouble concentrating on anything academic for a while now. Nothing seemed interesting anymore and sometimes it made her want to scream.

She looked closely at the two she'd be working with for the next couple of weeks. Isabel was slim, her shoulder-length brown hair pulled back into a ponytail. She wore no make-up and didn't need to, her only jewelry the small gold hoops in her ears. Her blue Converse tennis shoes, jeans and a well-washed gold-colored tee fit her petite frame well.

Sara had straight blond hair, blue eyes, and seemed quiet, serious even. She had on an outfit that shouted designer. Everything matched from her purse to her shoes and showed off her curves.

Professor Saunders approached. "Just checking in to make sure you've made a good start."

"All set," Jessie answered, hiding the pain of a steadily growing headache behind a smile.

Isabel raised her brows but said nothing.

The professor moved on to the next group. Jessie picked up her pen and looked at the handout. Her brain didn't cooperate. Her thoughts kept circling back to the music and she shuddered again, despite the flowing long-sleeved top, leggings and boots she wore.

Maybe her late nights were finally catching up on her. She was bored, which meant she accepted every invitation to go out that came her way. A never-ending round of hanging out at clubs, lounges, concerts, or happy hours, then trying to catch up on assignments the next day. She supposed she should get her act together.

Isabel cleared her throat. "What time period? I say we do classical and Hellenistic Greek art. Most everyone else will probably choose the Middle Ages or Renaissance."

Sara shrugged. "It doesn't matter to me. Whatever you two want."

"Okay by me," Jessie agreed.

"That was easy," Isabel said with a grin.

"It's nice when everyone agrees. Sometimes working with a group can be difficult," Sara said, and then blushed. Jessie could tell she spoke from experience, and really, hadn't they all had to work in groups where lazy ones left all the work to others, or where one person wanted all the control? These two didn't seem to fall into either of those categories.

Isabel suggested pieces of art that could be included in the project and they all agreed on a statue of Aphrodite, of Hygeia, and the Nike of Samothrace.

"You know a lot about art, Isabel. " Jessie said, watching Sara write it all down.

"It's my major," was Isabel's reply.

"You paint?" Sara asked, eyes bright with interest.

"Draw. Mostly charcoal."

Jessie looked to Sara. "What about you? What's your major?"

"English," she answered, "although I don't know what I'll do with it. I just like to read and write. You?"

"Oh, I haven't decided yet." Surprised at what she'd just admitted to these two strangers before she'd told anyone else, Jessie felt the shift inside her again. Tried to ignore it.

They agreed on everything for the project easily enough, a feeling of comfort settling between them. There was an ease of working together she seldom felt with others.

Then the music began once more. This time a clear tenor voice sang along, adding to the stirring quality of the melody.

Once, she could explain. She was certainly tired. But twice? Yes, this was trouble. Green wavered at the edges of her vision, the fragrance of freshly cut grass around her. Looming shadows, tall and dark, rose up around her.

There was more? What was happening?

Whatever it was, it was creeping her out.

Through a haze of flickering light Jessie saw Isabel gripping her desk, knuckles white. She was pale and trembling. Sara was staring at her bare wrists in shock. Maybe something was happening to them too?

The music stopped unexpectedly, the green shadows vanished.

Professor Saunders gave some final instructions and dismissed class, but Jessie didn't hear a word of what was said. Her heart was beating like she'd just finished a run and her forehead was damp with perspiration. As the room cleared out, she got her breathing under control and came to her feet, looking at the others. "You have another class now?"

Sara answered first in a hushed voice. "In half an hour." She didn't move but Jessie could see her hands on the desk trembling a little.

"Me too," Isabel said. Her eyes had the glazed look of shock before they slowly came into focus.

Jessie wanted to know what just happened. She hadn't imagined it. "Can you meet later? Campus coffee shop?"

"What time? I work a dinner shift at the diner tonight." Isabel gathered her things together, stuffing them into her backpack.

"Three?"

"Okay, see you then." Isabel left, and Jessie didn't think she imagined Isabel's unsteady stride.

The room was empty now and for some reason Jessie didn't want to leave Sara there by herself.

Sara looked up, her voice wavering. "Go on." She cleared her throat. "I'll see you later. I'm fine."

As far as reassurances went it wasn't much, but she figured Sara must know how to take care of herself.

By the time Jessie walked across the lawn of the commons and got to her old Buick in the student lot, the brisk air had cleared away most of the desperation she'd felt in the classroom. She opened the glove compartment, found the Advil and downed three with what was left in her water bottle.

Hungry and tired, the first person that came to mind was Nana. The one Jessie had always gone to when she needed something but didn't know what. She wanted answers to the music and the memories. Her grandmother would make something for her and she could ask.

Jessie took the side streets, watching the big Victorians that surrounded the campus turn to modest middle-class two-stories and finally working-class, single-family homes. Mostly second-generation immigrant families lived in this neighborhood where she grew up.

She parked on the street in front of the small white residence she'd called home until last year. Now she lived in the back house of an old Victorian close to campus that she rented with a couple of girlfriends from high school. Maribel worked at her family's travel agency and Emily attended Marinello School of Beauty.

Her grandmother was in the kitchen and greeted her with a lavender-scented embrace. "Hello, love. What brought you here in the middle of the day?"

She hung on for an extra few seconds and felt the last dregs of unease wash away.

"What's wrong?"

"Nothing, I'm fine. I hadn't been by in a little while, that's all."

"You want some lunch? I'll fix you a sandwich."

"I was hoping you'd say that." Jessie sat down at the table, tossed aside the newspaper and arranged the woven placemats while Nana got out the bread and ham.

Nana, her father's mother, had lived with them as long as Jessie could remember. She'd pretty much raised Jessie while her mother worked full-time as a paralegal. Her mother's late hours in a law office meant Nana had been the one to go to parent conferences, bake cookies for after-school treats and help Jessie with homework.

As she watched Nana put together plates of food, memories from her childhood swamped her. She'd gotten into a lot of mischief as a young girl and her grandmother had been the one to bail her out. She'd sat right here more times than she could count and listened to Nana, who although strict in her lectures, when it came right down to it hadn't been in her punishments.

Jessie had learned all the family stories here, too. According to Nana, the one feature she inherited from her father was her smile. In every other physical way she was like her mother. The story she liked best was how her mother, a smart Puerto Rican beauty, had captivated her father, a tall dark-haired Irishman, from the first moment he set eyes on her at a small political rally.

"So what's on your mind?" her grandmother asked, setting the sandwich with a side of chips in front of her.

Jessie took a first bite. "I didn't realize how hungry I was. I haven't eaten all day."

"I was afraid you weren't going to eat well out on your own. You must come home more often. It's not that far."

She gave her grandmother a smile as she got up to get some iced tea from the fridge. "That's the whole point of living on my own. Learning to manage the money in my account. Along with everything else."

"You're my only granddaughter. I can worry if I want." Nana sat down and they ate in comfortable silence. "Your father wanted you to use all that money for college," she continued after a while. "You know that's why your mother saved it for you."

Why had she brought that up? Jessie grabbed another handful of chips from the bag on the counter. "I'm spending it wisely. Tell mom not to worry."

"We know you are. I guess she hopes no one is still tempting you not to finish." Nana rose and started to put things away.

Okay, that was way too close to how she'd been feeling lately. And she knew exactly who her mom hoped had disappeared from her life. Time to change the subject. "I heard some music this morning that reminded me of Dad. I was hoping you could tell me why."

Nana looked up from rinsing plates in the sink. "You know your father sang to you a lot. Your mom and I used to listen from the living room as he sang you to sleep. He had a nice voice."

"Can you tell me what the songs were?"

"He sang show tunes. Sinatra, folk songs from the 60s, Jimmy Buffet..."

"What about one that goes like this?" Jessie hummed some of the mysterious tune.

"Hmm. It doesn't sound familiar."

Jessie hid her disappointment, leaned in and kissed her grandmother's cheek. "I'm off." She grabbed her purse from the floor and fished out her keys. "Thanks for lunch."

Even though she'd gotten no answers, a jolt of energy came with the idea of solving a puzzle. Back on campus, her cell phone rang as she approached the steps of the campus library. Mario's name showed on the screen. Just the person her mother was afraid was tempting her.

"Hey, handsome, what's up?"

"Just thinking of you," he answered.

She sat down on the steps, letting the timbre of his voice fill her. She'd met Mario Cervantes when he'd transferred junior year to Foothills High School. They'd become fast friends and a great support to each other during a tumultuous senior year. He had moved to San Francisco after graduation and was already on his way to making a name for himself in the music industry.

"I need a favor. I'm going to send you a song I just finished. Let me know what you think."

"Sure, but isn't that what Phil's for? Make him work for the outrageous producer fee you're probably paying him."

"He doesn't get any money from me 'til the album's sold, you know that. And I'll ask his opinion. I just want yours first. You have an ear for my music."

That made her smile, as he knew it would. He'd often used that phrase in moments that had nothing to do with listening to his music.

"All right. How'd it go last night?" she asked.

14

Mario and his band were performing weekly at different clubs while working on their new album. Their first one, put out the previous year, had gotten a Grammy nomination and won them a short interview with Rolling Stone magazine.

"There was a line out the door."

"Told you."

"Jess . . ." he paused.

Something in his voice was too much for her. Pushed another memory at her that she didn't want to think about. "Listen, I'm meeting some friends."

A beautiful pair of suede Jimmy Choo boots that Jessie recognized came into view. She looked up and smiled at Sara. "Really, I've got to go. I'll call you later." She ended the call and stood up. "Class over?" she asked Sara.

"I left a little early. I couldn't concentrate." Sara fell into step beside her as they headed toward the student union.

When they met up with Isabel, Jessie snagged a table in a back corner, while the other two got drinks. Everything was swirling in her head and she couldn't contain her curiosity much longer. When they returned she decided to get right to the point. "So, what happened at the end of class?"

Isabel said nothing and instead pulled her hair out of its ponytail and redid it with swift, sure strokes.

"Why are you asking?" Sara blew on her tea and sipped, her eyes looking wary and tired.

"Something really weird happened and I thought maybe all the late nights were starting to get to me. But then it seemed like something happened to you, too. You both looked... a little strange."

Neither answered. Jessie sighed. "I heard music. Surround sound, like in theaters."

"I knew she wasn't listening," Isabel muttered.

"Did you hear music?" Jessie asked. When they shook their heads in obvious disbelief, she took a risk and said, "See? No one else heard it except me. And then I saw a flickering images and a flash of green and dark shadows. There was this smell, like fresh-cut grass in the summertime."

She waited for them to say she'd probably just imagined it. Or was crazy. Or on drugs.

"What do you think it means?" Sara asked.

Jessie looked at her in surprise. "I have no idea. What happened to you?" She looked back and forth between them. "Sara?"

Sara rubbed her wrist, the gesture nervous. "Nothing. Why do you think something happened to me?"

"Because you're rubbing your wrists now the way you were then."

Jessie eyed the two of them. Maybe the direct approach wasn't going to work. Or maybe it would. "Fine. If you don't want to admit it, I get it." She shrugged for emphasis. "You don't know me, so why be honest? But we do have to work together for the project. Besides, you two didn't seem like the usual crowd."

Isabel turned her gaze to the window. Sara kept staring at the floor.

What would it take to get them to open up? And why did it matter?

Jessie's impatience got the best of her. "Well, I guess I'll go then." She started to get up.

"I felt chains wrapping around my legs and wrists." Sara blurted out. "Like a snake slithering up me." She took a couple of deep breaths, finally raising her eyes to meet theirs. Uncertainty and fear shone bright. "It sounds creepy but it wasn't. It was like they were there to protect me, like, I don't know, armor or something."

Jessie shivered. Sara seemed okay now, but she remembered the fragility, the vulnerability she'd seen at the end of class.

Silence lengthened as they both looked toward Isabel. "Okay, okay." She shook her head as if to clear the image. "Mine was freaky, too."

"So you did feel something!"

"Actually, I thought I'd fainted for a minute. Everything around me was gone, there was silence, it was pitch black and I could smell water."

"Water?" Jessie repeated.

"You know, like creeks and rivers." Isabel leaned back in her chair holding her cup as if to warm her hands. "I felt enclosed in something, like walls all around, but I couldn't see anything."

They sat in silence for a minute, the din of student chatter swirling around them.

"I didn't get a lot of sleep last night because I had to finish a project. Maybe I just dozed off for a minute," Isabel suggested.

Jessie shook her head. "That doesn't explain how weird things happened to each of us at the same time."

Sara rubbed her arms, crossing them in front of her and said nothing.

Then it happened again, for the third time that day, right in the middle of the student union. Jessie knew it was trouble like she'd never experienced before. Or was it? And it didn't look like it was going to go away any time soon.

Two

Isabel

A strange feeling hit Isabel as she walked to the bus stop in the emerging dawn. She arrived just in time to board the crowded Number Fifteen and tried to shake it off along with the remnants of sleep as she sipped her coffee. It was a little after five but the early shift for many workers was starting soon. She stood in the back next to a guy in an overall uniform and watched the neighborhoods silently go by. It took her directly to the corner of Foothill and Broadway, the southwestern edge of campus, home of The Downtown Diner.

Friendly greetings from the kitchen staff followed her as she made her way through the back entry into the restroom to get ready. She tied her apron, checked her pockets and pulled her hair back to secure it. But, when the clip slipped to the floor and she bent over to pick it up, she realized it was happening again.

Damn.

The mirror reflected something different than what she knew was really there. The wall and floor became flat gray stone, not white tile. The sound of running water wasn't the toilet or the sink, but the echo of water moving back and forth.

It made her think of a cave.

She turned around, wondering if it would all disappear in an instant like last time. It didn't.

A bowl of red paint sat on the floor. She didn't know what made her do it but she reached for it. It was wood, uneven in texture, and felt heavy in the palm of her hand.

She'd never been as good with paint as she was with charcoal, but a sudden desire to fill the blank wall with the red was gripping and fearsome. It pulled at her as if necessary for her survival.

But, that was ridiculous. All this was just a figment of her imagination, wasn't it? She put the bowl down.

A knock sounded and the hostess called through the door. "Isabel, we're open. I'm going to seat some customers in your section."

When Isabel looked down, there was no stone floor or bowl of paint, just her backpack and the fallen hair clip.

Her hands shook through the first half of her shift. Which pissed her off.

At least the restaurant was busy enough to distract her. Tips were decent and the morning flew. At the end of her shift she debated what to do. After what had happened earlier, she needed to empty herself in drawing. She needed the total absorption of eye connecting with hand.

She caught the bus and got off after a couple of stops. She walked toward Crystal Springs Park where she'd played with her brothers and sisters growing up. It still had all the old equipment, metal merry-go-round and monkey bars. She hadn't been here in years. She watched as children played, laughing and squealing, while their parents sat on benches, for the most part ignoring them. One mother comforted a little girl in tears who was pointing at some boys. Just like her older brothers, Ben and Matthew, picking on her and her younger sister, Maggie. But there'd been no mother to run to because their mother had never gone with them to the park.

She got her notebook and pencils out and sat down to draw. As a child, it had first been crayons, then colored pencils that were her friends. She'd used any paper she could get a hold of: the back of someone's homework, reminder note, or school announcement. Out of the cacophony of noise at home, the television, the pots and pans, the radio in an upstairs bedroom, water from the shower or washing machine, images had emerged, layer after layer.

When she drew, Isabel let everything inside her and the images around her become visible on the page. Doorways, scratches on furniture, shoes peeking out from under the bed, trees, sky, mountains, and the creek by her house. As she'd grown, so had the images. She became good at faces. Now her style seemed to be a merging of people and nature, each blending with the other.

Her brothers and sisters had never paid much attention to her art other than to tease her for always using her allowance money on sketchpads and charcoal pencils. Except Maggie. Her younger sister had watched her draw while sitting in bed at night, their nightgowns billowing around them, hushed whispers and giggles in the air between them.

Her parents' only attention had been to her grades and her attendance in church every Sunday. There was never money for extra art classes, so the only instruction she got was in the occasional art class at the Catholic schools she attended. It wasn't until her junior year at Assumption High when a teacher displayed a few of her drawings in the main office that anyone had really taken notice. The school counselor had made her fill out numerous college applications for art scholarships that spring. The following year she'd been accepted to Stone College on a full ride, excluding room and board. Which at first hadn't mattered, until it did.

Isabel sighed with a mix of tiredness and relief as she finished a sketch of a girl playing in the sand. She needed a hot shower. Time to go home.

The shower washed off the day's grime but didn't really improve her mood. She was uncommonly restless and the mess in her room didn't help. She wandered to the window in an attempt to find . . . what? Inspiration? Answers? Twilight shimmered through the grove behind her house and cool evening air drifted through the crack in the window. She'd drawn this view many times through the years and something about it always soothed her. But not tonight. She was distracted. How could she concentrate when bizarre things kept happening?

At first she'd convinced herself she was just tired from work and studying late. Or that maybe she was coming down with something. But together with Jessie and Sara's craziness, she was giving up trying to explain it in any reasonable or logical way.

Had it already been two weeks since the first time? She'd felt faint, yet conscious of damp air, the taint of salt and water. But the second time, a week later while studying at the library, Isabel had seen the vague shape of a rock wall and heard the echo of water very clearly. And then there was today's incident.

She flopped down on the bed with a groan. Doors were slamming and water was running in an upstairs bathroom. She could smell the clams in garlic sauce her mother was making for dinner. The news program her father liked to listen to drifted up from the living room. He must be going deaf if she could hear it through her closed door.

"James William Cordova! *Siete in ritardo!* Get down here this minute!" her mother yelled at her younger brother in a mix of Italian and English.

God, she really had to move out of here soon.

Maggie knocked on the door and peeked her head in, her brunette waves bouncing. "What'cha doin'?"

"Nothing. What's up with you?" Isabel pushed herself up on her elbows.

"I'm off to practice. Mom's upset because I'm going to miss dinner. Again."

"Nothing new there." Isabel reminded her with a knowing look.

"It'd just be nice to be supported for a change."

"Maggie, you're going to be great."

"You know what I meant. You're coming to the competition?"

"I switched shifts so I could make it."

Maggie gave her a brilliant smile and left, closing the door behind her. All the other girls on the cheerleading squad had family show up at the games and competitions, and although Isabel couldn't make it to everything, she tried to get to the important ones. Maggie was tall, athletic, strong and graceful. Popular, too. So different from Isabel. But as the two youngest females in the family, they stuck together and understood each other best. Like when her sister had encouraged her to move on campus freshman year. Maggie had known that for Isabel, continuing to live at home probably wasn't the best option. But because Isabel's scholarship hadn't covered dorm expenses, she'd decided to stay at home and work to save money and not get into debt.

Now she was quietly going crazy.

Her phone vibrated on the desk and she glanced at the incoming text from Jessie.

"Wanna go out? Meeting Sara @7."

"Sure," she wrote back.

"I'll pick u up."

"Ok." It'd be better than dealing with her mother tonight, especially since Maggie wouldn't be around. And though she hated talking about things she really just wanted to ignore, the restroom-turned-cave incident had scared her enough to think she should tell Jessie and Sara.

She searched the closet for her favorite black V-neck. It hugged her body and was soft and warm enough that she wouldn't need a jacket. She slid into her newest pair of skinny jeans, dragged her black ankle boots from under the bed and pulled them on. She picked up her wallet, house keys and phone and headed down.

Her mother chose the exact moment she reached the bottom step to come out of the kitchen. She gave Isabel an appraising look.

Isabel scooted past her and the hall table her mother used as a shrine for the Virgin Mary. Besides the statue of Mary that had been blessed by the Pope himself, there was a small vase of flowers, three votive candles and a rosary. Scenes from Friday nights during Lent followed her down the hall. The whole family used to pray the rosary kneeling on the floor in front of that statue.

"Why are you going out? I made all this food," her mother complained.

"Don't start, okay?" Isabel really didn't want to have this conversation because it always ended one way. With her mother making her feel guilty, whether she gave in or not.

"Dio sopra de mi auito!" A litany in Italian followed her as she turned away. Something about the saints preserving mothers from the ingratitude of their children.

Her father glanced up from the TV as she passed through the living room. He was still in his work clothes, his bulky frame filling up the armchair. "Where are you going?" he asked, muting his program.

"Out."

"You're going to miss dinner."

"Next time."

The sound came on again as she pulled the door shut. She could feel her breathing ease once she left. She leaned against the neighbor's fence to wait.

What had Jessie said that first time after they'd all admitted something strange was going on? "We don't know why or how. Let's just see what happens." Well, Jessie and Sara might be comfortable waiting to see what would happen next, but to Isabel it was like kneeling on the floor praying the rosary. Agonizing. She wanted answers.

Jessie pulled up to the curb a few minutes later. Her long black curls hung loose, her olive skin held just a hint of makeup, and her dark chocolate eyes held more than a trace of recklessness. Her slim legs were clad in stretch pants and boots, paired with a flowing top and lots of jewelry.

One of the things Isabel had noticed about Jessie was she took pleasure in the moment, whether it was food or laughter or the weather. Since they all met, Jessie had easily convinced her and Sara to go along with things they didn't normally do. Like skip a class or eat frozen yogurt at ten in the morning or drive one of the many winding foothill roads just because.

She got in the front seat, tossing Jessie's school bag into the back. "Where are we going?"

"The Attic." Jessie looked Isabel up and down. "You'll do. Ever been there?"

"No. How's the food?"

"Not bad." As she waited for a light to turn green, Jessie reached for a music system that was incongruous with the rest of the 1990 Buick Regal she drove. "You like Muse?" She cranked the volume and then yelled over it, "Great, huh?"

Isabel agreed by nodding her head. While the song "Madness" played, she thought about just how different they all were. She would've thought they'd never find common ground. But they had. Little things sure, but mostly it seemed to be the experiences each of them had, starting the day they met, that no one else would believe.

When the song ended, Isabel turned the volume down a notch. "Can I borrow some lip gloss?"

Jessie picked up a slim silver tube, one of many from the compartment between the seats. "Here, this one is probably best for you." She handed it over. "We're in luck tonight. I'm making every green light."

Isabel swiped some on, noticed they were close to downtown, and began to look for a parking place.

Jessie slammed on the brakes and skidded to stop on the side of the road, barely missing a parked car.

Isabel felt her seatbelt yank her back and the lip gloss went flying.

"Oh my God, did you see that?"

Isabel struggled to get her thoughts and her heart beat under control.

"It was… I don't know what it was. It was a giant hedge. Or something. Bigger than the car." Jessie's voice trembled.

Isabel gripped the door handle and turned to look through the back window. Cars sped by, honking. Lights from signs and traffic signals held vigil around them.

"Where was it?"

Jessie held a hand over her heart, pressing. "It was in the middle of the road. Blocking our way. I thought I was going to crash into it."

"Jessie, there's nothing there."

Jessie turned and looked too. "But it was there. I swear I saw it."

A knock on the passenger window made them both jump. A man in a business suit stood there, his eyes questioning. Isabel rolled down the window a crack.

"Are you two all right? Anyone hurt?"

"We're okay, thanks." She tried to smile but wasn't sure if she pulled it off.

"I saw the whole thing. You're lucky you didn't hit that car. What happened?"

The concern was nice but she didn't think Jessie wanted to confess to seeing bushes obstructing the street.

"My friend saw an animal run into the road and didn't want to hit it." That was always a good excuse in this pet-friendly town.

"Might be better than crashing your car," he said and shrugged before walking away.

Jessie took a deep breath and pulled back into traffic. "That was scary, and you know what? I'm a little pissed. We could've been hurt."

"No kidding. Hey, there's a parking spot," Isabel said pointing to a car pulling out.

They walked a couple of blocks, which gave Isabel time to work on calming her still speeding heart. Jessie turned into a low-lit entryway and Isabel followed. The place was decorated exactly how she imagined an attic in one of those old turn-of-the-century homes on the hill. Books and antiques and dressmaker mannequins artfully furnished the area. Sara waited for them at a corner table.

The evening passed in a whirlwind of appetizers they shared and friends of Jessie's stopping by the table to talk. Isabel tried to relax, join in, even though it wasn't her usual venue. She didn't really have one, the more she thought about it. She rarely got out like this. But it was a definite snapshot into Jessie's social life. Sara was smiling, but quiet. From what Isabel could tell, Sara wasn't used to it either.

Finally, when the food was finished, Jessie turned serious. "So let's talk."

"I thought that's what we've been doing," Isabel couldn't resist saying.

Jessie gave her a sharp look. "You know what I mean."

"About what?" Sara asked.

"Something happened on the way here." Jessie pushed her empty glass away and picked up her purse from the seat beside her.

Isabel watched her pull a small mirror out of her purse and check her reflection. "I can't believe you waited so long to bring it up."

Jessie shrugged. "I needed to forget about it for awhile." Her glance toward Isabel was shrewd. "You were shaken by it too."

"Would someone please tell me what's going on?" Sara asked, calm, composed.

Isabel sighed. "Jessie's not the only one with something to share."

Jessie carefully shut the compact, her eyes lit with more than curiosity. "You've been holding out on us?"

Isabel's defenses rose. "It happened this morning. Maybe I needed time to process too. It was different than before. Much different."

"Like a hedge in the middle of the road?"

"I held a bowl of paint in my hand. In a cave. One minute it was there and the next it wasn't."

"Really? That's... way cool. You actually touched something. And it was real? Solid?" Amazement was clear on Jessie's face. "Now we're getting somewhere. It can't be just our imaginations." Then she frowned. "But a hedge in the middle of the road is frickin' dangerous."

"What?" Sara interrupted. "Did you hit it?"

"Almost," Isabel said.

Jessie filled Sara in on the details.

Sara sat forward in her chair and lowered her voice. "I don't think these incidents are going to go away. In fact it appears they're getting stronger."

"Bigger anyway." Jessie picked up her purse. "I just can't believe these things actually happen to us."

Isabel was having a hard time too.

"You both ready to go?"

As they made their way to the door, a muffled ring tone could be heard in the empty entryway.

"Whose is that?" Sara asked.

"Not mine," Jessie said.

Isabel dug into her jeans' pocket. "It's mine." She glanced at the screen without opening it. "It's a local number, but I don't recognize it."

"You're not going to answer it?" Jessie stopped at the curb and turned back.

"They can leave a message and I'll listen later."

"Aren't you curious?"

Isabel put her phone back in her pocket. "Nope."

Jessie shook her head. "You're a strange one, Isabel."

"See you tomorrow?" Sara asked. "We've got to work some more on the project. It's due in four weeks." Sara held her purse awkwardly while rubbing her arms for warmth. "It's cold out here."

"It is. I've got time around two. You Isabel?"

"That'll work for me."

Isabel walked with Jessie toward her car waving to Sara who headed in the opposite direction. Instead of turning up the music as she drove through the quiet streets, Jessie kept looking over at Isabel. "Go on. Listen to the message. Even if you're not curious, I am."

Isabel laughed. "It could be a wrong number, a telemarketer, another waitress wanting to switch shifts."

"Bet it's not. Could be one of my friends you met tonight."

"You didn't give my number to a guy, did you?"

Jessie laughed. "I might have."

"Jessie, that's crazy." Isabel scrunched down in the seat so she could pull her phone out. She opened it up. "They didn't leave a message. See. Just as I said."

"Call the number back." Jessie suggested as she turned down Isabel's street. "It's just after ten. Not too late."

"Sorry, not going there."

Jessie grabbed the phone as she pulled up to the curb.

"What are you doing?" Isabel figured Jessie was just pretending until she watched her push the call back button. She stretched out to take the phone away, but Jessie switched it to her other ear where Isabel couldn't reach it short of leaning over the steering wheel.

Isabel had to laugh. Jessie just didn't understand that she never, ever, got interesting phone calls.

Jessie held her index finger to her lips for silence. "Hi, I saw you just called this cell phone but didn't leave a message."

There was a pause, then Jessie's laugh. "You're looking for Isabel?"

Isabel shook her head madly. Whoever it was, she really didn't want to talk at the moment.

"Yes, this is her phone but she can't talk right now."

Another pause. "No, I'm not her sister, just a friend." Jessie grabbed a pen from the seat and waved at Isabel to find a piece of paper. "Hold on."

Isabel reluctantly tore off a page from a notebook on the floor. She couldn't imagine who it was.

Jessie jotted down a number. Isabel watched her put a name next to it. Michael. Michael who? Isabel only knew one Michael and it couldn't be him.

Jessie hung up and tossed the phone back to her. "He was very polite." Jessie pointed to the paper, "That number is the best way to reach him. It's a cell. Nice voice. Older, I think. Ring any bells?"

"Not a one." Isabel opened the door and got out.

She shut the door but Jessie leaned over and rolled down the window. Held up the slip of paper Isabel had dropped on the seat. "Here don't forget this."

Three

Sara

Chains held her suspended. Sara fought the familiar jolts of panic, shut her eyes tight and took a couple of deep breaths. When she was able to think coherently, she realized she was bound up like a cocoon, held secure and safe.

She wouldn't fall.

Smooth, cool metal against her skin, empty faded light around her, it felt like the chains were breathing, their hold tightening then loosening. She was frightened, but the silence was peaceful and non-threatening. Unlike the thought of a giant hedge in the road like Jessie had seen.

It was probably only a few minutes, but it felt like forever. Just hanging there.

Then she was back in her Honda parked in the medical building parking lot, her hands gripping the steering wheel like a lifeline. That was way more intense than the previous two times. Even though she'd been expecting something to happen again, it still took her by surprise.

It was appointment time, but her body refused to move. She told herself she wasn't going to freak out. She counted to ten slowly, rubbed her fingers together, and finally felt her shoulders and arms relax enough to undo her seatbelt and open the car door.

With early morning clouds hovering, she slowly went inside to the psychiatric group waiting room. She'd been here so often in the last two years she could find her way blind. Twenty steps from the outside door to the elevator. Three floors up. Twelve steps to the office window. She greeted the office staff as she approached. The friendly redheaded nurse who loved to talk waved from the back counter. The accountant, who never said much, nodded at her. The receptionist, who always wore the latest fashions, gave her a quick smile.

Sara hated waiting with the other patients because she dreaded running into someone she might know. Boulder was a small town after all. Mostly it was the darting glances, shifting bodies, and the impatient tapping of feet that made her nervous. She never got used to it.

What should she bring up in her session with Dr. Bernstein? Her psychiatrist knew all about the times she'd run out of class shaking from head to toe, cried alone in bathroom stalls, or couldn't remember getting home. He knew about the worst, when she'd collapsed on the bathroom floor at home. But what would he say about this thing that just happened? He might think she was hallucinating. He might prescribe more medication. No, she couldn't let that happen.

Sara heard the inner office door open. It was time.

"So, how are you doing, Sara?" Dr. Bernstein asked from the leather armchair in the corner. He was dressed in his customary buttoned-down shirt, khaki pants and brown loafers.

"Fine." From her place at the far end of the sofa, she looked around, as always, curious to see whether anything had changed. His framed diplomas lined the wall behind his desk, pictures of his wife and children sat on a side table by the windows next to his chair. It was all comfortably the same.

"Medication still working out?" he asked.

"Yeah." She'd been on Paxil, a standard anxiety medication, since the end of freshman year in high school when her parents had brought her to Dr. Bernstein to get her some help.

"Good. So, what would you like to talk about today?"

"I was wondering if I might try a smaller dose. You know, like we talked about last time." She knew she was pushing it, especially with all the new stuff going on, which she wasn't going to mention.

Dr. Bernstein wrote something on the notepad on his lap. "You've had no panic attacks?"

"Nope. Not one." The incidents with the chains were something altogether different, not panic.

"Sara?"

"Sorry, what was that?"

"Have you been using your meditation tape?"

"At least once a week, yes." The tapes had taught her to focus on breathing in times of stress. And to envision a safe and relaxing place she could go to in her mind if she went into panic mode.

"Hmmm." He looked steadily at her, his gray eyes showing understanding and warmth. "Okay, let's try it. However, if anything happens that upsets you and you panic, I want you to call me. You might have to go back to a full dose. You've been doing so well. I don't want anything to jeopardize your hard work."

Relief came in a rush, saturating her in its intensity. The panic attacks had ruled her life for so long, before she even understood what they were. Paxil had saved her, allowed her to do normal things she hadn't been able to before. Still, she hoped one day to be medication free. She wanted to control herself, not have medication do it for her. Her father and mother didn't think it possible, but Sara did.

She told him about meeting Jessie and Isabel. How they got along so well and how comfortable she was beginning to feel with them. "They're both really beautiful. Jessie's tall and thin and Isabel's slender and petite."

"That reminds me of the homework I gave you last time. Do you remember?"

She'd forgotten with everything that had been happening lately. Or was that just a convenient excuse?

"Sara? You seem distracted today."

Sara shook herself out of her own thoughts. "I'm sorry. I am a little, and no I didn't do my homework."

"I want you to make that a priority for next time we meet. Remember, look at yourself for a full minute in the mirror at least once a day."

She knew she was overweight and had to watch what she ate, and absolutely hated the exercise Dr. Bernstein wanted her to do.

"Tell me more about Jessie and Isabel."

"I guess I never thought I'd have friends like them. They're confident and outgoing. Popular, interesting. At ease with everything."

"What kind of friends did you think you'd have?" he asked.

Sara thought for a minute. "Serious, studious, ordinary. Like me."

"Safe, in other words."

"I suppose."

Dr. Bernstein looked at his watch. "We'll talk more about this next time." He rose to his feet. "Don't forget your homework."

Sara thought about his comment as she walked to the car. She wanted safe? Probably. Safe was her default button. But was that what she still wanted? She had no idea. This last week had been anything but safe.

She glanced at her watch. She'd have to hurry to her standing Wednesday lunch date with Quinn. If she hit all the lights she'd arrive right on time.

When she spotted him waiting on the bench outside the restaurant, she remembered the day they'd first met on the tennis courts. Tennis was the only physical exercise that had ever interested her. She felt graceful with a racket in hand and learning to play when she was a young girl had been her salvation in more ways than one. She'd first thought Quinn was just another handsome, blonde, arrogant rich kid, which usually sent her running. But to her surprise, he'd been genuine and nice. It wasn't until later she'd heard the rumor that he was gay. She'd relaxed even more around him after that. He'd been her one true friend through high school and now he probably knew and understood her better than anyone.

"Hey," he said, giving her a hug.

"I didn't eat breakfast so I'm starving. Let's go in." She followed the hostess to a booth and watched Quinn settle across from her.

"Did you thank your mom for me?" he asked.

"You should probably call her yourself. I hardly see her and we talk even less." Sara decided on a salad and diet Coke. "So, tell all. How's it going with the Stone Theater production?"

"Everyone is very friendly even though there are a few big egos running the show." Quinn smiled at the waitress, grabbed Sara's hand and held it while he ordered.

She smiled and pulled away when the waitress left. "She wasn't even making eyes at you. Who's the one with the big ego here?"

"Ah, c'mon, you know I'm just having a little fun," he said with a laugh. "Anyway, it's all going great and your mom's recommendation to the theater director was just in time. If he hadn't called me that night and offered me a stipend for doing makeup for the show I would've had to tell my apartment manager I couldn't pay the rent. That wouldn't have gone over well."

Sara understood Quinn's need for independence. He refused financial help from his parents even when things got tough. She wished she could do the same.

"It worked out with your other show schedule?" The civic light opera and a local dinner theater regularly contracted him to do make up for their shows.

"I'm making it work. Hey, that's what I'll do. I'll request a couple of tickets for one of the shows for your mom and dad."

"More than likely, dad and I would use them. Mom's never home. It's worse than when we were in high school."

Quinn's thoughtful gaze across the table made her uncomfortable.

"What?" she asked.

"You sound bitter," he answered.

"Maybe I am."

"It's too late, Sara. She's never going to change and you've got accept that."

"Besides, you have your father."

"Some things are hard to talk about with fathers. Although it probably wouldn't've mattered. Mom hates to talk about anything except business, you know that."

"Maybe you should move out. It might help you see things differently. You could always live with me."

The waitress set their food down and hurried to the next table.

Sara sighed and picked up her fork. "I stayed at home because I didn't know if I could really handle everything at college." She'd chosen safe.

"But you're doing fine, right?"

Sara nodded as she took a bite.

"So you could handle it? Moving out I mean."

"Maybe I could. But that would leave dad alone a lot. I feel bad for him. It's like he's got a part-time wife. Less than part-time."

"Sara, you can't make decisions for your life based on your dad and what you think he needs. You don't know everything about their relationship. Maybe he doesn't mind your mother's long work hours like you do."

His words irritated her. "How could he not mind?"

"Have you ever asked him?" Quinn took a sip of his Coke and finished eating.

They both knew the answer to that.

"All I'm saying is, just think about it. About talking to your dad and moving out."

"I'm sure getting a lot of counseling today," Sara grumbled.

"Quinn Blakely, therapist and make-up artist at your service," he said with a mock serious face. "Your outfit is great by the way."

She smiled and they finished their meal. On their way out Quinn put his arm around her as they left money for the bill on the table. Sara waved to him before getting in her car.

What would she do without him? He was probably right about talking to her dad. And although moving out sounded good, she really wasn't sure she could handle it.

Ten minutes later she pulled into her driveway. The house she'd grown up in was ranch-style with big windows, and a stone fireplace, set back from the street and surrounded by tall pines. Opening the front door, she recognized the hum of the vacuum in an upstairs bedroom. Brenda, their housekeeper, cleaned on Wednesdays, did laundry on Fridays and went food shopping on Mondays. Unfortunately for Sara's diet, she always left an edible treat, either one of her own or something from the bakery in the cookie jar. Sara grabbed one on a detour through the all-gleaming-stainless-steel kitchen then headed to the den. This was her father's retreat and the only room she felt comfortable in beside her bedroom. Probably because of all the books. Her mother's decorating style was sleek, modern, with lots of white and pops of color here and there. Definitely fashionable, but not relaxing, so she usually retreated here or her room.

Quickly and efficiently she took out her laptop from its case, set it down on her father's desk, and turned the printer on.

She breathed deep, the smell of her father's cologne a brief memory in the air, and waited for the ten pages of the paper due for her next class to print out. Sara studied the framed photograph on the desk of her mother and father on one of their rare vacations a few years ago. Slim, tan, dressed to the hilt at some fancy restaurant. She shared their coloring but the thin gene had definitely bypassed her. Fingers tapping impatiently, her eyes focused on an envelope to the side of the blotter. She recognized her father's handwriting but it was the name on it that made her heart tremble.

Violet Caldwell. To an address in San Francisco.

A memory struck so fierce, her knees buckled and she had to sit down before she fell.

The fight.

She heard the yelling, the voices growing in pitch and volume. Her sister storming out of the house after that. At six, Sara had been too little to remember what the argument was about, but sometimes she dreamt of a door slamming, harsh and final.

She never saw her sister again.

She'd wanted to. She'd begged her mother later to tell her something, anything about where Violet had gone or when she would see her again. But all she'd gotten was her mother's cold stare and more door slamming that had put an end to the questions. Her father had said he would try to work something out, but never had. At least that's what she'd thought. Until now.

The printer stopped, half of the pages falling to the carpet, the rest lying in the tray, waiting. She grabbed them blindly, remembering the sadness and anger of that time.

Brenda appeared in the doorway. "Oh sweet heavens, it's you. I heard a noise in here and it scared me to death." She lowered the silver candlestick she held in one hand, her other hand on her hip. "What are you doing home at this time of day? Shouldn't you be in class?"

"Sorry, didn't mean to scare you." Sara pushed everything into her bag and slung it over her shoulder. "I forgot to print out a paper for English Lit."

"Are you okay?" Brenda's shrewd eyes didn't miss much. She was as bad as Quinn.

Sara gave her a quick kiss on the cheek and scooted to the door. "Fine. Great cookies. Have a good weekend."

She fled the house without hearing Brenda's reply.

She was tired - exhausted, really - and it was only one in the afternoon.

Clusters of young women were scattered throughout the small amphitheater when she arrived a few minutes before class started. Any other day she would've taken copious notes on comments made by students and the professor, which helped later with papers and exams.

Today her thoughts kept returning to her cocoon. What it felt like and wondering when it would happen again. And Violet. Had she been in San Francisco this whole time? And what was her dad sending her anyway?

By the time class ended and she began the walk across campus to meet Jessie and Isabel, she felt like she'd run a marathon in her mind.

Jessie waved from a table near the front of the crowded student union to get her attention. "Hey girl."

"Hey." Sara slumped down into an empty chair. She reached into her bag and pulled out the research for the project. "Help me organize this the way we want it." She laid out sheets of paper across the table.

"I've got the pictures," Isabel said.

Sara pulled a colored copy out of another folder. "Oh, I almost forgot. I've got one more to add, if that's okay."

"All right, but that's it. We already have more than we need." Isabel held out her hand. "Let's see what it is."

The image she'd found while doing research was simple yet striking. A frieze of three headless women standing shoulder to shoulder, arms linked, naked. The broad band of stone was in the museum at the Parthenon.

Jessie came around the table to look over her shoulder. "Who are they?"

"They're the Three Graces," Isabel answered. "In Greek mythology they're daughters of Zeus, goddesses of creativity, the arts, and celebrations."

"So, what do you think?" Sara asked.

"It fits our time period." At Sara's nod, Jessie picked it up and examined it closely. "I like it. Three women, three of us. Nice."

"We could even use them as our theme," Isabel suggested. "So, this is it now, we're set." She put the copy with the rest of the visuals she'd compiled on the table so they could organize them. "What are you two doing tonight?"

Jessie took a sip of her latte. "Nada."

"I'm starving, but I don't want to go home," Isabel said, matching some of the art with the research.

"We could do take-out," Sara suggested. "Thai sounds good." She numbered the pages as Jessie handed them to her.

"Or someone could cook," Isabel suggested.

"I will." Jessie offered.

"Do you even know how?" Sara blurted out, then felt heat rising to her cheeks.

Isabel laughed out loud. "Good one, Sara."

"Of course. I'll prove it." Jessie closed her bag and grabbed her sweater from the back of the chair.

Sara hurried to explain. "I just meant... I could cook if you want me to. I enjoy it and I'm pretty good."

"You're on for next time. But believe it or not, I can make some rice and grilled chicken. Besides, you haven't been to my place yet." Jessie jotted down her address with directions. "C'mon Isabel."

When they'd left, Sara put the last of her papers in order, then got out her phone and called her father.

"Hi, darling. Where are you?" Her father's voice was low, which meant he was still at the office, probably on his way out.

"School. I know I said I'd cook tonight but something came up."

"No problem. I'll grab some take-out on the way home."

"No fast food. Remember? Doctor's orders." Sara knew he usually stuck to his low cholesterol diet but couldn't help saying it. She was as protective of him as he was of her.

"I'll be good," he chuckled. "I've got to go, sweetheart."

"I might stay over at Jessie's tonight."

There was a pause, his silence speaking volumes. "Okay. You know I worry. Be safe." Her father said with genuine concern.

Safe. The story of her life.

Sara waited till a group of girls got through the doorway before leaving. She buttoned her coat as the wind swept leaves off the trees and around her feet. After the sun went down behind the mountains, Colorado weather turned cold fast. Hurrying to the car, she wished she'd brought some extra clothes to change into something more comfortable. The new outfit Quinn liked so much, courtesy of her mother's online shopping, would have to do. Sara had long ago realized her mother believed giving her daughter clothes meant giving attention. Of course the clothes were nice, but they weren't the same in Sara's eyes.

She looked at the numbers on the houses and pulled up in front of a beautifully restored Victorian. Following Jessie's directions, she walked up the long driveway beside the house until she reached a back gate. Nestled among some pine and oak trees sat a small cottage. It was quaint, almost magical with little lights illuminating a path to the door.

"Let's see some of your latest pieces," Jessie was saying to Isabel when she opened the door.

Sara took off her coat and walked around the small open living area while Jessie opened a beer for each of them. The chicken smelled good and the music lightened her mood.

"Let's eat before we look," Isabel suggested.

"Plates are in that cabinet," Jessie said, pointing to the left of the stove, "and forks in that drawer. Help yourselves. I'm going to drink my beer first." She scooted up onto one of the bar stools at the counter.

Sara finished her inspection while Isabel got her food. The room was decorated in deep blues and creams, and the wood floors and fireplace created a cozy atmosphere. Framed photographs were everywhere. Even a vase full of pink roses sat on the corner table.

"My roommate's being pursued by this good-looking broker she met at a party," Jessie said, noticing her interest in the flowers.

"And you?" Isabel asked around her first mouthful as she stood at the counter. "We haven't heard about a boyfriend. You dating?"

Jessie sipped her beer and shrugged. "Nobody special. I've gone out with some of the guys I've met at clubs but that's it."

Sara got up on a stool next to Jessie, let the talk swirl around her, allowing the weirdness of the day to fall away as they finished Jessie's food. "Thanks for cooking, Jessie. It was great."

"You didn't eat much."

"I'm ah… watching my weight."

"Why?" Isabel asked. "You look fine to me." She got up from the counter. "What may or may not come as a shock is my lack of cooking skills. So I'll do the dishes."

Jessie piled all the dishes in the sink and filled it with soapy water. "You're on. But these can wait till later. C'mon." Jessie tugged Isabel along with her sketchpad to the sofa.

Sara joined them, looking over Jessie's shoulder. "Hey, that looks like Chautauqua Park." Boulder, a small valley town nestled up next to the foothills of the Rocky Mountains, was famous for its red rocks and scenic views from hiking paths just minutes from town.

"It's that lookout area off the Flatirons loop," Isabel said.

"These are really good, Isabel." Jessie turned each page slowly, through unfinished sketches to more complete pieces, until she reached the end.

"You're going to enter Stone's annual art contest, aren't you?" Sara asked.

Isabel set the sketchbook aside. "Maybe. I haven't really thought about it."

"You didn't enter last year?"

"Nope." Isabel snuggled into the sofa, wrapping her arms around one of the pillows. "Why?"

"Winning is a prestigious honor in the Boulder art community. I just think you should, that's all."

Jessie got up and lit a few of the candles placed around the room. "Sara, get comfortable. You guys are staying, right? No classes tomorrow."

Sara liked the softness of the light, the mysterious glow it gave to everything it touched. She thought about the last month getting to know Jessie and Isabel. It felt good to have new friends. She didn't have any really beside Quinn. She decided to tell them about the chains. "I had another incident this morning."

Isabel's attention sharpened, though she didn't move. "Really? Come on, don't keep us in suspense."

"We want it all. No summarizing," Jessie demanded.

Sara imagined she was writing it down, telling a story. "I was going to a doctor's appointment. As soon as I turned off the engine in the parking lot, I knew. It happened slowly, like time had stopped. I watched everything around me fade into nothingness until I was alone. The chains made this clicking noise as they slid over my arms and legs, wrapping around and around until I was in this shell and then the ground disappeared too."

Jessie and Isabel exchanged looks.

"What?" she asked.

Isabel pulled her sketchpad off the floor. "I can picture it exactly how you describe it. Hold on." She grabbed a pencil from her bag and began to draw in quick sure strokes.

Jessie went to the kitchen and came back with a box tied with ribbon. "I don't know about you two, but after hearing that, I need chocolate." She opened it, chose one and passed it around.

Knowing what Isabel was doing didn't prepare Sara for the shock of seeing it on paper when the sketch was finished and handed to her. "It looks like something out of a science fiction story." She stared at the image, seeing herself the way she'd felt it this morning. It was...disturbing. Downright frightening. "What about you two? Any more? Sara asked.

Jessie shook her head and reached for another piece from the box. "Any ideas on what this all means? Why we go to these crazy places?"

"You heard music that makes you think of your dad. Then the giant hedges. Maybe there's a roadblock you have to break through, Jess," Isabel suggested. Turning to Sara, she said, "And you have something keeping you safe, as you said, but it's really keeping you prisoner."

"Maybe," Jessie agreed, "but it's still so unbelievable. What about yours? Dark caves and painting?"

Sara frowned. "Her art, of course. But a cave? Maybe something is hidden, that she's got to discover." She put the drawing down and closed the candy box, retying the ribbon.

Jessie stretched her arms above her head and got to her feet. "C'mon. I'm going to get out of these clothes."

She was stripping down to her bra and underwear in her bedroom when Sara and Isabel followed a few minutes later. Jessie got two knee-length tees from a dresser drawer and tossed one to Isabel and the other to Sara. "You two can have the bed, I'll sleep on the chaise."

Sara hesitated, unsure of what to do. She'd never slept anywhere but her own house. The newness of everything lately started the fluttering of panic she recognized well. She breathed deep in an effort to hold it at bay. She wanted the safety of the bathroom, but sat down at the foot of the bed instead. The tee was huge on Isabel, reaching down to her knees, Sara noticed. She watched Isabel wander the room looking at all of Jessie's things.

"Where are your roommates?" Isabel asked. She crawled onto the bed.

"Emily said she was spending the night with her broker. Maribel's probably partying late."

"It's a nice place," Sara said, trying to add to the conversation. "Quiet."

"Not usually," Jessie laughed.

"What about you, Isabel?" Sara asked. "I can't imagine living with a big family like yours."

"Depending on which Cordova you talk to, you'll get a different answer." Isabel smiled with the words. "I'm third youngest of seven. I've always shared a room, worn hand-me-downs and been compared to all my older brothers and sisters at some point. Until Stone College."

"Anonymity can be a good thing," Jessie curled deeper into the blanket.

Isabel looked through some CDs sitting on the bedside table as she talked. "My younger sister Maggie's in a cheerleading competition tomorrow. I'll have to get up in time to get there by eight."

Jessie got up and grabbed one CD from the pile and handed it to Sara. "Here. Put this on."

Sara stared at the cover. A young man with strong lean features and shoulder-length black hair sat on the back of a motorcycle playing a piano on the edge of a cliff, the ocean on the horizon. "Who is he?"

"A friend I went to high school with. It's his first album. Great cover, huh?"

Isabel admired the picture when Sara handed it over. "Just a friend? He's hot."

They listened for a while as the candle shadows flickered on the ceiling.

"What do you think?" Jessie asked. "He writes most of his own music."

"His voice is mesmerizing. It draws you in." Isabel had her eyes closed, her voice sleepy.

"I've never heard anything like it." It was hard for Sara to believe Jessie actually knew someone with such talent. "He's really good."

"You can have it," she said, gesturing to the CD Sara still held. "I've got another one."

"Cool. Thanks." Sara went to the living room and put it in her bag. After using the bathroom, taking her Paxil, and changing into the tee, she returned to the bedroom and started working out the tangles in her hair with a brush she always carried in her purse. On one side of the bed, Isabel was chatting with Jessie, who was looking at a magazine.

"Hey, Sara, come look at this. Isn't this your outfit from the other day?"

"If you two are gonna talk clothes all night, I'm going to sleep," Isabel threatened.

Sara could do this. She took another deep breath, sat on the bed next to them. And felt the slide of cold metal against the soles of her feet, wrapping around her ankles. She swallowed hard. She wouldn't freak out. She answered Jessie's question with a smile. She *was* doing it.

Four

The Graces

Autumn 1820
Woburn Abbey, Great Britain

They could tell she was close by the scent she wore. Bloom rather appreciated that it was lilacs. As she came around the bend from the house, they watched the Duchess walk the dirt path that wound through the trimmed lawn to the small table and chair nearby. There she would sit, write and take afternoon tea in the garden as she so often did.

By Joy's estimate it had been three human years since the night their destiny changed; since they had been trapped in stone in the physical representation of themselves. Three months of that time they'd been completely covered and packed to ensure safe travel to their new home.

A time of darkness. Grief. Lament.

A time to question how this had happened to them. And by whose hand.

It could have been any of the gods, but they truly suspected only one.

Aphrodite.

They were her handmaidens and knew well her petty jealousies and the ways she wrought revenge. She had probably seen the statue in their honor and the admiration of the men and had done her worst. And since they knew her so well, there was without a doubt a way to be released. They would find it. They had to.

Brilliance would never forget the day the covers were withdrawn, exposing them to the open air, to the light. Nor the first moment Lady Georgiana laid eyes on them. The workmen had finished the pedestal where they were to be placed and she had rushed from the house with her husband, the Duke, following at a more leisurely pace.

"Oh my!" With flushing cheeks and an ardent gaze she'd taken to them immediately. And they to her. They'd known in that exact moment they could still affect people because they sensed in her a sadness and longing as great as their own. It had been a trigger of sorts. They began to sense the needs of everyone who came to see them and in that way it felt familiar. A homecoming laden with relief.

Yes, it was her husband who had commissioned the statue, but the Graces discovered as they looked into the Duke's heart that it had been commissioned for her. To win her over. And he succeeded brilliantly. The Graces made sure of it.

There was not much else for them to do except what they did best. Even from a considerable distance they could still work their magic.

Five

Jessie

Autumn   Present Day
Boulder, Colorado

Jessie pulled into the parking lot of the mini mall and wondered what would happen when she stood in the exact spot again. She wasn't scared, just curious. It was a test of sorts because she'd avoided this particular corner of her neighborhood since that day fourteen years ago. But hearing the music had made her think about her dad, made her think enough time had passed that she could come here without reliving it again.

She'd convinced herself she could.

Isabel and Sara, however, weren't certain at all about the plan. She'd told them about her father and this seemingly innocuous place that had changed her life so drastically. Now that they were here there was a collective hesitation about getting out of the car.

"You don't have to do this, you know," Sara said quietly from the back seat.

They watched groups of kids from the nearby middle school hanging around outside the convenience store while next door at the laundromat mothers with babies in strollers chatted and folded clothes.

"Looks so ordinary. Like ones we've all been to dozens of times." Isabel undid her seatbelt, waiting.

As soon as Jessie got out she knew fourteen years wasn't long enough. The loud hum of washers and dryers, the overpowering smell of detergent and bleach brought death to her senses. She wasn't going to escape it. The nightmare of her father's blood soaking her mother's pink floral dress came to her, as real as the moment it had happened.

She was a little girl with licorice pigtails watching other kids play jacks on the scarred linoleum floor when the shots sounded. Then, like now, her legs wouldn't move, but the other children screamed and ran. Voices shouted, cursed, or muttered prayers. An elderly couple hid behind a washing machine. She'd gone outside and seen her father on the sidewalk in a pool of blood, her mother on her knees, his head in her lap.

Caught in the crossfire of a gang hit, her father and the teenager they'd been after, died later that night in the emergency room of St. Luke's hospital.

Jessie heard Sara and Isabel slamming the car doors and moving in next to her. She could feel the stares of people skirting around them. Wave after wave of desperation hit her, the sheen of violence still there, invisible and insidious.

She'd thought the music might come back, or the hedge, something, anything to give her a clue as to how it all connected to her father. But only remnant images pressed in on her.

Isabel tugged on her arm, pulling her back to the car. "Okay, that's enough. Let's get out of here."

Sara turned her around and helped her in, saying nothing. Isabel took the keys from Jessie's hand, started the car, and backed out of the lot. Jessie stared straight ahead, afraid to close her eyes.

Sara leaned forward from the back seat. "Take deep breaths, Jess. Just listen to your breathing and pay attention to the air going in and out of your lungs. Don't think of anything else."

Jessie tried to think only of the movement of her chest filling up then draining out. Her heart slowly stopped galloping like a runaway horse. By the time she was able to focus outside the window the Pueblo-style architecture of Stone College was in view.

Isabel pulled into an empty space in the student lot and handed her the keys.

"Thanks." Jessie took them but didn't make a move to gather her things.

"Did you hear the music?" Isabel asked.

Sara pushed Isabel lightly on the shoulder. "Give her some time. It was obviously difficult for her. Maybe she doesn't want to talk about it right away."

Isabel made a face. "She can handle it. Can't you Jess?"

Jessie pulled down the visor to check her face in the mirror, wiping a finger under each of her eyes and smoothing back her hair.

"She was moaning back there, for god sakes." Sara sounded concerned, with a little fear mixed in.

Jessie tensed. "Was I really?"

Isabel got her wallet from the seat and grabbed her backpack from the floor. "Yeah, you were. Come on, we're going to be late for class."

She didn't hear one word of Professor Saunders' lecture on the Spanish Renaissance. Sara leaned over toward the end and whispered, "I'll share my notes."

"I guess revisiting the laundromat this morning wasn't a great idea after all," Jessie said as they walked out of class into the chilly autumn morning.

"So I take it you didn't hear the music like you hoped you would," Isabel said, buttoning up her coat and wrapping a scarf around her neck.

"Nope."

Isabel stopped where the path veered off in two directions. "I go this way. Catch up with you later?"

Jessie nodded.

"Where are you headed?" Sara asked as they continued on.

"I've got a meeting with my adviser."

Sara had on a beret that matched her knee-length navy blue coat and she stopped to adjust it on her head. "Wanna talk about it?"

"I really thought I'd dealt with it. I didn't think that place still held such power over me."

"You haven't gone there all these years. Some part of you must've known that."

"Maybe I should've gone back before. I hate that it's resurfacing again." She shuddered just thinking about the pain she'd felt emanating from that place.

Sara looked away, the wind tugging at her hair and the beret slipped again. She reached up to right it. "I know what you mean."

Jessie kept silent, not pushing, just waiting for Sara to open up. She needed something to distract her, even if it was someone else's problems. School work certainly wasn't going to do it.

"I have an anxiety disorder. I'm on medication and I see a psychiatrist every month." Sara's gaze traveled over the courtyard before coming back to Jessie.

"What's it like?" Jessie asked.

"When I have a panic attack my heart races out of control, my hands shake, I can't speak, my vision blurs." She gripped her hands together, knuckles white, and took a deep breath. "If it's bad, I get dizzy or pass out. But with medication, that doesn't happen anymore. So I understand what you mean about other things having control over you."

Jessie had a thousand more questions but she could tell Sara wouldn't say anymore now. On impulse, she stepped forward and gave Sara a hug. When she pulled back Sara's eyes showed surprise, but her smile said the embrace was welcome.

"See you." Sara turned as she walked up the steps to the Foreign Languages building.

Jessie gave a little wave. In another few minutes she was at Dr. Blackstone's office door waiting for her to arrive. From the moment they'd met, Jessie liked the professor's friendly smile, her open and direct approach. Still, Jessie didn't know why she had requested this meeting, unless it was to push her into declaring a major.

"Thanks for waiting. I'm running a little late." Dr. Blackstone hurried in, her keys jangling as she opened her office door. She signaled Jessie to follow.

Jessie sat in one of the two chairs along the wall, put her bag on the floor and waited.

Dr. Blackstone took off her coat revealing a crisp, black business suit. Her auburn hair was pulled up in the back and amber eyes looked Jessie over carefully as she opened a Thermos and poured what looked like tea into a mug on the desk. "I've got your transcripts and some notes from your instructors. You had excellent grades in the beginning but then they dropped." Dr. Blackstone took a sip from the mug. "How's everything this year?"

"All right."

"You don't sound too excited," she replied.

It probably wasn't what she expected to hear, but Jessie decided to be honest. "My classes aren't holding my interest. Nothing is. I feel like I'm not heading in the right direction. But I don't know which way that is either."

"Hmmm. Well you're not the first one to say that to me, but I have to admit, most Stone College students come with a plan because they already know what they want to do." Dr. Blackstone made a note in a folder on her desk then sat back in her chair. "When we talked last year you said you were leaning toward business or math."

"Yes, I'm good in those subject areas, but they don't...excite me."

"Is there some interest you haven't told me about? A secret passion or hobby? We have a great arts department. Music too."

Jessie hated this. Hated thinking about things she didn't want to.

Dr. Blackstone raised her brows waiting for a response.

Jessie shrugged in a defensive gesture. The weirdness of the last few weeks had given her a lot to think through. Figure out. She needed more time. There were no windows in the office and Jessie wondered how Dr. Blackstone could stand the lack of natural light. She looked at the Van Gogh prints on the walls and some photographs of two children playing in the park.

"My kids," Dr. Blackstone said, following Jessie's gaze. She pulled a pamphlet out of her drawer and passed it across the desk. "I'm sure you've seen this but it won't hurt to look again."

Jessie took the list of degrees and programs offered by the college and stood, slinging her bag over her shoulder. "Thank you."

"You really should've declared something last semester. Think on it and make a decision soon."

They shook hands and Jessie headed out.

Instead of the library, where she should go, she went to her car. She needed to run, despite the cool weather. Maybe it would help clear her mind. She didn't like being so indecisive and her jumble of emotions was starting to make her crazy.

At home she changed into her running pants and a long-sleeved tee. Out front, she checked under a rock in the fountain to make sure the extra key was still there, closed the door and started jogging down the drive. By the time she turned on Boulder Canyon Drive toward the mountains, she was breaking a sweat.

As she inhaled and exhaled, she remembered the breathing she'd done that morning to forget the pain. She'd never talked with anyone about how physical her memories were. When she thought about that time she felt as if a sheer, sharp edge cut her all over her body. Maybe death was like that for those left living. The way her mother had cried each night for months after the funeral told her it was probably so.

The aspens were almost finished turning to deep red and gold. In contrast to the dark green of the pines, they dotted the roadside and the hills beyond like confetti.

Her feet pounding the pavement became a wordless chant. She wished she understood the meaning behind the music she'd heard and how her dad had known it. Which reminded her she'd promised to listen to the song Mario had sent. She'd download it when she got home. If she didn't collapse first. She was pushing herself hard and her muscles were starting to hurt so she turned around and started back.

As twilight neared, she began to see wisps of her breath on the air. Her fingers felt stiff, her hands always being the first to feel the cold. She'd have to dig out her gloves for next time because winter was coming early. She was at the front door when she remembered she had to get the key. Turning around, she came face to face with imposing shrubs.

They stood tall, but not gigantic like the time in the street, with a single path leading around a bend. Like a maze or labyrinth. Her first instinct was to run, but her legs were so wobbly she didn't think they'd carry her far.

Seconds ago the air had been so cold she'd seen her breath. Now the temperature was balmy, almost tropical. She waited until her breathing and heart rate slowed, staring at the tightly woven branches in front of her. When her legs became steadier, she touched one of the leaves. Soft, smooth, and very real, it broke off into her hand just as the music floated like before out of nowhere. It was poetic and powerful and the allure came in wanting to sing with it. She'd stuffed that desire away for so long, its return shook her deep.

"Hey, Jess, what're you doing?"

Her roommate Emily's voice sounded far off even though Jessie knew she was only a few yards away.

The maze disappeared.

"Damn, you're crazy to be standing out in the cold. Get in here!"

The next thing she knew, Emily had dragged her backward into the house and slammed the door. In a black sweater, short checked skirt, black tights and high-heeled boots, Emily's hair fell in curves around her darkly defined eyes and brows and sharp cheekbones. She looked Jessie up and down and shook her head.

"Snap out of it, girlfriend. What's up with you?" she asked.

Jessie couldn't answer. It was like being unable to wake from a dream, where one world blended with the other.

"Let me guess. You went running, pushed yourself, stayed out too long, and now you're freezing to death."

Jessie nodded and moved toward her room, finally finding her voice. "Something like that."

"Go take a shower and I'll make you some tea."

Jessie turned on the shower. Somehow she managed to get undressed and under the hot spray. Even when her limbs no longer felt numb, her mind did. When she reached for the shampoo, she looked down to see a leaf on the tile floor. It swirled away down the drain.

She went through the motions of washing and rinsing her hair and body before stepping out and toweling off. A cup of mint tea waited for her on the counter. After putting on a white terry cloth robe and slippers she was about to go into the living room when she heard a male voice. Emily's boyfriend was over.

A glance at her phone showed a text from Isabel.

"R u ok?"

She sent a quick "yes" back, downed the tea, curled up on the bed under the blankets and fell fast asleep.

She was startled into wakefulness by a persistent buzzing noise. Her phone lay next to her on the pillow. She glanced at the time. Midnight. Mario's name lit up the screen.

"Hi."

"Did I wake you? You're in bed early," Mario teased. He knew she was usually a night owl like him.

She struggled to sit up; her muscles protested. "I went for a run."

"Had a bad day?"

"Yeah, kind of." Which was putting it mildly. "I was going to listen to your song and call you later."

"We'll get to that in a minute. First tell me what happened."

She didn't answer but listened for sounds from the living room, and when she didn't hear any, she went to the kitchen to make more tea. She cradled the phone between her neck and shoulder as she filled a cup and put it in the microwave.

"I've got all night. I'm lying here in bed, just waiting, nothing else to do," he said, his voice soft and low.

She laughed and didn't feel so weak any longer. She told him about going to the laundromat.

"Why did you suddenly have the urge to visit the place where your father was shot?" he asked.

"I've been thinking about Dad a lot lately, that's all."

"Maybe that place will always do that to you. No matter how much time's passed. Just don't go back. You don't really need to, anyway."

He was right, she didn't.

"Why haven't you listened to it yet?" Mario asked. His question didn't surprise her, but she still wasn't ready to answer.

"I promise I will tonight and I'll call you tomorrow."

"You didn't answer my question."

She could hear disappointment in his voice. "I don't know. I really don't."

Silence was his response.

She looked at the phone to make sure the call hadn't been dropped. "I'm sorry..."

"Forget it," he interrupted. "Phil worked out a few of the kinks with me and the band's been practicing it. We're going to play it Wednesday night at Fisher's."

"Where's that? Have you played there before?" she asked.

"I've got to go," and he hung up.

He was angry and she didn't blame him. He'd asked for a favor and she'd let him down. How could she tell him how hard it was for her to help him with his music and not be there with him? He was smart. Why the hell couldn't he figure that out by himself? She took her half-warm tea to the computer and sat down at the little desk in the corner of the living room to wait while it came on. Putting in her earphones, she clicked on the file and took a sip of tea.

Ten minutes later she crawled back in bed. She pressed on her eyes to stop the tears and gave herself a headache instead. He'd written a song about taking chances. Taking risks. About the kind of woman that wasn't confused, knew what she wanted, and went after it.

Jessie dreamed of giant hedges that kept growing taller and taller until they reached the heavens. But there was no music in the maze of her dream. She was enclosed, trapped, in an unbearable silence.

Six

Isabel

"There she is."

At the sound of their voices, Isabel turned from the canvas on the gallery wall.

Jessie's high-heeled boots clicked on the cement floor as she approached. "Sorry it took us so long. We walked the wrong way."

"It's okay," Isabel said. "You gave me time to jot down some notes for the assignment. Now I'm free to enjoy."

"Wow, look at that one over there." Sara pointed to a canvas with a mix of greens and gold in lines and swirls on the opposite wall. "Who's the artist?"

Isabel handed over the brochure she'd picked up on the way in. "One of my professors, Brian Dowling."

While Sara read the short bio on the inside of the pamphlet, Jessie followed Isabel to the price list discreetly placed on an antique cherry wood table at the other end of the room.

"He's had shows all over the Southwest." Sara gazed at one piece that took up half the wall. "Interesting."

Jessie leaned over and whispered in Isabel's ear, "Do people really buy this stuff?"

She smiled because she'd often wondered the same thing. "You don't like it?" she asked.

"I just can't imagine having one of them hanging in my living room."

The three of them critiqued each piece. Sara knew a lot about art: the balance, the movement, and what drew the eye.

"This one looks like a giant penis in the middle of a football field," Jessie said.

Isabel laughed. "What an interesting perspective."

Sara tilted her head to one side. "I guess everybody sees something different."

"She's just joking, Sara," Isabel said.

"No, I'm not."

They wandered into another section, a separate room off to the side of the main space.

"Is this a different artist?" Jessie asked, bypassing the information posted on the wall.

Isabel scanned the two paragraphs, Sara standing next to her. "No, this is some of Professor Dowling's earlier work." She glanced around before approaching the first sketch. "I didn't realize this room had his stuff, too."

"They're all charcoal. Kind of like yours, Isabel." Jessie stopped in front of a sketch in the middle that was slightly bigger than the others. "Hey, look at this one. He's good with people, too."

They wandered to where Jessie stood.

When Isabel saw it, the world seemed to slow, to narrow, encompassing just her and the sketch.

A young man, hair disheveled by the wind and coat collar turned up, looked at the sun setting over hills covered with trees.

A vise squeezed her heart.

A memory of a moment from the past came to her. She remembered the pattern of the sun on the floor of his office, smelled the faint scent of incense that clung to him. She saw how they greeted each other with the usual embrace. How she wanted to stay there, comforted.

How she wanted more.

Her cheeks flushed as she thought of how she'd clung a little too long. Then pressed a kiss to his chest without thinking. He'd pulled away, his expression puzzled, but before he could speak, she fled. He called after her, but she didn't stop. In the empty bathroom of the girl's locker room, with the steady drip of the broken faucet echoing from a sink along the wall, Isabel let her embarrassment cool as she steadied her uneven breathing and her racing heart.

She felt a hand on her sleeve.

"Isabel? Are you okay?" Sara asked.

"Did you go to your cave?" Jessie whispered.

She shook her head.

They each put an arm around her. It helped banish the images and brought her back to the present.

"Do you want to go or stay?" Jessie asked.

"I'm done. You guys?"

"Come on. Let's get out of here," Sara urged.

Isabel felt better once they stepped outside, though the memories kept pushing at her.

They walked past restaurants and boutiques, talking fashion, keeping the mood light. The afternoon sun was out from the clouds, the air dry and faintly sweet. They found a patch of grass along the narrow beltway that ran through the downtown area. Even though it was already brown, it looked comfortable enough. Tossing her bag down, Isabel sat and stretched out, happy to soak up some warmth.

Sara reclined more gingerly, probably in deference to her outfit.

Jessie sat on her bag, leaned back and closed her eyes. "This is much better than studying."

"Having a hard time of it?" Sara asked.

"I'm so not motivated and it's only fall term. How am I going to get through the rest of the year?"

Isabel exchanged looks with Sara. "I thought you had A's and B's in your classes?"

"I do."

Isabel rolled her eyes. "We don't want to hear any complaining then. If only we had it so easy."

Sara shifted slightly. "Hey, Jess, you never told us about the song."

"There's not much to tell. Nana doesn't recognize it. I've never heard it before that I can remember and I can't figure out why I think of Dad when I hear it."

"Maybe it's not the song itself," Sara suggested. "You said he used to sing to you. Maybe it's just that. You need to remember that for some reason."

Isabel watched Jessie intently, looking for a reaction, but she was turned away, looking out over the creek and path nearby.

Sara reached into her purse, took out her phone and looked at the time. "I hate to say this but I should get back." She got to her feet, looking around. "Half your stuff is out of your bag, Isabel."

"Which way you heading home?" Isabel sat up and gathered her things. "I have to stop by the art supply store. I'm almost out of charcoal pencils and I need a couple drawing pads."

Jessie reached out and grabbed one of Isabel's sketchbooks off the grass. "No kidding. This one has seen better days for sure." She opened it and began to look at the drawings.

"That's one I used in high school. I grabbed it out of my drawer this morning so I'd have something just in case." Isabel watched Jessie turn the pages.

Jessie closed the book and leaned forward to hand it over. A folded piece of paper slipped from the inside and floated to the ground. "Sorry. Can I see?" she asked, opening a faded, smudged charcoal print.

Isabel jerked back in surprise. Where had that come from? She hadn't looked at that particular piece since the day she'd drawn it and couldn't even remember putting it in that sketchbook.

"He looks like the guy in the picture at the gallery, right?" Jessie turned it around so Sara could see.

In a garden overgrown with lush tropical plants a man filled the side of the paper as if he were backing away.

Isabel rose, brushed herself off, and took the drawing, her hand a bit unsteady. Damn. There were just too many coincidences to ignore. She couldn't pretend any longer. First the phone call, which she'd guessed was him. Then the sketch in the gallery. She didn't know how Professor Dowling knew him, but that, along with her own drawing simply falling out, was completely upending her.

Isabel stepped onto the path and looked at Sara. "Which way you parked?"

Sara gestured toward one of the city's public lots a couple blocks down.

"Who is it?" Jessie put her arm through Isabel's and began to stroll. "You obviously know him."

Some kids on bicycles went by, their shouts covering Isabel's silence until they turned off the path and disappeared.

"His name's Father Michael Livingston."

"Father? You mean he's a priest?" Jessie asked, astonished.

Isabel smiled. She'd managed to shock Jessie, which wasn't easy.

"Was he the priest at your church?" Sara asked.

Isabel shook her head. "At Catholic schools there's a priest on campus called a chaplain," she explained, "who says Mass and stuff and is also available for counseling. Senior year I had all these questions about faith and didn't know who to talk to. So I made an appointment with Father Michael."

"Most of the priests I know don't come close to young or handsome," Jessie said with a grin.

Isabel sighed. "We had some great talks. Like he really understood what I was going through. How I felt things that didn't make sense with what I'd been taught."

"Keep going," Jessie encouraged.

Isabel hesitated. The memory of that day in his office was still fresh after her experience back in the gallery. No one knew about it, not even Maggie.

Hell, she might as well just put it out there.

Haltingly, it poured out. The embrace. The kiss. Her running away. "A part of me was ashamed that deep down I wanted more with him, more than counselor and student," she admitted. "More than a priest is supposed to have with anyone. But another part of me never stopped wanting it."

"So then what happened after you ran from his office?" Sara asked.

"I didn't see him for a week and when I did, he thankfully acted like nothing happened. He never brought it up and neither did I." Isabel crossed her arms, rubbing them briskly in the swiftly approaching cool night air. "He always asked to see my latest drawings. The hour each week we spent together would fly. He encouraged me to go to Stone College, you know. When I got the scholarship he was almost as excited as I was." Isabel remembered that vividly, too. She'd given him one of her favorite sketches and he'd had it matted and framed.

"Then a couple months later I graduated, and over the summer he was reassigned to some parish that needed help."

They came to a stop in front of Sara's light blue Honda and she opened the door with the remote. They didn't move to get in the car.

"Now that I actually tell the story, I don't know how it sounds. I felt so foolish. Still do a little," she admitted.

"We can't help who we're attracted to," Jessie said, shrugging. "He's good-looking and he helped you when you needed someone to talk to. Besides, nothing happened, did it? You both did the right thing."

Isabel remembered all the gossip among the girls in her class about the handsome priest. She'd been attracted to his warmth, the way he looked at her while she was talking as if what she had to say was important. She'd liked his laugh and the way he'd lovingly teased all the nuns. He'd even gotten the grumpiest of them, Sister Giovanna, to smile.

Sara went around and opened the driver's side. "Come on, I'll drop you off, Jess, and I'll take Isabel to the art store."

Sara put on some mellow music as they headed back to campus, which didn't help Isabel's mood. Thinking about that time in her life didn't ever do her much good. A couple of sketches she'd titled, Torn in Two, from that year of uncertainty were pinned to the wall in her room. What she wasn't able to put into words or would never talk about, always came out in a drawing.

"Hey, I just thought of something." Jessie turned off the music and shifted toward Isabel.

Jessie's excited voice jolted her out of her reverie. She turned from the window and looked to the front seat. "What?"

"Did you ever call your mystery man back?" Jessie asked.

Isabel sighed. "I knew you'd figure it out sooner or later." His face came to her clearly, even the sound of his voice. She was momentarily awash with emotions she'd tried desperately to forget. The fierce pull of longing and wanting. The guilt and shame.

"So you guessed all along. Why didn't you call?"

Sara pulled to a stop next to Jessie's car and glanced in the rearview mirror. Her eyes said she understood how shame could rule your actions. "C'mon, get in the front."

"Call me later then," Jessie said, getting out. With a wave she was gone.

Out in front of the art store, Sara parked and got a notebook from the back seat. "Go get what you need. I'll study while I wait."

Fifteen minutes later and forty dollars poorer, Isabel was back and they headed home.

"Are you gonna call him?" Sara asked as she turned onto Isabel's street.

"Even if I wanted to, I'm pretty sure I don't have the number anymore. I have no idea what I did with it." Isabel grabbed the plastic bag with her purchases and her school bag from the floor. "Thanks for the ride. The buses are always overcrowded this time of night."

"I've got you covered. Anytime." Sara looked tired but her smile was as genuine as always.

The lights were off in the living room, which meant everyone was at the dinner table. Isabel hoped to sneak up the back stairs with a plate of food but it wasn't meant to be. Her mother was already bringing empty plates from the table to the sink as she closed the back door.

Maggie and James were arguing over whose turn it was to do dishes. The front door slammed and then her sister came in the kitchen, which meant her brother had won the argument.

"I hate it when he's right," she said with a frown. Then her face lit up. "Isa! When did you get home?"

"Just now. What's up?" Isabel stood at the counter and ate a bowl of pasta, watching as her sister filled the sink with soapy water. Her mother, dressed in her usual dark knit skirt and cotton blouse, put things away, her movements brisk and efficient.

Maggie chatted happily about the latest gossip at school, the upcoming basketball season, and the new cheerleading uniforms. Isabel let her sister's talk flow and relaxed with a second helping and a sip of the red table wine her mother had left sitting in a glass on the counter.

"I'm stuck on my calculus homework. Can you help?" Maggie asked, as she set the last pot on the dish drainer.

"Sure. Go on, I'll just wash my plate and be right up."

Isabel listened to her sister say goodnight to their father, aware her mother was listening too and watching her even though she appeared not to. "The Bolognese sauce was really good."

"It's your father's favorite. Management accepted the union proposal today."

"That's great." Isabel looked at the remains of a cake sitting under plastic wrap and the almost empty bottle of wine. "So you had a celebration dinner."

"He deserves it. He's worked hard, putting in extra hours to help..." her mother waved her hand in the air, searching for the word.

"Negotiate," Isabel supplied.

"Yes, that's it."

Isabel washed her bowl and glass, adding them to the already full dish drainer.

Her mother untied her apron, the signal her kitchen duties were over for the evening. She crossed her arms and leaned against the counter. "He asked about you."

"I'll talk to him before I go up."

"The holidays are coming. I expect you to be around," her mother said.

"Finals are right after Thanksgiving so I'll have to put in a lot of study time." Isabel headed toward the living room.

Her father was asleep in his recliner, the TV on but muted. She watched him for a minute, the rise and fall of his chest, the slow relaxation of muscles as he drifted deeper in sleep. He looked old; the lines on his face visible even in the shadows, his thinning hair and veined hands in stark contrast to his muscled forearms.

"It was the second glass of wine that did him in," her mother said from behind her. She pulled the handle on the side of the chair, pushing it slowly back so that he was almost lying down.

Isabel felt like an intruder on an intimate moment, watching her mother untie and loosen his boots while her father slept. She'd never thought much about their marriage, whether they were happy, whether they still loved each other. It was only in moments like this, just glimpses really, when she felt anything for them. And how horrible was that? She'd never found conversation with them easy. Of all her brothers and sisters, she was truly at ease only with Maggie. Now there were Jessie and Sara. And for a couple months, when she'd most needed it, there'd been Father Michael.

She said a quiet "goodnight" and went to help her sister with calculus.

It was almost ten thirty by the time she got back to her room. Dumping her bags on the floor, she stripped down to her camisole and underwear and sank onto her unmade bed in the dark. The moon was a crescent surrounded by twinkling lights through her window. She tore off the packaging from a charcoal pencil and began to draw on a clean sheet from the new sketchbook. The outline of the window appeared, followed by the view outside, and in the corner, her father sleeping in his chair. As shapes and shadows blended together, she breathed easier, letting the details go because they'd been transferred to paper.

She set her finished piece aside and pulled the covers up as she scooted back against the headboard. Turning the light on its lowest setting, she stared at the collection of items lying on the bedside table. Half a pack of Carefree sugarless watermelon gum, a couple of quarters, a pair of earrings, a black ballpoint pen and a slip of paper.

She'd lied to Sara about his phone number.

Digging through the pockets of her jeans she found her cell phone. Her fingers caressed the dial pad while a tug-o-war assaulted her insides. Just so she could be free of the worrying and wondering, she dialed the number.

"Hello."
His voice was exactly how she remembered. "Hi."
"Isabel?"

"Yes, it's me."

"I was afraid you didn't get my message."

"No, I did. It's just that I didn't realize it was you. It's been a while." More lies. What was she going to say though? I didn't call you 'cause I was afraid?

"It has been, hasn't it?"

"You're in Boulder."

"Yes, I'm staying with a friend. I'd like to see you."

She paused, heart racing, lightheaded. "My days are pretty full but…"

"Isabel, please. Tomorrow?"

She forced her mind to think clearly. Fridays were usually pretty open. "Around eleven?" she finally managed.

"Great. Come here and I'll fix something to eat." He gave her the address.

"That's close to campus."

"I know." Then he paused as if searching for the right thing to say. "I…well, I'm glad you called."

Her sleep was so restless she didn't feel like she got much of it by morning. She went through her routine thinking solely of the upcoming visit. Consequently, she missed the bus and had to wait for the next one, making her late to class.

Jessie's eyes questioned her as she took the seat next to Sara, who handed her a cup of coffee. She smiled her thanks and took a first sip, settling into her chair as the professor reminded the class of the upcoming presentations of their project.

"I'll give you the rest of the class to finalize them," Professor Saunders said, "I expect to see a lot of creative and interesting projects next week."

"Well, since we're pretty much done with ours," Jessie said, leaning over, "let's talk about what's up with Isabel."

Isabel sipped her coffee and leafed through copies of power point slides Sara had printed of the final version. "Did you get the music to work with it the way we wanted?"

Sara nodded. "It looks and sounds great. Now it's just up to you two to present it."

"Why are you ignoring me?" Jessie asked. "I know something's up."

Isabel wondered if she really was that transparent. Or maybe Jessie was just exceptionally good at reading people. "Okay, okay. I was going to tell you after class, you know."

"Ladies," Professor Saunders approached, notepad in hand. "I'd like yours to be first in the line-up."

"I'm good with that," Isabel looked at Jessie. "You?"

Jessie smiled. "Perfect."

Under the cover of the clamor of voices around them, Isabel told Jessie and Sara about "finding" the phone number and calling, about her agreeing to meet Father Michael later.

"Are you excited? Nervous?" Jessie asked.

"A little nervous, yeah. What am I going to talk about with him?"

"You sure you're gonna be okay?" Sara asked.

"No, I'm not sure, but I'll be fine."

"You know you don't make sense, right," Jessie teased.

As soon as Professor Saunders dismissed them, Isabel got up to go.

"You wanna ride?" Sara offered.

"No, I'm gonna walk. It'll help clear my mind. I hope." Isabel slung her bag over her shoulder. "Meet you later?"

"Are you kidding? We'll want to hear all the details," Jessie answered.

The sky was gray, the air cold. Isabel pulled on her gloves and kept her pace slow while she headed into the neighborhood south of campus. She rarely came this way. A tree with gnarled limbs in an empty lot beckoned. She saw a multitude of scenes that wanted to be drawn. She'd have to come back again. She stopped when she got to the end of the directions he'd given her. 345 Marion was a one-story, simple in style, the yard neat and orderly like the other houses in the area.

Isabel rang the bell and waited.

"Isabel." Father Michael opened the door wide. "Come on in." He stepped back and gestured for her to enter. She swallowed hard and nodded.

Isabel walked past him into a small foyer and glanced around, curious. "Nice house." Then she looked at him. He was dressed in jeans and a white T-shirt, socks on his feet. She'd never seen him without his priest garb on. It was like looking at a completely different person.

"It's a friend's." He led her down a hallway to an open kitchen, dining room area.

"Professor Dowling. I saw his exhibition and there's a sketch of you."

"You saw that, did you?"

Isabel noted the sparse furnishings and the clean, orderly kitchen counters. A few pieces of art on the walls. She took off her gloves, unzipped her coat, set her backpack on the floor and turned to face him.

"Would you like something to drink?"

"No thanks."

They studied each other.

She wondered what he saw. Tried to keep her expression guarded as the sound of water roared in her ears.

Please, no. Not here, not now.

She blurted out the first thing that came to mind. "Why are you here? I mean, in Boulder. Weren't you on assignment in Sterling, or somewhere? Are you on sabbatical?"

He ignored her questions. "You're looking well. How's Stone College?"

She crossed her arms. It was a defensive pose, but she couldn't help it.

He took a deep breath. "All right. I'll go first. I've left the priesthood."

It was like a punch in the gut; the last thing she expected to hear. She moved to the window that looked out on the back yard and tried to get her racing thoughts in order. Finally, all she could manage was, "Why?"

"That is the big question, isn't it?" He paused for a long moment. "I thought it was the life I wanted, the life I was meant for. I was happy and content... the first few years, anyway, especially as chaplain at Assumption High."

"But?"

"But the more time I spent doing service to the poor, in my own solitude, in prayer, even saying Mass ... I realized being a priest wasn't feeding my soul the way I longed for."

Isabel was listening, trying to keep up, keep an open mind. "Go on."

"I want to help people find God, not condemn them with church dogma. I want to serve people, but I don't want to be lonely for the rest of my life."

She looked at him, then, really searched his eyes, his face, as if she could see inside to the truth there.

He sighed. "Most people hold you at arm's length, even more since…"

"The sex abuse scandals," Isabel finished for him.

"It's hard to be looked at with suspicion by some and reverence by others. Then a void started growing inside me, Isabel. It's hard to explain. I wanted the Church to fill it, believe me."

"What about God? God could fill it," she said, even though God wasn't in her own life much anymore.

"God, yes, the Church, no."

Isabel leaned against the windowsill, feeling the late morning sun on her shoulders, in her hair. Letting his words sink in.

"I had a lot of time for introspection. The last year and a half, pretty much. Talking with my superior, going to counseling. Yelling at God. Yelling at myself."

He stopped talking then, and she figured there was probably a whole lot more that he didn't want to say. He ran his hands through his hair, the gesture one she remembered. It made her smile. "You were always such a good listener when I had doubts. You always seemed to understand what I was going through," she admitted. "I can try to do the same for you."

He smiled and she saw relief pass over his face. It was probably very difficult to share with others what he'd been going through.

"Thank you."

"What are you going to do?"

"Find work that I love." He began to pace slowly around the room.

"What kind?" Isabel asked.

"Peace and justice work hopefully. Possibly at a non-profit organization." His voice held a passion she remembered from his sermons on the homeless and the poor. He'd been inspiring. Her senior class had sponsored a couple of food drives and soup kitchen visits because of him.

"Now it's your turn. Tell me about you, Isabel."

66

What could she tell him that didn't sound less than ordinary? "The college's art program is interesting, challenging. I'm happy with it."

"Good."

She smiled a little. "Waitressing, living at home still, hoping to move out next year." She shrugged, not knowing what else to say.

"Friends? A boyfriend?"

Up until the last month, her life had been extremely quiet. "No boyfriend, but yeah, friends."

"I spoke with..."

"Jessie." She smiled, thinking of the phone call in the car. "Yes. She's spontaneous and fun, and another friend, Sara who's very smart and interesting. You'd like them."

"It's important to have people in your life who really know you, who accept you for who you are."

She didn't know what to say to that. She didn't know if others really knew her or not with how far she let them in.

"You didn't stay friends with any of the girls from Assumption?"

Isabel shook her head. Then the silence turned awkward.

"Stay for awhile. Let's talk, eat," he invited.

A suggestion that made her panic. She hadn't been prepared for his news and it left her feeling unsure and uncomfortable. "I've got to get back. I have your number. I'll call you."

He looked surprised and a little disappointed. "All right."

She didn't remember leaving; only that she kept her feet from running until she'd turned the corner and gone around the block. By then her legs were trembling so much she stumbled to a stop. The roar came back and this time she couldn't stop it. She welcomed the dark, the smell of saltwater, the solid rock beneath her feet. Her hands touched cold shale walls as she steadied herself. Turning, she leaned back, listening to a far-off drip echoing in her mind or in the air around her, she couldn't tell.

She squinted so her eyes could adjust to the dim light. Reaching out, she traced the trunk of a tree etched in the stone. The tree from the lot she'd passed on the way to see Father Michael.

Except that wasn't who he was anymore.

But then again, she wasn't the same person she'd been three years ago, either. When the tree and cave walls disappeared, she was leaning against a chain link fence out of breath. Oh, God, now what?

Seven

Sara

"You should tell her the truth."

The words stopped Sara as she walked past her parents' bedroom. Her father's voice, muffled by the closed door, held an edge she didn't recognize. She stood in the hallway listening, even though she'd been raised to believe it wasn't polite to eavesdrop on other people's private conversations.

"I'm not going to talk with her about it. Just drop it, James."

Sara's heart accelerated like a racecar going from zero to sixty.

"Don't you think she has a right to know? And it should come from you. Not me."

Her mother's voice was firm, implacable. "We've been over this before. I'd think you of all people wouldn't want her to find out."

"She deserves the truth. She can handle it."

"Well, then, you tell her."

Sara slowly backed up into her room just inside the doorway where she couldn't be seen. She'd long suspected they kept things from her, but she'd never questioned her father about it, afraid of what she might hear. Maybe this truth her father thought she should know was about her sister, Violet.

She went to her bedside table and picked up the polished quartz lying next to her journal. Doctor Bernstein had suggested she find an object to calm and center her when anxious or nervous. The glossy, fluid surface of the rock was a work of beauty. Quinn had given it to her years ago. She couldn't remember the occasion, but since then it had saved her many times from succumbing to her fears.

She heard her parents' bedroom door open, then close. Clutching the stone, she waited. It opened and shut again. The hum of the garage door faded followed by her mother's Mercedes and a few minutes later by her father's Volvo.

She took a couple of deep breaths. The stillness and ringing silence filling her ears enabled her to find her way downstairs to the kitchen. Did she want to hear whatever it was her father thought she should know? Could she handle it? Even now, after all her therapy and the security of knowing the medication would keep her from going into darkness again, the worst memory came to her clearly.

It had started with a small, rumbling noise that turned to a deafening roar. She saw herself as she ran to the bathroom and was violently sick. Wave after wave of wrenching, wracking sobs followed, the tears dripping on her hands as they gripped the edge of the toilet. She remembered the pain, her whole body hurting, as she slipped to the floor and lay on her side on the cold tile.

That was how her father had found her when he got home. He'd gathered her off the floor as if she were three instead of sixteen. He'd stroked her hair and whispered words of love.

Sara grasped the edge of the counter and practiced her relaxation techniques until she felt she could move. Today of all days she didn't need to be caught up in that fog of fear. The culminating presentation for humanities class was this morning, and even though she wasn't giving it she was still nervous. If she didn't leave soon, she'd be late. And they were first.

Grabbing a bottle of juice from the fridge and an orange from the fruit bowl on the counter, she headed out. Dressed in velvet-smooth brown corduroys and a warm wool sweater covered by a brown down jacket, she grabbed her gloves and scarf from the hall closet, locked up and headed to town. She just missed getting stuck in a long line at her favorite coffee shop but still only made it to campus with minutes to spare.

The corridor outside the classroom was packed with waiting students.

"What's going on?" she asked one of the girls.

"The door's locked."

Sara spotted Isabel up front and with a little maneuvering made it over to her. Isabel was putting her gloves into the pocket of her down vest and greeted her with a smile.

"Is Jessie here?" Sara asked.

"You'll never guess what she's going to do."

Sara felt a little rush of panic and then remembered they were talking about Jessie. Of course she had something planned. But what? And why hadn't she told them about it?

Isabel must've read her mind. "She told me she got this great idea late last night. She texted you this morning but you didn't reply. So I told her to go for it."

She hadn't checked her cell. She looked around at the hallway full of students. "Is that why we can't go in yet?"

Before Isabel had a chance to answer the door opened and Professor Saunders stood waiting. She whispered something to Isabel, who slipped inside the dark classroom. When Sara made a move to follow the professor held up her hand, keeping anyone else from entering. The crowd quickly hushed.

"The first group to present today has asked that we enter in silence and darkness. As soon as everyone is seated they will begin. Please be respectful and find seats quickly." Professor Saunders was clearly enjoying being part of the drama.

Jessie came out dressed in a long sleeveless gown, her face lit by a single candle. She introduced herself as one of the Three Graces, a patron goddess of the arts, and announced that she would be taking them on a tour of ancient Athens and the Acropolis. Isabel started the music and the Power Point was projected onto one empty classroom wall.

It was perfect. Jessie had taken Sara's long hours of research, showcased in Isabel's visual format, and made their project unforgettable. Looking at Professor Saunders' face, she could guess what grade they'd get.

Outside after class, they made plans to celebrate.

"Meet here at our usual time?" Isabel asked.

"Let's get food and go to Red Rocks," Jessie said, excitement lighting her features.

Sara frowned. "You're not serious, are you? It's too cold to sit up there this time of year."

Jessie grinned. "If we have coats and gloves we'll be fine."

Isabel shook her head, trying to look serious. She rubbed her arms up and down as if already cold. "We'd be mental to even consider it."

"Come on, it'll be fun. If it gets too cold we can sit in the car with the heater." Jessie tugged on Sara's sleeve. "Say yes. I'll get the drinks and snacks."

Who could say no after the performance Jessie had just given?

"Okay." She waited while Jessie high-fived Isabel with a whoop of laughter. "But I'll bring some take out. You do drinks."

"You got it, girl." Jessie turned toward her car and then pivoted back. "It turned out great, didn't it?"

Isabel smiled but looked at Sara. "If we tell her just how well, she'll be even more of a drama queen."

"Hey, not true."

"Oh yeah, right," Isabel said.

"I have self-esteem issues," Jessie replied with a mock serious face, her hand over her heart.

Isabel rolled her eyes. "See, like I said. Drama queen."

They parted ways in the usual spot, mid-campus, and Sara joined the back of a group of girls heading into biology. The farther away from Jessie and Isabel she got, the more thoughts of the conversation she'd heard between her parents intruded. What was the secret? It must be about Violet. Confusion filled her and she couldn't contain the vulnerability that came with it.

Instead of her usual spot in the front of the auditorium she chose a seat in the back row and got out her notebook. No one sat next to her, which was good because she didn't think she could stand the proximity of another person when she felt so fragile. The lecture started but instead of notes, a letter poured out of her onto the page.

A letter to the sister she hadn't seen in thirteen years. Two pages full of grief and guilt and questions. Her eyes swam with tears and she wiped at them angrily. She left before class was over, anxious to get to the restroom, to be alone.

It took a while to get herself together. Finally, her face washed, her breathing even and her hands no longer shaking, Sara walked outside hoping the cold and a trip to The Chinese Dragon for take-out would pull her out of her funk. She got the notebook she'd hastily shoved into her bag and walked to the trash. A compulsion to tear out the letter and toss it into the bin warred with a strong desire to keep it. She'd never thrown away any of her writing, evidenced by the wall of boxes in the basement full of her journals and school papers.

"Are you okay?" a voice asked from behind. It held compassion and more than a little curiosity.

Sara pushed the notebook back into her bag and found a pair of emerald green eyes studying her. "I'm fine."

"If you say so." The voice was skeptical.

Sara nerves skittered at the young woman's closeness. She was Sara's height and build, dressed in black tights and boots, a red wool skirt and matching vintage jacket. Straight auburn hair framed her face. Sara felt a pull, like an invisible thread reaching from deep inside, tugging her toward this girl whose name she didn't even know.

She hoped this didn't bring on a panic attack.

"I'm Leslie, by the way," the young woman said, holding out her hand.

Sara shook it, trying to ignore the herd of butterflies stampeding in her stomach. "I'm Sara."

"We had a class or two together last year but I haven't seen you much this year. Different schedules I guess. I saw you go into the bathroom earlier. Looked like you were pretty upset so I redirected girls to the other bathroom in the building."

Sara knew she was staring but couldn't help it. Why would this girl she hardly knew do that for her? "Thanks."

Leslie waved her hand in a gesture that said it was no problem. "Are you free right now? Wanna get some coffee?"

Surprise that she wanted to and disappointment that she couldn't overrode the anxiety she felt at such an invitation. "I was ... on my way to pick up some Dim sum and meet some friends."

A sad smile flitted over Leslie's face. "Some other time then."

Sara bravely let her gaze linger on those deep green eyes. "Sure."

She watched Leslie walk back toward the science building, her hand idly searching her jacket pocket until she felt the smooth round surface of her quartz. She held onto it as she crossed campus to the restaurant and didn't let go until she had to in order to grab the two plastic bags of take-out.

She could feel her spirits lighten when she met with Jessie and Isabel outside the student union. She was hungry for the first time all day and she felt safer with them than on her own. Just their presence kept the harshest of emotions at bay.

Fifteen minutes later they were parking Jessie's car in the almost empty lot at the trailhead to Red Rocks. They stopped at the plaque set in the rock at the start of the trail, wisps of breath swirling in the air around them. Jessie ran her gloved fingers over the words in bronze. "The earth is your grandmother and your mother, and she is sacred," she read aloud. "Every step that is taken upon her should be as a prayer."

"Chief Lakota," Sara said.

Isabel started up the trail. "Come on, I'm starving,"

"You're always hungry," Jessie said, but her response lacked its usual teasing tone. Her mind was obviously elsewhere.

"I hope the soup's still hot." Sara followed Isabel, Jessie falling in beside her.

They reached the small clearing in minutes and found a fallen log to sit on. Isabel spread a blanket over it and soon they were all sipping hot wonton soup and Jessie was recounting how she'd come up with the idea to play the goddess. They gossiped about the other presentations as the early night sky turned black and a smattering of stars came out.

Isabel suggested a toast and they all clinked their cups together. "Cheers!" Isabel held her cup high. "To our great presentation."

Sara's hands trembled and the cup slipped, falling to the ground, her green tea soaking the dry earth.

Isabel reached for a napkin and handed it over without comment.

Jessie of course didn't let it drop. "Sara, what's wrong?"

To her horror her eyes misted up. She didn't want to lose her tenuous hold on her emotions. She wrapped her arms across her chest and looked up at the stars, waiting for the precipice of anxiety to disappear. She could almost see the exchange of looks between Jessie and Isabel. Somehow they'd gotten proficient in silent communication during the past weeks.

"So, a brilliant idea came to me down at the foot of the trail when I read that plaque." Jessie's voice brimmed with its usual vivacity and effectively drew the attention from Sara, allowing her to breathe a little easier.

"Well, you're one for one so far today. Let's see if you can make it two for two." Isabel poured the last bit of tea into her cup and offered it to Sara, but she shook her head.

"You're the last person I thought to hear using sports lingo."

"Brothers," Isabel said.

"Do you want to hear it or not?" Jessie asked, getting up and facing them. Without waiting for an answer, she went on, "We should take a trip. Get away. Just the three of us. Doesn't that sound fun?"

In the silence that followed, looking at Jessie's expectant face, Sara focused on unraveling her thought processes rather than answering. "How did Chief Lakota's words give you that idea?"

"Every step taken, something like that." Jessie gestured wildly around them. "We haven't seen anything beyond this. Going to Puerto Rico when I was little doesn't count. I want to see the ocean, walk the beach, hike different mountains. See something beyond this town. Don't you?"

It was a pleading look and Sara thought she saw a little desperation in Jessie's eyes but she couldn't be sure.

"Where were you thinking?" Isabel asked.

"We could go to San Francisco and stay with my friend Mario. Take a road trip down the coast. He says it's beautiful. Isabel, we could go to galleries and museums in the city and you could sketch all you wanted. And Sara, I know your first reaction is to say no but we'll be together and I think it would do us all some good to get away."

In a flash of stark clarity Sara saw that the giant steps she'd taken that day were way outside the secure box she'd made for herself. There'd been shock and tears and other things she didn't want to think about, yet she'd survived. It had been building in her slowly, but she knew she was tired of living within the confines of "safe."

"Let's do it." The words were out of her mouth before she could think of all the reasons she shouldn't.

Then she felt the chains, the sly way they came around her ankles and wrists, under her gloves and boots, creeping like a vine. The sensation was becoming familiar even though she knew if she looked she'd see nothing. They didn't tighten or pull this time, just lay on her skin with their smooth weight. She listened to Jessie and Isabel plan. They were exhilarated with the prospect of going somewhere together and she forced a smile so they wouldn't think anything was wrong. They packed up and walked back to the car, Sara glad to have them on either side of her in the black stillness of the hills. The chains were still wrapped around each leg like they were a part of her skin. It was frightening. Comforting. And how was that possible?

When she made it home a half-hour later, the house was quiet, a few low lights guiding her to her room and her bed where she'd always found peace and yes, safety. She straightened up a little and checked her emails before undressing. The smooth metal links were gone now. Not sure when they disappeared, she thought it might've been as she'd entered her room. She jotted down in her journal the time and place they'd appeared and when they vanished. She was trying to find a pattern, hoping that would help her find some answers.

She showered and got into bed but couldn't fall asleep. Her body was exhausted but her mind refused to turn off. Her parents' conversation kept intruding. Should she ask her father what the secret was? Would he tell her? She had no answers and wished she'd confided in Jessie and Isabel. She imagined what their advice would be. Probably yes to all of it.

On a sigh of frustration she reached toward the bedside light and knocked over the stack of journals she kept on the table.

"Shoot," she muttered as she slid from the warmth beneath the covers and bent to pick them up. The one from her years in high school had fallen open and she left it for last, curious to see what entry it happened to be. She'd carried this journal around like a protective shield, writing in it daily. She hesitated before reading, remembering the time that had led to Dr. Bernstein and medication.

Her handwriting hadn't changed much but she was surprised to see the conversations she'd painstakingly written, almost word for word. She'd been so compulsive.

She read a May entry from an afternoon at the tennis courts with Quinn. The day she'd met Camille. Felt nauseous to the point of sickness. The first time she'd ever had a fight with Quinn.

Sara glanced at the next day's entry: *"What did Quinn mean by you won't admit it, not to yourself or anyone else?"*

They'd never talked about it again. Even now, rereading it, she refused to explore the possibilities of that one statement. *You won't admit it.* She couldn't. She wouldn't.

Sara stacked the journals carefully before getting back into bed. When she closed her eyes she didn't know if she was dreaming or not.

She was back in the cocoon, the chains holding her aloft, with nothing above, below or around her that she could see. Just faint red lights, like neon streaks of blood, among the endless white. The links slipped. She screamed.

Eight

The Graces

Spring 1926
The Ranch, San Simeon, California

Another journey.

Well-wrapped in soft cloth, they were packed carefully and tightly in the crate before being carried away. The Graces hadn't any idea why they were shipped off from Woburn Abbey, but they certainly had plenty of time to speculate. News of a mysterious buyer had been passed around for some time before they were actually sent away. Judging by the length of the trip, whoever he was, he lived a world apart.

The tireless motion of travel, first truck, then boat, then truck again, appeared to be at an end. Thank the gods. The Graces were ready to see the sun and feel the air. To smell flowers and trees.

The truck's movement came to an abrupt halt, followed by much commotion. They felt the slow movement of the crate lowered to the ground. Three voices were distinct, two masculine, one feminine.

"Well, let's take a look, shall we?" the female said. An authoritative voice. Strong. Confident.

"Get the crowbar, Rotanzi," ordered a deep male baritone. "Stand back, Miss Morgan."

The Graces hoped the one named Rotanzi knew what he was doing. They held their collective breath. More in anticipation of seeing the outside world again than anything else. The wood of the crate fell away with a loud crash and complete silence descended as the last of the wrapping was pulled away.

Joy, the goddess of splendor, gazed with curiosity at the vast open land. Some of it well-manicured garden and some of it wild, light earth with pale shrubs and strange looking trees.

Bloom, the goddess of festivity, sighed, so relieved was she to see the sun again.

78

A small crowd gathered behind the three who'd opened the crate. Every one of them looked dumbfounded, at a loss for words.

Brilliance, the goddess of gracefulness and charm, thought their speechlessness delightful and the amazement on their faces sufficient welcome.

"They are called The Three Graces," the only woman, and obviously Miss Morgan, finally said. "Loorz, Rotanzi, get ready to move them to the spot we've chosen. Everyone else, help them as needed and then we'll have a break for lunch."

"Welcome to La Cuesta Encantada, Graces," said Rotanzi as he came forward and touched them. His skin was deeply tanned, his hands calloused, his smile genuine.

Loorz whistled softly. "They're beauties all right." He was tall, handsome and his touch sure and strong.

All three goddesses felt a yearning shimmer up through the heat. They recognized the heady mix of pleasure and desire that their presence evoked.

"Where are they going?" Loorz stepped around the Graces, a look of concentration on his face. He gave some orders to the waiting workers.

"In the small alcove behind Casa del Mar. Right off the walkway to the Main House," Rotanzi answered.

They were moved with care, the progress slow, which provided the sisters glimpses of brightly colored tile, paved walkways, an astounding variety of trees and the other statues in attendance. All the while, human hands touched, pushed and pulled on them, showering flashes of emotion like droplets of rain.

The Graces could hear the men breathing hard; smell the sweat of their exertion. With a signal of his hand, Rotanzi led the small group of workers around a bend where a pedestal waited. Once they were lifted up and settled properly, all the men drifted away. Rotanzi stayed, pulling a bandana out of his back pocket and polishing them with a delicate hand.

The attention and care was a balm that soothed. Brilliance, Joy, and Bloom were immensely pleased with this turn of events.

And perhaps this place held the answers they sought.

As the days passed, the Graces became quite enamored of their new surroundings. The weather was warm and they delighted in the frequent breezes, the faint smell of the sea and the sounds of activity that filled their days.

Brilliance liked looking at the handsome young workers with their tools as much as she liked being looked at by them. They reminded her of the footmen at the Abbey.

Bloom intensified the fragrance of the myriad flowers in the garden, pleased to have such a great assortment to work with.

Joy created a stir in anyone who came close to the small glen. It was enclosed by trees and hedges along the back but open to the path and close enough to the whitewashed house that they could see into one of the side windows.

One fine day a few weeks after their arrival, they discovered the identity of the mysterious buyer, the statue's new owner.

"The Chief has just arrived, Miss Morgan. He's looking for you," Loorz said as he walked in one direction and she in the other.

"Would you oversee the workers at the pool while I meet with him?" Julia asked. "He'll want to see all the latest acquisitions."

Sometime later, The Graces heard quiet footsteps and Miss Morgan, deep in conversation with a man, approached. The Chief was tall, his oval face and long straight nose framed by sandy brown hair. He examined them closely, as they did him.

"Perfect, Miss Morgan, aren't they?"

And that was that.

He often came by to admire them. When guests accompanied him, they called him Mr. Hearst, and there was always lots of laughter and playing around.

The ones the goddesses lured in most often were the three who had unveiled them. Loorz was a family man to the core. The longing that radiated from him was rooted in a wife and two sons he missed daily. He was in charge of the workers and the labor involved in each project. He visited the Graces when the early morning sun turned the sky pale, his long strides easy, and his mood always bright. "Morning, Ladies," he would say and nod his head in greeting.

Julia Morgan usually arrived in the late afternoons. Dark-haired and petite, her conservative hairstyle and dress were in sharp contrast to the many different women guests who wandered the gardens. What most set her apart was her humble authority. How unusual for her to be the one in charge of everyone and everything, except of course, Hearst. Even with him the Graces had heard her stand her ground. Over some modification they guessed, since the house seemed to be in a state of constant construction. When alone, Miss Morgan would settle on the marble bench, her mood a palpable presence in the air. The Graces ensured her comfort and creativity with each visit.

Rotanzi, the caretaker and keeper of the gardens, accepted them wholeheartedly into the family. Like a lover, he tended the earth, grass, trees, and flowers with his wise, capable hands. Every week he cleaned The Graces, humming pieces of simple tunes, and trust passed between them.

If fate left them trapped in stone, the Graces couldn't ask for a more beautiful home.

Nine

Jessie

Winter Present Day
Boulder, Colorado

Jessie sipped a Pelegrino, her fingers tapping out the electronic rhythm as Goldfrapp's "White Horse" pounded the air of the small club like a living, breathing being. Colored lights flashed over the darkened dance floor where a handful of couples were scattered.

"Come on, we're going to dance." She dragged Emily and Maribel with her.

Jessie led them straight to the middle, her body already whirling before the others caught up with her. More people flooded the floor, including Emily's boyfriend who joined them, grinning. Jessie knew it wasn't coincidence that he just happened to show up.

Jessie watched Eric's hand slide up the curve of her roommate's hip as they danced. She closed her eyes, not wanting to see anymore. The rhythm and volume of music created a vacuum around her. God, she missed Mario's hands on her. After he'd left Boulder, she'd dated more times than she could count and no one had been able to make her feel like he had. In any way.

From one pulse of music to the next, the club disappeared and she was alone with green shrubbery, night air cool against the perspiration that had begun forming on her brow. The DJ sounds, muffled but audible, followed her as she turned around in confusion.

This couldn't be happening.

She stopped and breathed deep. The calm quiet was insistent, almost urgent. Wet grass and crickets. Thick foliage, the green almost black in the night.

She was in the labyrinth.

She felt the smooth wax of a candle in her hand. A tiny spark of light in the all-consuming dark. A rustle of leaves from behind startled her. She turned, a scream in her throat. Then caught a glimpse of a shadowed male form that she recognized. Everything went numb. Her father was here? How could that be?

He disappeared around the corner of the maze. "Wait!" she called out.

She dropped the candle, the hiss as it was extinguished in the wet grass like a snake about to strike. She was running to catch up before she could think twice. The lawn was uneven. She stumbled. Stopped only long enough to step out of her heels that held her back. Then picked up the pace. The club's music faded, displaced by the evocative refrain of the mystery music. Down long corridors, around towering hedges, the figure got farther and farther out of reach.

Then the green swallowed him whole.

She tried to stop but her momentum took her straight into the tight-knit web of leaves and branches like a runaway truck.

"Girl, you must be on some kind of drugs, because that was really weird. And it doesn't even explain the..."

The rest of her roommate's words were swallowed up by the crashing intro of the next song. Maribel grabbed her elbow, dragging her off the dance floor and up the steps to the row of tables.

"What's the matter with her? How did she get like that?" Emily's voice, full of distress, brought her fully back to the moment.

Maribel still had a hold of her but Jessie pushed her hands away. "I'm okay, really I am." She sat down on the closest stool.

"You are so not okay," Maribel said.

Jessie felt disoriented. "I'm thirsty. Where's my water?"

"What's she on?" Eric asked. He looked amused. "And what's with the special effects?"

Nobody answered.

Jessie noticed the stares and curious looks from people passing by the table. She needed to get herself back together. She grabbed her small bag from the table. "Going to the bathroom."

"Go with her," she heard Emily say to Maribel.

"Alone," she said over her shoulder as she headed toward the entrance where she remembered seeing the restrooms as they came in.

"OMG," said a pink-haired girl, who stared as she passed in the corridor.

Jessie forced her eyes to meet her reflection in the mirror above the sink. Her hair was wild, flying in all directions with a sprinkling of leaves stuck in the curls. Her eyes were twice as big as normal and there were red scratch marks on her face, neck and arms. She looked like she'd just been in a catfight in the bushes. Picking the leaves from her hair took some time. Then she splashed water on her face and by the time she reapplied mascara and lip-gloss, the scratches had nearly faded like they'd never been there.

Her hands were barely steady as she straightened her dress but her heart sank when she realized she wasn't wearing her heels. How could she not have noticed until now? She knew exactly where they were, but could hardly go back and get them.

"Hey, you there in the black dress," said a heavy-set security guard. "You're going to have to leave." She pointed to Jessie's bare feet. "Unless you can find some footwear."

Perfect. She was being kicked out of the club. Probably just as well. She didn't feel like staying anyway.

"I was just on my way out," Jessie said with one last glance in the mirror. She looked pretty normal except for the shoes.

"I have to escort you," the woman said, waiting.

"Fine." Jessie followed her from the restroom, past a tall man in a suit that Jessie guessed was the manager, until they got to the bouncer who was sitting on a stool by the door. Waiting next to him were Maribel and Emily.

"You don't have to leave," Jessie said, reaching into her bag for her phone. "I can call someone for a ride."

They stared without saying anything. They must be having a hard time reconciling the Jessie they'd seen go into the restroom with the one that had emerged. Well, so was she.

Jessie glanced at Emily as she pressed number five on her speed dial. "I'm sure Eric wants to stay." She had to get out of here. She couldn't face the looks and the questions that would follow.

"No, we'll go with you. I drove so you have no way of getting home," Maribel insisted.

Finally Emily seemed to snap out of it. "And what the hell happened to the shoes I let you borrow? We couldn't find them anywhere on the dance floor or at the table."

"I don't know. Look, I'll pay you for them so just chill, okay? I'm calling a friend to pick me up." Jessie held the phone to her ear, praying Sara would answer. When it went to voicemail, she turned her back on the group that was curiously listening in. "Sara, I need a big favor. I'm stuck at the Illuminate Club on Broadway and 6th. Can you pick me up? Call me as soon as you get this message."

Maribel and Emily were arguing quietly about what they should do. Jessie knew Emily was pissed about her shoes, but Maribel didn't want to leave her alone.

"We need you to step outside now," the tall man said, approaching. The bouncer stood up, the stool scraping the floor with a screech. The security guard stepped closer.

"At least let her wait inside until her ride comes. She doesn't have a coat or shoes," Maribel insisted.

"I'll take care of things," said a voice from behind. A hand gently touched her elbow guiding her forward. The pressure was firm and strong. She looked up into friendly gray eyes framed by clean-cut features.

"Thanks, Phil," said the surprised manager. "You know her?"

"Yeah, I do," her rescuer said. His other arm came around her from behind.

"Jessie?" Maribel asked.

"He's a friend of Mario's," she said and introduced her roommates. "What are you doing here?" she asked him.

"In Boulder? Visiting family. Tonight? Looking into some new bands I'd heard about."

"Come on, let's go back in." Emily still sounded upset as she turned and walked away.

"You sure you'll be okay?" Maribel kept her eyes on Jessie though she moved toward the dance floor.

Jessie nodded. "Go on, I'll see you later." She put her hand on the arm supporting her and held tight. The cold air was a shock after the stuffiness of the club. She walked beside Phil past the line of shivering people waiting to get in. He stopped, took off his coat and put it around her shoulders.

"Thanks," she said, trying not to notice the ice-cold sidewalk beneath her feet.

"I don't suppose asking about your lack of footwear is a good idea right now," he stated seriously, although he was smiling as he said it.

"You always were a smart guy."

He was broad-shouldered, his muscles filling out the long-sleeved dress shirt he wore. He'd changed a lot since the last time she'd seen him. The day he and Mario had packed all their stuff into Phil's Toyota before taking off to leave for California hadn't been her best day. They'd been on a high, talking and joking about their plans despite hangovers from the graduation party the night before. She'd had to fight hard to keep from crying.

"Did you really make a call to get picked up? Cause I can give you a ride." He started walking again. "Come on, let's get somewhere warm."

They crossed the street and walked half a block to an all-night coffee shop.

"I don't think they want me in there, either."

"My parents own the place. Besides it's practically empty. Nobody'll notice." He led her through the door, past the deserted hostess stand to the first booth with a view out the window.

Jessie was trying to rub some feeling back into her toes and Phil was ordering from a tired-looking waitress when her phone rang. "Sara, thank god you called."

Jessie explained where she was and that she needed a ride and a place to spend the night. When she hung up, she noticed Phil studying her intently. Like she were a puzzle to solve.

"She'll be here in about half an hour. You don't have to stay you know. I'll be all right." Jessie found herself unable to look away from the eyes that held hers, steady, warm, and confident. She shivered.

"This'll warm you up." Phil pushed the cup of tea toward her that the waitress set down. "Mint, right?"

Jessie nodded. She'd never noticed much about him back in high school. He'd had a reputation as a talented and driven production manager of every show and concert the music department put on. But she wondered how many people had bothered to get to know the person behind it all. Mario had. He knew and trusted Phil completely.

"Tell me what happened back there," he said, pouring cream and sugar into his coffee. "If you're in some kind of trouble, maybe I can help," he offered.

"I'm not in that kind of trouble. I don't do drugs. That hasn't changed from high school." She shook her head. "I don't think you'd believe it."

"Try me."

"I haven't even told Mario."

"Why not?"

"It's not something you just spill over the phone. It's complicated."

"You're gonna tell him when you come out in a few weeks?" He sipped his coffee and shook his head when the waitress asked if they wanted anything else.

Of course Mario had told Phil about her trip. She sipped her tea, letting the warmth soothe her. "I haven't thought about it beyond dealing with it as it comes."

"You've certainly made me curious. Especially given what I saw."

Damn, she should've known. He probably witnessed the whole dance number. What she'd looked like, she could only guess. She hesitated, but had to know. "Tell me what you saw."

"You were with your roommates, dancing, and the floor was filling up fast. I was talking with a buddy of mine. He introduced me to a guitar player who's trying to form a band. When I looked back, there you were, eyes closed, still dancing, but there was something strange going on. I remember thinking maybe it was just me, but then other people started to notice."

As Phil spoke, she saw it all again, heard the music, felt a tightening in her chest. She held her breath, waiting.

"You were ...lit up, Jessie. I don't know how else to describe it. You were glowing. From within. It was one of the most amazing things I've seen."

She'd been afraid she'd run around the dance floor looking like a lunatic. "Then what?"

"I took my eyes off you for a second, that's it, and the next thing I see is your roommate dragging you to the table and you've got scratches all over and leaves in your hair."

Jessie breathed a sigh of relief. It wasn't as bad as she'd thought but she couldn't tell him that. "Pretty crazy, huh?"

"Crazy's tame for what I saw tonight."

"I'd appreciate it if you wouldn't say anything to Mario. Let me figure a few things out first."

"Talking it out with someone might help."

"I have two friends I've confided in."

"Your roommates? They didn't appear too supportive."

"No, not them. Sara, who's coming to pick me up, and Isabel. Friends from Stone."

"Good." Phil pulled out his wallet out, dug through the pockets and set a business card on the table. "Consider me a friend, too."

Jessie reached for it just as he held it out and their hands ended up tangled together on the table. His was warm and strong. They stared at each other for a moment. Jessie felt a current of energy run through his hand to hers, like an electric shock.

She pulled away, taking her time putting the card into her purse, trying to figure out what had just happened.

The door to the coffee shop opened but Jessie didn't look up until she heard Sara's greeting. She made the introductions, Phil gestured to the booth and Sara slid in next to her. Sara wore a coat of the softest material and she smelled like roses.

"You live in San Francisco?" Sara asked.

Phil nodded. "You're coming with Jessie in a few weeks, I hear."

Jessie leaned into Sara for warmth and said, "Along with Isabel, who I mentioned earlier. You guys better be ready to show us a good time."

"The band's got a few gigs and there's lots to do and see around the city. You're gonna love it."

"You said you were at the club looking over some bands and now you're probably missing them because of me."

"The incident of your missing shoes intrigued me and I decided to help out."

"Missing shoes?" Sara asked, looking at Jessie for an explanation.

"I'll tell you all about it later." She was tired and didn't want to talk about the confusing pieces of her night when one of them was sitting across from her.

Sara hooked her arm through Jessie's. "Ready to go?"

"Yeah, it's been a long night."

Philip walked them to the car. He shook Sara's hand. "I'm sure I'll see you when you're in the Bay Area. Have a nice holiday." He surprised Jessie by pulling her into an embrace. The contact was explosive. Jessie felt an electric charge jolt her , a surge of energy that broke only when he pulled away. Without a goodbye, he turned and left.

Sara already had the heater going full blast when Jessie got in. "Why didn't you tell me to bring some shoes?"

"Weren't you at a play tonight?" Jessie asked. Sara had told her about Quinn and his gift of tickets to the show currently playing at the Boulder dinner theater.

"Yes, but I could've gone by the house on my way here."

"I can stay with you?"

"Of course. I told you the offer's always open. My dad really likes you." Jessie had been over a few times to study for their humanities tests. They'd also hung out once and watched a movie. "I called Isabel and we're picking her up on the way."

Jessie snuggled down into the seat and wiggled her toes in the warm air blowing from below. She rubbed her hands up and down the leather lapels of the coat still around her. "I forgot to give him back his coat." She caught the scent of him, pine on a crisp winter day. She closed her eyes, needing to block out the world going by for a moment.

She felt a hand on her arm. "Jessie? We're here," Sara whispered.

"Time to wake up and tell all," Isabel said from the back seat.

"I fell asleep, didn't I?" she asked as she unbuckled the seat belt and opened the door.

"Yep," Isabel answered cheerfully. She got out and slammed the door. "Come on, I can't wait to hear."

"Stay here. Let me get you something." Sara ran in the house and returned a few seconds later with a pair of fur-lined suede boots.

"Oh my god. These feel great," Jessie slipped her feet into them. As Sara locked the car, Jessie slid her arm through Sara's and nodded toward the house and Isabel. "She's lively tonight."

"I think she's a little drunk," Sara said with a grin, stepping inside the back door.

"I heard that." Isabel came out of the bathroom off the kitchen. She looked from one to the other. "Okay, I am, just a little. The engagement party was more fun than I thought it would be. My brother looks happy and his fiancé is really nice." She took off her coat, revealing dark wool pants and a gray silk blouse. "I didn't have time to change. Can I borrow something?" she asked Sara.

"Sure," Sara took off her own coat. "I'm dying to get out of this dress. C'mon."

"I think I'm going to have a headache soon. Got any Advil?" Isabel rubbed her temples lightly.

"One-stop shopping, upstairs."

Jessie needed nightwear too, but took a detour to the cookie jar and grabbed a handful. Sara had showed her the secret stash one afternoon when they'd needed a pick-me-up while studying. She downed one, and then another; because she hadn't eaten anything since lunch and was starving.

"Our housekeeper makes them. Good, huh?"

Jessie almost jumped at the unexpected masculine voice. Turning toward the doorway, she saw Sara's father in a faded Colorado University sweatshirt and matching sweatpants.

"I was just about to make some tea."

She watched him fill the kettle and put it on the stove. "How was the play?"

"Well done, actually. I enjoyed it quite a bit."

It must have been the heady mix of events and the contradicting emotions of the night that made her see her own father making tea as she watched Sara's. She thought of the figure in the maze, a young man in a dark suit, like the picture Nana had of her father when he graduated college. What would he look like now? How would he have aged?

Sara came down dressed in pink flannel pajamas and ballet slippers. She gave Jessie a questioning look as she entered the quiet kitchen. The teapot whistled. "I got it." Sara took it off the burner and filled the waiting mugs.

Jessie stood to the side, observing father and daughter as they arranged everything on a tray. She envied Sara. Just like she'd envied Emily earlier. She wanted things she couldn't have and it was crushing her.

Sara headed up the stairs with the tray, Jessie following. " G'night, Dad," she called out as her father went into his study.

Isabel was already changed and curled up at the end of Sara's bed. As Sara rummaged through her drawers for another oversized t-shirt, Isabel looked Jessie up and down. "You should see yourself." A laugh escaped. "Those boots with that jacket, your low-cut dress."

"The jacket is Phil's and it saved me from freezing. Sara's boots are divine and I want a pair." Jessie sat on the bed next to Isabel and took a cup of tea from the tray.

"Who's Phil?" Isabel asked, munching on a cookie.

Jessie told them about her night, from the club to her trip to the maze and back.

"Weren't you scared?" Sara asked.

"For a second, but then it became more about catching the figure I saw. He looked like my father. Same build, height, coloring. And the music. It does something to me when I'm in there. Makes me feel like I'm running out of time." Jessie stood up and began to peel off layers down to a lace camisole and matching underpants. She pulled on the t-shirt and curled up under the covers.

"So Phil saw it all?" Sara climbed up on the bed, brush in hand, and motioned for Jessie to turn her head.

"Yeah," Jessie said with a sigh as Sara pulled the brush slowly and carefully through her tangles. She told them what he'd described.

"Really? You glowed? I wonder if that's what happens to Isabel and me," Sara said.

"Then this very confusing thing happened while we were sitting in the coffee shop. He gave me his card and told me to call if I ever needed anything. But when I touched his hand it was like an electric shock."

"Did it give you a bad feeling? Like you couldn't trust him?" Isabel asked.

"No. I don't know. It was just weird."

"Add it to our collection of freaky." Isabel slid under the covers.

"It's late." Sara scooted off the bed and wandered the room putting things away before turning down the lights.

Jessie closed her eyes but couldn't help getting one last word in. "Don't think I've forgotten to ask about Father Michael. I want details in the morning,"

"There's nothing to tell. I haven't called him." Isabel sounded stubborn even as she was falling into sleep.

When Sara came around to turn off the light, Jessie snagged her arm, moved over to the middle of the bed and pulled her down. "There's room, sleep here."

When Jessie woke up it was still early, pale morning light tingeing the sky. She had a lot to do, mostly study, because finals week was upon them. Laundry was high on the priority list too.

The others got up when they heard her shower because Isabel had to work and Sara wanted to go to the library. Jessie borrowed leggings, a sweater and, of course, the boots.

When Sara dropped her off, she was as quiet as possible getting her things together so she wouldn't wake her roommates. If they were even there, but she wasn't about to look. Then she headed home to do laundry. The only drawback to their quaint little back house was that there wasn't a washer and dryer.

Her grandmother was sitting at the kitchen table reading the paper when she walked in. Nana looked at her over the top of her glasses and smiled. "There's my girl. Early today, aren't you? Let me know when you're ready for pancakes."

"Bacon, too?" Jessie asked, dropping two mesh bags on the floor by the back hall.

"I'd better get busy." Her grandmother set aside the news and rose. "I'm done with global warming updates and fighting in the Middle East for today anyway."

Her mother rushed in, dressed in a slim blue wool skirt and matching jacket. She gathered keys, purse and briefcase, then saw Jessie and smiled. "Here to do some laundry?"

"Yep. It was starting to pile up." She frowned as her mother got a plate of enchiladas covered in plastic wrap from the refrigerator. "Why are you working today?"

"We have a big case coming up and there's still a lot of legwork to be done," she said. "You know how it is."

"Shouldn't that be an intern's job?" Jessie asked.

"Mr. Samuels counts on me to make sure the interns do it right. I'll be home by two." She grabbed a cup and poured herself some coffee, took a sip. "Hopefully."

Jessie watched her mother's balancing act as she tried to open the back door. "You could ask for help, you know." She grabbed the plate and the briefcase out of her mother's hands and followed her to the car. "By the way, I'm going to take off after Christmas this year." She might as well give her mother all of it. "With Sara and Isabel for a week to San Francisco."

Her mother set everything on the front seat before looking up. Brown eyes held hers for a couple of heartbeats. "I haven't even met these two girls." She pulled Jessie closer. "And why San Francisco? Because Mario's there?"

Jessie didn't answer, just leaned in and let the warmth of her mother's Chanel-scented embrace envelope her.

"Invite those girls for dinner tomorrow. I'll make your favorite." Her mother kissed her on both cheeks. "We can talk more then. You can tell me all your plans. Now get in the house, it's freezing cold out here without a coat."

Jessie meant to get started on her finals, but the morning passed quickly between loads of laundry, breakfast and talking with one of her aunts, who stopped by to share the latest family gossip.

"Mija, you'll never guess what your abuelita told me about the tenants in her apartment building." Even though Jessie had visited Puerto Rico with her mother only a few times as a young girl, she had no trouble keeping all the people and places straight. She'd grown up listening to stories such as this around the kitchen table. By the time her aunt left, the morning was gone and Nana had folded all her clothes and piled them neatly in her laundry bags.

"Can I study here?" Jessie was curled up on the sofa, her backpack unopened next to her. She didn't want to run into Emily until she'd gotten a replacement pair of shoes and she'd be less distracted here.

Her grandmother gave her a curious look. "Of course. I've got to run to the pharmacy and run some other errands, then I'll be back."

"Okay." Jessie remembered her mother's invitation and reached for her cell to text Isabel and Sara. "Mom's going to make dinner tomorrow for Sara and Isabel," she called out to her grandmother.

"She'll spend all day in the kitchen cooking then," Nana said with disapproval as she shut the front door behind her.

Jessie shook her head, smiling. Nana was very protective of her mother, just like she'd always been with Jessie. She sent a text to Isabel who should've gotten off at one. Sara was probably still at the library.

Their travel plans were mostly set, with tickets purchased on Sara's credit card and hotel reservations made for their stops down the coast. When she'd told Mario the news that he was getting visitors, he'd sounded surprised and pleased. They still talked every day, but never about that song, or him hanging up on her.

Her phone chimed with two incoming replies.

"Count me in," from Isabel.

"Love to. What time?" from Sara.

"B here @ 5," she answered and sent them her mom's address.

If she was going to be able to accomplish anything there had to be no distractions. No thoughts of the maze, the mysterious figure or Phil. She used her mother's laptop, writing all night, finally finishing her take-home finals by the time Sara and Isabel showed up the next afternoon.

The smells coming from the kitchen had tempted her but she'd stuck it out in her bedroom upstairs where her mother and Nana wouldn't keep offering her food to eat. The Guisado was worth waiting for.

When she opened the door for Isabel and Sara, the cold blew in behind them and a blanket of gray sky said snow was on the way.

"I hope you guys are hungry," Jessie said. She led Sara and Isabel into the kitchen, introduced them to her mother who was still wearing an apron over her Sunday church clothes and stirring a pot on the stove. Nana, who had just set the table, embraced them warmly and told them to sit.

Jessie put out fried bananas, yellow rice and red beans in heaping bowls and the Guisado, a beef stew, in a pot in the middle of the table. Just as she'd always found seated here with her mother and grandmother, there was the easiness of women's laughter and conversation. Often when family came over, her uncles and the boys would take their plates to eat in front of the TV, leaving the women to themselves. Jessie had missed her mother's cooking. The food tasted like heaven.

After a minute of silence in which everyone enjoyed the first few bites, her mother started in with the questions, gently prying information out of both Sara and Isabel. Jessie interrupted occasionally with a teasing comment or two.

Nana offered advice on school and boys. "You two study hard, don't you? It's the most important thing right now. Boys can wait."

"Nana, we're 21 years old. It's not boys we're interested in anymore," Jessie said and they all laughed.

"Speaking of boys," her mother said, "tell me all about your trip."

Isabel and Sara shot her quizzical glances from across the table. Jessie let out a sigh. "That was my mother's not so smooth segue into asking about Mario and why we are visiting him in San Francisco."

Jessie's mother just smiled as Sara went through their itinerary and places they hoped to visit in the Bay Area, Monterey, Carmel and Big Sur. "We turn around in San Simeon and head back."

"What's in San Simeon?" Jessie's mom asked. "I can't remember if I've ever heard of it."

Isabel set her fork down after the last bite on her plate. "The project we did together for our Humanities class focused on Greek antiquities. There's a whole lot of Greek figures at Hearst Castle, right outside San Simeon," she explained. "We thought it'd be fun to see."

"It sits on a hill overlooking the ocean," Sara continued, "and was the home of millionaire William Randolph Hearst. I'd never heard of him until I started doing research for our trip."

"Ah, that's right. He made his money in newspapers and magazines, wasn't it?" Nana asked.

"At first it was newspapers in San Francisco and New York in the early 1900s. He printed these really sensationalized stories and a lot of opinionated articles."

"He became known for what's called yellow journalism," Jessie added.

"Today Hearst corporation runs magazines like *Cosmopolitan*, *Seventeen* and *Elle*. Even *Oprah* magazine."

"Sara, didn't you tell us Hearst lived at this castle with an actress, Marion Davies?" Jessie asked.

"That's right. She was his lover and companion for many years. They entertained there while he just kept adding more and more rooms and art. All sorts of famous people stayed as his guests. It's sad that he left his wife, although they never divorced."

"I'm most interested in the architect," Isabel added. "A woman named Julia Morgan."

"When did she design Hearst Castle?" Nana asked.

"Starting around 1920, something like that."

"That was probably quite astounding back then. A female architect."

"It was," Isabel agreed. "She was the first woman to attend the best art school in Paris at the time and to get an architectural license in California. Before she started the Hearst Castle project, she'd already become famous for her designs after the San Francisco earthquake and fire destroyed over half the city."

"Well, it sounds like you've all done your homework. It'll be a lovely trip," Jessie's mother said. "Promise me you three will be cautious and keep each other safe."

"Of course, Mama," Jessie replied, rolling her eyes.

"But you still haven't told me about Mario," her mother reminded her.

Jessie got up and began to pick up the empty plates. "What exactly do you want to know?" she asked, hearing the tension in her voice.

Isabel shifted in her seat and Sara rose, picking up the empty bowls on the table. "Let me help," she offered.

Her mom waved her back to her seat. "No, no, you're the guests this evening. Besides we still have coconut flan for dessert. Jessie, go make some decaf."

Glad to escape, Jessie put the dishes in the sink and turned on the coffee pot. She got the flan out of the refrigerator and took it to the dining room.

"Jessie and I have this disagreement over Mario, you see," her mother was explaining to Sara and Isabel. "I think all kids should go to college. But Mario chose not to, even though he's a very smart young man. He could've majored in music if that's what he wanted."

"He's already made a name for himself in the music industry and he's doing what he loves," Jessie said.

"Fame and fortune don't last forever. He'll need something to fall back on in ten or twenty years and he won't have it," her mother argued quietly.

Jessie turned to Isabel and Sara. "My mother thought Mario was a bad influence on me. She was afraid he'd tempt me out of going to college."

"By asking you to go to San Francisco with him," Sara said.

"And did he?" Isabel asked.

Jessie hadn't told her mom or Nana much about their relationship. The things they'd done, what they'd wanted to do together. She could still see the look on Mario's face when she'd told him her final decision to stay and go to college. It hurt her more than she'd thought possible. And had been messing her up ever since.

She went to the kitchen and returned with small plates, forks and the coffee.

No one spoke.

"I'm here, aren't I?" she said as she cut the first piece of flan.

Ten

Sara

The ring of the phone disrupted the comfortable silence. Sara finished rinsing the last plate, put it in the dish drainer and moved to the back window as her father took the call. Outside, snowflakes quietly drifted, clearly visible in the dark yard beyond.

"Do you want to talk to her?" Her father laughed quietly, then said, "I'll give her the message." He hung up and wiped the counter with a towel. "Jessie's been trying to get a hold of you, wondering why you don't pick up your cell."

"What'd she want?" Sara asked.

"To remind you to pack your swimsuit."

Sara grimaced. "I was going to conveniently forget."

"You'd better not. Knowing Jessie, she'll bring two and make you put on one of hers."

"It'll be too cold to swim anyway, even though the weather in California is nicer than this."

"I looked at the forecast. You might get rain. But who knows?" Her father put the towel in the laundry room and returned to stand beside her at the window, a smile on his face. "Jessie said something about a hot tub at one of the hotels where you're staying."

"There is. But I don't have to get in."

Her father switched off the light and Sara followed him to the den.

"Nervous about your trip?" Her father adjusted his reading glasses, picked up his book and sat in the corner of the sofa.

"A little." Sara wandered to the bookcase lining one wall and ran her fingers over the spines of one row of books. She loved their touch, found comfort in the weight and feel of them.

"As long as you take your medication, you'll be fine."

"I wish I didn't need it."

"Some people spend their whole lives on medication. It's nothing to be ashamed of."

"Easy for you to say. You're not the one on it." It sounded harsher than she intended so she softened her tone. "But you're right. I'll be fine."

She pulled her favorite classic from the shelf. *Jane Eyre.* That would distract her well enough. She glanced at the clock on the mantle. Her mother was really late tonight. What was it, the third night in a row? Even the holidays didn't deter her. "Everything okay with you and mom?"

"Of course." His usual answer.

"Not that you'd say if it wasn't," she muttered, heading to the stairs.

"Sara." Her father's voice had a tone that stopped her going any farther. "You can't say that while you're walking away."

She turned. "Why don't you tell me the truth?"

"I did."

"I don't want to be treated like I can't handle things." A rush of anger came out of nowhere, the threat of tears.

"I don't think I do." Her father rose from his chair, removing his glasses to look directly at her.

"You keep things from me so I won't have a panic attack."

"What do you think we're not telling you?"

"About Violet. Maybe other things."

Her father stayed silent. He ran a hand through his hair in a gesture that said he hadn't expected that.

"Why does mom work such long hours? She's not here for us, for you. Why is work more important than us?"

"It's her dream. What she always wanted. It doesn't mean that she doesn't love us."

"Could've fooled me."

Her dad gave her a sharp look.

Sara wasn't going to back down. She'd always had an easier time standing firm with him than with her mother.

"You have a right to know about Violet." He moved to the window, looking out into the dark night while his reflection stared back at her. "I told your mother you needed to know."

Sara leaned against the doorjamb; her legs felt weak. "Why don't you tell me?"

Her father hesitated, clearly torn. "I know it's sometimes hard for the two of you, but if you ask she will."

"You just don't get it. She won't. Ever." Sara thought of the argument she'd overheard. A puzzle she didn't understand. She wanted to know what had happened all those years ago and why.

Her father remained stubbornly silent.

"Does mom know that you write to Violet? I never understood how you could side with her, how you could just drop your own daughter out of your life. It was so unlike you. But you didn't, did you? You've kept in touch with her all these years." She tried to keep her voice steady, but her courage in bringing it all up was slipping.

Her father turned to face her, a frown marring his features. "You've been looking through my desk?"

"No, I just happened to be printing something for school and saw an envelope you left out." Sara watched her father stiffen, anger visible in his stance. "You knew how much I wanted to see her, talk to her. How could you not let me?"

"I wanted to. Please believe that. But it's really for your mother to say."

"That's what I don't understand," she said in frustration. "Why her? Why not you? Violet and I are your daughters, too."

Her father eyed her warily from across the room. "Sit down for a minute, Sara."

Sara's heart hammered at a frightening rate as she sank down into the nearest chair. Maybe she'd convinced him. She could see that he was debating how much to say. "Daddy, tell me," she whispered.

His eyes pleaded with her to let it rest.

"Please."

He sank back down onto the sofa, his sigh of resignation loud and clear. "Actually I'm not Violet's father. Your mother had a one night stand right out of grad school, got pregnant. We were already engaged by then so I persuaded her to keep the baby, we got married and a couple months later Violet was born."

The paintings on the walls, the books, the furniture and carpet, everything in the room vanished. She felt the familiar weight of the steel chains, her body encased inch by inch. She hung in that empty dim white space that was becoming quite familiar now. This time the streaks were blue and dripping.

No, no, no. She didn't want this to happen. It wasn't fair, not when she was finally getting some answers. She struggled against the hold, but the chains didn't budge. She breathed deeply through a wave of panic and tried to focus on her father's words, which came to her as clearly as if she were right next to him.

"As to your mother's work hours," he was saying, "I don't like it either. You always seemed so busy with school I didn't think you minded."

She'd missed something in her panic. Something important about Violet, she was sure. She twisted and turned as the fear she'd kept back earlier blanketed her until she couldn't breathe. The smooth metal links held fast.

Then she was in her father's arms, his clasp tight, and the chains vanished. The smell of his cologne and the rasp of his five o'clock shadow sent a shudder through her.

"I'm sorry," he whispered in her ear. "Don't hate me. Or your mother. You were so young. It just never seemed the right time to say anything."

Overwhelmed by his words, she pulled from his embrace. It felt too much like the chains. Should she ask if this was why her sister ran away that night long ago? Searching for answers in her father's eyes, she saw weariness and guilt. She got to her feet, stumbled a bit on the couple of stairs that led to the bedrooms. Held up a hand when he reached for her. "I'm okay." Her heart felt hollow and she ached all over.

"You should lie down, honey," he said from behind.

"I will." She closed her bedroom door and stood in the dark until she heard her father's footsteps fade down the hallway.

Her night table held the two things she needed: her phone and her quartz. One in each hand, she hesitated only a moment before making a call.

"Hey, can you come over?" She didn't recognize her own voice. With shaking hands she clutched the stone tighter until her nails dug into her skin. When she heard Quinn's, "Of course," she felt relief pour through her.

Her phone rang as soon as she ended the call.

"Jessie?" She heard something about sharing toiletries on the trip so they wouldn't all have to bring the same things.

"Hey, are you okay?" Jessie finally asked.

"I don't know." Her voice sounded too loud, too high.

"What happened? Wait. Stay there. I'm coming over," Jessie told her.

"Quinn's coming."

"Good." Jessie hung up.

Sara curled up on the bed, her gaze on the closed door, sightless. Her mind going in circles. Violet had a different father. But what did it matter? She couldn't imagine her sister being so angry over that she'd leave and never return. There had to be more.

When a knock sounded and the door opened, she focused on Quinn like a lifeline. He was dressed in jeans and a wool sweater and brought in the scent of snow and fires. He frowned briefly, shut the door behind him, stood against it and surveyed first her, then the room. Two suitcases were open on the floor, already half-packed. Otherwise her room was neat and tidy like she always kept it.

"It's about time you called when you needed something other than a tennis game or a lunch date. Not that I don't enjoy those, but..." He sauntered to the bed and told her to scoot over. Making sure his boots were off the comforter, he stretched out beside her. Lay there waiting.

When a knock sounded a little later, Sara called, "Come in," and Jessie peeked in, her eyes widening, probably at the good-looking blonde next to her on the bed.

"Hey," Quinn said, without moving a muscle or breaking his contemplation of the ceiling, "you must be Jessie."

Propped on her elbows, Sara watched Jessie step inside followed by Isabel. They took off their coats and tossed them onto a chair. The next thing she knew Jessie was helping her sit upright and plumping pillows behind her and Isabel was putting four tablets in one hand and a glass of water in the other.

"What was it?"

"Just something to help you sleep. Your dad gave it to us."

Sara watched Isabel and Jessie take off their boots and get comfortable at the end of the bed. Quinn settled against the headboard beside her.

"Spill, Sara. You'd better tell us everything, and no holding back or I'm gonna be pissed," Quinn threatened.

Jessie watched him with obvious appreciation. "You know, Isabel, maybe we should've tried the hard-line approach with her."

Isabel's eyebrow rose. "We've yet to see if that tactic works."

Sara sighed, trying to gather her courage. She chose her words carefully, attempting to reconstruct the evening, not didn't mention the chains.

"Of course you were surprised," Jessie finally concluded. "But it's hardly shocking. It happens to a lot of women."

"You wouldn't say that if you knew her mom," Quinn replied.

"And you still don't have an answer to the argument between your sister and your mother. Could it have been that?" Isabel asked.

"I was only six. I see flashes of it, images and sounds but no words. But no, I don't believe my sister would take off because of what dad told me."

Jessie reached out and squeezed her hand. "You were probably too young to understand."

"You've got a lot of questions to ask if you want to know the whole story," Isabel said.

Sara lay back against the pillows, crossing her arms.

Quinn laughed. "She might never get answers then."

"Why?" Jessie asked.

"Because her dad probably told her she has to talk to her mom. And that's not going to happen," he replied. He gazed thoughtfully at Sara. "Unless she braves a confrontation."

"We live in the same house and I never see her."

"You could if you really wanted to," said Quinn countered.

Sara knew it was true but didn't like it so blatantly pointed out. "I'm going to change."

From the bathroom, she heard them talking and laughing as she washed her face, brushed her teeth and ran a comb through her hair. She undressed and put on her favorite pink cotton robe. When she emerged, Quinn was standing by the door.

"Since you're in good hands I'm gonna take off." He gave her a quick hug and kissed her on the cheek. "Be good and call me from somewhere fun in SF so I can imagine I'm with you."

"I will," she said softly as she walked with him into the hallway.

"And no cheap souvenirs. I want something nice."

That made her smile. "Of course. Only the best for you."

"Damn right." He held out his arm, blocking her way. "I know my way. You don't need to see me out."

In the silence that followed Sara heard the faint tones of her mother's voice coming from the kitchen. "Thanks."

He stepped away, then turned back. "You've made some good friends," he said with a glance toward her bedroom. "Try and forget tonight and have some fun on your trip. Do something outrageous," he advised.

She watched him go down and listened. He greeted her parents. Imagined him saying something witty and charming like he always did. She heard her parents laugh. Quinn to her rescue. Again.

She returned to Jessie and Isabel completely sprawled on her bed. Jessie tossed one of her journals through the air and Sara caught it.

"We're gonna play twenty questions. The ones you need to ask your mom to get all the answers."

"Write 'em down so you don't forget," instructed Isabel.

Sara picked up a pen from the desk on the way to the bed. Okay, she'd write them. But whether she ever actually asked them would be another story.

Eleven

Isabel

Isabel was counting saltshakers and sugar caddies when she heard the diner door open. The hostess was gone so it was up to her to seat and serve any customers before closing in half an hour. The cook and dishwasher were doing their cleaning up and she hoped it wasn't a big party that would keep them here for two extra hours like last week. The holidays were crazy that way.

When she glanced up front, her heart leaped. In profile, against the backdrop of snow flurries through the window, Father Michael waited there, handsome in a long suit coat and leather gloves. Wiping her hands on her apron, she walked to where menus were stacked.

His smile was warm and engaging, so she couldn't help but smile in return. It was the first time she'd seen him since that day at his house more than a month ago. She'd certainly thought a lot of about him, trying to wrap her mind around the fact that he was just Michael now. She gestured to the counter and he sat on one of the stools.

"You want anything?"

"Hot chocolate would be nice."

He undid the top two buttons of his coat and she could see a dark blue dress shirt that matched his slacks. He'd been out somewhere nice. Seeing him like this caused a flurry of unnamed emotions inside her. She turned to the diner's new espresso machine and made it with steamed milk, taking her time so she could get her thoughts together.

"I saw you as I was walking by," Michael explained when she set the cup in front of him. "Funny, I've been in here a couple of times and never seen you."

Isabel settled on the edge of the seat next to his and brushed away some imaginary crumbs from the counter. "I usually do early morning shifts the days I don't have class and on weekends. Occasionally a dinner shift, like tonight."

"How have you been?"

She felt guilty she hadn't called him back like she'd promised. "Busy. Final projects, final exams, the holidays, you know how it is."

"How's your family? How was Christmas?" His questions evoked memories of all their talks in his office at Assumption High. She tried to let herself relax into that same comfort and ease.

"My family keeps getting bigger. One of my brothers just got engaged and my oldest sister is expecting again." Her fingers played with the edge of her apron as she watched him take a sip. Whipped cream stuck to his upper lip and she pushed a napkin his way. "Christmas was noisy and crowded. It's my mother's favorite time of year so she goes all out with food. I did so many dishes my hands feel permanently wrinkled."

He laughed. "Sounds nice. The food and family and all. Not the dishes."

"And you? Are you still staying with Professor Dowling?"

"Yes. Mine was quieter than yours, but nice. Brian and I and a small group of friends. I did most of the cooking so the dishes were left to everyone else."

Two things hit Isabel simultaneously. The first was that she didn't know him at all. His thoughts and beliefs about certain things yes, but not his day-to-day activities or likes and dislikes. The second surprised her but was true. She wanted to know these things about him.

He asked her about her art classes and she talked as he finished the hot chocolate. She asked if he'd found work and he told her about some non-profits he'd been checking into.

Her manager started locking up and she waved to the cook as he left.

"Time to go?"

Isabel nodded, standing. Michael towered above her small frame, and as she looked up at him she noticed the curl of his hair over the collar of his coat, the small lines at the corner of his eyes, the smile he was so generous with.

"It's on me tonight," she said.

They walked to the door and stopped.

"Thank you. How are you getting home?"

"The bus." She nodded toward her manager who was locking the cash register. "Bob makes sure I get safely on and it takes me straight home."

"Let me give you a ride." He held up his hands in defense of the stubborn refusal she started to give. "Otherwise I'll worry about you out there in the cold."

She held his gaze and considered for a moment. "All right. Give me a minute to punch out and get my coat and bag."

The ride home was shorter than she wanted it to be. She directed him to the right street and told him to pull over a few houses away. "Here's good. I'm really glad you stopped in."

"Me too." He looked serious, like he wanted to say more, but didn't.

"Are you having a hard time, with...not being a priest anymore?" She found the courage to ask.

"Some days are harder than others. Whenever someone recognizes me, I can't seem to find the right words to say, so I end up saying nothing."

"Did you ever consider moving somewhere where no one knows you?"

"I did, but it felt too much like running away. Like I'd done something wrong."

"Are there more good days than bad?"

"Yes."

"I'm glad." She gathered her stuff. "I'm taking a trip tomorrow with my girlfriends, Jessie and Sara."

"Really? Somewhere warm, I hope."

"San Francisco and a couple of stops along the coast. For a week.

"You know, your face lit up just now when you told me that."

Sometimes the things he said floored her. She looked out the window, down at her lap, anywhere but at him. "It'll be my first time away. I'm excited."

"You'll have a great time. San Francisco is a beautiful city."

Isabel didn't want to say goodbye. She wanted to stay and talk for a while, like they used to. She put aside the reservations that had kept her from calling before. "Can I see you again when I get back?"

"I'd like that." He got out before she could stop him and he came around to open her door.

"Thanks for the ride."

He smiled in response, waiting until she walked to her house and opened the her front door to before he got get back in the car and drove away.

The house was warm and the Christmas lights still on. The tree and the crèche under it were cast in a soft colorful glow. The quiet enchantment of it filled her, like it had so many times in her youth, yet it felt new, almost unreal, like a dream.

Darkness descended swiftly and completely.

Caught off guard, she heard her bag drop, the sound harsh and brisk on stone floor. Cool damp saltiness assaulted her, the physical signs of the cave breaking down the resistance in her mind. She shuffled, arms outstretched, and encountered familiar rough walls on either side. At her touch they lit up in soft reds and greens and yellows like a the Lite-Brite toy she'd played with as a girl. There was no image, she noticed, just a messy mix of color.

In a rush like a tidal wave, water roared from behind her and rose over her head.

"Isabel? What are you doing?" With that whispered question she found herself half kneeling, half sitting on the floor by the Christmas tree in the living room. She swallowed the tight knot in her throat that had formed with the water and the panic.

Her sister put her arm around her shoulders and guided her up the stairs. "You're freezing." Maggie rubbed Isabel's arm, the gesture comforting, solid and real.

Isabel's mind was in turmoil but she found focus with one detail that now came to her attention. Her sister had just gotten in, too. "It's past your curfew." Isabel kept her voice low as she unzipped her coat, turning toward her sister. "You have to be careful. You don't want to be grounded over New Year's."

"I know." Her younger sister unwound the red wool scarf from her neck and pulled off the matching hat and gloves. She reached out to push a stray lock of hair away from Isabel's face. "No wonder you're so cold, your hair's wet."

Maggie looked as startled by the realization as Isabel felt. She scrambled to come up with an explanation her sister would believe but decided on distraction instead. "I'm going to be leaving early tomorrow. Try to stay out of trouble while I'm gone."

Maggie laughed softly. "Only if you promise to get into some. You need a little excitement in your life, Isa."

If her sister only knew.

Isabel said goodnight, closed her door, laid down on her bed and collapsed into an exhausted sleep.

The next morning she woke before her alarm, showered, dressed in black jeans, boots and a sweater and packed in under an hour. She had a cup of coffee while she waited for Sara's dad. He'd offered to drop them off at the airport because it coincided with a meeting he had in Denver. A honk out front was right on time. Isabel grabbed her bag from the foot of the stairs and almost collided with her mother.

"Come." Her mother pulled her to the prayer table in the hall. Small pine branches wreathed the Advent candles her mother lit every Sunday in December.

"Mom, they're waiting for me," Isabel protested.

"This will just take a minute," her mother said. She took Isabel's hands, placing them on the Virgin Mary statue and closed her eyes.

The Fatima prayer was her mother's favorite, softly murmured in Italian. Isabel waited for her mother to finish with the sign of the cross over her forehead, heart, her left and right shoulders, and finally her lips.

Her mother looked tired and older this morning than Isabel had taken the time to notice lately. Her hands were rough, her dark, gray-streaked hair had been hastily pulled back, and her slippered feet looked slightly swollen. Isabel tried to shake the mix of pity and exasperation her mother stirred in her.

"Say 'bye' to dad for me."

"Call and let us know you're safe," her mother instructed.

After throwing her bag in the trunk of the car, she got in the back seat and was instantly better. She felt like a seed ready and waiting to burst under soil that had been left dormant too long. Jessie chatted, drawing them all along in her growing excitement. Once they were dropped off, she led them through check check-in, the long security line and to the terminal. She wore a gray cowl sweater dress with a delicate, chain belt, her long legs clad in black tights and knee high boots. Her model looks were in sharp contrast to Isabel's own casual attire, jeans and a light-weight V-neck sweater, and Sara's elegant brown, wool pantsuit that probably cost a week's worth of Isabel's tips. They stopped at a newsstand to buy magazines for the flight. Isabel watched the flow of people, taking it all in, filled with images and scenes like snapshots on a camera.

Sara sat on the aisle, Isabel at the window and Jessie between them as the plane took off and rose above the clouds. Jessie shared stories of what she remembered from trips to Puerto Rico as a girl. Sara had traveled some, but seemed reluctant to share. They ate the small packets of snacks that came with their drinks and gossiped over ads and pictures in the airliner magazines.

The scene out the window was nothing like Isabel expected. All white, the sky was endless up here, no horizon. She got a sketchbook and pencil from her bag to try and capture it.

She was in her own world and Jessie and Sara let her be.

When the pilot announced their descent a while later, Isabel turned to Jessie, "You nervous?"

"It's been a year and a half since I've seen him," Jessie admitted, looked up from her cell phone where she'd been checking messages. "A lot can change. We talk all the time, but sometimes it doesn't feel real. I think I'll know when I see him, and he will too."

That confirmed what Isabel had guessed, though Jessie had never come right out and said it. They were more than friends. Which made Isabel wonder about her and Michael. Is that what she wanted? Did she want more? She had before when it was impossible. But now?

Then the flight attendant's voice came over the intercom and they listened to the announcement about baggage claim and connecting flights. It was while they were waiting for everyone to file off the plane that Isabel noticed a new text message in her inbox. From Michael.

"Don't miss the Museum of Modern Art. There's a spectacular exhibit you'll love."

Jessie leaned over her shoulder, read the text. "Haven't talked to him, huh?"

"Just last night. I was waiting for you to stop talking so I could tell you." Isabel teased back.

"C'mon. Tell us while we wait for our bags," Jessie ordered on the way out.

Twelve

The Graces

Winter 1937
The Ranch at San Simeon, California

Brilliance felt their presence before they came into view and gathered her sisters closer.

Joy listened intently.

Bloom settled herself firmly into their circle and the warmth of their embrace.

Human voices filtered down the garden path.

"So, I guess that's it then." Loorz took his hat off and held it in both hands. "I'll be leaving to for Santa Monica tomorrow."

"Good. You have the plans. I want the same quality work on the pool and tennis courts there that you've done here." Julia carried a small wrapped box. Her fingers played with the bow as they walked. "You're one of the best, George. I'm counting on you."

He acknowledged her compliment with a nod and smile. "And you, Miss Morgan? Your new designs for the Wyntoon Estate coming along?"

"Yes. The Chief is as demanding about that project as this one." She laughed softly.

"Demanding is a polite way to put it," Loorz drawled.

Julia stopped at the bench below the Graces and lifted up the box. "May I?"

"Of course." Rotanzi held out his hand to take the paper as she pulled it off.

Julia lifted the necklace up with a sound of pleasure. Three strands of ribbon intertwined, each falling to a different length. The yellow band held a small gold medallion of a sun, the blue cord a silver moon pendant and the red velvet ribbon had a ruby rose stone.

"It's very unique." She touched each with a small smile. "Like a piece of art."

"A small token of my appreciation." Loorz turned to look up at the Graces. "My wife picked it out. She has an eye for jewelry and that sort of thing."

Julia watched Loorz's face as he looked at the statue. Rotanzi took the box and paper, put them in his pocket and looked at Julia. They stood in silence for a moment, the morning air quiet. No guests were here today. The Graces listened as Julia mentioned Mr. Hearst's declining health.

"Do you remember the day they came to us?" Rotanzi asked.

"Yes." Julia said as a breeze stirred the trees overhead. "Many days blend into each other around here, but that one stands out."

"I can't put my finger on it, but it seems they're different from any of the other acquisitions," Loorz agreed.

"Everyone feels it. I've seen guests that can't seem to move from this very spot." Rotanzi took Julia's elbow and guided her a step closer.

The breeze picked up strength, ruffling hair and jackets.

"The Chief often said says that as well," Julia said.

Loorz came to her side, so the three stood facing the three. "Well, I'd better finish getting my things together."

The Graces held on a little longer, soaking up the appreciation. The connection they'd always felt between these three humans was about to be broken and it saddened them. Joy sighed. There was a power in each one of them and together the sisters had hoped it would somehow be strong enough to break the bond that held them trapped in stone.

Brilliance wanted to try, at least once, to forge their own limited powers with the humans. Otherwise the sisters would never know if it were possible? She pushed the clouds away with effort, and the sun dazzled, blinding all in the courtyard. Bloom pushed at the earth and it rumbled. Joy pulled on Julia, Loorz and Rotanzi, until they were so close every breath and heartbeat pulsed against the stone that trapped them.

Energy drained out of the Graces into the humans, swirling between marble and flesh, ancient and new.

Then the connection snapped, ending as suddenly as it had begun.

Julia smoothed her jacket, stepped away and straightened her glasses.

"Well," Loorz cleared his throat and loosened his tie.

Rotanzi bent to pick up a stray leaf off the walkway.

If only they had touched the statue, the sisters thought. That might have done it.

Rotanzi looked at the Graces again. They could see the questions in his eyes.

Loorz offered Julia his arm and she to Rotanzi. With a final look at the statue, the power the Graces had released was returned a hundred fold. Then the three humans were gone.

The power exhilarated and gave them hope.

They had connected physically to something alive and real in this time and place.

The Graces thought about the many lives touched throughout the centuries, their gifts given and without question. But, this meeting of three and three had not happened since the day they'd been trapped. It intrigued them, and the desire to do it again grew in them like hunger craving sustenance. It was the key to their freedom. They were sure of it.

Thirteen

Jessie

Winter   Present Day
San Francisco, California

She did not do fear. She didn't like it controlling her life in any way, and in the years since that bloody day outside the laundromat she'd done a pretty good job of it, too. The maze, which had provoked curiosity, annoyance, even anger, had never scared her. Right now, however, Jessie couldn't stop the fear from rushing in. As she walked out of the airport, rolling her luggage behind her, Isabel and Sara on either side, it gripped her hard, squeezing so tight she felt like throwing up.

It didn't matter that she talked to him almost every day. Like she'd told Isabel, she'd know the minute she saw him just how it was going to be.

She scanned the area looking for a red Mercedes like his text said. Since their luggage was the last to come off the plane, the area was almost deserted except for a taxi or two.

"Hey, Jess, isn't that him?" Isabel asked, pointing.

He stood by the curb against the car, legs and arms crossed, waiting. When their eyes met, something flashed through his, dissolving the fear in her immediately. Her knees weakened and she had to stop and lean on the handle of her suitcase for support.

He walked toward them, a smile creasing his face. Seeing it, her strength returned and she broke into a run, throwing herself at him.

His arms felt like a homecoming.

She laughed with relief and a joy that had been pent up too long. She kissed him hard. She couldn't help it. God, he tasted good. Finally, she pulled back, turned and made the introductions.

At six-foot-two Mario was lean and well well-muscled. He wore his signature look: black jeans, black boots, and a black V-neck T-shirt. He looked intimidating but Jessie knew his abuela had raised him to be gracious and polite. He shook hands with Isabel and Sara, welcomed them, grabbed their suitcases and headed back to the car.

"Even your pictures don't do him justice," Isabel whispered, as they followed.

Jessie linked her arms through theirs, watching Mario try to figure out how to get all the luggage into the trunk.

Glancing at Sara, she asked, "You good?"

Sara's smile was genuine, but the wariness Jessie recognized lingered. "Sure." Then Sara stepped forward and offered some advice to Mario, and to Jessie's surprise she bonded with him over trunk space.

They piled in, Isabel and Sara in back, Jessie in front.

"Great car," Isabel said, settling into the comfortable leather seat.

"It's Phil's. He got a good deal on it. We're still trying to break into the business and it impresses all the right people." Mario revved the engine and pulled out into traffic.

"I told you about Mario's motorcycle, didn't I? You know the one on the cover of the CD I showed you." Jessie was dying for a ride. Another thing she'd missed.

The sight of the bay out the windows soon held their attention as Mario took them sightseeing through the city's famous hills, pointing out legendary Victorian homes and the Golden Gate Bridge. He drove to the famous Fisherman's Wharf, parked, and gave them a walking tour of the city. Jessie bought chocolate at Ghirardelli Square, Isabel got a book featuring full-page photos of the most scenic views near one of the historical parks, and Sara picked out a necklace of silver intricately woven with tiny shells at Pier 39.

"Sara's got a lot of style. It comes naturally. She's not even aware of it," Jessie said to Mario as they waited for her to pay. "I would never wear something like that, but it'll look great on her." She linked her arm through his and they strolled to a bench right outside the store.

Mario glanced back inside, at Sara handing over her credit card and Isabel trying on some bracelets as she'd said, 'just for the heck of it.' "They're really nice, Jess, down-to-earth. Different than I expected, but I like them."

"Yeah, me too." It meant a lot to hear him say that.

Mario turned her, drew her closer so they were touching, forehead to forehead. "God, it's good to see you," he whispered.

She'd stopped breathing the second his large frame came into contact with hers. She wanted to ask so many things but stayed silent letting the embrace fill up the spaces instead.

"Enough of that you two," Isabel teased from behind them and the moment was gone.   Mario kept his arm around her and steered them down the pier to an observation deck. Sara tucked her new purchase into her bag and got out her camera. They messed around, with Sara taking pictures of Jessie and Isabel in crazy poses with the seals on the rocks behind them.

For dinner, Mario took them to his favorite pizzeria where long communal tables were lined by wooden benches and people were grouped together like one big family. They got the pepperoni with extra cheese and pitchers of Coke. Jessie smiled as she listened to Isabel and Mario teasing each other while they waited for their order.

"Italians don't know a thing about pizza. It's an American invention," Mario said.

"It's not. Have you ever been to Italy? It's different than what we get here, but only Italians do it right."

The crust was thick, the cheese dripped off each slice and Jessie couldn't remember enjoying pizza more.

When Mario finished the last piece, he wiped his hands on a napkin and rose. "Gotta go. Early rehearsal and set up before the show."

"So, how do we get there and what time?" Jessie asked.

"Walk south to the end of the block, make a right and it's the second entrance. I'll save you a table. Show starts at 10."   He kissed her cheek and headed out the door.

"So what do we do with a couple of hours to kill?" Jessie asked Sara when Isabel left the table to use the restroom.

Sara rested her chin in her hand and looked out at the darkening sky beyond the window. "Don't you just love this time of day? When the last of daylight has faded and yet it's not quite dark? The city lights come on little by little, casting a glow over everything." Jessie moved to sit next to her so she could have the same view. "How poetic you are tonight," she said, the loud buzz of conversation around them accentuating their quiet exchange. Jessie took notice of how little Sara had eaten and how pale she appeared. "How are you? Holding up okay?"

Sara turned from the view and smiled in reassurance. "Once I have the chance to freshen up a bit I'll be fine."

"That's not what I meant."

Sara nodded in understanding, rummaged in her handbag and extracted a small gold box with a black lacquered cover. She took out a small white tablet, put it in her mouth and swallowed it with a drink of water.

"Why do you put them in there?" Jessie asked.

"Because it's pretty and I hate carrying prescription bottles. Plus I have to cut the pills anyway, since I take half a dose." She rested her chin in her hand and gazed back out the window.

"Who's that?" Jessie pointed to a piece of paper stuck to the side of Sara's wallet. The name Violet and a phone number. Jessie recognized the San Francisco area code.

Sara turned to face her. "That's my.... sister,"

"Really? She lives here? Why didn't you say so?"

"Maybe because I haven't seen her or spoken to her in over fifteen years."

"What? That's crazy!"

"Tell me about it."

"Hmmm. A long lost sister. You're just full of surprises."

Sara nodded to the slip of paper. "My dad gave me her number this morning."

Jessie couldn't contain her curiosity. "Are you going to call her?"

"Maybe," Sara answered, her smile sad and just a little mysterious.

Jessie watched Isabel making her way back to the table, wanting to ask more but the moment passed.

"You know what?" Sara started to organize her purse. "I think this has been one of the best days ever."

Isabel sat down just in time to hear Sara's comment. "I agree." She sank down on the bench across from them and reached for her bag under the table. "It's like a dream. I have to keep telling myself it's real."

Jessie thought about the lightness she felt in being in Mario's company and the comfort and closeness of Isabel and Sara. "We've got six more days. Each one's gonna be better than the last."

"Would you like me to take your picture?" The waiter asked as he approached, pointing to Sara's camera on the table. Isabel joined them by the window and he took a couple of different shots.

"Thanks," Jessie said as he handed the camera back to Sara. "We'll take the check now."

"It's already been taken care of," he said with a grin. "Have fun tonight."

Isabel opened the sketchbook she'd gotten out of her bag and glanced toward the doorway. "There's no one waiting, so can I draw for a minute?"

Jessie grabbed Sara's hand and pulled her up. "Sure, we'll be back in a few."

Inside the women's restroom, a long counter ran under the mirror to the side of the stalls. Jessie opened her purse and pulled out two small, velvet-zippered bags. They contained a mini toothbrush, toothpaste, and a complete makeup kit from foundation to lipstick.

Sara opened her bag and pulled out a similar assortment of items. "We are a pair, aren't we?"

"Girl, it had to be your secret to always looking so put together, even at the end of a long day. I can't believe I didn't find you out earlier." After a serious study of her face, Jessie opened the mascara. She didn't need much of a touch-up. She brushed her teeth, spritzed herself with jasmine and adjusted her jewelry while Sara did her thing.

A memory from the night at the club came to her, how she'd had to pick leaves from her hair in the bathroom.

That was when black-and and-white images of the maze began to flicker back and forth with the bathroom scene before her. Like a fun house with a room full of crazy mirrors and strobe lights that distorted everything in view, she saw two different worlds in tandem. Sara was putting her bag back together and going into one of the stalls while hedges were crowding her in, the smell of vegetation colliding with her favorite perfume. Back and forth it went on, the instrumental sounds of the now familiar melody at war with a flushing toilet.

"Jessie? Did you hear me?" Sara turned from washing her hands at the sink.

The flashes of the labyrinth continued but Jessie saw the instant Sara realized something was going on. Confusion over what to do warred with concern in Sara's eyes. Jessie opened her mouth but no words emerged.

Sara stepped closer. "Phil was right, Jessie. You have a glow." She put out a hand but didn't touch. "It's amazing."

The bathroom was fading fast, the maze encroaching on the one view, inserting itself almost completely in front of her eyes. The whole flashing picture thing made her a little nauseous. Jessie lifted her hand toward Sara, wanting the contact and the return to the bathroom. She couldn't see it anymore, but an instant later felt the cool touch of Sara's fingers wrapping around hers.

Instead of Sara taking her back, she took Sara with her to the labyrinth.

They stared at each other, eyes wide, surrounded by thick foliage, a grassy path beneath their feet.

"Oh my god, oh my god, oh my god," Sara whispered, looking around her in awe. "You never told us it was this beautiful."

"Listen." The music soared in the space around them.

Sara nodded. "I hear it."

Jessie took Sara's hand and pushed it into the closest hedge.

"Yes, I feel that too," Sara said, with a laugh that matched the light and the weightlessness of the air. She suddenly went still. "Jessie, look over there." She pointed to where the end of the path disappeared around a bend.

Jessie saw her father, covered in shadow. It was difficult to make out detailed features but she was sure it was him. Her legs wanted to take flight toward him, but Sara's hand held her back.

"Wait, Jessie, think. Last time you ran to him, he disappeared. Just look at him, talk to him from here. See what happens."

Good idea. Jessie lifted her voice a little. "I'd like to talk to you." The figure made no sign that he heard. She took a step. "Why do I come here? Are you trying to tell me something?"

As soon as the questions were out of her mouth, she heard a door open, followed by the sound of high heels on tile floor. "Excuse me," said a feminine voice.

When Jessie blinked, she was in the bathroom again, holding hands with Sara, blocking the way to the stalls. A young girl of no more than sixteen smiled expectantly at them. Jessie pulled Sara with her against the wall and smiled at the intruder. "Sorry."

They simultaneously faced the mirrors, inspecting themselves, conscious of being alone no longer. Jessie picked up her bag that had fallen to the floor and gestured to the door. Sara quickly followed her out.

These episodes happened at the worst possible times. And they'd discovered nothing new to solve the puzzle. If only they weren't interrupted they might stay long enough to learn something. Frustrated, Jessie hurried Isabel out of the restaurant into an ocean of city lights. She breathed deeply of the chilly air and fought for composure. Sara still held her hand and Jessie understood she needed the contact so she didn't let go.

Isabel suddenly stopped in the middle of the sidewalk. "All right. What's up? Tell me now."

"That obvious, huh?" Sara asked.

"You're like an open book," Isabel replied, then turned to Jessie. "And you hurried me out of there so fast my head's still spinning."

They walked in the direction of the club, passed it, and kept going. Jessie told them about the blinking images of the maze. They stopped at an empty plaza still lit with Christmas lights. Jessie and Sara sat on a bench while Isabel wandered the small area.

"What is it with bathrooms?" Isabel asked. "One of the first times in the cave was in the restroom at work."

"I haven't even gotten to the good part," Jessie told her.

"There's a good part?" Isabel asked.

"These things that happen, the places we go, they aren't all bad," Sara pointed out.

Before Isabel could disagree, Jessie interrupted. "Sara saw the glow, just like Phil described. Then she touched my hand and went with me."

Isabel jerked around, her eyes wide in disbelief. "No way."

"I couldn't believe it myself, but it's true," Sara said, her voice low and a little shaky. "Just thinking about it makes me shiver. I mean, it wasn't scary or anything, just surprising, I guess. And the maze was so lush and green, like springtime in winter."

A crowd of young people, clearly dressed for a night on the town, passed by, their laughter loud in the small space.

"Have you seen his performance before?" A young woman asked another.

"No. Everybody at work keeps talking about him, so of course I had to come check him out."

Jessie's eyes followed the group down the street. "Any guesses as to where they're going?" She pulled out her cell phone out to check the time. "Let's go find our table and get a drink."

"So what do you think triggered it?" Isabel asked as they walked back they way they'd come.

"I was thinking about cleaning leaves out of my hair."

"And last time, when you were dancing and went to the maze, what were you thinking about then? Do you remember?" Sara asked.

Yeah, she remembered. But things had changed now that she was here. She didn't want to think about how she'd felt that night.

They were silent until the entrance of the club was in view.

"Come on, Jess." Isabel said, stopping.

Jessie could feel a thread of tension running through the three of them. Sara turned so they formed a small circle at the edge of the sidewalk. They watched a few couples stroll by and two groups of girls go into the club after being carded at the door.

Isabel went on, "It's all very random. We don't know why it happens, and when it does it's freakin' weird. Tonight things changed, pretty radically. It might be important or might not, but you can't hold back."

Why did Isabel have to be so damn sensible?

"Fine. Emily's boyfriend had his hands all over her and I wished Mario was there with me. Satisfied?"

Isabel's smile was tight. "Yes."

Sara looked grim, silent as she always was when tensions ran high.

"Can we let it go for the rest of the night? I just want to enjoy the performance." Jessie pulled them into the small line that had formed at the door. When they got to the front, she pulled out her ID to show the bouncer.

"So you're the Jessie we've heard so much about," he said, checking her name off a list.

His remark cheered her immensely. Mario had been talking about her and that was good. "Don't believe everything he's said about me," she teased.

He looked her up and down without hiding his appraisal. "He got the beauty part right. I imagine the smarts part is also true. These two your friends?"

"Yes. Sara and Isabel."

"Nice to meet you. The name's Sam," he said shaking hands with each of them.

"Hey, are we going to have to stand out here all night or what?" a male voice complained. The line behind them had become even longer.

"I might not let you in at all if you don't shut your trap," Sam said to the young man. He shook his head in disgust. "Some people are so rude."

Jessie couldn't stop smiling, her earlier tension fading fast.

He called out to a woman inside the darkened entryway. "Janet, these three ladies are going to the reserved section. First drink on the house." He gestured for them to go inside. "Enjoy the show. And Happy New Year."

Once seated in a booth with a clear view of the stage, Jessie relaxed back in the leather seat. The club was almost full of people, all ages and cultures, the talk and laughter loud and excited. Mario's band had a following.

Isabel looked up from her phone. "Michael sent a New Year message."

"That's sweet," Sara got hers out of her bag. "Quinn sent one to me."

"I've never been to any of the clubs in Denver, you know, only one of the campus hangouts." Isabel surveyed the room with interest. "You, Sara?"

"Quinn tried to convince me to go clubbing with him a few times but I always said no." Sara sipped from a glass of water with lemon. A few minutes later two bottles of beer appeared in front of Jessie and Isabel and a Diet Coke in front of Sara.

"Tell me what you think of Mario." Jessie drank slowly, watching Sara and Isabel take in the atmosphere.

"He's great, Jess," Sara answered, but she was clearly distracted by something on stage.

"Even if he does think pizza is American," Isabel teased.

One thing Jessie loved about Isabel was she let things go easily, no hard feelings, the earlier friction forgotten.

"Who's that?" Eyes still on the stage, Sara watched a young woman in a skin-tight leather outfit pick up a guitar and start to tune it.

"Caryn. The one female in the band." Jessie watched Sara's reaction with interest. There was a flush to her cheeks and she picked up the drink napkin and folded it over and over again.

The rest of the band came on stage and the lights dimmed.

The audience was rowdy and clearly devoted. Each band member took turns introducing a song. They were funny, sometimes serious, all of them comfortable with each other and the audience. Jessie felt like she knew each one by the time they took a break and made their way through the crowd talking to friends and fans.

Smiling to everyone he passed, Mario came directly to their table, to the obvious disappointment of the female population in the club. He didn't sit down but leaned over her, his kiss long and unquestionably intimate. Jessie couldn't be sure but thought she heard a catcall or two.

Mario straightened and nodded toward the drinks at the table. "Another round?"

"Sure," Isabel answered at the same time Jessie did, which made them laugh. She pushed the empty bottles to the edge of the table, where they were picked up by a passing waiter.

Jessie's heart was racing, her thoughts keeping time with it. She was trying to relax but it was hard. She blamed the bathroom incident. And why had Mario kissed her like that here? And in full view of everyone?

Another familiar male voice intruded on her thoughts. "Jessie." Phil slid into the booth next to her. "Sara, right?" At Sara's nod, he turned to Isabel. "And you must be Isabel."

Introductions were made and the rest of the band soon appeared at their table, scooting in or leaning over the back of the booth, shaking hands with them and welcoming them.

"This is Mitch, who rents the second bedroom at Mario's place," Phil said, as a handsome blond pulled a vacated chair from a nearby table and sat down.

Jessie decided she liked him right away. He had baby blue eyes, a smile full of charm, and dressed with a lot of style. "Thanks for letting us stay at your place. Hope we're not crowding you out."

"It's no problem. I'm gonna stay with my girlfriend, who's glad to get some extra time with me," he said with a glance toward a brunette mixing drinks behind the bar.

"Mario never told me he had a roommate."

"Really?" Mitch gave Mario a punch in the shoulder as he came back with the drinks.

"Watch it. I'm delivering the goods." Mario handed them around.

Jessie took her beer and clinked the bottle against Mario's then Mitch's in a silent toast. "Yeah, I mean he talks about all of you a lot. But I thought he lived alone."

"Guys don't think of sharing the details." Caryn leaned in, joining the conversation. "I was the last to join the group and it took me months to get everyone figured out. Who works where, who's dating who, you know what I mean."

Sara excused herself from the table and headed toward the restrooms. After a minute, Caryn got up, too. "Nice meeting you. See you around," she said to Jessie and Isabel, then glanced Mario's way. "Backstage?"

"Yep. We're back on in five." Mario gave the signal and they all downed their beers.

Jessie became acutely aware of Phil's tall frame next to her, a quiet heat emanating out from him to her. God, was she in trouble. The band took their leave, Mario's hand lingered on her shoulder from behind then he followed them to the small door that led backstage.

"What do you think of the show?" Phil asked, his eyes steady, unblinking. They seemed to pierce right through her.

Sara quietly rejoined the table and Isabel talked about the band's talent, how it strengthened Mario's music. They were just now coming out again onto the darkened platform. They took their places and the lights came on low. Mario sat behind his keyboard relaxed, ready and waiting.

"Eyes are drawn to him," Jessie finally responded to Phil's question. "Then his voice pulls you in." The first notes of a song sounded, clear and light. "It's always been like that. Or is it just me?"

Phil shook his head. "No, it's not only you. That's why he's gonna make it. Big."

Jessie recognized the intro before Mario started singing. Her throat tightened. She fought to keep a smile on her face. Why did he have to do this song tonight?

As if sensing her struggle, Phil moved closer. "Are you okay?" he asked quietly in her ear.

She couldn't speak so she nodded.

When the song ended, the applause went on and on. Jessie knew it was one of his best, she just wished it didn't hurt so much to hear it. When the audience quieted, Mitch said something that had everyone laughing. But she was too busy trying to figure out the very strong attraction she felt around Phil. Maybe it was because he'd seen her when she'd gone to the maze and he'd come to her rescue when she'd needed it. Yes, she decided, that was it. Jessie tried to focus on the show. Only half succeeded.

A few minutes 'til midnight the waiters walked around offering glasses of champagne and Mario did a countdown. His eyes met hers from the stage as everyone toasted the New Year. Phil gave her a kiss on the cheek and Jessie almost bolted out of her seat. His touch was so charged it unnerved her and made her tense.

After two encores, Phil handed Jessie a fifty and Mario's house key and told her he had a cab waiting to take them home. "They're going to be a while and you all look like you could use some sleep. We got your luggage, too."

"How'd you manage that?" Isabel asked.

"I brought my car around earlier and some of the crew unloaded your stuff," Phil answered.

Twenty minutes later they were walking up the steps to Mario's front apartment. Isabel and Sara turned in almost immediately. Jessie waited for Mario's return. When she heard a soft knock sometime later, she looked out through the curtains to make sure it was him. He stood on the back step grinning at her.

"What?" She opened the door and smiled back.

"Wanna go for a ride?"

"I thought you'd never ask. I've missed your motorcycle, our rides."

"Just that?" Mario asked.

"I don't know, let's go see." Jessie pulled on the boots she'd taken off by the door and grabbed her coat.

He locked the door behind them and led her to a shed on the side of the house. With only the porch light to guide them through the shadows, he wheeled his motorcycle out of the dark interior, got on and held out his hand. She climbed on.

Riding behind him, the warmth of his back and the mingling of their hair in the wind, pushed her adrenaline into overload. She was breathless and laughing when they finally stopped and got off. A round structure with pillars and carved details shrouded in darkness stood at the far end of the park, a multitude of trees around them.

Mario pulled a blanket out of the storage case on the back of the motorcycle. He grabbed Jessie's hand and led her to a spot next to a tree where the streetlights didn't reach.

Jessie sat on the blanket first, leaning her head back for a view of the black, star-dotted sky.

"Remember riding up the dark roads into Boulder Canyon and catching a view?" Mario lay down and put his head in her lap.

Images flooded Jessie as her fingers slid through his hair. They were silent for a minute and then she said, "San Francisco is beautiful; the people are really nice. I can see why you are happy here."

Mario rubbed the inside of her elbow.

She'd missed that. Something as simple as his touch. "I wondered what kind of greeting I'd get this morning," she admitted.

"You never have to worry about that. I'm waiting for you to come to your senses. To be here with me."

Jessie felt a flutter deep inside at the strength of his words, but didn't want to have that discussion tonight. His fingers moved to the seam of her pants. Obviously, he didn't want to talk, either.

"I'm waiting for you to show me how much you've missed me." She laughed as he rolled and pulled her down so they were both sprawled on the blanket. "We've got tonight and tomorrow night, possibly my last night here, too."

"I'd better get busy then." He kissed her, his hands moving over her in ways that were familiar but bolder than she remembered.

Her senses went on overload.

She unzipped his jacket, pulled his t-shirt free. What started out light-hearted turned serious fast. She sensed a sudden intensity in him as his grip on her hips tightened. They fought to see who was going to lead and who would follow.

Then he slowed, his breath a feather along her shoulder and neck. "You still inspire my music, even from hundreds of miles away."

She'd known he wasn't going to play fair. "You've got so many fans I'll have to wait in line just to get an autograph." She struggled to say the words and pushed her coat aside and her sweater up impatiently to give him better access to her skin.

"But you're the only one I want to do this with." His hands slowly worked her pants from waist to hip. "You still on the pill?"

She nodded.

He pulled a condom out of his jean pocket as she undid the buttons on his Levi's. She decided to give in this time, let him lead, because the ability to think was fading fast. "Hurry," she murmured, at least having the last word.

Fourteen

Isabel

Winter   Present Day
The Pacific Coast, California

Isabel's eyes and hand connected as if they were one. Somehow the simple act of moving pencil on paper put the world in perspective. Basic forms took shape, details of light and shadow giving energy and life to the whole. When she finished with the view of pounding surf and lone seagull, she looked out over the crashing waves and decided she was pleased with the results.

Next to her, Jessie's eyes were closed, her headphones plugged in to her iPod. Sara reclined in a lounge chair opposite them, journal in hand.

"What are you writing?" Isabel asked.

"About the last two days. I want to remember everywhere we've been, everything we've seen."

New Year's Day they'd toured Muir Woods before shopping in Sausalito. The next day more sights, lunch, then the museum. Mario had cooked Paella and the whole band came for dinner. Yesterday, after renting a car, they'd driven down the coast to Monterey, explored the aquarium and had lunch at Hog's Breath Inn in hopes of seeing Clint Eastwood. They hadn't, but it was fun all the same. There'd been silence in the car on the famous seventeen-mile drive along the coast as they watched all that beauty go by. The most unforgettable, in Isabel's opinion, was the sunset from Carmel Beach. The shimmering ball of red and orange hovering on the horizon with ocean stretching as far as the eye could see was imprinted on her brain. She'd already tried to capture it on paper a few times, with varying degrees of success.

This morning she'd made them stop three times on the drive through Big Sur. At two lighthouses and to see the elephant seal rookery. Now they were happily settled in their hotel in San Simeon with another glorious view of the beach.

Isabel noticed how radiant and relaxed Jessie looked. Mario had a lot to do with it. On the drive yesterday she got Jessie to give them details. Isabel figured she'd been dying to tell them anyway.

"It was like we'd never been apart. We fit. We're in tune with each other. I don't know how else to describe it." Jessie's eyes shone with memories and anticipation of one more night in San Francisco before going home.

"You had safe sex, right?" Isabel asked.

Jessie rolled her eyes. "Of course."

Isabel remembered the sex talks given by the dean her sophomore year in high school. "Just say no," and "Wait until marriage," had been the mottos. Advice that most girls she knew hadn't listened to. She'd have to think about it someday she supposed. Her visual mind leapt into a picture of Michael naked on her bed, the two of them together. Okay, push that thought away. She was so not going there. Yet.

Sara closed her journal, a smile on her lips. Now that Isabel thought about it, at some point, Sara's usual caution had vanished too. Maybe because everything was going along perfectly. Sara worried about things like that. Or it could be the massage she'd gotten earlier this afternoon at the hotel spa, but Isabel was just glad this trip they'd put their hopes on wasn't disappointing.

"Let's get in the hot tub tonight." Jessie sat up, pulling the headphones out of her ears. "Time to put on the swim suits."

Sara groaned and reached for her water bottle.

"It'll be fun, Sara. You'll love it. What are you working on, Isa?" Jessie asked.

She showed them the sketch she'd just done.

"You have to enter the competition at Stone, Isabel."

"Yeah, I know," she mumbled.

"You should submit a mountain scene. Or maybe one of your portraits." Jessie suggested.

"I like the one of the trees by the creek," Sara added.

"Or maybe…"

"I'll think about it when the time comes." Isabel gave them her sternest look. "No school talk on vacation. Are you ready to eat? Come on, I'm starving."

After dinner, wrapped in white hotel towels, they walked the well-lit path to the pool area. Sara eased into a lounge chair, but Jessie in a red bikini and Isabel in a jade-colored one, laid their towels aside and stepped right into the bubbling hot water. There were a few friendly hotel guests willing to share the space in the tub, but they didn't stay long. In no time, Jessie, Isabel and Sara had the area to themselves.

Isabel shifted so that one of the jets was in the middle of her back. Jessie urged Sara to get in. She stepped gingerly onto the first ledge and sighed. Isabel thought she looked good in her coral-colored one piece, with her hair lifting away from her face in the breeze coming off the ocean. With the steam rising around them, Isabel gazed at the palm trees overhead and the half-moon shining like a beacon in the sky.

That was when the lights went out.

"Hey, what's going on?" Isabel could just make out Jessie's silhouette as she stood and moved closer to Isabel and Sara's side of the hot tub.

Everything was dark; the walkways, the pool area, even the hotel, Isabel realized, looking around.

"Isabel?" Sara's voice wavered from where she stood.

"I'm right here." Isabel moved through water unexpectedly soundless and motionless, until she felt them next to her.

The air was no longer cool on her shoulders, but damp and musty. Then, like someone had pulled the plug on a drain, the water slid away.

"What the...?" Jessie moved in closer.

"Isabel, is this...?" Sara clutched her arm.

The gritty bottom beneath her bare feet confirmed what her senses had told her the minute the lights went out. "Yep. The cave."

"It's so dark I can barely see you two and you're standing right next to me," Jessie said.

"There's a faint light to the left." Isabel was trying to remain calm. That and the fact that there was no water at their feet, and that Jessie and Sara were here with her helped.

"Well, we can either stand here waiting for something to happen or move. I say let's go toward the light."

"As long as we promise not to let go of each other." Sara's agreement came with a tight grasp on Isabel's hand.

"Okay, here we go."

The light became brighter, growing larger, spreading out from a center point within the stone as they approached.

"It's like one of those hidden caves where ancient drawings were found," Jessie said in awe when they stopped, side by side.

Rock surrounded them, images emerging on the expanse of it as high as Isabel could see. With the sweep of an invisible hand, mountains, oceans, trees, blended with faces and people, disappearing and re-emerging with different colors on a different place on the wall.

"Look there." Sara pointed to a spot on the right. "Isn't that your picture of the foothills?"

Isabel released Sara's hand and moved closer to the picture of hills and trees, a rocky slope and a trickle of a waterfall. Her heart pounded madly in her ears as she touched the familiar scene with gentle fingertips. It faded, and before she could blink, a new one bled through the stone.

"Hey, there's the one of your sister Maggie that you showed us." Jessie pointed to a space high above their heads.

"Is that us?" Sara asked, as two young women appeared, hair windblown across their faces, hiding most of their features except their eyes and a glimpse of their lips.

Isabel realized she'd been holding her breath. "Yes. I did it after our walk up Chautauqua." She turned to look more closely at a family picnic scene she'd done in high school when a hand grabbed hers.

"Over here." Jessie pulled her to the opposite end.

A close-up of a man, his head turned away so only one eye, part of his forehead and cheek were displayed.

"Michael?" Jessie asked.

Isabel nodded. She'd done it the afternoon after her visit to his house.

"Do you hear that?" Sara asked.

Isabel heard the low rumble at the same time the ground beneath her feet sent vibrations shooting up her legs. Jessie pulled her and Sara together into a huddle away from the wall of pictures. A crack like a gunshot tore the air as a deep fissure spread from one end of the rock to the other, splitting apart the picture of her family, the ocean scene she'd done that morning and the one of Michael.

An arrow of pain pierced her in the chest at the sight. It was so physical she looked down to see if she was actually bleeding.

The wall continued splitting into thousands of tiny fractures, the sound like ice breaking on a lake.

"Do something. Make it stop," Sara pleaded.

Isabel watched the fissures spread. "I don't know what to do!"

"Stop!" Jessie yelled at the top of her lungs, the words vibrating through the air until the echo finally faded.

For a moment there was absolute stillness. No more shaking or cracking.

Then the water returned.

Jessie and Sara were looking at her from the other side of the hot tub with a mix of relief and surprise on their faces. She gripped the tile edge for support and sat down, causing water to slosh up over the sides.

"Everybody okay?" Jessie asked.

Sara nodded.

Isabel took lots of deep breaths and let the pulsating water calm her. "Damn, but that was scary. And weird."

"It was cool the way the stone lit from within." Jessie ducked under the water and came back up. "But you're right. I was afraid too."

"When the wall started to break I felt a very real pain." Silence followed Isabel's pronouncement.

"The stone was a view of life from above, or outside. Nature, seasons, family, children, friends." Sara leaned back against the ledge, the water bubbling up around her shoulders. "Your work, Isabel. Your life. Of course it hurt. Art is everything to you."

"But why the water, why the cracks in the wall?" Concern shadowed Jessie's eyes.

"It's interesting that what seems to be the focus of Jessie's maze is her father. The past. But Isabel's cave? Is it about the past?" Sara asked her directly.

"I don't know, but I've had enough of it for now. For a long while."

Sara slowly got out, holding the rail for support. Dried quickly before covering up. "Wow, it's midnight," she said, checking her watch.

"Time for a real swim." Jessie's smile was mischievous as she hopped out. "Hope the pool's heated," and she swiftly stepped out of her swimsuit. "I dare you two to join me," and dived into the deep end, her long lean body arching over the water before smoothly flowing into it.

Damn, she loved how Jessie could turn things around. After a cave encounter, what was a little skinny-dipping? In one fluid motion, Isabel had her bikini off and she was in, catching up to Jessie who was swimming back and forth. It was heated, although compared to the hot tub it actually felt cool. She mirrored Jessie, stroke for stroke.

They tried to get Sara in but she stubbornly refused. There was lots of splashing, laughter and daring each other to do other crazy things. Eventually, exhaustion overcame each of them. Isabel turned over in the water and allowed her body to float. Her mind drifted on calm nothingness as the palm trees above swayed back and forth above, and the stars and the cool air blanketed her. Finally, she swam to the shallow end and noticed Sara heading back to the room and Jessie picking up her suit.

Isabel slowly followed and went through all the motions of getting ready for bed. Sleep came instantly, enveloping her in dreams that she couldn't remember when she woke the next morning.

Isabel was showered and dressed before Jessie and Sara, so she went to the hotel lobby to grab some muffins and coffee to take back to their room. They sat on the balcony while they ate and Sara read from the research she'd found and sent to each of them on Hearst Castle.

"This says Hearst dreamed of building a house like the castles he'd seen traveling as a boy throughout Europe. He collaborated with architect Julia Morgan for more than twenty years on the estate. It has 165 rooms and 127 acres of gardens, terraces, pools and walkways. Hearst entertained the elite of Hollywood, politics and sports there, even while it was under construction."

"I'm glad you talked us into coming here, Sara. It sounds cool." Jessie grabbed another muffin off the tray. "Don't even say it," she warned when Isabel started to mention her increased appetite. "Sea air makes me hungry."

"Read more," Isabel prompted Sara.

"Apparently Morgan supervised all aspects of construction, including the purchase of everything from Spanish antiquities to reindeer for the castle's zoo. She personally designed most of the structures, grounds, pools, animal shelters and workers' camp."

"What are we waiting for?" Isabel finished the last of her coffee. "Let's go. At the hotel desk they said it's really close."

Just as promised, the drive was short and they arrived at the parking lot as it was beginning to fill up with early morning tourists. Bags slung over their shoulders, they followed the painted pathway toward the visitor center.

"Look!" Sara pointed.

The early morning fog was lifting. A castle sat at the very top of the mountain, majestic and proud. They stood a moment admiring it.

"I feel this pull, like it's calling us, inviting us in," Jessie said.

"I'm so excited to see it all. Come on." Sara grabbed each of them by the arm, towing them inside.

After deciding on the Grand Rooms Tour, they wandered through the exhibits and saw the video on Hearst in the visitor center theater. Then sat in the back of the bus that would take them up the long winding drive to the castle. The guide was short and balding, wore white pants and a blue blazer with the Hearst Castle logo on it and introduced himself as Vincent.

"What you see before you was open wilderness in 1919 and known as 'Camp Hill.' Camp they did, in quite luxurious tents for sleeping and eating and called it 'roughing it.'"

That got a laugh out of everyone.

"Hearst hired Julia Morgan, the famed San Francisco architect, and this is what he said, 'Miss Morgan, we are tired of camping out in the open at the ranch in San Simeon and I would like to build a little something."

Vincent timed his story perfectly. The shuttle went around the final bend and the whole castle came into view. With a dramatic flourish Vincent said, "I give you, Hearst's little something."

More laughter.

"It was named La Cuesta Encantada, The Enchanted Hill. Now we will proceed with our tour."

Everyone filed off the bus, couples and families, some asking questions, some taking pictures. Isabel was last, having taken a seat in the very back of the bus. Vincent kept the pace easy, talking as he walked. "Marion Davies was hostess here to a constant stream of visitors from the entertainment and political elite of the 1920s and 30s. She threw lavish parties, flying guests into a private airfield or hiring a private car. The house rules were that all guests had to attend dinner in the dining room each evening followed by a newsreel and movie in the theater. We will be seeing those rooms when we reach the main house."

White marble steps led to a creation of tile, a sculpture and water called Neptune's pool. Vincent pointed out the colonnades, statues, and Italian carvings. "It is speculated that many guests used the lounge chairs at this very pool at night for romantic liaisons," Vincent remarked while everyone took one last look at the pool and the view.

"Why not?" Jessie whispered to Isabel. "I bet it's really cool with the pool lights on at night."

As the tour continued into the gardens, Vincent described the guest houses and the history of some of the art pieces they passed. Isabel pictured working with Hearst as Morgan had, deciding on details of color and material, where the art would go. He'd had extravagant tastes, room after room filled with art and antiquities. And then there was the statuary of the gardens. Roman and Greek gods, cherubs, lions, Adam and Eve as they fled the Garden of Eden, and the most famous, the four statues of Sekhmet, the warrior goddess of the ancient Egyptians. All were beautifully kept.

Isabel only half listened as Vincent launched into another story. She stopped, letting others in the group pass her while she studied the detailed tile work on the corner of the guest house called Casa del Mar. She heard the call for everyone in the group to keep up right before she felt the hand on her arm pulling her back. It was Jessie, her face serene, glowing.

"We're supposed to stay with the group," Sara scolded, even though they had already been left behind.

"You've gotta see this." Jessie pulled them into a secluded recess Isabel hadn't even noticed.

Straight ahead, a statue of three women stood together as one, so stunning Isabel simply stared.

"Guess who." Jessie's voice was hushed, her gaze reverent as she moved closer.

There was a heartbeat of silence before Sara answered. "The Three Graces."

Fifteen

Sara

Hearst Castle
San Simeon, California

Set on a short pedestal, surrounded by a low wall of flowering trees, the statue shone brilliant white against the greenery behind them. Every line of ankle, knee, thigh, hip and arm drew the eye toward them.

"The Three Graces," Sara repeated with less surprise, more certainty. "We found them." Compelled to study every detail on the life life-size sculpture, she moved closer, her steps light, her breathing fast.

They were naked. The hair on their heads curled in front, the length pinned up in the back. The middle Grace was the tallest, her arms around the other two, along back and shoulder. The goddess on the right faced inward, both arms around her sister. The one on the left rested her cheek against her sister's forehead, an arm reaching across the front, her legs crossed.

Sara felt like she was intruding on a scene of quiet intimacy between sisters.

The courtyard was absolutely still. Sara watched the tableau before her as if the echoes of years past halted time. Isabel approached the middle figure. Jessie's fingers were already on the tangle of arms. Sara was captivated by the smaller figure on the right. The young woman's features seemed to be offering help, advice, and solace. It was a face of compassion. Drawn closer by some invisible force, she reached the statue, her own hand upon smooth, cool marble at the same time as Jessie and Isabel's.

The rumbling of the earth jolted her and a gust of wind burst through. As the ground continued to shake, the marble under her hand turned flesh. Soft, warm, pulsating with life. She held onto Isabel with one hand and watched as the figures moved from their embrace of each other, reaching out to each of them. Sara felt something like hope flood her, even as she stood there completely confounded.

Jessie was touching one Grace's cheek. It glowed at the contact, her expression enraptured. Isabel's muscles felt taut under Sara's hand as surprise and bewilderment flitted across her features.

Thoughts intruded inside Sara's head that were not her own. Another voice meshed with her voice. A thousand scents, flavors, and textures she'd never smelled, tasted nor touched assaulted her. It was too much and not enough all at once.

Then she couldn't move.

She wasn't alone.

It was a comforting thought, despite the attack on her senses, and she forced herself to breathe into the sensation of it.

Sara.

Her name. Someone was calling her name.

Then there was stillness. She felt it penetrate her skin, down through every muscle and organ in her body, into her very blood.

And because of it, she was completely unprepared for the semi-circle the figures led them into and the scene that suddenly appeared in the Spanish tile courtyard.

A little girl in pigtails came running. Unmistakably Jessie, at a very young age. Anger and grief etched into her features. She kicked off her shiny black shoes, unwound a dainty pink boa from around her neck, and threw them all in a big trash bin.

A kitchen appeared. A much younger but recognizable Isabel, in a plaid skirt and white blouse, trembled, although her face gave no indication of any emotion. An older woman, her face full of anger, snatched a sketchbook and pencils from the bag on the counter, stashing them away in a drawer.

A tennis court took its place. Sara in a yellow tennis skirt and top, racket in hand, stood next to Quinn who was talking to two girls. Sara said nothing, her face impassive, immobile, until the two walked away and Quinn gave her a little shake.

Sara met Jessie and Isabel's questioning stares, but only for an instant.

Another voice – shouting - intruded. Like quick slaps, footsteps sounded on the marble walkway behind her, jolting and imposing on the sanctuary that had been created.

Sara returned to a "before" that was the same, yet distinctly different. Isabel and Jessie tried to steady themselves and each other. The stone figures were back, their beauty enticing, but Sara turned to face what was coming.

Vincent, their guide had noticed their absence and returned to find them. He reproached them with a, "Tsk, tsk," when he saw them, as a parent might to naughty children. He kept up a stream of polite admonitions as he led them back to the group.

And the tour continued. Sara moved next to Isabel and Jessie while her mind lingered on the statue. Of the scenes she'd witnessed. Of the intensity of emotion. She barely registered Vincent's parting story of Hearst's final days and how the castle came to be a state park. When she sat down on the bus for the ride to the visitor's center, she breathed deep in a concentrated effort to come back to the present.

Jessie reached across the aisle to grip her hand and that helped. "Are you okay?" she whispered.

She nodded and looked at Isabel who was staring out the window. "How's she doing?"

Isabel sighed and turned. "Fine."

"I feel like the world has been rearranged and my brain is trying desperately to process it." Jessie searched Sara's eyes for confirmation. "They moved, right? Touched us?"

Sara nodded again, words escaping her for the moment. She took stock of her heart rate, hands that appeared almost steady and stomach that wasn't too clenched. The most extraordinary thing had just happened to her and she was handling it.

143

"We've got a lot to talk about," Jessie said.

Isabel's brown eyes looked troubled. "Not here. Not yet." She rubbed her arms up and down a few times as if chilled, though the bus was warm.

"I know," Jessie said, rewrapping her black scarf around her neck as the tram slowed.

When it stopped, they got off last. In uncustomary silence, they walked slowly through the visitor's center.

Sara stopped by the double door entrance to the gift shop. She couldn't leave without taking something with her from this place. "Wait a minute. I'll be right back."

"I hope she isn't going to buy some cheap souvenir," she heard Isabel say as she sat on the bench outside to wait.

At the sound of Jessie's laughter, Sara knew things were returning to normal. She went straight to the book section and without even having to search, found exactly what she wanted. She bought three.

They drove down the road to the small town of Cambria to eat. "Let's just get a smoothie from this place and stroll," Isabel answered as she pulled into a just-vacated parking spot. "I can't sit in a restaurant right now."

The sun on Sara's face seemed to warm not just her skin, but deep inside where she still felt chilled by what had happened. Isabel got caught up in the art of one gallery so Jessie pulled Sara along the sidewalk to the clothing stores. She figured they wouldn't last much longer. Jessie was fairly bursting with the need to talk about what had happened and Isabel's eyes had that sharp look she got when she was fed up and wanted answers.

"I'm tired. Can we go?" Sara asked.

"Fine by me," Isabel answered, and without waiting for Jessie's reply, crossed the street to the parked car.

Back at the hotel, Sara put the card key in the slot and entered their room first. "I'm going to shower." Throwing her purse down, she laid her suitcase open and sorted through for a clean shirt and underwear.

Isabel lay face down on one of the beds and was instantly asleep.

Jessie peeled off her clothes, found her bikini, and put it on with quick jerky movements. "I'll be at the pool," she said, towel in hand.

The shower's spray of hot water massaged Sara's neck and shoulders and she finally relaxed her hold on herself. Which was a mistake. She'd shut out the statue turned-living- breathing flesh until she could talk it over with Jessie and Isabel. The image that came sharply to mind was another memory she'd tried to bury.

The hallway leading to the restroom at the club three nights ago.

She'd left the table to escape the suffocation. Too many people at the table or maybe just the one person she didn't want to think about or be close to. At the end of the hallway the back door was open, so she took deep breaths of fresh air to pull herself together. When she looked up, Caryn was watching her.

"You okay?" Caryn had asked.

Sara nodded. "Fine." Tried to still her shaking hands. "You all are really good."

"Thanks." Caryn took a step closer, then another and another.

Sara didn't say anything to stop her because her heart was pounding so fiercely she couldn't think. She wanted to look away but couldn't do that either.

"Are you afraid?" Caryn trailed her fingers along Sara's arm as she examined Sara from head to toe.

The boldness shocked her. Excited her. "Yes." She should tell Caryn to back up, give her some room. Or she should move, now before it was too late.

"I'm going to kiss you," Caryn said, reaching her hand up behind Sara's neck. The pressure was warm and made Sara shiver.

Her mind screamed one thing and her body another. Rational thinking usually won. Or was it fear that usually won? The need to feel safe? This time it didn't.

145

Warm lips descended upon hers, moving slowly, delicately. Tongue and teeth teased her until she couldn't take it anymore and kissed back.

"Caryn, let's go. We're on," said a voice from the other end of the hallway.

Links of chains clicked against each other as they covered her legs and arms even before Sara turned her face in the opposite direction to hide her shock. At the sudden presence of the restraints or the kiss she'd allowed to happen, she didn't know. Caryn stepped back, put a stickie with a phone number in Sara's hand and walked away without a word.

Now, as Sara turned off the shower and reached for the towel, she thought about the looks Caryn had given her the night when they'd all had dinner together. She'd hated it and loved it and didn't want to think about what it meant. Sara dried off and was just getting dressed when through the closed bathroom door she heard Jessie return and Isabel say, "God, that felt great. Just what I needed, a little nap. Hey, Sara, open up. I've got to pee."

"Hold on, I'll be right out."

"Hurry!"

Sara gathered her things and opened the door. Isabel rushed past her. Jessie sat in a chair by the window wrapped in a towel, a diet soda can in hand.

"Hot tub nice?" Sara asked.
"Great."
"You've got to loosen up, Sara," Isabel called through the still open bathroom door.
"Isabel," Jessie's tone was one of exasperation and warning.
A minute later Isabel walked out, her pants up but undone, pulling her shirt off. "We're all girls here, in case you hadn't noticed."

"So what?" Jessie shot back.
"What is she so afraid of?"
Sara opened her mouth, but no words came out. The last thing she wanted right now was an argument.

But Jessie didn't stop. "We didn't grow up the same, that's all. Sara's not used to walking around in her underwear like you and I are."

"From what I've seen there's nothing wrong with her body. Why should she be afraid to show it? Especially to us; we're all friends."

From somewhere, Sara found the strength to say, "Chill, you two." Both looked at her in surprise.

Isabel lay down again on the bed, clearly still annoyed, but Sara knew it really had nothing to do with her.

"If we talk about it, we'll all feel better." Jessie obviously had the same idea.

The winter sun was beginning to set, creating shadows on the walls. Through the window, Sara watched other guests coming and going. Remembering what she bought at the gift shop, she got the bag from the floor and handed Jessie and Isabel each a copy of an interpretive guide to Hearst Castle.

They looked pleased and Isabel immediately began paging through it. Jessie joined her on the bed and patted the space next to her. Just like at home, Sara flopped down next to them.

"I think they're on page fifty-eight," she said, opening her own copy.

And they were, displayed in all their beauty on a full-page spread.

Jessie began to read the text on the opposite page. "The Three Graces was sculpted by an Italian artist, Antonio Canova, in the early 1800s. They were called Charities, and personified grace and charm. Although most often depicted as a trio, each represented a quality revered by the ancient Greeks."

Sara looked at the small print under the picture. "Look! The caption under the statue says they are named Brilliance, Joy and Bloom."

"Sara was standing in front of this one here, Bloom." Isabel tapped the one on the right. "I was standing in front of Joy, and Jessie touched Brilliance."

"I felt pulled, connected by some invisible thread, to get closer, to touch them." Jessie told them what she remembered from her first startled glimpse of the statue. "It was like a homecoming. I knew them. They were a part of me. Touching them was the only thing I could think about and you two had to be with me. When I finally put my hand on the marble, there was energy and it kept building inside me until I couldn't hold it any longer. A fire with a life of its own."

Sara took herself back to the moment in the garden, describing how she touched the figure, felt the earth shake and heard a voice calling her name. She tried to relate the rush of scent and flavors on her senses, but there were no words that fit.

Isabel's version was shorter. "Ditto, to what both of you said."

"Come on Isa, not fair." Jessie shifted to sit cross-legged and closed the book.

"We were all there, seeing the same things, feeling the same things, with a few variations."

"What about what we saw at the end?" Sara asked.

Isabel scowled. "I don't want to talk about that."

Jessie sighed, "I know. I don't either, but it's gotta be important."

"How?" Sara asked. "I don't understand what mine has to do with anything." Except she did remember that day. She'd been embarrassed. Felt panicked. That flutter, that confusion when meeting the girl Quinn talked to was similar to what she'd felt with Caryn the other night. No, she really didn't want to think about it. "Do you remember when you were that young, Jessie?"

The silence was so long Sara thought she hadn't heard or was ignoring the question.

"I'm getting a headache." Jessie rubbed between her eyes. "You were much older in the scene we saw you in, Isabel. Why did your mother do that?"

148

Isabel sighed in annoyance. "When my brothers and sisters got in trouble they were grounded from TV or from going to dances. Stuff like that. I was grounded from drawing." She waved her hand vaguely. "That happened a lot when I was young. Then I learned to be sneaky and draw in my school notebooks."

Sara couldn't imagine how lost Isabel must've felt without her drawing tools.

"It'll be cold but let's take one last walk on the beach," Jessie suggested.

"Cold?" Isabel laughed. "When I talked to Maggie yesterday she said they got a foot of snow back home. This is heaven."

They found a well-lit trail from the back of the hotel straight to the beach. The empty sand stretched for miles and the water that led to the horizon was a dark gray blue.

"The water feels more powerful at night, doesn't it?" Off the path onto the sand, away from the lights, Sara stepped into the mystery of the darkness. A little like how she felt about her life right now. There was no longer predictability or routine, that was for sure.

"I think I've fallen in love with the sound of the sea," Jessie said, her voice soft and dreamy. "I feel calm inside when I'm here."

They walked to where dry sand met wet. Close together facing the water, they sat for a while, the roar of the ocean the only sound between them.

Tomorrow they'd return to San Francisco where they'd stay with Mario one last night before flying home. The thought made Sara sad. She'd been scared to go on this trip in the beginning, true. She'd never believed she could travel or meet people like she'd done with Jessie and Isabel. Now that it was coming to an end, she wished it were starting all over again.

Jessie brushed her windblown hair away from her face. "So we felt drawn to this statue. And the experience was similar to the others we've had, where one minute we're here and then we're not."

Isabel uncrossed her legs and stretched them out. "I need to draw them. I don't want to forget how they looked."

"You have the book," Sara reminded her.

"You guys are going to think this is totally weird, but…" Isabel hesitated.

"We're way past weird here," Jessie said. "Besides who was the one who said we have to be honest with one another? Not hold back?"

Isabel frowned. "Fine. It's just that… since touching the statue I see what's there, like you do, but at the same time, I see something different." She shook her head, frustrated. "I can't explain it right."

"We get it. I think." Jessie gave Isabel a slight push in the shoulder with a smile.

"And you heard music, Jess?" Sara prompted. "Was it the same?"

"No, but it's kinda like what Isabel said; there seems to be notes or a tune in my head. It won't go away."

"I don't understand why this is happening. To us." Isabel's gaze moved from the water, to Jessie, then to Sara. "Do you?"

"I keep seeing my father in the maze, hearing the song," Jessie offered. She seemed about to say something else, but hesitated.

"Did you grieve for him, Jess? You were so little, maybe you didn't," Isabel suggested. "You could never face going back to where he was killed."

Sara watched emotions dance across Jessie's face in the silence that followed.

"What about all those pictures in the cave?" Jessie asked Isabel. "Your family, some of your sketches."

"Yeah, yeah, I know. Then the wall cracks right through them," Isabel said.

"Do you feel separate, somehow different and so apart from your family, Isabel?" Sara thought she must. From everything she'd seen and heard, Isabel didn't feel she fit in with them.

"There she goes again, saying things that make total sense," Isabel remarked with a wry smile. "And my mom didn't help, as you saw earlier."

She wanted to understand, to help Jessie and Isabel understand, but it felt like a puzzle with too many missing pieces.

Jessie leaned into Sara but kept her focus on the ocean. "Have you been caught up in your chains since we've been on our trip? I hate to say this, but I don't really want to go there with you."

Isabel shuddered. "Me neither, sorry."

"I don't think you will. When I'm caught up in the chains, I'm completely alone."

Jessie looked like she was beginning to see. "You said you were in emptiness, completely isolated. How you've felt your whole life."

Sara thought of her father and Quinn. Not completely alone. But since they'd promised to be honest she had to admit it. "Pretty much."

"But not anymore," Jessie said. "You've got us."

Sara felt her throat tighten with emotion at Jessie's words. Then came the slither of cool metal under her pant leg, wrapping up and around beneath her coat. She waited, her heart beating frantically, fear at the edge of her consciousness. She said nothing, afraid Jessie and Isabel would get up and run if they knew, especially after what they'd just admitted.

A squeeze on her hand refocused her attention. "Thanks," she managed to say and the constriction around her loosened.

"Who was Quinn talking to? Do you remember the day that we saw, Sara?"

"Just some girls from school."

Isabel rose, brushing the sand from her pants. "I'm starving. Let's get some dinner."

Jessie pulled Sara to her feet. The chains disappeared completely and her breathing evened out. "I'll do some research about the Graces." The wind picked up, blowing her hair this way and that. "Maybe I can find something that will help."

"Help how?" Isabel asked.

"I don't know," Sara answered. "I just feel like I have to do something."

"What can it hurt?" Jessie rubbed her arms.

Sara breathed the salty sea air into her lungs. Out of her normal place and routine, not without doubts and fears but not ruled by them either, she saw herself living two lives. One familiar; the one she'd been living and one was new, which was the one she desired.

She joined hands with Jessie, who took Isabel's, and they watched the waves roll in and hit the shore one last time.

Sixteen

The Graces

Present Day

Hearst Castle, San Simeon, California

It was a miraculous day.

They could move beyond the marble.

It had taken an incredible amount of effort, true. But so worth it.

Luring the young women had been easy. They hadn't even tried to resist the compulsion the Graces used upon them. As if they were accustomed to the strange and inexplicable. Which the sisters soon discovered they were.

They needed guidance, like so many Brilliance, Joy and Bloom had helped over the centuries. When Jessie, Isabel and Sara had touched the surface of the statue, some of the barriers that held the Graces had broken. But not all.

The girls were the key. But how were they to find them again?

The silence of the garden lengthened as twilight shimmered on the hill.

"Sisters," Brilliance whispered, sensing an energy that beckoned, called, from somewhere nearby. "Can you feel that?"

"Of course," the other two responded in unison. A picture of a woman from years gone by slid into the Graces' memory. One of their three, Julia, coming to sit with them the day she said goodbye.

"She carried the necklace, the gift, and put it in a box," Joy remembered. The sky had been gray and full of dark storm clouds, the air blanketed with sadness, an ache that seemed to weigh heavily on every plant, animal and piece of art on the entire grounds.

"Then she hid the box under the bench in front of us," Bloom added. "I believe it is still there."

Since they'd been touched by the three young visitors that morning, The Graces' powers were returning little by little. As goddesses of not only beauty and mirth, but also of adornment, they could feel the energy now of this hidden necklace. It had been freely given. First to Julia in friendship, and she in turn, had left it for them. At the time, they had puzzled over her actions. Now they knew that whatever had led Julia to do it, whether instinct or some other force, they were meant to use the necklace. And doing so would help them.

A blast of sparks flew upward. The pendants, three in one, were in their hands, spurring the goddesses to put together a plan. When the time was right, they would set it in motion.

Seventeen

Jessie

Present Day

San Francisco, California

"Jessie! Let's go," Mario yelled from the living room.

"Where are you going?" asked Isabel, who was curled up on Mario's bed.

Jessie checked her reflection in the mirror above the dresser one last time. "I don't know." She turned to look at Sara, who was leafing through her Hearst Castle book on the floor next to the bed. "Are you sure you don't mind? I feel like I'm abandoning you two on our last night here."

Sara looked up. "It's okay, really. Go."

"That means get outta here." Isabel waved toward the door.

"I'm gone," Jessie said with a laugh. She stopped by the kitchen when she saw Mitch stirring something on the stove. She leaned in and gave him a kiss on the cheek just because she liked him and knew it would make him smile. Which it did.

Seeing two men waiting by the front door stopped her in her tracks.

"What's going on?" Jessie asked.

"Mario wants to show you around the studio," Phil answered. "Then I'm going out with some friends who'll meet me there. You guys can use my car for the night."

Jessie looked suspiciously at Mario. He hadn't mentioned anything about this earlier in the day when they'd returned and he asked her out.

"Don't worry, you're gonna love it," Mario said, his eyes meeting hers.

She'd been hoping not to see Phil again. He had that electric awareness that unsettled her, only because of its similarity to what she felt with Mario. It looked like tonight she was in for double jeopardy.

Phil drove and Mario insisted she sit up front. She teased them like always and laughed at Phil's biting commentary on a band they'd all heard about. But seriously, couldn't they feel it too? She breathed easier when Phil finally parked and she was able to get out of the car.

The studio was all glass, steel and concrete softened by surrounding trees, which gave it a solitary feel, despite its location in the business section of town. A hushed air greeted them as Phil unlocked the door.

"You may be able to find your way in the dark, but we need a little more light," Mario said, pulling Jessie to his side and holding her there.

"Give me a second." Phil hit some buttons on a keypad to turn off the alarm to the right of the door.

Mario was warm, smelled wonderful, and she loosened up a little at his touch. She looked up at the exact moment he looked down. With his free hand he pulled her face to his for a kiss.

Dim lights came on around them. She could feel Phil's gaze, knew he was watching. She drew away, still holding Mario's hand. "Nice place," she said, looking around. The first floor opened into an atrium, offices lining the outside walls. Wide staircases were on the right and left.

"The studios are below," Phil explained. "Let's go."

She led the way down the stairs but stopped at the bottom. Numbered doors were scattered along both sides of the hall going in both directions. Mario and Phil headed right.

"All of the recording studios vary in size. This one," Phil said, opening one of the last doors, "offers the best mix for smaller bands." With a flick of a switch the room lit up.

Jessie couldn't move. Her heart was racing and it had nothing to do with the two men next to her. Something inside her was shaking. Expanding and growing. Sleeping Beauty awakening from a deep sleep.

The dark pine of the walls gave the room a cozy cabin feel. A baby grand sat in one corner and sound equipment in the other. Through the glass wall to the left she could see the area where the sound engineers worked. "I told you she was gonna love it." Mario moved around her, grabbing her hand and pulling her inside. She turned around a couple of times trying to take it all in.

"I don't think I've ever seen her at a loss for words." Phil pulled out two mic's and some cords and set them up next to the piano.

After checking out every corner, Jessie went through the connecting door and sat in one of the chairs in front of a huge console. She ran her fingers lightly over the many switches and lights. A string of notes came from the piano in the other room.

"Jess, come back," Mario called out.

She didn't move but sat there imagining Mario and his band recording their music here.

"It's a lot of work and takes a group of dedicated people to get it right," Phil said from the doorway, watching her.

She'd tried to guard herself, didn't want him to see how he unnerved her. It felt impossible now that she'd entered this studio.

"He wants you to sing with him." Phil continued to stare, almost as if he were daring her.

Jessie was not surprised by the request. He'd been asking her ever since he'd found out she could sing. By accident, really. She'd been messing around in his basement studio toward the end of their senior year, waiting for him to get back from a food run. She'd been picking out notes on one of his guitars and started singing, not knowing he was standing there listening. After that, they'd sung together some, just to mess around, for fun. He'd asked to record her and of course she'd said no. But she hadn't expected Phil to know about it.

"It'll make him happy, Jessie. And what harm is there? He just wants it for himself, that's all."

She stood up and turned away from the door to watch Mario through the glass. He was playing in earnest now, a medley of songs, a mix of his own and others.

She hated that Phil was right. It wouldn't hurt anyone. Except, she'd be breaking a promise. The vow of a little girl, frightened and confused, who missed her father and the things they shared. Music had been the biggest. She thought of her father's figure in the maze and the music she'd heard there. The day she threw away her boa and dance shoes was fresh in her mind, too. That promise made so long ago. Everything hinged on that. She was sure now.

What to do? If she protested, it might break the fragile bond with Mario she was trying to strengthen again. Still, she'd never pursued music like he had. Her voice was untrained.

"It's the only way to get him to stop talking about it, and to be honest, I'm tired of hearing him go on and on," Phil said in a low voice.

When she turned, she saw the teasing look in his eyes. "I hate you," she said, pushing past him. His laughter followed her into the other room.

The music stopped abruptly. Mario kicked his leg around the piano bench so he was straddling it. Jessie sat down facing him. He pushed a strand of hair away from her face. "Will you do it? For me?"

"I don't know why you want this so much," she whispered, tracing a finger along his cheek, his jaw. In a louder voice, because she figured Phil had turned on all the mikes and could hear everything. "But I'll do it for you." She looked around but didn't see music lyrics anywhere. "What are we singing?"

Mario gave her a little push. "Go stand by the mic and look at me. You already know every piece I want to do."

Jessie didn't have time to think. Mario started playing and when he nodded, she sang.

It just happened. And like breathing, it was the most natural thing in the world. When one song came to an end, he began another.

She was flying. From ballads to R&B. With his harmony.

There was freedom in letting the words pour out.

Exhilaration and terror reigned inside her.

She lost track of time.

When Mario finally stopped playing, Jessie couldn't move, couldn't take her eyes from his. The sudden silence was a vacuum, encompassing them.

Then she heard Phil moving around in the other room, shutting everything down. "Set the alarm when you leave," he said, and then he was gone.

Jessie couldn't think beyond the one thought of what should come next. Saw the same need in Mario. She pulled off her sweater, then the boots and leggings. She stepped over Mario's shirt where he'd just dropped it on the floor next to his belt. The one light left on, a spotlight on the piano, highlighted every fluid line as Mario turned on the padded bench so he faced her. Without either saying a word, she climbed on his lap, her legs on either side of his. Nothing compared to this. To the way they fit.

This time, she led and he followed.

Eighteen

Jessie

Winter, Present Day
Boulder, Colorado

Jessie couldn't get her mind on studying. She dreaded the workload in her classes and was having a hard time focusing. Nothing new there. Images of San Francisco, of Mario, of that night in the studio, occupied her mind at least a dozen times a day. She thought about the Three Graces and wished she could see them again. And she worried about the fact that she hadn't gone to the maze in the week they'd been home. But since neither had Isabel been to her cave or Sara suspended in chains, she tried not to think about it too much.

Emily and Maribel seemed to have gotten over the club incident. Last night when Jessie gave Maribel shoes identical to the lost ones, all was forgiven. The three of them stayed up late talking and laughing like old times. Jessie was hit with doubts that wouldn't go away. Was she happy? Should she stay here, study and get her degree as planned?

What kept creeping in, insidious in their torment, were Mario's whispered words to her on the bench in Phil's studio.

"Come be with me. Make your life here with me."

She'd kissed him and said she'd think about it. In fact, she couldn't think of much else. But he didn't realize how much those words tore at her, made her question the plan for her future. She was supposed to graduate college and get a good job. Her father had, but no one in her mother's family had done it yet. She'd be the first. The expectation had always been there and she'd never questioned it. She could imagine the disappointment if she didn't come through. She'd forever hear about it.

She sipped her coffee in the quiet morning light, figuring a good run might clear her head. With a black wool headband covering her ears and matching gloves on her hands, she headed out. A slight wind caught her unaware as she turned the corner of her block. Even with long underwear beneath her sweats she wasn't going to last long. After about a mile through the neighborhood, she'd had enough and made her way back. Jogging in place waiting for a light, she heard her phone ring.

"Hey girl, what's up?"

Sara offered a ride to school since Jessie's car had been acting up.

"In 45? Sure, I'll be ready." If she hurried.

It wasn't until she entered her small yard from the gate that she remembered the time she'd gone for a run and ended up in the maze, right here.

Stopping to catch her breath, she waited. Nothing happened. She waited another minute. Still nothing. Fine. It didn't matter anyway. She didn't know why or how it happened and she wasn't going to waste any more time figuring it out.

Inside, she got more coffee, showered and dressed. Munching on a granola bar while waiting for Sara, Jessie glanced at the newspaper she'd brought in.

Her kitchen went completely black for a flash and then split into a half-lit, half-dark passage of the maze. She stood still in shock, the snack bar falling from her fingers. She'd almost convinced herself the labyrinth wasn't coming back, yet here she was again. She straddled the line of light and dark, shading her eyes, as she looked right and then squinted as she looked left. Music abruptly came from the right, the melody familiar. Within the inky shadows to the left she saw the figure of her father walking backward, away from her. A tugging sensation from each direction pulled at her.

It all felt wrong somehow.

Peering into the darkness, Jessie could've sworn the figure beckoned to her. She took a tentative step to see better, and then the maze went dark.

161

"No!" She yelled instinctively. A scratch on one arm and then another halted her. She could barely see but could hear the maze closing in. A hundred leaves and twigs pushed into her clothing as if to go straight through her.

She screamed again.

A faint voice chanting, "Wake up, wake up, wake up," intruded into her consciousness. It was Sara and she sounded really worried.

Jessie opened her eyes and looked straight up into Sara's shocked features, blonde hair falling forward.

"Look, she's awake," Sara said, with obvious relief.

"What happened?" Jessie asked, struggling to sit up. She looked around and discovered she was on the kitchen floor.

"You tell us," Isabel said.

Sara helped her lean against the refrigerator. "We heard you screaming, but the door was locked. Then I remembered where you kept the spare key," she finished on a breathless note.

"Her hands were shaking so much I finally had to take it from her to open the door. Otherwise we might've caught you." Isabel handed her a towel.

"What's this?"

"I think you hit your head."

Sara was gently prodding her scalp. "Yep, here's the bump."

Jessie frowned and put the ice on the side of her head.

"How many fingers am I holding up?" Isabel asked.

"Oh, stop that." Jessie swatted Isabel's fingers away. "I'm fine."

Sara looked at Jessie, her eyes serious. "It was a terrible scream."

"I went back to the maze," Jessie said. She told them about her morning and how different the maze looked and when she got to the part about the branches crowding her, pushing into her, she actually had to take a deep breath before she could finish.

162

Sara was squeezing her hand so tight she was losing feeling in her fingertips. "You can let go now, Sara."

"Sorry, it just sounds, I don't know, so different than what I saw with you."

"It was. I knew something was wrong but I couldn't figure out what."

"Well, there goes my morning lecture," Isabel said looking at the clock on the kitchen wall.

"Mine too," Sara said.

"Sorry." Jessie didn't want to think about the maze or her classes or anything else right now. "Can we go get a latte and just hang out?" She didn't want to be alone.

Sara drove to their favorite café. While snowflakes fell, they had coffee and muffins and talked about the latest movies they wanted to see. By the time they got to campus the sky had cleared as if the snow had never been. Sara gave her a hug and Isabel surprisingly did too before they parted ways. Since she had a lot of studying to do she headed to the library.

At the big double door entrance her phone went off so she pulled it out quickly and looked at the number. Her mother.

"Hey...yeah I'm fine...how's everyone?"

Her mother gave her all the latest family gossip in the time it took her to get to the second floor of the library. Plus an invite to dinner. Knowing her mother would ask a lot of questions about the trip made her decline. She used her ready-made excuse that she had a lot of studying to do.

"I promise to drop by sometime over the weekend."

"You'd better, Jessie," came her mother's cool reply. "Your Nana misses you."

That certainly made her feel guilty, as her mother had known it would.

Settling on a couch in a corner, Jessie began to leaf through her books and the hefty readings her instructors had assigned. There was so much. She closed her eyes with a frustrated sigh and wondered for the thousandth time what she was doing here.

The Graces stood before her in a room of pure white, no doors, windows or walls, just a single ray of sun shone down, casting luminous light everywhere. Brilliance stepped forward, hand held out. Jessie recognized the feel of it, the warmth. She looked carefully at the perfectly carved features, at her skin and how her body moved smoothly beside her. Fragrance floated on the air, musical voices, too, like a gentle hum in the background.

They walked as if wading through water. The wash of pure emotion kept coming and going, like ripples at the edge of a lake. It felt like her own heartbreak, her own joy. It would've been too much but somehow the presence of Brilliance beside her made it bearable.

She wished Sara and Isabel were here.
Then Brilliance let go of her hand.

Wait! Don't go yet!

Jessie felt the sofa beneath her and heard human voices. She sat there a while, keeping her mind stubbornly empty. She wasn't ready to return to the world yet. She hadn't had enough time with the Graces.

Something warm around her neck forced her return. With a light touch she discovered a necklace. Grabbing her compact from her purse, she held up the mirror to get a better look. A gold, silk ribbon with a small, gold pendant lay on her chest. The little charm was round, with the rays of a sun shooting out in all directions. She got the feeling it was very old despite its luster and the way it seemed to glow against her skin.

She studied her face. She touched the pendant again. The worries that had been building up over the past week were fading. What she really wanted, more than anything else, was becoming clear. Now she just had to figure out how to make it happen.

Nineteen

Isabel

Isabel was putting away her supplies at the end of class when one of the art department teacher assistants slipped into the back of the room and handed her a folded note.

"Come to my office after class."

Dowling's scrawled signature filled the bottom corner.

Now what? Dowling was her adviser but since she'd already planned out all her course work, she couldn't imagine what he wanted to talk about.

Professor Burns started his closing remarks. Isabel tuned out because he tended to say the same thing every time. Her phone vibrated in her bag and she glanced at it quickly.   Michael.

Since her return, they'd gone to lunch once, had coffee twice and talked almost every day. Seeing him was new and weird and messy. Weird because a small part of her remembered him as a priest, even though she was getting to know the man. Messy because he'd originally said he wanted to be friends but she still felt that old pull of attraction and couldn't decide if he felt it too.

Now Burns was talking about the art competition. Yeah, yeah, yeah. Four categories, oil, watercolor, sculpture and charcoal prints. She'd already heard about it in two other classes and didn't need to obsess about it anymore than she already was. She couldn't decide what to enter, and her indecisiveness was starting to piss her off.

"How are the winners chosen?" A student asked from the back of the room. Everyone had heard comments from classmates whose work hadn't won in previous years. Talk had gone around about the judges playing favorites.

"By the faculty. Two from the art department; this year Dowling and Freeman. Two from other departments; I believe Saunders and Stapleton from Humanities. I expect each student to submit one piece and you don't have much time. The deadline is Thursday," the professor warned, then turned to go.

"Two days," Isabel said to Silvia, who sat next to her. They skirted the drawing tables and stools on their way out the door.

"Have you decided which pieces you'll enter?" Silvia asked, falling into step beside her.

"Not yet. You?"

"Nah. I'll probably pick out a couple the morning of." Silvia stopped for a quick drink at the water fountain. "What about the application?"

"Yeah, got that."

"Me too. You're not stressed about it, are you?"

The question was a little too close for comfort.

"I didn't enter last year but now it's kind of important. I'm not sure why."

"It's a way in to meeting the right people," Silvia answered.

"I guess."

"All the Boulder art critics will be there."

"I'm going to pretend I didn't hear that."

"There's more than one way in." Silvia shrugged and gestured toward the north door. "I'm going this way."

Isabel looked toward the faculty offices. "I've got to stop here. See ya."

She walked into the reception area and saw the TA from earlier.

"Is he there?" Isabel asked, nodding toward his open office door.

The young woman nodded.

Brian Dowling stood staring out the window. He turned at her knock.

"You wanted to see me?"

He gestured to a paper sitting on his desk. It was her writing assignment for Saunders' modern art class. She'd turned it in just days ago. Some comments were written on the cover page in Saunders' hand next to her grade. Isabel noticed the "A" but didn't read the rest. She forced herself to meet his eyes. She couldn't tell what Dowling thought about her assessment of his paintings in the gallery. She'd been honest with her praise and her criticism, but she hadn't expected Saunders to show it to him. Unease settled quickly in her stomach.

"You don't mince words, do you? Your analysis is thorough and incisive," Dowling said, moving to sit at his desk. "Have a seat."

Isabel sat on the edge of the nearest chair and waited, still unsure of where the conversation was going.

"Saunders wants to submit this to the Boulder Daily News."

Floored, Isabel's mind raced in a thousand directions. "Okay, but why'd she give it to you?"

"Her instincts are right about your piece. I can almost guarantee the paper will publish it. But she's new and we're a small, close-knit faculty. She didn't want to blind-side me."

Isabel laid the paper back on his desk feeling awkward. Michael had muddied the waters here, too. Knowing they were friends rattled her for some reason.

"I'll let you talk with Saunders about that," he said eyeing the paper.

Did that mean he was all right with it? She tried to remember everything she'd said in her essay. She really should've chosen someone else to write about. What had she been thinking?

"You're entering Stone's art competition." He wasn't asking.

She rose, grabbing the paper from the desk. "Yes. Is that all?"

"For now."

Isabel turned to go and noticed the long table on the other side of the room. A number of drawings were laid out next to several standard black portfolios. Wondering if Dowling would object, she stepped closer, interested in the style of one in the middle. The others were quite ordinary and not that good in her opinion.

"Whose are these?" she asked, setting her things down and picking up the one for closer inspection.

Dowling joined her by the table. "Admission submissions. Part of my job as faculty chair. What do you think?"

Isabel set it back after a moment. "That's the only interesting one out of all of them. Good technique and the style is subtle, which makes it stand out. The others are trying too hard to be bold."

They talked about the work for a few minutes and she was surprised at his willingness to listen. She'd taken one of his classes last year and met with him only twice to be advised on the requirements for her major. Not really enough time to connect with him on a personal level like she'd heard some students did with their advisors. Surprisingly, he agreed with most of her opinions about the drawings.

Dowling glanced at his watch. "I'm meeting Michael and some friends for lunch."

Isabel felt her cheeks flush at the casual mention of his name. She gathered her things. "I should go," but she hesitated. Something he'd said earlier kept nudging its way back into her mind. "How long have you been faculty chair?"

"Four years."

So, he'd had a part in her acceptance to Stone College. She knew nothing about the how the process worked but her mind kept jumping to conclusions anyway. What if Michael had persuaded Dowling, pressured him? Would he do that? And more important, why?

She left the office without a goodbye. Her thoughts sped ahead with the implications of what she'd just discovered. She wandered into an empty classroom, the smell of wet clay permeating the air, three large kilns lining the far wall. She sank onto one of the stools.

Something wet and cold drenched her feet right through her shoes. She looked down and her world went black.

Hell, not again.

Water rose higher, up to her ankles.

She stood, the water surrounding her with sloshing sounds against the cave walls. Her jeans were already soaked and clinging to her legs. Her knuckles scraped on the rough stone. She turned around, shivering as water rose to her waist.

She dragged her legs, feeling her way along the wall. How was she going to get out of here? Should she wait it out? The freezing water reached just beneath her chin now and she was treading water. She looked up, hoping the ceiling was far above. She gave a yelp of surprise as she was lifted off her feet by the sheer force of water that was pouring in. Right before it covered her head.

Kicking strongly, she went in one direction, then another, in search of air. Turning her head this way and that, trying to see something beyond the all-consuming dark.

The high-pitched sounds of girls' chatter followed by loud laughter broke through her struggle. She opened her eyes. Where water had been, now there were only tables, stools, and an incoming tide of freshmen. Isabel tried to clear away the terror of almost drowning.

After a few minutes, she stopped shaking. Yep, her clothes were only slightly damp now, and drying quickly. But the whole incident had so unnerved her, she continued to sit there as the ceramics class started, trying to make some sense out of it.

There'd been no light, no color, no pictures in the cave this time. Just darkness and water. She'd come close to dying. At least that's what it felt like.

She ran a comb through her hair and tidied herself in the restroom down the hall, then made her way to their meeting spot, sure Jessie and Sara had given up on her now that she was half an hour late.

They waved from the library steps.

"What's up?" Isabel asked, catching up to them.

"When you didn't return my text we got worried," Jessie said, looking at her closely. "Everything okay?"

Isabel was unprepared for the torrent of emotion the simple question evoked. She told them everything, the weight of it slowly lifting. They walked, one on each side of her, their arms through hers. After they got their drinks, they wandered into the bookstore to stay warm. Being with them felt cathartic. That, along with the caffeine in her system, made her feel somewhat whole again.

"Let's decide on the drawings you're going to enter in the contest," Jessie said to Isabel, stopping near the art book selection.

"I think you should enter The Graces," Sara said.

"You didn't tell me you'd finished it." Jessie frowned at her. "Show me."

Isabel set down her cup on one of the shelves and opened her portfolio. She really liked the final effect she'd created. The Graces moved through a very fine veil, no harsh edges, everything streaming from one entity into distinct arms and legs. Isabel had illuminated the garden where they'd all been together by putting the background edges in shadow.

"They're beautiful," Sara finally said. "You're amazing, Isabel. It's really one of your best pieces."

Jessie touched the drawing briefly, right in the middle where the Graces were intertwined. "I agree."

"I don't know if it is, but anyway, I like how it turned out." Isabel slid it carefully back into her portfolio.

Jessie glanced at her phone and sighed. "I gotta go."

Sara looked surprised. "Already? I've got something to show you."

"What?" Isabel asked.

"Just a little research I've been doing," Sara said.

"Hand it over and I'll look later." Jessie pulled her gloves out of her coat pocket, put them on, and grabbed the folder Sara handed her.

"Where you off to, Jess?"

"Family dinner. I couldn't put off my mother any longer."

"Yeah, sounds tough. Let me go instead. I'll eat the terrible food your mother's making."

"The food's the tempting part. And seeing Nana. But I really don't want to have to dissect my time with Mario with my mother."

"So don't tell her everything," Isabel suggested.

"You haven't seen my mother give the third degree." Jessie grabbed Sara's hand. "Be careful. I had a really scary episode and so did Isabel. You're next. Call me later," and she took off.

"You need a ride somewhere?" Sara asked Isabel.

"Home, if you could."

They were silent on the walk to the car and on the ride home until Sara pulled up in front of Isabel's house.

"So, any chains recently?" Isabel asked, curious.

Sara hesitated then finally admitted, "They wrap around me a lot. In class, at home, anywhere, anytime. Not completely into the cocoon, just around my legs and arms."

"And you just, what? Ignore them?"

"Pretty much." Sara reached into the back seat for her backpack. She handed Isabel a manila folder. "Take a look and see what you think."

"Thanks for the ride."

The usual turbulence that was the Cordova family greeted her when she walked in. Her brother Ben, his wife and one-year-old son were there for dinner. Maggie and her youngest brother, James, were sitting at the table too. It was nine o'clock before she made it to her room.

"Playing with little Ben was fun," Maggie said from the doorway.

"That's because we could hand him over when he got fussy," Isabel reminded her.

"What are you doing?" Maggie asked as Isabel cleared her bed of a pile of clothes and smoothed the comforter out.

Isabel opened her portfolio and laid a couple of sketches on the bed. "There's a contest. I have to choose a drawing to enter."

Maggie stood by the bed and watched Isabel set out her favorite pieces. "I bet any one of these will win."

"That's why I keep you around, Sorellina," Isabel said, using the affectionate name in Italian for little sister. "You've always been my biggest fan. If you had to choose, which one would it be?"

Maggie looked them over and pointed to The Graces.

"Why that one?"

Maggie shrugged. "It's cool, in a really weird way."

Isabel laughed. "Fine. That'll be the one then. Besides, Jessie and Sara like it, too."

"I wanna meet your friends. Can I hang out with you guys sometime?"

Isabel pretended to think about it. "Maybe," she teased. "Now go do your homework or whatever you have to do."

She spent a few minutes cleaning up her room but left the drawings out on the bed. Despite what she'd told Maggie, she still wasn't completely sure The Graces was the one she'd enter.

Her phone beeped with incoming texts. She got back to Jessie saying she was fine. She told Sara she'd look through the folder before she went to sleep. She was just about to send a message to Michael when there was a knock at her door.

Her mother came in with an armful of folded laundry.

"I would've done that," Isabel said. She took the clothes and opened her dresser drawers.

"A simple 'grazie' is enough," her mother said. "Besides it's been sitting in the laundry room for days taking up space. I was about to donate it to the poor if no one claimed it."

Isabel smiled, knowing her mother would do it, too. "I'll remember to check more often." Isabel started to rearrange her drawers and re-fold the mess inside each one.

"I never understood your need to draw," her mother said quietly from the other side of the bed.

Isabel turned, startled.

"This one is good of your sister," she said pointing. "These are your girlfriends, right?" She gestured to another.

"How'd you know?" Isabel asked, leaving the clothes and joining her mother.

"I watched from the window when they came to pick you up for the trip you took. You should've brought them in."

Isabel sighed, remembering her need to escape that day. Maybe someday she would bring them over, when all the family was here and Jessie and Sara could meet everyone all at once. Yeah, wouldn't that be fun.

Her mother picked up a sketch. Examined it closely. Here we go, Isabel thought.

"He looks familiar. Wasn't he the chaplain at Assumption?" her mother asked.

Her mother remembered every bishop, priest, and nun the Cordova family had ever encountered.

"Yes. His name's Father Michael." This charcoal sketch showed his face in fragments, with jagged shards of rock and wood shadowing his eyes. A river ran beneath his chin and the mountains were subtle shapes behind him.

"Why did you draw him like that?" she asked.

Isabel sat down on the edge of the bed and gathered her art pieces. "I draw what I see in a particular moment."

Her mother shook her head. "Strange eyes you've got. How you're a child of mine, I don't know." She moved to the door. "I'd ask why there's more than one of him on that bed, but I don't think I want to know."

The door closed quietly behind her.

Isabel counted six, subtle but stinging reprimands, all in the space of a five-minute conversation. She thought she'd gotten used to it, become immune to it, but no, it still felt like she'd never measure up.

A half-hour later she began filling in the shadows on a pencil drawing due the next day. Frustration swelled. The shading just didn't look right and after the day she'd had, she almost crumpled it up.

Then something moved in the corner of the paper.

Isabel blinked.

It happened again.

The flock of birds sitting in the topmost branches of a tree slowly took flight and disappeared off the page.

She fought to drag air into her lungs.

There was a crunch of gravel. Leaves moving in the wind. The flutter of birds' wings. She blinked again twice before she fully comprehended that she stood in her drawing. A steep path veered to the left in a canyon full of oak and maple, with an endless sky of clouds overhead.

Joy beckoned from farther in and Isabel, conscious of every step, walked slowly to meet her. Joy was clothed in shimmering blue that changed hues as she moved. It was like watching moving water.

Face to face, she searched Joy's eyes, hoping to find answers. There was a wisdom in the depths of blue, but mostly she saw lightness and laughter. Her unease slowly drifted away like a balloon in the hands of a child.

Joy held Isabel's drawing, birds and all. Without warning, she tore it up, the pieces slipping through porcelain fingers, floating to the ground.

173

Stark white bits of paper littered the dull brown of her bedroom carpet. Isabel stared, her legs weak and her heart beating unevenly. What did it mean? What was she supposed to do now? The muffled sounds of night in the Cordova house intruded, along with the insistent ring of her phone sitting on the dresser.

She reached for it, the mirror catching the reflection of a glint of silver around her neck. A blue cord fit neatly beneath her collarbone, a half moon-shaped pendant cool against her flushed skin. A gift from Joy. Just like Jessie's from Brilliance. She fingered it, peering at the etched details as she picked up the phone.

"Hello?"

"Isabel. It's Michael."

"Hi." She backed up and sat on the edge of her bed, gazing at her image in the mirror.

"How was your day?"

She didn't even know how she would begin to tell him.

"Hmmm. That stressful, huh?"

She sighed. "Yeah, a little."

"It's late but, could I see you?"

Twenty minutes later she was waiting for him at the end of her block. He wore a leather jacket and jeans that were a little loose on his slim frame. He parked, got out, came around to the sidewalk before leaning against the back of his car, watching her all the while.

Isabel in a black fleece pullover, jeans and boots, looked up at the gray clouds drifting overhead, enjoying how the earth felt like it moved when she watched them.

"You probably don't need one more person asking you if you've decided which drawing to enter in the contest."

She kept her eyes on the clouds. "Nope."

The quiet stillness of the night reminded her of the walk in her drawing but her heart refused the serenity now.

A minute or so passed.

"It looks like more snow's coming in," she finally said.

"We've been reduced to talking about the weather?"

That made her laugh, which felt so good it was like being given a reprieve. "Talk to me. Tell me about your day," she said, moving to lean back on the car next to him.

174

He'd volunteered at the downtown soup kitchen that morning. "Brian and some others met me there for lunch and we hung out for a while."

"Really? Was it their first time?"

Michael nodded. "You should come again some time."

Isabel shifted her gaze to him. "Have you had any regrets about your decision?"

"In occasional odd movements, yes. But mostly, no." He put his hands in his pockets, a thoughtful look in his eyes. "Do you remember what I told you the day you gave me the drawing of the valley?"

Isabel shook her head. She'd never forget the wide, open grassland vista she'd made for him, but his words from that moment she couldn't recall.

"I told you it was going to take a lot of hard work, but never to doubt yourself."

Which was what she'd been doing all day. She couldn't make up her mind which piece to submit because her insecurities kept getting in the way.

Michael put his hand on her arm. It was a gesture of empathy but instead a frisson of awareness rocked through her. She forced herself to meet his eyes, found her body sliding into him.

His hands were gentle but firm as they skimmed over her chin to cup her face. He held her gaze for a long moment, tracing her lips with his thumbs.

Isabel was completely still, knew what would come next if she didn't pull away now. She was afraid to want and then be disappointed. She was afraid to take the next step because she couldn't see where it would lead.

"Stop thinking," he said. Chocolate brown eyes locked with hers. "We're both novices at this, I'm guessing, but I've wanted to do it ever since I saw you again."

His words reassured. And scared her to death. Closing her eyes as he shifted closer, she felt the unusual weight of Joy's gift around her neck, on her skin, and that helped too.

It wasn't anything like she'd expected. The anticipation had been building for so long that she swore her lips were trembling. So she grabbed his coat and pulled him hard against her. Turning the first tentative touch into a demanding search.

175

To Isabel's way of thinking, the necklace and the kiss made the rest of the day worth it.

Twenty

Sara

"Hi Sara."

The greeting jolted her. She glanced up, surprised. She hadn't seen Leslie since the day outside class when she'd been crying. "Oh, hi."

Leslie eyed the books on the table. "A lot of work already, huh?"

Reading about the blazing Greek sun and hillsides of bleached stone houses was fresh in Sara's mind. She'd walked with the ancients, learning details of Sappho's poetry and Homer's legends. Her legs were actually a little numb from sitting so long.

Sara smoothed her hair back from her face, self-conscious about how she looked. "Uh, yeah. You too?"

Leslie sat down in a chair, her slim frame covered in a deep purple long-sleeved dress, black tights and thigh-high boots. "Not so much. Hey, have you heard the latest?" Leslie asked. "Red Hill Dorm got trashed last night. Toilet-papered rooms and girls waking up covered in shaving cream."

"You're kidding," Sara said. "I thought that only happened in high school. Or summer camp."

"It happens every year at least once or twice and is just all in fun. Everyone's speculating on what the retaliation will be."

"You live in a dorm?" Sara asked. When Leslie nodded she continued, "Which one? You didn't wake up covered in shaving cream, did you?"

Leslie grinned. "Nah, I'm in Blue Arrow, the ones who did it." She dug some bills out of her backpack. "You want coffee? I'm going to get some."

"Sure. A Chai tea latte. Thanks." Sara reached for her purse but Leslie had already gone up to the counter.

Tired as she was, the chains made her jump when they slipped slowly up her calves and around her knees. She'd sort of gotten used to their coming and going the last few weeks, but today she wasn't prepared. She sat back and closed her eyes to breathe deeply, wishing they would go just as quickly as they'd come.

When Leslie returned, she looked Sara over carefully. "You okay?"

Sara flushed at the scrutiny. "A little tired, that's all."

"So, have you heard of Golden Key?" Leslie handed Sara her cup and sat down again.

The name sounded familiar but Sara wasn't sure. "Is it a college club?"

"No, an honor society. You didn't get a letter of invitation?"

That's what it was. A piece of mail she'd thrown away without even opening it.

Leslie continued, "Your name was on the list and I wondered why I hadn't seen you at any events."

Sara took a sip of her tea and let the warmth slide through her. "What kind of events?"

"You know, guest speakers followed by cocktails and hors d'oeuvres, that sort of thing. The speakers are pretty good and it feels so grown up to stand around drinking with the professors."

It was something Sara never would've considered going to in the past. But now?

They chatted some more until Leslie finished her coffee and rose to go. "How about going to a movie sometime?"

"Ah..." Sara couldn't think she was so startled by the question. It sounded a lot like being asked out on a date.

"You do like movies, don't you? There's that new comedy playing at the campus theater tomorrow night."

Maybe Sara was imagining it but she'd swear Leslie's eyes said one thing while her words conveyed something different. It'd happened before, once in high school and just recently with Caryn by the bathrooms at the club. Although Caryn had been clear about what she wanted, Sara felt so confused. The same nervous butterfly feeling attacked her full force now. She knew her face was blank while she struggled to reply. She wanted to say yes but hated the ambiguities swirling between them.

"Oh. I get it. You're one of those," Leslie said.

Sara frowned. "One of what?"

Leslie swung her bag over her shoulder and turned as if to walk away. Sara was unsure what to do or say.

Leslie looked hurt and more than a little disappointed when she moved around the table to stand right next to Sara. "It means you haven't figured it out yet, or if you have, you're still hiding it."

As Sara watched Leslie leave, the talk and laughter and people at the other tables vanished. From one instant to the next, the booth beneath her disappeared, leaving her dangling in the chains wrapped around her arms and legs. The breath was sucked right out of her.

The smallest motion on her part tilted her precariously. She crested the first wave of panic spilling through her. Used to it coming out of nowhere, she put all her survival mechanisms in place: the deep breathing, repeating a calming refrain in her head, picturing her quartz in her hand.

Leslie could've meant only one thing. Pursuing that meant discovering exactly what Sara feared, what confused her and had for a long while now.

She forced her hands to unclench and tried to loosen her shoulders. But that only made her tip backward. Before she knew it she was upside down, her golden hair hanging free, in the void of nothingness that she'd come to know well. Except for the drips of purple, in rivulets like rain, coming down from the endless above.

Sara willed the coffee shop back with closed eyes and a begging chant on her lips. The aroma of espresso and the buzz of conversation returned to her senses. Looking around, everything appeared as before. No stares or whispered remarks. Gathering her books, Sara stood on trembling legs and forced herself to walk out. Tears threatened but she thrust them back. She couldn't afford them now.

She was late but made it to class. Sitting in the back, she distracted herself with the lecture and discussion, hearing but not knowing if she'd remember any of it later. She didn't even try to take notes because her hands were still shaking.

On her way out of class, she turned in the first assignment for her creative writing class. It'd been easy to write once she started, but would be difficult to let go. The story was about her sister and memories Sara had long buried. Most were sensory, like the smell of bacon and Saturday morning breakfast in pajamas. The sound of wind chimes on their back patio and watching the stars come out at night. The taste of green apple gum and Violet teaching her how to blow bubbles. She'd looked up to her sister, idolized her.

Looking at her watch she knew she had to hurry. She still had to pack. Her mother had invited her along on a last-minute business trip to Chicago. Since Sara had successfully traveled without them, her mother seemed to think she was ready for more, and as usual, Sara didn't know how to say no to her, much less anything else.

An hour later, as dusk began to fall, Sara settled next to her mother for the long ride to the airport. Her mother, in a magenta suit, blonde hair so like Sara's expertly pulled back, looked like she'd just walked out of a salon instead of a long day of meetings.

"I knew that outfit would look good on you," her mother said, eyeing Sara's dark blue pants and beige wool sweater with approval.

"It'll be comfortable for the long flight and I won't look wrinkled when I step off the plane."

"Yes, we'll be getting in late, but it can't be helped. At least you can sleep in tomorrow. There'll be a car to take you around the city. I hear the exhibit at the Art Institute is fabulous. Then we'll meet for dinner and some night sightseeing."

As usual, her mother had it all planned. After the day Sara had, a strange city sounded overwhelming, but she reminded herself it was also exciting. If she could just put the coffee shop incident out of her mind, she'd be okay.

She texted Jessie and Isabel about her plans. She really wished they were going with her. Not only because it would be more fun but also because she really didn't know how to be alone for so long with her mother. She got her quartz out of her bag and rubbed its smooth surface before digging out the book she'd brought along.

She read on the flight and dozed a little before her mother nudged her as they were touching down. When they finally reached the Drake Hotel, one of Chicago's oldest and finest, sleep claimed her swiftly. It was so deep Sara didn't remember dreaming, nor did she hear her mother get ready and leave in the morning. A note on the bed contained information on the car.

Sara thought about the night before. She hadn't braved a serious conversation, despite the many opportunities during the car ride and the flight. She was such a coward when it came to dealing with her mother. She'd made that list of questions for her, but wondered now if she'd ever ask a single one on it.

With a sigh, she got ready for the day. Coffee, a muffin, a little shopping and the museum, in that order. The weather was cool and the Chicago sky overcast. But she had her own driver who knew all the best places and that did a lot to alleviate her qualms.

She took a picture of the coffee shop, the mannequins in the Bloomingdale window and had to sneak one of an ancient Greek mosaic at the institute to send to Jessie and Isabel. Back at the hotel later that afternoon, Sara wrote in her journal for the first time in days. Mostly she put down impressions of the city and the art she'd seen. Looking back at her previous entries, she realized she'd never written about Jessie and Isabel getting necklaces from the Graces. Jessie's golden pendant and Isabel's silver one fit them perfectly. Sara wanted to see Bloom again and she wanted a necklace of her own more than she could say, but she didn't get her hopes up. Whenever she did, she was usually disappointed.

After dinner at a crowded Italian restaurant, they went on a tour of the city as promised. Her mother pointed out Segway and Millennium Park, and asked the driver to stop so they could get out at Buckingham Fountain and walk around.

"How many times have you come here on business?" Sara asked as they watched the lights dance in the fountain's spray.

"A few. The city has a nice feel, doesn't it?" Her mother kept a slow pace as they mingled among other tourists. "Your father mentioned you had a panic attack before your trip to California."

Taken aback, Sara stopped. Her mother never broached difficult topics. "Just a small one." Which wasn't quite true.

"You haven't had any since, have you?"

"No. Uh...did he tell you why I had that one?"

"You were going to be away from home for the first time," her mother replied, "so of course you were nervous. But you've done so well this time I really don't understand what your father was worried about."

So her father hadn't mentioned he'd revealed the secret they'd been hiding all these years. He was leaving that part up to her. "Actually, it wasn't that. He told me about Violet."

Sara held her breath, waiting.

"You need to make sure you take your Paxil regularly and stick to your routine to minimize your stress level."

Had her mother not heard?

"I know you've been going to Dr. Bernstein because I get the bill every month," her mother continued. She patted Sara's arm and continued walking, heading back to the waiting car. "I think you're doing fine, considering."

It wasn't the first time her mother had ignored an issue she didn't want to discuss. But why even bring it up? Sara tried to shake it off, to let it go, but their close proximity made it difficult.

They returned to their room. Sara's father called just as Sara was turning out the light to try and sleep. Her mother spoke softly for a few minutes then hung up.

"Dad said to tell you he loves you."

"Thanks."

Her mother shifted on the bed, settling into the pillows. Sara did the same, staring at the sliver of streetlight that fell on the wall in the dark.

After a while, her mother's breathing evened out. The noises in the hallway faded away. Clutching her quartz stone, she closed her eyes, finally able to unwind. When she heard a soft shushing sound next to the bed, her eyes flew open wide, her heart leaping.

Bloom, in a cloak of blood-red roses, took Sara's clenched hand and pulled her out from the covers. Sara had never seen such kind eyes. Startling blue, shaped curiously like her own. Bloom's touch was like medicine on an open wound, burning at first then soothing, almost numbing, until Sara relaxed enough to get her feet moving.

Bloom led her out the balcony doors into the night. The lights of the city were like jewels around them. Wind whipped their hair and Sara, overcome with emotions, couldn't hold in any longer so she laughed out loud while tears rolled down her cheeks. After some time, she wiped her eyes and stood with arms outstretched, breathing deeply. A wash of peace fell over her.

She woke up sometime later and looked at the clock. Two in the morning.

She caught a whiff of roses.

Turning over, the neckline of her nightgown caught on something. She slid out of bed to look in the mirror. A long, crimson, velvet ribbon hung around her neck. It held a ruby red stone in the shape of a rose in bloom.

Sara sensed Bloom's presence when she touched it. She stared at her reflection, her pale features and golden locks like a halo against the dark backdrop of the room. The pendant felt like a safety net, easing her fears of the last days in a way she couldn't describe, a way her medicine never did.

She slipped back into bed and fell immediately to sleep.

The next morning Sara and her mother had coffee and fruit in the Drake dining room before checking out. They made one stop so her mother could sign some papers. Then it was back to the airport.

On the flight home, her mother's constant, low-voiced business calls began to fray her nerves. Sara's fingers returned again and again to touch the stone and ribbon around her neck. It helped. She retreated into herself, desperate to talk to Jessie and Isabel. There was too much to say in a text. Once they landed, picked up their luggage and got into the car, Sara tried to ignore the rush of emotions building inside her but couldn't. Her instincts told her to run and hide and forget it all. But if she didn't take this opportunity to get some answers, she would regret it. She would hate herself. She really would be a coward.

She couldn't look at her mother sitting there so calmly leafing through her magazine, so she gazed out at the passing scenery. "I know Violet is my half-sister. Dad told me you got pregnant after a brief affair. Then you married Dad right before she was born."

Her mother's hand stilled and when she finally answered her voice was crisp and cool. "That's all in the past, and while your curiosity is normal, it isn't really your concern."

"I think that's why you and Violet fought the night she left. Maybe you didn't tell her that and she found out and was angry too." Sara heard her voice rising and tried to control the tone even though she couldn't stop the words now that they were finally coming out. "And it is my concern because she's my sister and I've wanted a relationship with her all these years."

Sara risked a glance but her mother's gaze was averted. In profile she looked pale and tired, something Sara had never noticed in her mother before. She wasn't about to stop now, though.

"What did you fight about? What was so unforgiveable that has kept her from us all these years?"

"Enough, Sara." Glittering hard eyes met hers. "I had my reasons and I don't want to discuss them with you."

"Dad's in contact with her."

Her mother looked startled but she must've known. Maybe she was just surprised that Sara knew.

"Call her if you want. But don't be shocked at what you find. Don't say I didn't warn you." Anger flowed across the space between them.

What in the world did that mean?

Her mother went back to the magazine, her movements jerky, unlike the smooth calm she usually displayed. Sara sank back into the leather seat with a sigh and closed her eyes, knowing she couldn't push her mother any further. She hadn't gotten any answers, but that just made her even more determined to track down her sister.

Sara escaped to her room as soon as she got home. Letting her suitcase drop on the floor, she dug through her purse and pulled out her cell. A text from Jessie read, "Hey, u home yet? Call me."

The minute Sara heard Jessie's voice, her eyes welled and her throat closed up.

From the other end of the line she heard: "I'm coming over. Meet me outside."

Twenty minutes later Sara watched Jessie's car park a couple of houses down. She opened her door, listened, then walked quietly down the hall and out the patio door. Shutting the side gate slowly and quietly because it often squeaked, Sara made her way to the waiting car. Isabel was in the back seat.

Another half a pill after Jessie's call was helping her feel a little more in control. And she'd wanted to reduce her dose. At this point she couldn't see how that was possible. "Thanks for rescuing me."

Once parked near one of their favorite spots, they huddled for warmth wrapped in blankets. Outside the periphery of light cast by Jessie's mini Coleman lamp, the trees and hills blended with the black night.

Isabel and Jessie told stories of sneaking out of the house in high school that made Sara smile. "That's my problem. I never did anything most teenagers do, like sneaking out of the house or breaking curfew or making out in the back of a car."

"Everyone has different experiences, Sara," Isabel assured her.

"Yeah, so tell us more about going out with an ex-priest," Jessie teased.

Isabel sighed. "Give it up, Jess. There are no juicy details to share. It's just nice to talk and laugh with him and not worry about what I do or say."

"Haven't you kissed yet?"

Isabel laughed, pushing Jessie lightly on the shoulder. "Yes, you moron. But there's more than that."

"Sounds serious." Jessie raised her brows in mock surprise.

Isabel rolled her eyes. "No, don't even go there."

Sara smiled, relieved to be here, away from all that felt rigid and restrictive. She looked up at the stars. "I always get a sense of déjà vu when I'm out here with you two."

"We come here a lot. It's becoming almost a ritual," Jessie said.

"It's beautiful and...comforting here." Sara pressed her temples to ease some of the tension from the day.

"Mario asked about you two today. He wanted to know which piece you submitted in the competition, Isabel."

"You told him about that?"

"Of course. He had his own ideas, but since I don't know because you haven't told us," Jessie emphasized, "I couldn't tell him."

"Fine. I entered The Graces."

"You did?" Sara asked.

"Don't look so surprised. I thought you liked it."

"I do," Sara said. "We do, don't we, Jessie?"

"I think that was the perfect choice. Hey, I forgot to tell you," Jessie said to Sara, "I saw you in the commons the other day talking with some redhead. Who was it? You looked like you enjoyed talking with her."

It was the last thing Sara wanted to talk about. They both looked at her expectantly.   "That was Leslie."

"Leslie who always wears black or some variation of it, long red hair with an eyebrow piercing?" Isabel asked.

Jessie nodded. "Sounds like her."

"She's cool. Very up front and honest," Isabel said.

"I don't know her well. She seems nice enough." Sara told them the story of the dorm fight, Leslie's description of the honor society, and finally the movie invitation.

Jessie and Isabel eyed each other across the blanket but didn't say anything.

Just as she suspected. She didn't really want to hear their answer. She shouldn't have brought it up because now she couldn't escape.

"Sounds like a casual invitation to do something fun to me," Isabel said.

"Girl, she was asking you out," Jessie said.

Sara could feel the panic pushing from inside, wanting out, wanting to take over.

"Did you say yes? What'd you say?" Jessie asked.

"Nothing. I kinda froze. It felt like hundreds of butterflies were in my stomach. And then she said I was hiding something and walked away."

"Butterflies mean it's something good. I get them when I see Mario."

"I don't know. The last time it happened to me, I ran to the bathroom and hid until they went away." Sara fought a little wave of nausea now.

"When was that?" Isabel asked.

Bright spots of memory flooded her. She couldn't seem to keep the words in, as if a dam had burst somewhere inside her. "There was a party senior year. Quinn invited me. It was all right at first, then I started feeling, well, like you said, and I went to an empty bedroom hoping it would go away." Sara's voice trembled. "Some of the other girls made some rude comments and Quinn overheard, so he found me and took me home."

Isabel moved the lantern farther away so their faces were in shadows. "It wasn't a panic attack. You know the difference. Who'd you meet at the party, Sara?"

Jessie grabbed Sara's hand. "Come on, Sara. Leslie was right. You are hiding something. You know it; we know it. Just say it out loud."

Sara's eyes widened. They had thought it, too? Her anguish was so deep and searing she felt raw.

"A lot of things scare me, Sara." Isabel admitted. "Like entering the contest. Dating Michael."

"Sometimes I think I'm scared to be truly happy. I'm afraid to say yes to Mario," Jessie added, her eyes luminous in the dark night.

"Say yes to Mario about what?" Isabel asked.

Reaching for the rose stone beneath her jacket, Sara pulled it out and instantly felt lighter. Less like she was going to suffocate.

"Hey, you got one," Jessie said softly.

Sara pulled off the necklace and dangled it so they could see it, touch it. She told them of Bloom's nighttime visit. For a flashing moment, Sara felt suspended in the chains with nothing below her to catch her, save her. Then she was able to get her breath back and with it came clarity. The shame and confusion she'd hidden and ignored over the years couldn't be denied any longer.

She slid the velvet ribbon back over her head and faced the hills. She looked at the red rocks turned black in the night and the outline of evergreens she'd loved all her life.

She decided to let go and hoped she wouldn't crash.

"Her name was Camille and she was a new student. She transferred senior year, made friends easily and got good grades. I'd met her once before on the tennis courts. You know, the scene we saw with the Graces that day we touched the statue. I felt it then, but at the party it hit me hard. I didn't know what to do. I didn't know what it meant."

Jessie squeezed Sara's hand again.

She took a couple of deep breaths, testing, weighing. The world was right side up and she hadn't fallen. At least not yet. "It's just one more way that I'm not…."

"It's called attraction and it's normal. It doesn't matter who it is, really." Jessie said. "Besides, who defines what is right for you? Only you."

Isabel shifted closer, leaned in. "That's right. You can't let other people define your life for you."

Crickets and rustling leaves sounded unusually loud in the silence that followed. "What am I going to do?" she whispered, afraid the universe would hear.

There was a collective hesitation as they all thought about it.

"Wait. Get comfortable with it yourself, then figure out the rest." Jessie paused, then added: "Sara, your best friend is gay. Probably why you've always felt so safe with him. I'm sure he's known all along. Ask him."

Of course. Quinn had known the truth about her even when she couldn't admit it to herself.

"And Caryn liked you, too," Jessie said. "Mario told me she kissed you."

It was too much. The tears flowed freely now and she couldn't stop them. Sara leaned into Jessie, hiding her face in Jessie's shoulder, the sobs shaking her whole body.

"Whoa, it's gonna be okay, really." Isabel rubbed her hand along Sara's back.

When she finally quieted, she breathed easy. The chains were gone.

"I know. Let's see if the Graces will come to us again. All together," Jessie suggested.

Sara was glad for the space to wipe her eyes and inhale the sweet night air.

Isabel looked skeptical, but pulled out her pendant. "Come on, Jess, we've never been able to make anything appear. You know that. It just happens."

"You in, Sara?" Jessie asked.

Sara nodded and held her rose.

Looking at each other, they waited.

And waited.

Twenty-One

Jessie

Spring, Present Day

Mario's strong hands held her hips. She was at the edge, breathless, on the precipice, and looked through the veil of her curls because she liked to hold his gaze in the final moments. So he could see what she couldn't say aloud. But the eyes that gazed back at her were Phil's. A cry of shock echoed in her head as she was pulled away, backward into blackness.

"Jess, wake up. Wake up. You're okay."

The dark tunnel she'd fallen into disappeared with the shake on her shoulder and Sara's words. She brushed her hair out of her face and sat up, unnerved by the dream that seemed so real, feeling cheated out of the orgasm she'd almost had.

Isabel rubbed her eyes and gave Jessie a look that said she didn't appreciate being woken up.

"You were shouting 'No!' pretty loud," Sara explained. "What were you dreaming? Do you remember?"

Oh, yeah.

"As long as it wasn't the maze, can we go back to sleep?" Isabel asked.

"It wasn't."

Isabel turned over in the big bed, pulling some of the covers with her. Sara lay back down too and closed her eyes.

Jessie looked at the clock. Five in the morning. She didn't think she'd be able to sleep again. They'd gotten back from Chautauqua around midnight after an unsuccessful attempt to summon the Graces.

Jessie crawled over Isabel and headed to the bathroom to use the toilet and brush her teeth. Trying to be as quiet as possible, she put on some yoga sweats and a long-sleeved tee. The kitchen looked like a tornado had blown through. She ignored the mess and made coffee in a pot on the stove with cinnamon sticks for flavor. It wasn't long before the aroma she'd grown up with filled the kitchen.

A faint chime told her a text was waiting. "U up?" Mario asked.

What was he doing awake so early? She pressed the call back button. "What's going on?" she asked, her voice low so she wouldn't wake anyone.

"Couldn't sleep. All these ideas for a new project kept running through my mind. You know how I get."

"What kind of project?"

"The kind that features you."

"I told you I'm just coming out to see how it feels."

"It's going to be good, Jess. Phil's already booked us for a couple of gigs."

Damn. That was fast. She'd just told him her decision a couple of days ago. "Really? Where?"

"I'll send you the links to both places. One of them will be just you and me. Piano and voice at some ritzy place I've never played before. The other is with the band at a bar out in Oakland."

Jessie smiled at the excitement in his voice. It pulsed through the phone. She latched onto it like someone lost in the desert might seize water. It was going to be good. Joining him in San Francisco was the right thing to do.

"Have you told your mother yet? Isabel and Sara?" he asked.

"I don't know how to tell my mom, Mario. You know how she is."

"Since when have you backed down from a challenge?" he asked.

Jessie heard her phone chime with another incoming text. She glanced at it. Her mother. "She's texting me about breakfast. Sara and Isabel are invited too."

"Perfect time to tell everyone if you ask me."

"I'll tell Isabel and Sara. I don't know about Mom. Maybe I'll just wait and call when I get there."

"That would be cowardly and you know it," Mario said.

She sighed. "But so tempting." Jessie promised to text Mario later and hung up. She couldn't explain the dread that rose up in her just thinking about it. Her mother had tried to be both mother and father, yet working so hard to support them had made her more of an absent parent than not. Seeing her come home every night late, exhausted and weary, had created a fierce love between them even as an equally fierce resentment had settled in Jessie's heart. At her mother or her father, she couldn't say.

Turning toward her bedroom she almost ran into Sara standing in the doorway.

"Tell us what?" Sara asked, belting one of Jessie's terry cloth robes.

Jessie almost dropped her cup, sloshing coffee all over her hand. "God, you scared me."

"Sorry." Sara reached for the towel hanging on the refrigerator door. "You didn't burn yourself, did you?"

"No, I'm okay. What are you doing up? It's still early." Jessie dried her hand then refilled her cup and poured one for Sara.

Sara leaned back against the counter next to her and sipped. "Don't think you can get away with not answering."

"I was going to tell you last night but it didn't seem the time."

Sara rubbed her eyes. "Yeah. Sorry."

"No apologizing. It's a relief it's out in the open. You did the right thing, you know."

"Maybe you should take your own advice. You need to tell your mom something?" Sara poured herself more and added a little sugar.

"Yeah. I guess it's why I really understood you last night. My mom's going to be mad. But mostly hurt. I don't want to see her that way again. Because of me."

"What are you talking about?" asked a sleepy voice from the doorway. Isabel yawned loudly then pulled her hair back into its customary ponytail, securing it with a scrunchie. She poured herself some coffee and stood facing them in her bare feet, a pair of Jessie's running shorts and a camisole hugging her small frame.

"Jessie's got some news to share," Sara said.

"Let me get a little caffeine in my system first." Isabel blew on her coffee and took a first tentative sip.

Jessie wondered about the best way to tell them. She reached for a couple of CDs sitting on the counter and gave each of them one.

"What's this?" Sara frowned at the blank cover.

"A copy of a recording. Remember our last night in San Francisco?"

They both nodded.

"I told you Phil and Mario took me on a tour of the studio." Jessie picked up a third CD from the counter and headed to the stereo in the living room. She put it in the player and adjusted a few knobs to get the best sound while Sara and Isabel plopped on the sofa.

She watched both of them try to focus as Mario's piano intro started. Their eyes widened when a clear soprano voice filled the room instead of Mario's tenor. They listened for a minute.

"Who is that?" Isabel asked suspiciously.

"Oh my God." Sara turned in disbelief. "It's you."

"It can't be," Isabel said with a shake of her head.

Jessie pushed the power button and the room became quiet. "Yeah, it's me."

"Why the hell didn't you tell us?" Isabel sounded shocked and angry.

Jessie shrugged. "It never came up." She could tell they didn't believe her from the looks on their faces, but it hadn't occurred to her. She told no one about that part of her life. She'd kept if from everyone.

"So, what now? Phil and Mario make this CD and . . .?"

"You know I've had a hard time concentrating on my studies," Jessie said. "I've decided to take a break and see if I should do this instead." She decided to leave out the part about how Mario asked her to join him.

"Why not major in music?" Sara asked.

Yes, there was that route. Jessie had a feeling her mother would say the same thing. It wasn't the pursuit of music that her mother wouldn't understand but how Jessie got there.

"And what kind of a break are we talking here?" Sara asked. "You're not going to finish out the year?"

Jessie smiled, thinking of Mario's obvious high when she'd spoken to him earlier. "I just need to see if it's what I really want. Mario did it and I think I can too. I'll come back if it doesn't work out."

"I've got to shower and get to work," Isabel said abruptly, heading into the bedroom.

Sara shrugged as if to say, 'Don't worry about her,' then grabbed her bag from the floor. "She's going to need a ride. We can talk more later."

That hadn't gone as smoothly as Jessie hoped. No words of encouragement or support. They probably just needed time to adjust to the idea. But if Isabel and Sara got all weird about it, there was no way in hell she was telling her mother. That decided, she could go have breakfast at home stress free.

When she got there around nine, stacks of waffles lined a platter on the kitchen table next to a bowl piled high with bacon. Her mother and Nana were visibly disappointed that her girlfriends hadn't come along. But it only took one phone call and a five-minute wait for her aunt and cousins to come over and help eat all the food.

"You saved me from having to cook." Her aunt kissed Nana, then her mother in greeting. "Why have you been a stranger?" she asked, enveloping Jessie in a strong embrace.

"You know how it is, Tia. Just busy, that's all."

"I never see her either," her mother added. "It's so quiet around here."

Her cousins looked like they'd just woken up. Amanda, a senior in high school and Victor, a junior, quickly grabbed plates. There was lots of talk and laughter while butter and syrup were passed around and everyone began to eat.

"So, what's going on with you guys?" Jessie asked Amanda.

Her cousin gave her a glare. Her aunt sighed loudly. Something was going on.

"What? You must be the only one not following this whole thing on Facebook," Victor joked. "Amanda's decided to go to beauty school instead of college."

Uh oh. Jessie could imagine the arguments over that decision. Well, she might as well try and smooth the way for Amanda.

"Which one? You know my roommate is finishing at Martinelli's."

Amanda perked up. "That's the one I'm hoping to get into."

"She loves it. It's been hard work and long hours but she's already got a spot at a salon cutting hair in Longmont."

"Cool. I'm excited."

Jessie gave Amanda points for ignoring all the glares coming from the mothers at the table.

"There's already too many hair stylists if you ask me," Victor said.

"Nobody's asking you," Amanda said.

Victor shrugged. "If that what's you really want to do…" He didn't seem aware that he'd just agreed with his sister and Jessie but she was glad he'd said it instead of her.

"It is."

Jessie asked her aunt about one of the nieces in Mexico and talk turned to the latest family gossip. It was nearly eleven before they left.

"I'm glad you came," Nana said as she washed the frying pan.

Jessie got her purse and stopped to give her a kiss on the cheek. "Me, too."

"Why did you have to encourage Amanda like that?" her mother demanded as she wiped down the kitchen counters.

"She's already made up her mind."

"You could talk her out of it. She'd listen to you."

"Why would I do that?"

"Because it's a mistake. She's an intelligent girl. Like you. College would take her further than beauty school."

Jessie reigned in her impatience with the conversation. It was exactly this attitude that she'd come up against if she told her mother her decision.

"College is not for everyone and Amanda seems happy enough."

"She won't be in a couple years," her mother countered, her voice rising, getting hard. "She'll be making little money for long hours of work and she'll regret her decision then."

She hated how her mother thought she knew the future and what people would feel. Her mother had used that very argument to convince Jessie to go to Stone College. She'd said Jessie would never get another chance and it would be a mistake to let it pass by. Something pent up inside her burst free.

"People change their minds. If Amanda tries out beauty school and she's not happy and decides to go to college in a few years, she can." Jessie was yelling but couldn't seem to stop. "College isn't always the right choice, you know. Sometimes it's boring and unfulfilling. I know I'm hating it."

"What?" her grandmother gasped.

"Jessie, don't say that. You are not," her mother said in shock.

"Yeah, whatever. You're right. I don't know my own feelings. But you do." Jessie slammed the back door and went out through the garage.

"Let her go, Adriana. Call her later," Jessie heard her grandmother say. "What got into the two of you?"

God, what a mess. Her temper rarely showed, but when it did it always caused trouble. She got in her Buick, put on her favorite Linkin Park CD, rolled the windows down and cruised up the twisty back roads of Boulder Canyon for a nice long drive. She revved the engine and sailed through the curves like she had in high school when she first inherited the old car.

The wind cleared her head. She stopped at an overlook and admired the view from the hood of her car. Drowsing in the early afternoon sun, watching the puffs of clouds dotting the sky, Jessie pressed her sun pendant against the skin on her chest as if to imprint it there.

The smooth marble was cool beneath her bare feet. Pure white emptiness held only one figure, naked, hand outstretched. No longer clothed in the leggings and flowing top she'd put on that morning but now naked too, Jessie followed Brilliance across an expanse of red that turned subtly to orange. The silence was so deep, so complete Jessie could hear her heart and lungs working together in rhythm. Sunset oranges turned to summer yellows. Her clenched stomach loosened at the beauty of it. They stopped when the yellow became so bright it hurt her eyes to look.

Substance became invisible as Jessie watched, the shape of Brilliance's body wavering into voices and images. The yard where she'd played tag with her cousins every afternoon and evening growing up. The voice she loved.

"Daddy, Daddy, look at this!"

"What's my girl got for me today?"

"I found a kitten behind the fence."

"He's cute all right."

"Can we keep him?"

"Who will take care of him while you're at school?"

The images flickered, changing. A familiar bedroom with a flower print wall.

"Time for bed, my *chica bonita*."

"Daddy, only Mama speaks Spanish to me."

"Why can't I call you my beautiful girl?"

"You just did, silly!"

"I'll tickle you if you call me silly."

"Silly!"

Jessie reached out to touch her father. There was no one there except Brilliance, her fingers smooth and warm on Jessie's cheek.

Jessie watched the sun hover on the top of the foothills, owning the memories of her father, glad to have some at last. She had plenty of stories but none that were hers alone. Brilliance had given her that. She felt lighter than she had all day and so ignored the chimes of incoming text messages. She got in her car, turned around, headed back, finally stopping at a small roadside market for a drink.

As she sipped a Naked Juice, she read a text from her mother that said, "Sorry, xoxo." Another from Nana said, "Don't be too hard on her."

Sara's said, "Chick flick. My house @ 7." The final one was from Mario. "Going for a long ride. I'll call later."

Jessie checked the time. Almost 6. She didn't bother replying to any, just drove in the direction of Sara's house. Isabel was walking up the drive when she pulled next to the curb. They faced each other on the front step.

"You're still mad," Jessie said.

"Maybe I don't have a right to be, but I am."

"That I didn't tell you about the singing or that I'm leaving for a while?"

"Both. But it's selfish of me to wish you'd stay," Isabel conceded.

They turned to find Sara waiting with the door open.

"Then I guess I'm feeling selfish, too." Sara admitted.

"I'm sorry." Before the three of them had met, Isabel and Sara had been going their own way doing their own thing without many friends. Sara had Quinn and Isabel was close to her sister but the three of them had bonded so quickly because they really had no one else. It was going to be hard on both Isabel and Sara, especially if the cave and chain experiences continued.

They followed Sara up to her room where the smell of popcorn filled the air and the menu on the TV screen showed "The Princess Bride."

"One of my favorites," Sara said. "It's like comfort food." She already had on her pajamas with matching pink ballerina-like slippers.

Jessie laughed. "Perfect choice then. We could all use a little of that." She tossed her things into the corner and began to change. It felt so good to get out of her clothes and into her favorite tee.

"Yeah, especially after my day. The tips weren't the greatest and my feet are killing me." Isabel dropped her bag, kicked off her shoes and plopped on the bed.

"What do we do if the Graces come to us and you're not here, Jess? Or what if they don't because we aren't all together?" Sara was busy plumping a bunch of pillows against the headboard and pulling down the duvet, but Jessie still heard the distress in her voice.

"They certainly didn't show up last night, did they," Isabel said dryly, grabbing the bowl of popcorn on the bedside table.

Her visit from Brilliance and her father's voice were still with her but she didn't mention it. More important was getting them to understand her decision to leave.

"I don't have any answers, I just know that I'll go crazy if I stay." Jessie pulled Isabel over to sit on the bed next to her. "Singing with Mario in the studio opened up something inside me. And now it's just sitting there waiting for me to use it."

"I get that. It's like if I hadn't ever picked up a pencil. But it doesn't make it easier on our end."

"I know. You see, Nana has this picture of me when I'm three, all dressed up in black tights and my best Sunday dress. There's a boa around my neck that my mother got at a thrift store. Nana used to tell how my father and I would sing together or I would put on shows for him." Jessie hadn't told another soul what she was finally voicing. "And then he died."

"You never sang after that?" Isabel asked in surprise.

"I was never the little girl in the boa again, no matter how much my mom or Nana tried to coax me into it. I just couldn't do it. It was too hard not to think of him when I sang. The day at Hearst Castle you saw how I was so upset I threw the boa and shoes away. I put it all aside for a long time. Can you imagine how mental they must have thought me when I started dating a musician?"

"You are mental, Jess. We just didn't realize it."

Jessie gave Isabel a push on the arm, which sent the bowl of popcorn tumbling.

"Hey, watch it," Isabel grumbled, catching it deftly with her other hand. But a smile was beginning to show and Jessie knew then it was going to be all right.

"How did Mario find out you could sing?" Sara asked.

Jessie grabbed a few pieces from the bowl before Isabel could pull it out of reach. "By accident." She told them the story. When they'd finished the popcorn, Sara offered to get more drinks.

Jessie stretched out her legs on the bed while she waited for Sara to return. "So… you're scared about dating the ex-priest." Isabel was finally looking relaxed so maybe it wasn't the best time to bring it up but Jessie was curious.

Isabel closed her eyes and sighed. "You were supposed to forget that. I just said it to make Sara feel better."

"I'm sure it helped. But it's also true."

"Maybe."

"So what's going on?" Jessie pried gently.

A small smile played across Isabel's face. "I enjoy being with him. It feels better than I'd ever thought it would."

Jessie was glad to hear Isabel admit it. "Hmmm. And the contest?"

"I won't hear for a week or so."

"You told us that. I meant how do you feel about it?" Getting Isabel to open up was hard work.

"How do you think?" Isabel asked, a little frustration creeping into her voice. "I'm trying to focus on other stuff 'cause if not, I'll go crazy wondering if I submitted the right piece or what more I could've done. And part of me is disgusted with myself for caring so much about a damn contest."

Sara returned, passing them each a bottle of water.

"Michael's probably a good distraction," Jessie teased.

"It's kind of weird though, Michael knowing Dowling, don't you think?" Isabel asked.

"Boulder is a small town," Sara said.

"If his connection gets you in, I say use it for all it's worth," Jessie said.

"I want in on my own merit."

Sara went to her desk, sorting through the neatly organized piles before pulling out three folders. "My father says success depends a lot on who you know, not just your talent."

"Mario will tell you the same thing. Is that more research?" Jessie asked reaching for a folder from where Sara had put them in the middle of the bed. But instead, her fingers touched grass and the sweet smell of it turned the bedroom into an open field.

Sara's voice came from a long way off. "More images of the Graces. Paintings, sculptures, you name it. And stories too."

They didn't notice anything wrong. Jessie watched Isabel open one of the folders.

"Hey, you guys..." Jessie began. Vines moved past her and the creaking of branches building the walls of the maze around her, stopped the words in her throat. Then the music started, like that very first day in Humanities class, the others oblivious to what was happening.

"That's by Botticelli, called 'Primavera.' Spring," Sara explained as Isabel looked at the first picture. "It's in the Uffizi in Florence. There they are, to the left of Venus."

200

"I've studied this painting. I forgot about The Graces being in it."

The hedges grew taller. Jessie could barely make out Isabel's next comment.

"They're standing in a circle, holding hands."

"It's the way they're most commonly depicted," Sara said, before turning in her direction. "Hey Jess, are you okay?"

"Jess," Isabel said, her voice sharp. "Snap out of it." She shook Jessie's arm. "What the...?"

Then, Isabel was sitting beside her, Sara quickly following, with a touch on her other shoulder. They looked around in amazement, then a slow dawning trepidation.

"Why is it so dark in here?"

"What is that noise?"

The creaking and snapping of tightly woven branches, so tall now they blocked the sun's light, had Jessie shivering, too. Farther down the path directly in front of them a figure appeared. Jessie's heart began a mad gallop like a horse shooting out of the gate. It wasn't her father this time, but she knew every line of muscle and strand of hair intimately of the man before her. Why in the world was she seeing Mario in the maze?

"It can't really be him, can it?" Sara asked in a whisper.

"No, of course not," Isabel replied.

He didn't move and neither did they. A cold ball of fear settled in Jessie's gut. The last of the aria faded away and for one moment there was complete silence.

A thunderous crash drew their attention to the right. Cave walls were breaking apart where a hedge wall had been moments before.

"Jessie! Quick!" Isabel pulled her and Sara aside and stepped back. They barely escaped being crushed by a huge slab of rock. Sara clung to Jessie's left, her breathing uneven in Jessie's ear.

Jessie looked down at the image at their feet. Half of a house. "Look." She pointed, but Isabel's attention was on the part of the wall still standing. Amid the dust, Jessie could see the other half etched in stone, lit from within like they'd seen before, but this time flickering like a faulty wire.

Sara started to cough from the rising gray soot in the air.

Everything vanished. They stood huddled together in a void of nothingness.

"Oh no, not this," Isabel muttered.

Something crept up their legs. Smooth as silk, light in weight, chains bound them quickly together in a shell. An armored cocoon.

Sara's body was trembling. "I'm so sorry about this," she whispered.

Isabel's hold on her arm tightened. Jessie's own breathing was shallow even though being bound up like this wasn't as bad as she'd imagined. Like the beginning of an amusement ride they were lifted slowly off the ground.

"You okay, Isa?" Jessie managed to ask.

"I guess. It's just so freaky."

"Don't move," Sara instructed, "or we'll fall upside down."

Then the chains began to unwind, sliding over their bodies, twisting and turning them until Jessie was almost dizzy. They were all panting from the sheer terror of it by the time only a single chain was left holding them in place.

"Please no," Sara groaned.

A faint ringing made its way into Jessie's consciousness. "What's that?"

"Sounds like your cell," Isabel answered.

Jessie blinked and they were back in Sara's room staring at each other. The ringing stopped and a beep said her voicemail picked it up.

"That was crazy. Intense." Jessie pushed her hair out of her face so she could look at her phone. A restricted number.

"That was way more than intense," Sara said, her voice shaky.

"I think it should stop. I've had enough." Isabel said, still breathing hard. She collapsed back onto the bed and turned over face first into the pillows.

Jessie listened to the message. A lot of background noise, a hesitation, then:

"Jessie, it's Phil. Call me immediately. Here's the number 'cause I don't have my cell with me." His voice sounded strained, tired, as he repeated the number.

Phil without his cell? Something crazy must've happened. But he was not the man she wanted to talk to. She looked through her texts but Mario hadn't been in touch since the one hours ago. Probably still out riding.

Jessie's heart rate slowed but her hands still shook a little as she wrote a quick reply to Mario and sent it off before dialing the number from Phil. She couldn't shake the unease that had settled on her from the first moment in the maze.

Phil picked up before it rang once.

"It's Jessie. What's up?"

"Where are you?" he asked.

"At Sara's. Why?"

"Your girlfriends are with you?"

"Yes. What is it? If it's about those gigs you set up, it's fine, really. Mario's out riding, which I'm sure you know, but I talked with him this morning and told him whatever you guys thought best."

"I'm not calling about the gigs."

Her mouth got dry at his serious tone. "You're starting to scare me."

"There's been an accident. Mario's dead."

Twenty-Two

Isabel

"Can you give me a ride? I know it's late but... the buses don't run at this hour and I didn't know who else to ask."

"Of course." Michael's voice went from sleepy to alert in an instant. "Are you okay?"

"Yeah, I'm not hurt or anything."

"Where are you?"

Isabel gave him Sara's address.

"It shouldn't take me long."

"I'll be waiting outside." She got her things from the floor and stood at the foot of the bed watching Jessie sleep.

"I gave her one of my sleeping pills." Sara joined the vigil at her side.

"Good idea. I'm sorry I have to go but I've got the early shift and I didn't bring a clean uniform top with me."

Sara grabbed her hand and gave a squeeze. "It's okay. She should just stay, don't you think? She shouldn't be alone at a time like this."

Isabel didn't want to be alone either. She was exhausted, not only from being on her feet the whole day. The maze, the cave and the chains had been hard enough to deal with but then had come the phone call and the night had gone to hell. She couldn't think straight anymore.

"My dad can give you a ride."

"I just called Michael. He's on his way."

"It's one in the morning."

"I know." She was going to be a mess tomorrow.

"Could you call in sick?" Sara asked.

"Nah. Anyway, I need the tips." Isabel took a good look at Sara. Pale, straight blond hair hanging limp around her face, dark circles under her eyes. "You get some sleep, too."

"I'll try."

Isabel escaped the confines of the room, knowing she'd never feel the same about being there again. She pulled the moon pendant from under her shirt as she left the house, holding it while she waited in the driveway.

When Michael pulled up a few minutes later, she could only stare at him, no words forming in her mind, or on her lips. She forced her legs to walk to the door Michael held open for her. He didn't drive directly to her house but to a small park a couple of blocks away. The playground equipment was a silent giant shadow, the lone streetlamp casting an eerie glow. He followed her when she got out and headed to a giant oak tree.

"There was this really rude father with his three kids who complained about everything and then stiffed me after I'd gone out of my way. Everybody seemed to be tipping low today. How is anyone supposed to make a living that way?" She talked about that part of her day because she could, but she really wanted to tell him about the other part. The maze where they'd seen Mario before they'd known he was dead. Her house broken in half. Held prisoner in a cocoon of chains. He wouldn't believe it. He'd think she was crazy. Maybe she was. Maybe they all were.

He slid his hand into hers. Sara had done the same in solidarity. Michael's offered comfort and a kind of protection from the worst of it.

"Jessie..." she cleared her throat. "Remember I told you about our trip and Jessie's boyfriend, Mario?"

"You said he's a gifted musician and treated you like queens and that Jessie is lucky to have him." Michael remembered all the details.

"He's dead. Killed in a motorcycle accident this afternoon."

Michael didn't offer any words, just pulled her into an embrace that was as gentle as it was crushing. His hand stroking her back caused her body to convulse in deep shudders that she couldn't control. Isabel and Sara had held Jessie as she'd gone through the same thing earlier. No tears, no angry denials like Isabel had expected, just the deep tremors. Probably because they'd seen him in the maze, and Jessie knew Mario really *was* dead.

"It's good you were there for her." Michael's lips were against her hair, soothing her with soft kisses.

"She sat there, her eyes blank, and we knew something was wrong. It was terrible hearing that news and knowing I couldn't really do anything to help. To make it better. I tried, but I didn't know what to do."

Isabel breathed in, caught some faint spicy citrus smell and fresh detergent. "You're used to dealing with death," she murmured, thinking of how people always turned to priests in times of grief.

"But you never get used to it." He tilted her face up so she was forced to look at him. "You did an extraordinary thing tonight just being there with her."

She put her cheek to his, suddenly desperate for skin on skin. "I want to forget everything, even just for a few minutes," she said, pulling herself closer.

"I'm glad you called me."

The first touch of his lips on hers was tender. She felt empty and needed his warmth and the simple pleasure of his mouth on hers.

Then it wasn't gentle anymore. The kisses became desperate and his hands on her body made her feel strong and weak at the same time.

They stopped a while later in some weird kind of silent mutual hesitation. His breathing was hard and she could almost hear her blood rushing through her veins in the stillness of the night. She didn't know what to say but something had held them back from going any further.

"I guess we should talk?"

He nodded, taking a step back and a deep breath. "Yes, we should, but not tonight. It's late."

"You're right. I have to be at work at 6."

"What? Why didn't you say something?" Clearly exasperated, he pulled her by the hand toward the car.

"And miss that back there?" she answered. "I think it was just what I needed."

She must've fallen asleep in the car because she didn't remember the ride. Finally, after sneaking in the house, undressing in the dark and making sure her alarm was set, she got in bed.

She heard someone slipping past her door. If the house wasn't so quiet she might've missed it. Probably Maggie missing curfew again. That girl was going to be in so much trouble if their mother found out. Right before she drifted off she heard her door open and shut. Without looking, she held open the covers for her sister to slip in beside her.

"I couldn't sleep," Maggie whispered.

"I have the early shift."

"Okay. I won't talk."

"Close your eyes. It'll come."

Maggie sighed and Isabel willed herself to let go.

Her early morning shift passed without incident and people seemed to be tipping better than the day before. She was glad for the constant stream of tables because it was a distraction. Sara texted her saying Jessie was still there but that her mom insisted on coming to see her sometime in the afternoon. Isabel had a feeling that wouldn't go over well. At the end of her shift she had the line cook make her a couple of sandwiches to go and caught the bus to Sara's house. She found Sara and Jessie on the back porch.

"Sara made some lunch already," Jessie said with a vague, empty smile, when Isabel offered her one. "But thanks anyway."

"I'll eat it," Quinn said from the doorway. He kissed Jessie's cheek in greeting, grabbed one and sat next to Sara, telling her about the tennis game he'd played that morning.

Sara's dad came out a few minutes later. "Jessie, your mom's pulling into the drive."

"I told her not to come."

Mr. Caldwell's smile said he wasn't going to turn her away or make any excuses.

"Is it okay if she comes out here?" Jessie asked.

"Of course. Stay as long as you need." He looked at Isabel and then Sara pointedly.

"Thanks, Dad." Sara got the hint, stood up and pulled Quinn with her.

"Don't leave, you guys." Jessie pointed to the chair and Sara sat back down.

"I'll go talk to your dad." Quinn went inside but left the screen door open.

"What do you want to do, Jess?" Isabel asked.

"You can stay here," Sara offered.

"Or we can stay with you at your place, but I think you'd be better off with some company right now."

Jessie stared at the mountaintop that rose above the line of the back fence and said nothing.

"You'd better decide quickly," Isabel warned, hearing voices in the kitchen.

Jessie's mom wore a flower print skirt that swirled around her legs as she walked, matching high heels, and a smile that to Isabel's eye looked forced.

"Why are you so dressed up?" Jessie asked.

"Victor's confirmation, followed by brunch at your Tia's house."

"Oh yeah. Sorry, I forgot."

"Call your aunt and tell her." Jessie's mom sat down and scooted her chair close. "You look tired."

"Sara told you?"

"Yes."

"I'll be okay. Sara and Isabel are gonna stay at my place," Jessie said.

"Hmm." Her mom gave her a long searching look, lightly brushing a strand of curls back from Jessie's face. "Everyone missed you today. Asked about you. I thought you'd come even with the news you got yesterday."

Jessie looked blankly at her mother as if her words didn't make sense.

Isabel could tell Jessie's mom was clueless about Jessie's true relationship with Mario. Jessie was certainly good at masking her feelings.

Mrs. McIntyre looked frustrated at Jessie's silence. She looked toward Sara and Isabel as she got up. "Girls, walk me to my car, please."

Jessie rolled her eyes but stayed put. Isabel recognized the mother tone of voice that wouldn't put up with any excuses. Sara rose, said she had to get something from her room, and would meet them out front.

Jessie's mom thanked Mr. Caldwell and nodded to Quinn as they passed through the living room, then they continued the rest of the way in silence, as Isabel had no idea what to say. Sara met them on the drive, something in her hand.

Jessie's mom sighed audibly. "So, maybe you two can let me in on," she gestured toward the house, "all that. I mean I know she's upset about Mario's death. It's tragic. But…"

"Here," Sara said shyly, handing over what Isabel now recognized was Jessie's music CD. "When you listen to this I think you'll understand."

"What is it?" Mrs. McIntyre accepted it with a frown.

"Jessie singing," Sara continued bravely. Isabel understood how difficult confrontation was for Sara, but she was doing great. It was brilliant really. No one could listen to Jessie singing with Mario and miss what was between them.

Mrs. McIntyre shook her head. "Jessie doesn't sing."

"When we were in San Francisco, Mario's manager Phil gave her a tour of the production studio," said Isabel.

"And?"

"They taped her singing."

"Why?" Mrs. McIntyre looked skeptical.

"Because they know she's got talent. It took doing that," Isabel pointed to the CD, "and hearing it, for her to figure out she's not in the right place and should be pursuing what she's really good at."

"That's ridiculous. She's never even studied music," Jessie's mom said. "It's just a phase. She'll figure out what she really wants to do and then she'll graduate from Stone with a degree to help her get there." She shook her head. "I knew he was a bad influence on her."

Isabel looked to Sara. How much were they supposed to say?

Mrs. McIntyre sighed. "I know they were close in high school, and that you all had a great time on your visit out there, but I thought she'd decided a long distance relationship wouldn't work. She's dated other guys."

"Just listen to that, then call her in a couple of days." Sara seemed to know just what to say.

"She'll let you know about the funeral. I'm sure she'll want you there," Isabel added as Mrs. McIntyre turned away.

After she left, Isabel heard Sara take a few deep breaths and shake her shoulders a bit. It'd been a rough two days on everyone.

"Great job, by the way." Isabel put her arm around Sara as they walked back.

"For what?"

"Everything. Taking care of Jessie, thinking of the CD, talking to her mom."

"It wasn't so bad."

Isabel stopped in the kitchen, opened the fridge and took out a bottle of iced tea. Downing half of it, she watched Sara throw out the food wrappers from lunch. From out back, Quinn and Jessie's voices could be heard. "Another good idea," she said looking out the window.

"Quinn's the best in difficult times, believe me, I know." Sara moved to the screen door and paused, listening. She motioned Isabel over.

"I had a younger brother," Quinn was saying. "Five-year age difference. I knew he looked up to me and I used to let him hang with me and my friends 'cause he was a good kid. But when I got to middle school I kinda brushed him off. Didn't spend much time with him. I was having too much fun. He was hurt. Crushed really."

That had happened with her and Maggie, too, Isabel remembered, until her sister had grown up a little. Then they'd somehow become best friends without either of them really trying.

"My sophomore year in high school, he was in fifth grade. He was riding home from school one day and got hit by a car. He died before they got him to the hospital."

"And you regretted not spending more time with him," Jessie said.

"I was guilt-ridden for a while."

There was silence outside and in. Isabel watched Jessie reach over to squeeze Quinn's hand.

Quinn scooted closer. "Maybe you feel sort of the same. Like you wish you'd spent more of the last two and a half years with him."

Jessie looked at him with eyes that reflected her grief. "How can I not think that I made the wrong choice? I should've gone with him after high school. We would've been so good together."

211

"Maybe. Or maybe not. But you couldn't know that then. The only way I got through my brother's death was to remember all the times I let him tag along. All the fun times."

"All my memories of Mario taste bittersweet now. I can't stop wondering 'what if?'"

"I think that's natural. Just don't let it change your perspective on the present. Or the future."

Isabel looked at Sara. She was right about Quinn. He gave good advice.

Sara opened the screen and said to Isabel, "I've got a test tomorrow. You?"

Isabel jumped right in without missing a beat. "Lots of reading. Should we meet later at your place, Jess?"

"Fine with me," Jessie replied.

The bus ride gave her time to try and piece together the cave incidents and The Graces' visits. The questions, the uncertainty, seemed to be piling up, out of control. The incidents were getting scarier. Even with the necklace gifts, which seemed to help them at least feel calmer, they didn't know how to make all of it stop or go away.

When Isabel got home, she went in through the garage and side door into the kitchen.

"You can't do this to me! I hate you!"

She recognized Maggie's high-pitched voice. A door slammed upstairs and the whole house descended into silence. Her mother and father turned from the table where they sat when the latch clicked behind her. Still in his church clothes, her father looked tired, almost defeated. Her mother appeared ready to take on the devil himself.

Isabel had a pretty good idea what had landed Maggie in trouble, but what was the punishment? They watched as she set her bag on the counter. The silence grew. They were waiting for her to ask what happened.

"You're to blame for this, Isabel Cordova."

She wasn't surprised at her mother's words, but the sting of it cut deep.

"With your late hours, and sometimes not coming home at all, you've set a terrible example for your younger sister," her mother continued.

"I'm in college. And twenty-one."

"But still living under our roof."

"Well, it's a little late setting the rules now, isn't it?"

Isabel's sarcasm didn't go over well. She saw her mother's face harden. "It's gotten worse in the last few months. And that trip had something to do with it no doubt."

Her father got up and took off his tie and jacket, frustration creasing his brow. "Maggie's always been the sweet one. Never got into trouble like this before."

"Well, she'll just have to deal with the consequences," said her mother. "We've taken away her cheerleading privileges. Should've done it sooner."

"What?" Isabel blurted out. "She's worked so hard to make captain and to take her team to the final competition."

"Her arguments exactly. But it doesn't change our minds," her father said, walking out.

"You know how much it means to her, don't you?" Isabel asked.

Her mother tied an apron around her waist and set a pan on the stove. "She should've thought of that before she missed curfew three times. I found cigarettes in her pocket, too."

"Find some other punishment," Isabel heard the pleading in her voice and hated it. She never begged for anything for herself but she had to try for her sister. "No cell or TV or computer."

"We're not changing our mind." Her mother's glaring look pierced Isabel's heart. They were punishing her too. She didn't know who to be more mad at, her sister for her stupidity or her parents.

When she reached the first stair, she hesitated. Her sister's sobs could be heard all the way down here. She didn't know if she could handle any more after what she'd been through with Jessie.

"They weren't cigarettes," her father said from behind.

Great. Maggie had really done it this time.

"Did you ask her about them?"

"She said a friend borrowed her jacket and must've put them there."

To Isabel that sounded right. She knew her sister wouldn't do drugs, even pot. "You don't believe her."

"The neighbor saw her with an older boy, Lorenzo Brunelli. God knows where she met him. She's hanging out with the wrong people, Isabel, and needs straightening out." Her father hung his jacket across the railing like he always did and returned to the living room.

Maybe her sister did, but they were going about it the wrong way.

She opened the door to her sister's room without knocking. Maggie lay face down on the bed.

"Go away," came her muffled voice.

"It's me."

Maggie came into her arms in a rush of more tears, clinging to Isabel like a lifeline. Once Maggie calmed, the whole story tumbled out. Lorenzo was involved, it turned out. Her sister thought she was in love and was willing to do anything to keep his interest.

"Whose weed was it?" asked Isabel.

"Mom thinks it was cigarettes."

"Dad knows."

"No wonder he took her side. If it was just the curfew he could've talked her into just a grounding."

"So?" Isabel pushed for an answer.

Maggie had the sense to answer honestly. "Lorenzo's."

Isabel threw up her hands. "God, you were stupid."

Sadness filled Maggie's eyes again. "I know."

"So, what are you gonna do?" Isabel asked.

"What can I do? Sneak out to rehearsals? The competition? Mom's gonna be watching me like a hawk."

Isabel pulled her sister back with her onto the bed and together they stared up at the ceiling, each lost in her own thoughts. Like old times. Her mind kept spinning scenarios on how to get her sister out of this mess. Isabel felt so angry. Why couldn't her parents see that what they were doing was pushing Maggie away, tearing her down, not helping her? A freezing cold sensation on her chest made her bolt upright.

"What's the matter?"

Isabel searched under her shirt for the silver moon and held it out, dangling from the blue ribbon. Like an icicle, it shone clear, Isabel and Maggie's faces reflected in it.

"That's beautiful. Where'd you get it?" asked Maggie.

"It was a gift."

"From a guy?"

"No."

"I just poured my heart out to you about Lorenzo and you won't tell me anything," Maggie complained with a teasing pout. It was a sign that her sister's spirits were coming back. Still if Isabel didn't do something, Maggie would either fall into depression here at home, angry and resentful, or run away to twenty-year-old Lorenzo, who was working and living on his own.

"I'm gonna shower." Maggie picked some clean clothes out of the dresser. "Don't leave, please?"

"I won't." Isabel watched Maggie look up and down the hallway before heading to the bathroom. Grasping the moon, she closed her eyes, hoping for inspiration. It stung her hand but she didn't let go. She had an idea and tried to think it through, but her eyes closed so she lay down and let herself drift off.

The sweet smell of shampoo and a dip in the bed told her Maggie was back. Her sister's red, puffy eyes said she'd done more crying in the shower.

"I have an idea." Isabel sat up, yawned and stretched.

"What?"

"Your birthday's next week."

"Right before the competition. It was going to be so cool celebrating with some of the other girls who've already turned eighteen. Graduation's a few weeks after that."

"Hopefully my idea will work 'til then and when you turn eighteen it won't matter any more." Isabel should probably tell Jessie her idea first, but knew there wasn't time. They had to do this today. Isabel explained what happened with Mario and the bad shape Jessie was in.

"That's so sad," Maggie said, her eyes misting.

"Don't start crying on me again."

Maggie sniffled. "I won't."

"You're gonna stay with us at Jessie's too."

Maggie thought for a moment. "But then what?"

"You'll continue going to school as usual and do the competition."

"What about Mom and Dad? Can they force me to come home?"

"No. Mom will be so embarrassed by the whole thing she won't force the issue, especially not at school. She hates making a scene, you know that. They'll just be glad you're finishing school."

"I shouldn't tell anyone then, huh?"

"No one, especially at school. Just go on as though nothing's changed. Except for one thing. No more Lorenzo." Isabel glared at Maggie so her sister could see how serious she was. "I won't do this if you're gonna see him. I'll leave you home to rot."

Maggie sighed. "I had a feeling you would say that." She pulled Isabel into a fierce hug. "Thank you," she whispered.

"Promise?"

"I swear."

Isabel pulled back to look at her sister. "God, I hope this works."

"It will." Maggie got on her hands and knees and reached under the bed to pull out a big duffle bag. "Mom's gonna hate you for this, you know." She gathered her school and cheerleading uniforms from the closet.

"I think she already does," Isabel said, then headed to her own room to pack.

They left a letter saying Maggie was safe with Isabel, that she would continue school and had promised to give up Lorenzo. Then snuck out of the house, which was easy enough since her father was asleep in his recliner and her mother busy cooking in the kitchen. By the time they got off the bus close to Jessie's, it was dark. The little yard in back with its string of lights, fountain, table and chairs was a welcome sight. Jessie's little cottage, however, was dark.

"I thought they'd be here by now." Isabel got the spare key, opened up, and after they put their bags in Jessie's room, she sent off a text:

"Where r u? I m at J's."

It was a few minutes before Sara replied:

"Shopping. B there soon. BTW, it's ok with roommates."

That was a relief. Except that now she was adding one more person into the mix.

"This place is so cool, Isa!" Maggie was in awe, examining every inch of the place, especially the photos.

217

"It isn't always like this, believe me," Isabel said with a laugh. "One of her roommates must've cleaned up."

"We can find a place like this to live together."

Even though she was exhausted, there was a light again in Maggie's eyes that Isabel was relieved to see.

"I was thinking the same thing. Maybe with Sara too."

"I can't wait to meet them," Maggie said.

"Come on, let's go wait in Jessie's room."

It wasn't long before Maggie was asleep in the middle of the big bed. Thank God. Isabel wanted to talk to Sara and Jessie alone first. If it wasn't going to be cool with the roommates that Maggie stay too, she was going to have come up with plan B. How had life become so complicated? Plus, she hadn't gotten any reading done yet for class tomorrow.

Her phone rang. Digging it out of her pocket, she checked to see who it was. "Hi, Michael."

"Hey. How are you? How's Jessie?"

It felt like years instead of hours since she'd seen him. She liked the way just hearing his voice made her feel. Like she'd found something valuable she'd lost. They talked awhile and then Isabel finally got up the courage to tell him what happened with her sister.

"Did I do the right thing?" she asked after giving him the details of the drama.

There was a short silence and then, "First of all, I'm glad you shared this with me 'cause I know how hard that is to do sometimes. But none of us can really walk in another's shoes. I don't know what I would've done in your place Isabel, but now that you've set out on this path, you have to make it work."

"It just all seemed so unfair."

"Parenting is hard."

"I know. But to punish her?"

"We have to take responsibility for our actions."

"Yes, by living with the consequences. They didn't give her a chance to do that, to see that. I gave her a choice: Lorenzo or cheerleading. If I'd left her to her punishment I just know she would've run away out of spite, anger and resentment."

"Do you think your parents will call the police? You and your sister don't need that kind of trouble."

"Mom doesn't believe in looking to others for help. She won't even call the school."

"Would she go to family counseling?"

"She doesn't believe in it."

"You took on a big weight."

I know." Isabel sighed. "It feels heavy already."

"Just take it a day at a time. And keep your sister close."

After saying goodbye, Isabel grabbed her sketchbook and pencil and went outside to wait. Drawing calmed her, as she knew it would. The night was cool but it felt good to sit under the lights with the sound of running water and let her hand move over the paper. Let images emerge.

The broken cave wall with her house in two appeared at the bottom with a few quick strokes, followed by shapes of people moving away, their faces averted. All except Mario who stood at the far right edge looking back.

"Hey, Isabel." Sara's voice came from up the driveway.

Jessie approached, shopping bags in hand. "Who's this?" she asked with a small sad smile aimed at a sleepy Maggie who stood in the open doorway.

Isabel knew she'd done the right thing. Now if only everything and everyone would fall in with her plan.

Twenty-Three

Sara

As soon as Sara closed the front door, Jessie seemed to snap out of the numb trance she'd been in since hearing the news of Mario's death. She took a good long look at Maggie in that way she did when taking on a new project. Sara saw the worry and fear in Maggie's features and knew just how she felt.

"So you're the sister we've heard so much about." Jessie set her packages down and pulled Maggie to the couch. "You're beautiful, athletic, tall. Very different from Isa, but I can see the resemblance."

Maggie laughed and Isabel settled herself on the arm of the sofa.

Sara couldn't move from where she'd stopped by the door. The chains were creeping up around her legs, heavier than she ever remembered. Squeezing ruthlessly. She must've made a small sound of pain because Isabel glanced her way in concern.

Isabel was next to her in an instant. "Are you all right? Are the chains on you?" she whispered.

Sara grabbed her arm and held tight. "It's hard to breathe," she murmured, her chest hurting.

"Damn, you're pale," Isabel said, turning Sara roughly to face her. "Look at me. Good. Now inhale."

Sara struggled to get her lungs to work, her eyes on Isabel's, concentrating on the simple act.

"Now, exhale."

"What are you guys doing?" Jessie called out. "C'mon Isabel, Maggie says you'd better tell us what's up."

Sara felt her body respond as the chains loosened. After a moment she nodded, Isabel gripped her arm one last time and returned to the living room. Sara stayed where she was, one hand reaching into her pocket for her rubbing stone, the other instinctively going for the pendant around her neck. She shuddered as the chains slipped away.

There was a narrow window next to the door with a perfect view of the yard.

Bloom's image shimmered there.

Call Violet

By the time her fingers touched the glass Bloom was gone.

She'd tried to call her sister, she thought in exasperation. Four or five times in the last couple of days. No answer, no machine. She'd almost given up. Was she willing to trust the voice and try one more time?

Isabel was talking to Jessie and Sara moved in closer to hear. Love, hurt and anger, she knew, made people do things they later regretted. She'd never doubted her mother's love, but she knew her mother didn't really understand anything Sara went through. It seemed Isabel and Jessie's mothers were having a hard time understanding them, too. Why did it have to be so difficult?

"So, why is cheerleading so important?" Jessie was asking Maggie.

Maggie gave her a strange look. "You know, I don't think anyone's ever asked me that. My body feels strong and alive when I'm out there." She shrugged. "It feels good to lead a group of girls in doing something difficult and pulling it off."

"And what's up with Lorenzo?"

"He's cute, confident, has a good job."

"You know he only wants you for sex, right?"

"He said he cares about me," Maggie defended.

"Guys his age only think about one thing." Jessie looked her in the eye. "It's okay to have sex if that's what you really want. You use protection, right? But believe me, it's better when it's with someone who's good at heart and will take care of you. Is Lorenzo that kinda guy?"

"He's been kind to me," Maggie responded thoughtfully, "but he doesn't think well of others. And too well of himself sometimes."

"I think that's your answer," Isabel said.

Jessie sure knew how to put it all out there.

Isabel rubbed her sister's arm. "We'll take the sofa tonight and see what tomorrow brings, okay?"

Jessie headed toward the bedroom. "C'mon, both of you. I think I have some extra pillows and a blanket."

Sara was left with only the voice in her head for company.

Call Violet.

Okay. Fine. She would. Sara dug through her purse and dialed her cell before she could talk herself out of it. A low raspy voice said hello after two rings.

Sara held tight to the ruby rose. "Hi."

There was a pause. "It's late. Who is this?"

Sara almost hung up, but braved on. "I'm sorry. Is this Violet?"

"No."

Sara breathed a little easier. She didn't like the sound of that voice and was glad it wasn't her sister. "Can I talk to her, please?"

"She's not available." The voice was even more impatient than before.

"Tell her it's her sister, Sara. My number is..."

"Hold on."

There was an abrupt silence that went on and on. When Maggie came back with blankets and pillows and lay down, Sara got up and moved outside. What was taking so long?

"Hello? Sara?"

Her heart was racing madly now even as her spirits lifted. Her sister's voice sounded just as she remembered. "Yes, it's me."

"Oh my god, I can't believe it."

Neither could she. "I'm sorry I called so late, it's just I've been trying to get a hold of you."

"We didn't recognize the number so we didn't pick up. You're still in Boulder?"

"Yes. I'm going to Stone College."

"Not an easy school to get into. You must be smart."

Sara smiled. "You live in San Francisco?"

"Yep. In a small house close to the Bay."

"Sounds nice. I was just there with some girlfriends about a month ago."

"Really? How'd you get my number, anyway?"

"Dad."

"Finally took things into his own hands, huh?"

In the silence that followed, Sara realized it was bitterness she heard in her sister's voice.

"Listen, I have to get up early for work tomorrow," Violet said.

Sara needed more than the last few minutes. Fifteen years was a long time. "Can we talk again? I have so many questions. There's a lot I don't know."

"Did you ask?" There was that sharpness again.

"I've had...health issues for a long time."

Silence.

"Please." Sara wasn't above begging.

"Okay." Violet sighed. "I'll call you in a day or two. My work schedule's really tight right now."

Sara wanted to ask what she did, but settled for, "Thank you." Finally, she'd be able to put the pieces of her life together. And hopefully get her sister back.

When she returned to the house, Isabel sat on the edge of the sofa talking quietly with her sister. Sara locked the front door, picked up the bag she'd left there and headed toward Jessie's room.

"Goodnight, Isa, 'night, Sara," Maggie said softly.

Startled, Sara turned to see Maggie hugging Isabel and then settling down, her eyes closing.

"Sweet dreams, Maggie," Sara whispered back.

Isabel followed Sara, shut Jessie's bedroom door behind them and began to undress, dropping her clothes on the floor.

Sara moved around the room straightening things before she took the outfits from her bag and hung them in Jessie's closet. Isabel sat cross-legged at the end of the bed and told them about holding on to her moon pendant and getting the idea to bring Maggie here.

"I saw my father and me when I was a little girl," Jessie said, and told them about the scenes she'd seen with Brilliance.

"I saw Bloom in the window." Sara laid her jewelry on the dresser and brushed out her hair while they talked, the ordinary tasks calming her, offering a comfort she was willing to take at the moment.

Isabel stretched out and kicked her shoes off. "So, not only do we go to these strange and frightening places but we've got Goddesses paying us regular visits. I don't get it."

Jessie heaved an impatient sigh. "Don't you? C'mon Isabel."

Isabel didn't rise to the bait. "I'm tired. I don't want to think about it anymore tonight."

Pajamas and toothbrush in hand, Sara paused by the bathroom door. "Let's talk tomorrow, okay?"

When she emerged ten minutes later, Jessie was sound asleep on one side of the bed and the living room was quiet. Sleep beckoned, so she climbed under the covers on the other side and turned out the small bedside light.

She was in a game of hide and seek. Bloom, clothed in flowers of every kind, led her on a chase through a forest of pines, and disappeared through the door of a small cabin. Sara followed. Inside, a large cherry wood desk faced a row of windows that lined one wall. She stepped onto plush carpet and gazed up at the high ceiling. It was quiet and warm, with deep colors and soft light from a single lamp. She moved to the desk, sat in the chair and put her hands palms down upon the surface, as if she could soak up wisdom and knowledge from the tree it was made of.

On the corner of the desk lay a garland of daisies, like the ones she glimpsed covering Bloom. Beneath the flowers lay a green, velvet-covered journal. She traced the leaf design on the front then ran her fingers over the blank first page. In the top drawer of the desk lay pens in a myriad of colors.

She sat and began to write the first words that came to mind. It wasn't until hours later, when every page of the book was filled, that she lay her head down upon it and slept.

The next morning there was no time to tell anyone about the room or the journal. Only a rush of taking showers and sharing mirror space in Jessie's small bathroom so they could all get out of the house on time for their different classes. Jessie appeared to be going through the motions.

"What's up for today?" Sara asked her brightly, trying to distract. Isabel and Maggie walked on ahead, discussing schedules for the afternoon.

"I don't know." Jessie held her phone like she was expecting a call. "I texted him this morning out of habit," she confessed. In leggings, flats and an emerald cotton top, she looked thinner than she had even the day before.

"How about a muffin and coffee before class?" she asked, wishing she could get Jessie to eat.

"Coffee. You have time?"

"Sure. I'll drop Maggie off at school and meet you at our usual place. You take Isabel. She's got an early class."

They split up and Sara followed Maggie's directions to the high school. There was an awkward moment when she pulled up to the curb and they sat in silence watching other kids talking in groups on the front lawn.

"Thank you." Maggie took a couple of deep breaths.

"Are you afraid? It's okay if you are, believe me I can relate."

Maggie looked relieved. "Yeah, maybe a little. I don't know why, cause nothing's really different since yesterday."

"Except that you were grounded from the thing you love the most, ran away from home, slept on someone else's sofa and you're not sure what will happen today."

Surprise lit Maggie's face.

"You like school, right? Have friends?"

"Yeah." Maggie waved to a passing group of kids. "What do I do?"

"Act as if—as if everything is normal. Chances are, nothing's gonna happen here, so if you spend all day worrying it'll be a waste."

"Isabel was right about you."

Sara couldn't imagine what Isabel had said. "Oh, yeah?"

"She said you were really smart." Maggie finally got out and shut the door. "I like your jacket." She turned to go, then whirled back. "See you tonight?"

Sara smiled, deciding she liked Isabel's little sister a lot. "Sure thing."

Back on campus, she got coffee and found Jessie lounging on one of the sofas in a quiet area of the student building. They watched people come and go and Sara told Jessie about the phone call with her sister.

"What do I do if she doesn't want to talk to me again? Never calls?"

"Don't push. She'll come around." Jessie set her empty cup down. "I know Isabel rolls her eyes when she talks about her big family, but I wish I had a sister to be close to like her and Maggie."

"She's very sweet. But we can't keep living with you forever. Isabel and I should get an apartment."

Jessie looked up in surprise. "You're ready for that?"

The idea didn't scare her like it used to. Smiling, she answered, "Yeah. Too bad your roommates look like they're going to be around a while. Now that you won't be moving to San Francisco, will you stay at Stone?" As soon as the words came out, Sara realized her mistake. "I'm sorry, Jess. I shouldn't've brought that up. I'm sure you haven't thought that far. And you don't have to yet."

Jessie stood abruptly, grabbed her things. "Gotta go. Later." She was gone before Sara could say another word.

Sheesh. Usually she was so careful about what she said. Or didn't say.

After taking the test in her morning class she hadn't studied for, she got a salad from one of the small shops at the edge of campus. A table outside was free so she read the assignment for the next class while she ate. She'd just finished gathering her things to head back when she spotted Leslie waiting to cross at the corner.

She hesitated, knowing she could take another way back to campus or wait 'til Leslie left. That was something she would've done last year. Now, she let her feet take her to where Leslie stood. Shifting her bag to her shoulder, she moved in alongside her.

"A long light, isn't it?"

Leslie turned in surprise. "Sara! How's it going?"

Sara smiled, taking in Leslie's black sweater, leopard print skirt, black tights and ankle boots. That thread of attraction she'd felt before pulled her again as they chatted and crossed the street. That's what it was, she admitted. What she'd always feared and tried to ignore.

Mostly Leslie talked, but Sara didn't mind. She fingered Bloom's gift hoping for some advice. Leslie was funny and interesting and Sara wanted to go out, just once to see what it would be like. But Leslie probably wouldn't ask again. It would be up to her.

"A mailing went out last week about an event sponsored by the Golden Key day after tomorrow," Leslie mentioned, stopping where three campus walkways came together.

"Hmm. I haven't been home to look at the mail lately. What is it?"

"An art walk. Don't you live at home?"

"I do, but I've been staying with a friend."

At Leslie's raised brows, Sara realized she'd given the wrong impression. "My friend Jessie, her boyfriend died, and she needed some moral support."

"Oh. Well, that's nice of you." Leslie motioned toward the science building. "Gotta get to class."

"Yeah, me too." Sara took a deep breath, still wishing for Bloom's voice to tell her something.

"See ya." Leslie took a few steps, her eyes still on Sara's.

Should she? Did she dare? Sara felt an odd tremble through her body. She stiffened, waiting to feel the slide of metal links up her legs. Knowing they would come. Leslie was already turning away when a whisper echoed through her head.

Ask her.

That was all, but it was enough.

She called out: "Do you want to go to that art walk? Get something to eat after?"

Leslie stopped. Hesitated before turning back.

Sara waited, her heart frantic.

"I'm already meeting some friends. You could join us."

She would hate that. "Okay."

"And I'm free after." Leslie pulled pen and paper out of her bag, wrote something down and ran back to Sara. "Here's my number."

Sara took the paper. "Great." At least the chains weren't so tight this time.

Leslie hurried off in one direction while Sara went more slowly in the other. The professor was already handing out papers and didn't seem to notice when she snuck in the back. But she couldn't concentrate on the discussion, barely took any notes and in the end felt like she'd just wasted an hour and a half.

"Sara? Stay after class a few minutes, please." Professor Jamison was white-haired, demanding and often unrelenting in his criticism. Sara didn't want to hear what he had to say, today of all days. He shuffled a stack of papers on his desk while the other girls left in groups, their chatter mingling with noise in the hallway before the room finally emptied and fell silent. He held out a paper.

"I haven't had a writer like you in my class in a long time, young lady."

What? What did he mean? "Is that good or bad, sir?" She looked down at the large quantity of comments in red filling the margins.

"What's your major?"

"English."

"Going to grad school?"

Sara hesitated. What was he getting at? "I haven't thought that far ahead."

He closed his briefcase, finally giving her his attention. "Well, done. That's a fine piece of writing."

Astounded at the praise she knew he rarely gave, she held up the paper. "There's a lot of red here."

He nodded. "Rework it a bit and that piece will get you published."

In a daze she watched him walk out.

Her phone rang and she fumbled getting it open.

"Hey, Quinn."

"Wanna play a set this afternoon?"

"What time?"

"In an hour. I'll pick you up at your house."

She meant to get there sometime today to pick up some things, so that worked. "Perfect." Quinn was just the person she needed to talk to.

Then the reality of what Professor Jamison said hit her. Published? She'd never imagined that. It made her pulse throb at her throat in fear, yes, but there was excitement there too. Caught up in doctor visits, taking medication and getting through each day without a panic attack had been her focus for the past three years.

Now, just maybe, she could plan a future.

Traffic was light and she made good time getting home. Turning the key in her front door, she noticed something wasn't quite right. Everything looked the same but a strange feeling hung in the air.

On her way past the den, she heard her father's voice. That was odd. What was he doing home at this time of day? She peeked her head in.

"Hey, what's up? You okay?"

"Hi, darling. Feeling a bit under the weather, that's all. Working from home."

"I'm taking him to the doctor, actually, Sara."

Sara turned in complete surprise. "Mom." Then looked back at her father. "That sounds serious."

"She just wants to go to make sure all the right questions are asked," he replied. "And it isn't serious. What brings you home?"

"Meeting Quinn for a game."

"Go, have fun and call me later," her father shooed her out of the room ahead of him.

Sara watched as her mother and father went toward the kitchen. He looked fine, but she knew that looks could be deceiving. She changed into her tennis skirt and top, grabbed her sneakers and a few other clothes for the next two days and threw them into her tennis bag.

Quinn opened the door to her room a few minutes later. "Hey, gorgeous."

"I didn't hear the bell."

"Your dad let me in."

"I can't find the new can of balls I just bought. I don't know what I did with it," Sara complained.

Quinn smiled. "No problem. I've got some."

"Mine are nicer." Sara straightened from where she'd been searching. "Don't give me that look."

"What?" he said, innocently. He walked to her desk and opened the notebook sitting there.

Sara's mouth fell open at the sight of the green velvet cover. Where had that come from? She struggled to remember exactly what she'd written in that room last night. It still felt like a dream but obviously wasn't.

He read for a minute, then closed it. Pulling a chair around, he sat, and propped his feet on the bed.

"What do you do with all your writing notebooks?"

Sara opened her closet, rummaging through her stuff. "Keep them."

"You must have a room full," Quinn said, his gaze intent.

"A basement full. Ah-ha! Found them!" She tossed aside a sweater she sometimes wore after a game when the weather turned chilly and grabbed the can.

"You should really think about being a writer."

"That's just journaling." Except Professor Jamison had liked her writing, too.

"Sara, what I just read is better than most of what's published out there."

Sara smiled at the second compliment she'd gotten in one day. "You don't read much except People and Vogue and they don't count."

He laughed and took her bag. "True. Ready yet?" he asked, heading toward the hall.

Following, she felt a tug at the back of her neck. The silk ribbon of her pendant was caught in some of her hair. Stopping, she loosened it then allowed her fingers to slide down to touch the stone. Images of Quinn spread like fire in her mind. All the times they'd spent over the years, how he'd come through for her when no one else had, the comfort she found in being with him. Suddenly it was imperative she tell him what she couldn't hide from any longer.

"Quinn, you've known all along, haven't you?"

He halted, turned back. She could almost feel him holding his breath. Waiting. His deep green eyes full of understanding and hope.

"How did you know that I…" her voice faltered.

"Say it, Sara." he said, patiently.

He was only a few paces from her, but it felt like miles.

"That I'm…" she paused, swallowed, and forced herself to say it, "gay." The word hung in the air. Sara glanced around, but the world was steady. And the chains were gone.

Quinn dropped the bag, his arms at his side. Then she was in them, his hold strong and safe.

"Breathe," he whispered in her ear.

She laughed and took big gulps of air.

"It's going to be okay." Quinn held her back so he could look at her. "The people who love you always will, no matter what."

"You do."

"Of course." He touched her cheek with one finger. "I guessed pretty much the day I met you."

"How long have you known that you're gay?"

"I figured it out when I was twelve."

"But you dated all those girls in high school!"

"I like girls, Sara. I had a good time and it was easy and fun. But I never slept with any of them."

"Do your parents know?"

Quinn still held her in the circle of his arms. "We never had the discussion, but yeah, my older brother told me they guessed."

Sara thought she heard a sound on the stairs but when she looked over Quinn's shoulder there was no one there. She hoped her parents had left. "They don't approve?"

He shrugged. "It doesn't matter. We just don't talk about it."

"I can't believe it took so long for us to have this conversation." Sara hid her face in the front of his shirt, embarrassed now at all the fears that had held her back.

"It's not one you force on a friend. I had to wait 'til you were ready."

"I can't tell Mom. She won't understand." She glanced up. "What about my dad?"

"Honestly? I think your father has guessed. He's said some things that made me wonder."

A flush of embarrassment overcame her again. "I'm that...transparent?"

Quinn shrugged. "All that matters is you be yourself from now on."

"I'm still trying to figure it out."

"Yeah, me too."

She laughed again, the sound of it light and freeing. "I've been thinking that maybe the reason I have panic attacks is because I've buried who I really am for so long. " Sara took a step back, confident she could stand on her own. "What do you think?"

"You certainly have a lot to talk about with your therapist," Quinn remarked, bending to pick up her bag again.

Hand in hand they started down the hall. A thundering crash tore through the quiet house.

Sara looked at him in alarm. "What was that?"

Her father came rushing up the stairs, out of breath. The sound of breaking glass came from her parents' bedroom. He threw open the door as Quinn ran over, Sara in tow.

"How could this be happening?" Her mother stood by the dresser, eyes on fire, visibly shaking, a ceramic vase in her hand poised to let fly. "It's cruel."

Hand outstretched, Sara's father took a step into the room. "Darling, it's okay."

"No, it's not," her mother practically growled.

Sara had rarely seen her mother so emotional, let alone like this. On the verge of a meltdown. Maybe already in it.

Focusing on Quinn from across the room, her mother took a deep shuddering breath. "When I saw you holding her in the hall, I thought, finally they're moving in the right direction."

A weight fell on Sara's heart, so hard she thought it would shatter. She felt sick. Her mother had overheard their conversation.

Quinn clued in, too. His arms snagged her roughly against him, his voice in her ear. "You're strong, Sara. You can handle this."

Could she? She didn't know.

Her father gave them a sharp glance, then moved slowly across the plush blue carpet until he was close enough to gently pry the vase from her mother's fingers. "What did they say that upset you?"

"Why?" she asked. What sounded like a sob escaped with the question. "How?" Her mother resisted his attempts to pull her into his arms before finally giving in. "It's not possible, is it? Tell me I heard wrong." She looked at Sara. At Quinn.

Then Sara was being dragged down the stairs, across the living room and out the front into the afternoon sun. Quinn held her steady while he opened the car. "Tell me where to go." He tore out of the driveway, tires screeching.

"Tennis?" she suggested on a whisper.

"You can think about tennis at a time like this?"

"I need a distraction. A big one."

He glanced over at her. "Okay." He turned the corner, slowing down once they were out of sight from the house. "What's that you've been holding this whole time?"

Bloom's gift was clasped in her hand, close to her heart. She hadn't felt the chains once since she'd touched it back in her bedroom. "A necklace I got in Chicago." Which was true.

"I've never seen your mom like that." Quinn shook his head, as if to clear the image from his mind.

"I have." Only one other person had caused such a reaction in her mother. Sara deserved some answers after what happened today and Violet was the one to give them to her.

Twenty-Four

Jessie

The congregation stood when the procession bearing Mario's casket entered the back doors. The priest's words and the sweet smell of incense reminded Jessie she hadn't been to church in a while. She looked at Mario's family lining the pew in front of her. Like Jessie's, they came from working-class immigrant roots and still clung to the Catholic faith. His parents had died when he was two and his *abuela,* and *bisabuela,* grandmother and great-grandmother, had raised him with the help of the rest of the family. Jessie thought about her and Mario growing up fatherless. He'd been so smart, sure of himself, and much less scarred than she was.

As the readings finished and everyone sat for the sermon, Jessie glanced around the small church at a very mixed group of people. Sara and Isabel sat with her, some teachers and many former Foothills High students behind them. Jessie's mother and grandmother were somewhere among the crowd and she'd glimpsed Sara's dad, too. A number of people from San Francisco had come, including the members of his band, who sat in a side aisle. They were all here, which proved Mario had been right when he'd said they were not only great musicians but also good friends.

The chill off the walls seemed to settle into Jessie's bones. She wore a sleeveless top draped across her breasts that wound around her waist tying in back. The matching skirt in deep plum, with gold threads running through it, fell mid-thigh. Mario had liked this dress a lot, so she'd worn it even though the weather was really too chilly for it.

Unable to concentrate on the priest's words, Jessie glanced to her left. Phil had insisted on sitting with her, and of course Mario's family knew him well, so she could hardly refuse. She observed the shadows beneath his eyes, the sadness around his mouth. He'd dealt with many of the responsibilities that had come with Mario's death and it showed. In a casual black suit with a bolo tie, Phil stared straight ahead. She didn't think he was really listening, either. He turned, his eyes met hers, and that electric frisson happened again.

Not here, too. She decided staring straight ahead was a good idea.

Sara leaned over and whispered in her ear, "We're right here."

Jessie willed herself to relax. She felt brittle, like old glass that breaks easily. Mario's grandmother had persuaded her to say something after the priest finished. She wondered what she'd been thinking at the time, because she didn't know now how she'd ever get through it.

Isabel reached across Sara and squeezed Jessie's hand. "I think it's your turn, Jess."

She stood up, scooted past Sara and Isabel and moved into the aisle.

Green hedges, dark and fragrant blocked her way. She stopped abruptly, as music drifted to her from all sides, the church fading in the humid air. She reached down and touched the pendant from Brilliance, warm and vibrant against her skin.

A familiar hand cupped her elbow. The way to the altar cleared. Phil stood beside her, murmuring gently, "You were glowing again. C'mon, I'll go with you. We'll do this together."

She didn't want what she felt with him, the electricity, or the comfort and safety. She'd once known that with Mario. How could it be there with his best friend, too? The sound of her heels clicking in time with his boots on the stone floor held everyone's attention. When they reached the pulpit, she looked out in silence at the faces gathered, watching and waiting.

"You can do it," Phil whispered beside her.

Jessie sought out the tiny, wrinkled woman who was Mario's great-grandmother. Her eyes were sad but she smiled at Jessie with Mario's smile. Whatever she did would be right. The fear that had somehow claimed her, left in a rush giving her the strength to begin.

With a song.

Her clear voice floated out over the congregation, the astonishment on their faces vaguely registering. Mitch moved from pew to piano, easing into accompanying her as naturally as Mario would have. Surprisingly the wonder and joy were there, as they had been that night in the studio.

The silence following her last note pulsed, trembling and aching. Then Phil's deep voice filled the void, introducing them in his quiet way, telling stories with a humor and grace that was distinctly his own. Jessie stood by his side, his hand gripping hers, listening and reliving her time with Mario, her grief a persistent heaviness weighing on her heart.

Leaving the church later, Jessie kept Sara and Isabel close, from the graveside to the small luncheon served in Mario's grandmother's back yard. They sat in folding chairs at tables covered in flowered tablecloths, ate enchiladas, drank *cervesas* with lime, and silently passed strength to each other.

After an hour, Jessie figured she'd stayed long enough. An incoming text said Phil and the band were on their way. She gave Isabel and Sara the signal it was time to go. "I've got to say goodbye to Mario's family. Then use the bathroom. Meet you by my car in ten minutes?"

Weathered hands gripped hers tightly as Jessie murmured her goodbyes to Mario's grandmother and great grandmother. Without asking permission, she descended the steps to the basement where she'd spent a lot of time during senior year in what was then Mario's studio. Empty now, cold and dark, it made her shudder. In the tiny bathroom she touched up her hair and make-up, changed into her usual leggings, a tank and long sweater. With one last look at the cracked mirror, worn carpet and faded wood paneling, she ran back up the stairs, closing the door, closing the past. She steadied her breathing and went to find Isabel and Sara.

And ran into her mother, Nana, and Sara's dad on the back porch.

"You stunned the whole congregation," Mr. Caldwell said, his embrace warm and reassuring. "I don't think I'll ever forget that moment."

"It was beautiful," agreed Nana, her eyes misty, pulling Jessie close.

"I'm sorry." Her mother embraced the two of them and lay her forehead on Jessie's like she had when Jessie was little.

She let that be enough for the moment.

Pulling away, Jessie said, "Sara, Isa, and I are going to spend some time with the band. I'll call tomorrow."

Both women looked disappointed she was getting away so quickly, but Jessie couldn't do anything else. She needed her mountains. And to be distracted by friends, their conversation and hopefully, laughter.

A group stood in a circle in the middle of the quiet street. Caryn, Mitch, Carl, and Steve had arrived and were talking with Isabel and Sara. And Phil.

"You guys are hungry, right? Go and get some food, pay your respects to the family, and meet us later," Phil told the band.

"What about you? Where are you going?" Caryn asked.

"Where are we going?" Phil turned to Jessie.

She raised an eyebrow and didn't answer. The current between them warred.

He didn't take his eyes from her, his voice tight. "I have something to give you."

Jessie gave in. It was difficult to find the energy to fight him. She turned to Caryn. "Take the main street out there, Broadway to Boulder Canyon Drive and go west. Once you cross the river, you'll see a sign for a turn off called Red Rocks. Park and head up the path and you'll see us."

"We won't be long." Caryn headed toward the house with the rest.

Jessie gave Phil a dark look. "Isabel and Sara are with me."

Water spilled over the rocky riverbed dripping winter's slowly melting ice. The sound soothed her frayed nerves. Wrapped in a warm wool shawl, Jessie sat in her usual spot, Isabel leaning against a boulder beside her. Sara opened a diet Coke, the pop loud enough to startle a group of birds into flight.

"Mario first or you first?" Phil asked.

"What about Mario?"

"Did you read the copy of the police report I gave you the other night?"

"Yeah." Jessie crossed her legs to get more comfortable. "It says it was an accident. Is that all you wanted? To talk about how it happened? Cause I really don't want to do that."

"Hell, Jessie, he was my best friend. Give me a break." He didn't sit, instead paced restlessly next to the path that led to the stream. "One minute he was with me, making jokes, showing me a new piece, excited about you coming out. The next time I see him he's on a slab at the morgue."

A small sliver of guilt prodded Jessie over giving him such a hard time, but she knew he was going to push her into making decisions she wasn't ready to make yet.

"The band and some of our other friends have been talking. They think you should have Mario's things. His instruments, his music. His furniture. His family agreed, so we're hoping you're still coming out as planned."

Jessie hadn't expected that tact. He seemed to know just what to say to get her to do what he wanted.

"Damn, you're good, you know that," Isabel said mildly, but Jessie could tell there was steel beneath her words. "You've made it almost impossible for her to say no. Once she's there, you'll work on making her stay, right?"

First with Maggie and now for her, Isabel was coming to the rescue. Jessie laughed and it felt good seeing the look on Phil's face. He hadn't imagined Isabel would play offense.

He held up his hands in a gesture of surrender. "She can come whenever she wants, in three days as planned or a year from now." To Jessie, "But you need to come. We all know it's what he would want."

Sara sighed loudly, getting their attention. "I think Phil's right. You should go Jess, when you're ready."

"Christ, Sara, how..."

Sara kept right on going. "I want her to stay as much as you do, Isabel, but she can't stop singing now that she's started."

Phil was as startled as Jessie that Sara was his ally in this. Not that Jessie had asked anyone's opinion. Sara sat on the blanket next to her. "Sorry. You didn't want to hear all that, did you?"

Jessie touched Sara's arm, acknowledging her apology. "You didn't start it."

"I'm going to head out to spend some time with my parents," Phil said, with a glance at his watch. "Jessie, this is for you." He reached into his pocket, pulled out an envelope. "I don't know how much Mario told you about my production company. My parents gave me half the start-up money so we're full business partners. I choose who we represent and do all the work, but if it weren't for them I wouldn't have gotten it off the ground. Anyway, they came out to see me three weeks ago and Mario told them about you." He handed her the envelope. "This is the note he sent them along with a copy of the recording you did. My mom thought you should have it but she didn't want to give it to you at the service."

The sound of a car approaching had them all looking toward the road.

"Call me later," Phil instructed.

The band arrived, Carl at the wheel. Phil waved a hand in farewell as he pulled away.

Isabel did some quick texting. "Maggie says hi. She's almost done with practice and will head back to your place to finish a paper. She can use your computer, right?"

"Sure." Jessie quickly tucked the envelope in her bag.

Caryn and the guys piled out with a case of beer and a small bag of what looked like pot joints. It didn't matter to her what they did, she only wanted to lose herself in their company. Soon the quiet evening was loud and raucous with conversation and laughter. The stories, all of them, had Mario at their center, and each and every one made her heart ache. But they made her feel closer to the last years of his life too, and for that she was grateful.

Two hours later, Jessie, Isabel and Sara watched the band leave to head back to their hotel. Finally alone, they sat on top of Jessie's Buick with only a flashlight to see by.

"You doing okay, Jessie?" Sara sat close, concern in her eyes.

"Not really. You?"

"Tired. Overwhelmed," she admitted.

"Multiply that by three," Isabel leaned in. "Read the note, Jessie, I can't stand the suspense anymore."

Jessie hesitated, then slit the envelope open and took out the small single sheet of paper. Passed it to Sara.

"Are you sure?"

When Jessie nodded, she took it and read aloud:

Wait 'til you hear her. She'll be one of Phil's greatest successes. One day I'm gonna talk her into marrying me and we'll spend our days making great music together.

Mario

"It's so unfair." Isabel's voice was hard, angry.

Jessie heard Sara sniffing and handed her a tissue. A cricket's song filled the air. Jessie listened to the breeze lifting the branches around them and let Mario's words sink deep, imagining the life he'd wanted. It sounded good and right and what she wanted too if she were really honest. Now she didn't even have a choice. It had been taken from her, stolen, by a rain-slick street and the turn of a wheel.

"Jess, in church today, you paused in the aisle on the way to the altar. Do you remember? For a moment I thought you'd decided not to go up." Sara's hand trembled slightly as she wiped her eyes.

"It was the maze, wasn't it?" Isabel said.

"Remember that time in the car?" When Isabel nodded, Jessie went on, "It was just like that. Giant green hedges blocking out everything."

A bird screeched, its dark shadow swooping low over the trees on their left. Sara grabbed Jessie's hand. "What was that?"

"A hawk. Or an owl."

Isabel scooted closer, scanning the area. "Did you hear that song you always hear?"

"Nope. But when I touched the sun pendant Brilliance gave me, it all went away."

Sara straightened. "It's like they're coming to our rescue. Every time I feel the chains, what helps most is holding the red stone rose."

"I don't know. The last time I saw Joy, it kinda hurt when she tore up my picture," Isabel said.

"She was telling you to chill out about the contest, that's all. What about when the whole thing was going down with your mom?" Jessie asked.

Isabel rubbed her arms for warmth. "I guess. When my pendant turned ice-cold. I pulled it out, showed it to Maggie, and that's when I got the idea to take her with me."

"See!" Sara nudged Isabel's arm. "She is helping you. They're guiding all of us. Bloom told me to call Violet."

"Your sister hasn't called back yet?" Jessie asked.

"She said to give her a couple of days."

"I don't know how you can wait," Isabel sighed. "Sounds like your mom went pretty crazy the other night. I'd want to know why."

"That's just it. I keep replaying what she said and I can't figure it out."

"What was it?"

"She said it wasn't possible it was happening again."

Isabel leaned over to look at Sara. "Again? Who was the first?"

"I didn't really stick around to ask." Sara grew thoughtful and quiet.

Jessie closed her eyes, too tired to keep them open any longer but not wanting to leave yet. She leaned her head on Isabel's shoulder. "Aren't the contest winners posted soon?"

"Don't remind me," Isabel groaned. "And you won't believe what Dowling told me the other day. The winning pieces, displayed at the reception, can be bought if the student's willing to sell."

Sara seemed to snap out of whatever daydream she'd been in. "I...ah, heard that too. How much are you going to sell your piece for, Isa, if someone's interested?"

"Are you kidding? Why would I do that? It's the one of The Graces."

Jessie smiled. Isabel was smart but sometimes she just didn't get it. "Because artists sell their work."

"But I..."

Isabel never got to finish. The dusty rocky path in front of them was suddenly swept clean. The air shimmered, fragrant with orange blossoms.

Platters of steaming food sat in the middle of a wood table set for six. Tapered candles flickered, spicy succulent aromas mixed with the citrus, and a lone guitar plucked out a soothing melody in the background. The Graces beckoned them forward with outstretched arms.

Their beauty took her breath away. It was like when the mist cleared for a view of the castle on the hill, and the first glimpse of The Graces in the garden, all over again.

Jessie realized she was starving. For food, yes, because she'd eaten so little all day. But as she surveyed the steaming dishes and the faces around the table, she knew she'd been hungry for something else for a long time.

Jessie gave Sara, then Isabel, a little push into cushioned high-back chairs before she sat down herself. Sara's eyes were wide in astonishment at the variety of food on the table. Isabel touched the rim of a plate lined with gold. Jessie watched Brilliance serve her from a steaming pot. The spoon felt like butterfly wings in her hand when she picked it up and the creamy rich soup tasted unlike anything she'd ever had.

The pleasure on her tongue and before her eyes was so intense it was almost unbearable. Yet something kept her from giving in to complete enjoyment.

She wanted to, but her questions were still unanswered. Maybe it was stress, probably grief, but she couldn't just go along with things anymore. She wanted to know how she could see The Graces after what happened in the garden at Hearst Castle. And what really happened anyway? Were they spirits? Did they live inside the statue? And, what was she going to do? Stay or go?

The hawk, or maybe it was an owl, screeched again from a nearby tree, and they were back. To the dark, pine-scented, dusty path in Red Rocks Park.

Twenty-Five

Isabel

Isabel woke up knowing she had only two things to do and they both sucked. First was to go to the art department building on campus to see the posting of the contest winners. She wanted to place at least. But if she didn't, well, she wasn't going to go there. The other was to go back home to pick up clothes and toiletries. She didn't know if she was up to facing her mom but it had to be done.

The hardest part of the fallout from taking Maggie away was something she hadn't anticipated. Her mother called every day, but never left a message when Isabel didn't answer. Her father too. Every one of her older brothers and sisters had called or sent a text telling her to take Maggie home. Their youngest brother, James, the only one still at home, had all but pleaded with her, saying it was unbearable without them.

Isabel shook Maggie awake to get up and shower, then went to the kitchen for a cup of coffee. Sara, wearing a dress that flowed down to her ankles and dainty ballet slippers, sat at one of the barstools texting, her forehead in a frown of concentration. Or worry. Probably both.

"Your dad again?"

"Yep. He says Mom is working too much and unwilling to talk about anything. But he wants me to come home."

"And that would help matters how?"

Sara sighed and put her cell in her bag. "He doesn't think it will, really. He just misses me."

"And you miss him?"

Sara gave her an uncertain look. "I don't know. Meeting him today will be the first time I've seen him alone since that afternoon."

Isabel reached over and squeezed Sara's hand briefly. "Your father's cool. He'll be okay with it."

"With everything that happened I never asked him why he was going to the doctor that day. I'm kinda worried. What if it's something serious?"

"You didn't ask him at the funeral?"

"No, we didn't really get a moment to ourselves." Sara regarded Isabel for a moment. "So if Jessie decides to go, we're staying here?"

"You want to?"

"Maybe just you and Maggie should. Quinn's offered me a place with him."

"Sure, if that's what you want." Isabel turned away to pour herself a little more coffee and waited to hear Sara's answer.

"It's crowded here, but I like it."

So what was she saying? Isabel waited for her to get to the point.

Sara cleared her throat. "I think I'll be more comfortable here."

Isabel sighed in relief. She'd gotten used to having them around, and even if Jessie left, Isabel wanted Sara to stay. "I was hoping you'd say that."

Isabel glanced at her watch. "I gotta go or I'll miss the bus. I'll text you later."

Sara had offered to take Maggie to school every morning, which was a big help and they seemed to have hit it off, so Isabel was grateful for that. She walked the block to the stop that would take her to campus first. Twenty minutes later she was outside the art building, her stomach a tight bundle of nerves. She leaned against the low brick wall next to the entrance to prepare herself either way for the results.

"What are you waiting out here for?" Her classmate, Sylvia, said in greeting as she approached from the cafeteria side of campus.

"Have you been inside? Seen the posting?" Isabel asked.

"Nope. Just got here." Sylvia looked at Isabel closely. "You okay?"

"Not really. I feel like I'm gonna throw up." Isabel hated herself like this, she really did.

"C'mon. We'll look together. Chill. How bad can it be?"

There was a crowd around the decorated board where professors posted monthly news. They waited until a few students stepped away before getting a closer look. Isabel recognized almost everyone whose eyes searched the list of the winning entries; it was a small department in a small school. They were all serious about their art and this contest would make it possible for a few lucky students to have their work shown in a well-known public space.

Isabel stuck her hands in the pockets of her jeans, squared her shoulders and looked for the notice of the winners in the drawing category.

Where was it?

Someone gripped her arm.

She spotted her name under first place and felt her heart take flight and the nerves dissolve. Thank you, God.

"We did it," Sylvia whispered excitedly. "Your drawing? First place? Congrats. I got first place painting category!"

They high-fived. Isabel took a good look at Sylvia's flushed face and laughed. "Yeah, right, chill. Look at you. You were just as worried as I was about this thing."

"Okay, so maybe a little. But I'm better at hiding it than you."

They went back outside. Sylvia headed in the opposite direction, calling over her shoulder, "See you at the winners' reception."

Isabel felt lighter than she had in days. And ready to share her good news. At the bus stop she texted first Maggie, then Sara, Jessie, and finally Michael. Smiling to herself as their responses came back, she boarded the number 19 that would take her home.

The good news buoyed her along until she reached the house. Nerves struck again as she stared at the driveway. She didn't remember there being quite so many cracks in it and wondered when she'd stopped noticing. As a girl, she'd used them as marking points for hopscotch, jump rope and races with her brothers. Now dandelions sprouted between them.

Her mother, in a short-sleeved black dress covered with her usual checkered apron, was sweeping the front porch. When she finished, she held the door open and looked at Isabel.

Musty stone smells and a roaring rumble of cracking rocks came and went. Isabel's eyes never left her mother's from across the yard. She forced her feet to move. Inside, the living room appeared different as well, but Isabel couldn't say exactly what made it so. One hand still holding the broom, the other on her hip, her mother blocked the stairs.

Sitting on the arm of her father's reclining chair, Isabel concentrated on keeping her heart and her voice steady. "I came for more of our things."

That was met with silence. Then, "Why are you doing this?"

"For Maggie. This isn't about me."

"I don't believe that. You've made it all about you."

"No, Mom. You did. You blamed me. Said it was my fault."

The clock on the mantle ticked loudly between them as they studied each other.

"Maggie answered our calls."

"I know. She's doing well. She's keeping her grades up. She stopped seeing Lorenzo and, most important, she's getting ready for the competition coming up."

Isabel noticed the candle lit on the prayer table in the hall. Her mother was holding vigil and Isabel could guess why. For some reason it made her angry. She couldn't resist adding, "So what we all wanted has happened, but without forcing her to give up what she loves."

Isabel's mother set aside the broom, picked up a cloth from the end table and began dusting. "So you think you're a better parent now, is that it? You're just giving her what she wants without her learning that mistakes have consequences."

"You didn't trust her enough. She's smart. She's figuring it out without missing out on something that's important to her."

"Why it's so important, I don't know. She should be doing something better with her time."

"Just because you don't understand means it's okay to take it away from her?" Isabel felt her body tense. She took a deep breath and forced some calm into her voice. "You've had the same attitude about my art. You think I should be doing something else with my life."

246

Her mother moved the dust cloth over and over the same spot on the table. "She should be here where she gets a decent meal every night and there are rules about homework and a curfew. That's what she needs."

"Have you ever asked her what she needs?" Isabel wasn't just talking about Maggie anymore. "A decent meal can't make up for what you don't give her in respect and love and trust. Some interest in what she's doing and support." She'd wanted to say these things to her mother for so long, but didn't feel better once they were said. Her mother would probably never understand.

When her mother finally looked up, there was disapproval and disappointment lingering in her eyes, hardness in her voice. "I thought I raised you girls to respect and listen to your parents."

There was no reply that wouldn't make things worse, so Isabel headed toward the stairs before her mother could block the way again. She didn't want to talk anymore.

Her mother didn't try to stop her.

Isabel opened the door to her room and let childhood memories swarm around her. Like bees in a hive, they were noisy and all consuming. And because she was alone, she allowed the tears to come as she emptied her drawers before going to Maggie's old room to do the same.

Back on the street with a duffel bag over each shoulder, she called Michael to see if he was home. She needed a place where she didn't have to be strong or have all the answers. Walking up the drive to his house she remembered the first time she'd come to visit him. So nervous and unsuspecting of what he'd say. They'd come a long way in the last couple of months. She didn't know what the future held, but winning the art contest meant her career just might've been given a jump-start.

Michael opened the door before she had a chance to ring the bell. He grabbed the two heavy bags she held. "Hungry?"

"Very." She stepped past him with a grateful smile. Into a very different scene than the last time. There was some instrumental jazz playing, the tantalizing aroma of BBQ filled the air, and he'd added a little of his own style to the house in a few pieces of art and furniture.

"Whatever you're making smells heavenly."

"What do you want to drink? It's going to be another few minutes before it's ready." He wiped his hands on a towel when they got to the kitchen and opened the fridge. "We have to celebrate."

"I can celebrate with iced tea." Isabel washed her hands at the kitchen sink, took the glass he held out and wandered around looking at things. She studied the bold strokes in brilliant colors of one of Dowling's paintings. Someday her work would be hanging in someone's home, too.

"Sit down and relax, Isabel."

She forced herself to slide into the nearest chair and focus on how effortlessly he moved around the kitchen. "You obviously know what you're doing. I should hit you up for food more often."

He laughed and shook some seasoning on the potatoes. "Maybe you should wait 'til you taste it before handing out the praise." When the chicken, potatoes and salad were on the table, he sat down beside her. Clinking his glass to hers, he said, "To the first of many wins."

She sipped her tea and confessed: "I was a mess this morning. So nervous I thought I was going to be sick."

"Is that usual?" he asked. He reached over and pushed a lock of hair behind her ear.

She stilled at his touch. Oh boy, was that distracting or what? "I've never entered an art contest before. But, yeah, I'm always a bundle of nerves when Maggie has a cheerleading competition."

"Really? I wouldn't have guessed that about you." He picked up her fork and handed it to her. "You said you were hungry, so dig in."

She ate, allowing a comfortable silence to settle between them, and letting herself sink into the taste of the food. If she could draw flavor, what would it look like? She closed her eyes and pictured it. The room got silent, even the jazz had stopped. Her eyes flew open and her cheeks flushed when she saw his intent look. "Sorry, it's just that I could see the taste of this in my mind." She reached for a napkin.

He cleared his throat. "Don't be sorry. That look on your face was a better compliment than words." He took another bite, never taking his eyes off her. "You can really do that?"

She shrugged, suddenly self-conscious. She couldn't tell him about Joy and how since that day in the garden at Hearst Castle her sight had metamorphosed practically overnight. She was so tempted to come out with the whole thing, the cave and The Graces that she got up from the table in a hurry and offered to clean up.

Her movements were those of a practiced waitress as she cleared dirty dishes, wiped counters and filled the sink with soapy water.

"What happened, Isabel?"

She searched for a sponge and started in on the pans. "I went home today. Talked with my mom. Tried to, anyway."

"Ah. I thought maybe it was something like that."

"Really? And since you figured that out you probably know how it ended."

"Let me guess. She didn't hear a word you said. You're at an impasse and probably always will be."

"Know it all," Isabel teased, and rinsed the final dish before setting it in the drainer.

She studied his lean length and graceful walk as she followed him into the living room. She wanted to draw him. Again. Like this, with him looking at her over his shoulder.

"Have you ever drawn me?" he asked.

How did he always seem to know what she was thinking?

"Sure," she answered as casually as she could.

"I've never posed for you, so you do it from memory?"

"It's hard to explain, but sometimes when I draw I don't think, my hand just works on its own."

He put a new CD on and turned it low.

"Before I studied technique with Dowling and others, drawing was…" She hated when she didn't have the right words.

"Instinctual?"

She laughed at the expectant look on his face. "Yeah, I guess that's it. Instinct." She sat on the sofa, toed off her tennis shoes, and curled up in the corner with one of the pillows. "Now I guess it's a little of both. Technique I've learned and instinct."

"Your winning piece was stunning." He sat close, but on the edge of the sofa. Blocking her in.

A small familiar knot of dread formed at his words. She hadn't shown it to him. "How do you know?"

"I was in Brian's office the day all the submissions were brought in." He raised a brow. "Is there a problem with that, Isabel?"

"Yes!" she said, trying to get up.

He put a hand on her arm. "Why?"

"I don't like to think that I won on anything other than my own merit." She pushed at him again and he moved so she could stand up and go to the front window, trying to get her emotions under control. She really didn't want to fight with Michael. She'd come here to feel better, not worse.

"Why would you think otherwise?" He came up behind her, put his arms around her.

She thought about pushing away again but didn't because it felt so good. "You've never talked with Dowling about me or my work?"

"Of course we have." He held tight. "But as you wrote about in that article of yours, Brian's got a mind of his own. I couldn't influence him when it comes to art even if I tried."

She breathed easier but not for long. He turned her around and kissed her full on, hard and demanding. Pulling back, he glared at her. "Don't doubt me."

"Okay, I won't." Then she couldn't help herself. "Did you know who the winners were before I did?"

Cupping her cheeks with both palms, he whispered, "No." And kissed her again, softly this time, his lips as persuasive as his words.

When he pulled her into a hug, she held on until the tension eased from both of them. What a rollercoaster her emotions had been on all day. She felt drained and exhilarated at the same time. What she needed was her usual distraction of pencil on paper.

"Would you draw me now? I don't want you to have only drawings of me from memory."

"Sure. Sit over there." Isabel pointed to the armchair next to the bookshelves and got her bag from the floor by the front door. Pulling out one of her sketchpads and a pencil, she studied the direction of the light coming in from the window, seeing the angle she wanted to draw.

Fifteen minutes later, only details in the background were left to complete. "I'm done with you if you want to move." She put the work aside and stretched her arms and rolled her shoulders to loosen a knot she felt forming at the base of her neck.

"I'll get us more tea." Michael went to the kitchen.

Like a bolt of lightning, exhaustion hit Isabel. Had her lying back on the sofa, yawning, and closing her eyes. She heard Michael opening the fridge, pouring the tea into glasses. Then a hand touched her.

It wasn't Michael's.

Joy was tugging on her arm.

"Wait!" she whispered. "Why are you here? Where are we going?" The last thing she saw of the living room was the sketch she'd just done.

Joy was smiling, her diaphanous gown in a mix of blues and greens glimmering in light that was rapidly fading. She led Isabel from the living room, out the front door, into a room of a completely different sort. An artist's space, with sculptor's tools covering one table along the wall and huge pieces of stone in various stages of progress scattered around.

Lit candles were everywhere, the scent of wax mixing with the sound of far-off voices, laughter and violins. Isabel didn't know exactly where they were but taking it all in at a glance, she knew it wasn't the present, but a long ago past.

She wandered by a few unfinished pieces, and some small tables with drawings and half-empty glasses. Joy moved through an archway out of sight. Even though she wanted to stay and explore more here, Isabel didn't want to be left behind, so she followed.

She halted abruptly at the sight of the statue of The Graces surrounded by three men. They were dressed from a past era, but Isabel didn't pay much attention to that. She was drawn to their faces. Suffused with awe, joy, and a sadness she didn't understand, they gazed at the three figures. It took a moment for it to register that they were speaking in Italian. And that they couldn't see her. The men were laughing and toasting with glasses of champagne when the rumble began.

Like at Hearst Castle and in her cave.

Beside her, Joy clasped her hand and the men and the room vanished.

It was daytime, in a garden. A woman sat on a wrought iron chair sipping tea from delicate china. The statue sat amid the topiary. Isabel took in the looming house that flanked her on three sides, the quiet except for birdsong, like she was watching a scene from a movie. Joy reached out and touched the woman's shoulder. Isabel had a moment to study her beautifully serene features before a man in a black uniform appeared escorting two other women.

Joy took Isabel's hand once more and the garden changed. The trees became palm, not alder or ash, the flowers were iris and morning glory not primrose or dogwood, the benches stone not iron. How she knew that, she couldn't explain. It was just there in her mind as she looked at The Graces to her left and the stone house on her right.

The swiftness of the changing scenes was so disorienting, her brain felt like it was on sensory overload. But if she saw with her artist's eye only, the one Joy had given her, maybe, just maybe, she wouldn't feel like she was going crazy. Trying to refocus, Isabel sensed an urgency in Joy that made it imperative she remember every detail.

Two men and one woman rounded the corner at a leisurely pace, deep in conversation. Isabel identified them at once from the pictures in the book Sara had given her. The tall blond man was the construction manager at the time Hearst Castle was almost finished. The other was a gardener from the look of his clothes. The woman was the designer and architect, Julia Morgan.

Julia was unwrapping a box, lifting out a necklace, smiling. Isabel could see the genuine affection they had for each other. The gardener stepped over to the statue of The Graces saying · something with a grand gesture and the other two moved beside him.

The images impressed themselves on her mind, a stamp of possession Isabel could do nothing to stop. She sensed the rumbling seconds before it began again.

Michael was whistling somewhere in the house, a sweet little tune that Isabel recognized but couldn't name. Sitting up, she grabbed her sketchpad without a moment's hesitation. The need to capture what she'd seen was a drug in her veins propelling her movements. Everything else, forgotten.

She went to each place again through her hand and what emerged on paper. The artist's workroom, the men's faces, the three lifting their glasses, the delicate china cup, the woman's tranquil features, her smile of pleasure at the arrival of her friends, the corner of Casa del Mar, the three admiring the statue.

Rubbing the last shadow in the final piece, a prickling awareness brought her back to the living room and the quiet presence of someone watching her. With a glance to the window, now dark, and the lamps lighting the room, she asked, "What time is it?"

"Seven."

That jarred her. "You're kidding." She set the charcoal pencil aside and dug through her bag for her cell. Yep. Three missed calls and five texts.

"You slept for about an hour, I think. The next time I looked, you were in a daze, a trance almost. You've been drawing for three hours." Michael pointed to the sketches scattered over the carpet as he sat beside her.

Isabel massaged her drawing hand absently, trying to think what to tell him. How could she explain? She hardly believed it herself, yet here on the floor was proof. The doorbell rang startling them both, but he didn't move to answer it. They just sat looking at each other.

"I had the most vivid dreams and when I woke up I had to get them on paper. Before I forgot anything."

"I've been studying them. They all involve this statue. The same figures in your winning drawing. Where did you see them?"

"At Hearst Castle."

He gathered a few of the drawings together on his way to the door. "I wonder why you dreamed about that."

"I dream about it a lot, actually." Which was true, but oh, there was so much more.

The bell rang again right as he opened the door. And the house came alive with female voices. Jessie, Sara and Maggie had come in search of her.

Michael gave her an apologetic look. "Jessie called you and I answered because it had rung so many times already. They were worried about you. So I told them to come over."

She introduced Michael to Jessie and Sara. Her sister hugged her and plopped down on the sofa, with a grin. Isabel wondered what she was thinking, because that kind of smile usually meant mischief. She probably recognized Michael as their former chaplain from her one year at Assumption as a freshman before he'd been reassigned. Sara went to admire one of Dowling's paintings while Jessie wandered the room asking Michael questions.

There was talk of ordering pizza for dinner and Isabel realized she was starving again. She quickly covered each drawing with a thin piece of tissue paper then slipped them into separate pages of her portfolio.

"When did you do those?" Sara asked softly from behind.

Isabel turned from the others and lowered her voice to match Sara's. "Wait 'til I tell you what happened. You're never gonna believe it."

Twenty-Six

Sara

Sara thought about lunch with her father as she drove along Foothill Boulevard. It hadn't gone as well as she'd hoped. He was understandably upset about how everything had played out. But it wasn't her fault, even though the sly slip of the chains up her legs had made her doubt that. She hadn't asked for anything but the truth. Why was that so difficult for her mother to deal with? Plus, she was still waiting to hear from Violet, which didn't help matters. Her father had also tried to reassure her that he had no serious health problem, but she still had her doubts.

Designated as the one to make a frozen yogurt stop on the way home, Sara pulled into the Pinkberry's parking lot, grabbed her wallet and went in.

"Sara!" A voice near the front counter called out. Leslie was walking toward her carrying a giant cup of chocolate frozen yogurt covered in gummy bears.

"Hey, there." Sara smiled at Leslie's look of anticipation.

"Have you ever had this? It's amazing." Setting the cup down on the counter, Leslie dug in with a plastic spoon and held out a bite. "C'mon, you gotta try it."

Sara looked around, self-consciousness. He legs tightened in anticipation of the chains.

"Open up," Leslie ordered, moving in close.

They still did not come.

Sara took an unsteady breath.

The spoon was there, so she did as she was told. Leslie wore some spicy vanilla scent, and the smell of it mixed with the velvety smoothness of the chocolate in her mouth. Sara felt a tingling rush through her and shivered, hoping Leslie would think it was the air-conditioned store and the yogurt.

As Sara chewed the nearly frozen gummies, Leslie waited with a smile, taking a few more bites. "Come sit with me," she invited, pulling her to the nearest chair. "Let's talk about what we're going to do tomorrow night."

Tomorrow night? Sara couldn't believe she'd forgotten about their date. As Leslie went to the counter for another spoon, Sara tried to think back to what they'd planned.

"You didn't remember, did you?" Leslie handed Sara a spoon and scooted in beside her. "The horrified look on your face spoke volumes. Besides you haven't called."

Sara blushed. Tried to think up a quick escape. Honesty came out instead. "I'm sorry. I usually don't forget a thing. But life has been a little crazy lately."

It all came out about Mario's funeral, Jessie's grief and unhappiness at Stone College, Isabel's family troubles, her own mother freaking out and how they all ended up living at Jessie's house.

"You win," Leslie said, taking the last bite of melting yogurt. "I thought my life was complicated but yours and your friends' trump it. By a long shot."

"How is yours complicated?" Sara asked. Her phone rang loudly in the now almost empty Pinkberry's. "Sorry, I'm expecting a call from my sister and I didn't want to miss it." She looked at the name on the screen. Maggie. Sheesh, the yogurt run she was supposed to have been on.

"Hey," she answered.

"Thank God we haven't lost you, too! I have my heart set on chocolate mint with Oreos on top."

"Sorry, I ran into a friend. I'll be there in fifteen."

Leslie reached over and grabbed her hand as she hung up. There was that tingling again. "There's gonna be a bunch a people there tomorrow night, so if you don't want to come I understand."

Was that the pressing of chains around her ankle?

She ignored it. "I do want to spend more time with you. I enjoyed this."

"So, if you show up around six, cool. If not, that's okay. Call me later and we'll make a date, just the two of us."

"I'd like that. Besides I need to hear about your complicated life." Sara watched Leslie throw her cup and spoon away then shook her head as Leslie held open the door for her. "I've gotta get some stuff to go."

"Okay. See ya," and with a little wave she was gone.

Sara made it back to Jessie's in a little over fifteen minutes. In the kitchen, she unpacked everything while Maggie and Isabel waited.

"I'll forgive you being late 'cause you got me an extra large." Maggie dug in with an enthusiasm that made Sara laugh.

"I know. It's like she's addicted to it," Isabel said, taking a spoonful from another one. "So, who'd you run into? Leslie?"

Sara nodded. Leslie had no problem talking, but she'd been a good listener, too. Sara had only ever confided that much in Quinn and lately Jessie and Isabel. It said a lot about Leslie. Or maybe she was just getting better at opening up.

"Where's Jessie?"

Isabel glanced toward the bedroom. "Said she was tired."

"She's so very sad," Maggie said. "You can see it in her eyes. Even when she tries to smile."

"It's only been a week since the funeral. I'm sure it's gonna take her a long while to get over this." Sara said softly. She noticed Isabel looked sad, too. And exhausted.

Sara's phone rang again.

"Think that's loud enough?" Maggie teased.

"I don't want to miss my sister when she calls." Sara grabbed her cell. "It's her."

Answer it.

With the thought came the unmistakable scent of roses.

Isabel nodded toward the door. "Go outside in the garden. It's a beautiful night."

Sara pushed the answer button and went into the yard. "Hello? Violet?"

"Yeah, it's me. Got back into town this morning."

It was the perfect opening for Sara to ask about her work. She discovered Violet owned a designer jewelry business and had showcased some pieces at a recent fashion show. As she talked, long forgotten memories swamped Sara. Her sister sounded just the way she remembered, in the lilt of her voice and the expressions she used. It felt right, this reconnecting. Or maybe she was being overly romantic, but she'd missed her sister for far too long.

Sara relaxed into the lawn chair, listening, and stared up at the stars dotting the sky. Despite Violet's break with their mother, she hadn't been able to escape the love of fashion and style they seemed to share. She wondered if her mother knew. Or cared.

Violet asked her about classes and her plans after college. Sara told her what the professor had said about her story and getting published.

"So have you re-worked it yet? Is it ready to send to literary magazines?"

"Not yet." It seemed like every time she sat down to work on it, she got interrupted.

"Sara?" A voice called from the drive.

"Yeah, it's me," she called out to Maribel, who pointed to the eye-popping heels she wore. Sara never would've guessed she'd get along so well with Jessie's stylish roommates. They'd all bonded over shoes the other night, and it appeared no matter what Jessie decided to do, she and Isabel were welcome to stay. "I'm talking with my sister. I'll be in soon."

Maribel waved and headed inside.

"Where are you?" Violet asked.

"Sorry about that. I guess you could say I've moved out of the house. I'm staying with some girlfriends."

There was a long pause.

Violet finally broke it. "Wow, that's a surprise."

"So you knew about my panic attacks then."

"Dad told me. He was always very worried about you."

"I really don't understand anything anymore." Sara sighed at the admission. She was so tired of trying to figure it out on her own.

"So I'm guessing they told you nothing."

"I know pieces. I just found out about Mom's one night stand and getting pregnant with you."

"Pretty amazing, huh."

"I never would've believed it about her. When did you find out?"

"When I was in first grade. I had to do a family tree project for school and Dad told me how he adopted me and that if I wanted to get to know my biological dad I could. I guess he lives in Denver. Or did then, anyway."

"Did you?"

"Nah. Dad felt like my real father all along."

There was another silence, as if her sister debated how much and what to say.

"You remember the night I left?" Violet asked softly.

"I watched from the stairs. You and Mom were yelling at each other, but I didn't know what the fight was about. Then you ran to your room and slammed the door. The last thing I remember was you hugging me before you left."

"I guess I should say sorry. Even if she hadn't kicked me out, I had to get away."

It was nice to hear an apology, but there were still so many questions. "What did you fight about?"

Another pause.

Then, "She found out I was dating a girl named April."

Sara's mind blanked in astonishment.

She'd never expected that answer, but as it began to sink in, there was almost an audible click as the pieces of the puzzle fell into place.

With it came a surge of anger and disappointment at her mother, melded together, coursing through her. "Why was that so terrible? I mean, surprising maybe, but why couldn't she deal with it?"

"It wasn't as acceptable as it is today. And the CEO of the company she works for is a conservative, traditional guy. Pretty religious, too. It was probably hard enough for her as a woman to make it as far as she did without him finding out she had a gay daughter."

Sara hadn't known any of that. "So she put her career first. I can't imagine an employer caring about something like that."

"There are a lot out there like him. Mostly I think Mom just wanted what she thought of as a normal family."

"You sound like you've accepted it all," Sara said, still in shock.

"Don't think too badly about Dad. He's not like Mom. He was okay with it and he came after me, tried to get me to work it out with her, but I just couldn't. It was all too hurtful and once I moved here, it became easier not to go back."

Sara's heart felt heavy, a sadness pressing down on her, bringing tears to her eyes. She wiped at them, focusing on the anger she felt instead. "And me?"

"I sent you some letters that later Dad admitted Mom never gave you. By then I guess your panic attacks had started and every time Dad brought it up, Mom refused to tell you, saying it wouldn't help. That it would only make it worse."

Sara took some deep breaths and reached into the pocket of her coat for her quartz. She'd done well without it tonight, but the comfort of it still helped a little.

Tell her.

The sweet smell of roses was almost overpowering.

Violet sighed. "So, you sound like you're okay with having a gay sister."

Say it.

"As long as you are okay with having a gay sister, too."

Sara held her breath. Waited.

Violet laughed, a light, tripping sound that went on and on and made Sara smile too. "Oh my god, what perfect irony. Mom kept us separated, yet we're alike in the one way she hated most."

Sara remember that terrible afternoon and her mother's plea, "Why is this happening again?" and finally understood it all now. "I have a lot more to tell you. Can we talk again? Soon?" Sara asked.

Violet promised to phone again in a few days. Ending the call, Sara realized her sister needed time to get used to having her in her life again. Maybe dredging up the past was as difficult for Violet as it was for Sara. She didn't want to push too hard.

The quiet midnight air was a balm Sara gratefully accepted. She took stock of the day, marveling at how she'd dealt with everything that had come up, big and small, without reverting to old behaviors. Oh, she'd wanted to a couple of times, but she hadn't. A tiny flutter of happiness came alive deep inside her.

When she went inside, Vampire Weekend's *Contra* album was playing. Maribel, Emily and Maggie were dancing recklessly in the living room. Isabel watched with a smile from the kitchen doorway. As soon as she saw Sara, Isabel looked toward Jessie's room. Sara nodded, knowing Isabel wanted to check on Jessie, make sure she was all right. After that, she talked with Maggie, Emily and Maribel about shoes and clothes. They were especially excited with the latest package her father had given her that afternoon. A Marc Jacob handbag her mother must've ordered before she'd found out her youngest daughter was gay. Just like her oldest daughter. Sara was still astonished by it all.

Finally, Maggie declared she had to get some sleep because the final rehearsal for her cheerleading competition was after school, and Emily and Maribel headed to their rooms too. Isabel reappeared, gave her sister a goodnight hug, and pulled Sara back into Jessie's room. The floor was littered with the drawings Sara had only gotten a glimpse of earlier at Michael's house.

"It's about time. I thought you guys would never stop talking."

Jessie pulled her earphones out and sat up. "I wanted to join you but Isabel needed company."

"Yes, yes, poor me. The only one who doesn't care about spiked versus wedged heels. I don't know how anyone wears them at all." Isabel lounged against the bed and gestured to the floor. "I've got more important things to deal with at the moment."

"Give Sara a break. She's enjoying herself." Jessie said, a little too sharply.

"I finally talked with my sister and had a lot of fun right now with yours," Sara said to Isabel, "so don't ruin it, okay?"

"Fine." Isabel threw up her hands in defense.

Sara tried to scowl, but couldn't pull it off. And couldn't be mad. Laughing, she asked, "Do you want to hear the big revelation, or not?"

She filled them in on the conversation with her sister and was secretly pleased to see their shock over Violet's disclosure. At least she wasn't the only one who hadn't seen it coming.

"No wonder your mom freaked the other night." Jessie said.

Sara sighed. "I know. But until she's willing to talk to me I can't really do much, can I?"

"Maybe she'll come around eventually," Isabel said.

"Yeah, right," Sara said in disbelief. "Just like she did with Violet? I don't think so."

That was met with silence, filled with a sadness Isabel probably understood considering her recent break with her own mother.

"Sara, take a look at Isabel's drawings and tell us what you see." Just like Jessie to turn the conversation when it was most needed.

"Start there," Isabel pointed to the one by the dresser, "and go right."

When Sara was bent over the last picture, Jessie suddenly rose to her knees. "There's one missing. It's been bothering me since I first took a look and I finally figured it out."

"What do you mean?" Isabel asked with a frown.

"It's so obvious I can't believe it we didn't see it," Jessie eyes lit up. "It's a history, right?" She quickly opened her bedside table drawer and dug through it. "Here's all the info you gave us, Sara, on the history of the statue." Jessie opened it and scanned the first page.

The sweet smell of gardenias permeated the air.

Sara grew flushed with a sudden excitement as she realized where Jessie was headed. Taking off her cardigan, she sat beside Jessie on the bed. "I get it. Wasn't the sculptor's name Canova?"

Isabel brought the first three pictures over. "Yes. So he's one of these three?"

They studied the one of the men toasting, the statue front and center. "If you drew their clothing accurately it could be him. He made the statue around 1815, something like that." Jessie glanced at Sara's notes again.

"There were two. The first one was given to Empress Josephine. Some duke commissioned a second one." Sara looked over Jessie's shoulder at the information, even though she remembered most of it.

"Our statue is the second one, made for the Duke of Bedford," Isabel said with certainty. "That night," she pointed to the picture, "was the unveiling. The presentation of the statue to the Duke."

"Is the Duke one of these three? Jessie asked.

"I don't think so. I overheard one of them say the Duke wanted to get things going. The other one said it was Canova's best work, something like that. My Italian is very rusty. And theirs was very formal."

Sara went with Isabel's train of thought. "Let's just say it's the second statue. Here's Canova and two others. They're friends and they come to admire the statue. Then what?"

"They raised their glasses in a toast. The floor shook and this loud rumbling started. From one moment to the next, I went…" Isabel bent to the floor and retrieved the woman in the garden, "here. It was so crazy and fast, it took me a minute to catch up."

Sara took it and examined it closely. "It's a traditional English garden. The details are amazing. Did you know there's a letter B etched in the stone above each window?"

"You're kidding. Let me see that."

Sara passed it to Jessie.

After a moment, she agreed. "Okay, so it's the second statue. B is for the Duke of Bedford." Jessie examined it at arm's length. "This woman must be the Duchess. She's beautiful. Content, peaceful."

Sara picked up another one. "And here, she's obviously happy at the arrival of two friends." Pointing to the Hearst garden scene, she said, "Then you went there?"

Isabel nodded. "It was the weirdest thing. I knew all the names of the plants and flowers in each garden."

"Wasn't there information on these three in our book on Hearst Castle?" Jessie pointed to Julia Morgan and the two men.

"There were many gardeners, you know, and even a couple of construction managers on site over the years. It could be any one of them. But there was one head gardener there for many years who was loyal until the end. And one manager who lasted for quite a while and did other projects for Hearst." Sara lightly traced Isabel's rendition of the famed architect. "Only Morgan was there through it all."

"Just seeing all her drawings and sketches in the exhibit and the Castle itself, you can tell how talented she was," Isabel flipped through some of the other sketches in one of her drawing pads as she talked. I was thinking earlier that even though I connected with Canova on some level, it is Morgan that really inspires me."

"You did get a glimpse of her that no one else has, Isabel. One more gift from The Graces," Jessie commented thoughtfully as she studied the last picture next to Sara.

"They were giving her something?" she asked Isabel.

"A necklace."

Sara peered more closely. "Wait a minute. See how it looks layered. Like three strands with something different at the end of each." The rose stone on the red ribbon around her neck grew warm.

Without warning, Jessie grabbed Sara's arm and even Isabel looked up quickly from her book.

"What is it?" Isabel asked.

"My sun pendant is vibrating against my skin." Jessie slowly pulled the yellow cord over her head and held up the necklace. "Look."

Sure enough Sara saw it trembling. She took off her own. "My rose is warm and almost glowing."

Isabel held hers up, the cool blue of the moon shimmering.

They looked at each other in shock.

"Do you think it's possible?" Sara whispered, awed and just a little afraid.

"Not only possible, but part of the puzzle, part of the whole that we need to figure out," Jessie answered.

"But if you think about it, it makes sense. They had to get our necklaces somewhere, right?" Isabel held up the drawing in one hand and the necklaces in the other.

"Do you know how crazy this all still sounds?" Jessie shook her head as if to clear it.

Write it.

The voice didn't faze Sara this time. If pressed, she wouldn't've been able to say whether it was her idea or Bloom's. She got her school bag and pulled out her new journal. "Tell me and I'll write it down, from the beginning again and describe everything. No detail is too small."

Jessie got back under the covers. "You know which one is missing, don't you?" she asked Isabel.

"If you're right..."

The image Isabel had drawn of the three of them with the Graces flashed through Sara's mind. It was the final piece of the story. And it was somewhere in the art building on campus in preparation for the winners' reception.

Isabel started her story once more, putting the sketches in order, telling everything she could remember.

Sara took Isabel's words and made them her own.

Twenty-Seven

Jessie

Questions haunted her sleep as Jessie tossed and turned. Her mind kept replaying the past couple of days and all they'd learned as if she'd missed something important that she needed to know. Her heart was like lead, her life turned upside down, and she hated it. Getting up, she slipped a sweatshirt over her camisole and let her fingers stroke the ribbon of Brilliance's gift. What should she do? She wished The Graces had given her some kind of answer because she didn't want to have to make a decision on her own. She wanted to go to San Francisco. She wanted to sing. But could she possibly do it without Mario? Did Phil really think she was as talented as Mario had?

She picked up her phone. Three a.m. Maybe she should take Tylenol P.M. to help her relax and sleep.

She quietly went to the kitchen and was opening the cabinet where she kept vitamins and pain relievers when Emily emerged from her room.

"Hey girl, what's up?" Emily wore a red, almost sheer robe with a matching teddy underneath, which meant her boyfriend had shown up.

Jessie looked toward the sofa where Maggie and Isabel slept and answered in a whisper, "Needed something to help me sleep. You?"

Emily's eyes flicked back to her closed door and she smiled. "Just having some fun. Hey, I got some weed if you want it. It'll relax you for sure."

It was tempting. "I'll pass. This should work." Jessie pulled out the small plastic bottle she'd been searching for. "Thanks again for letting them stay. Isabel paid me some rent money." She downed the pills with a cup of water.

Emily leaned against the counter. "If I'd had a friend in high school I could've lived with instead of my parents, I would've too."

"I didn't know it was that bad," Jessie said, surprised. "You never said anything. You could've stayed with me."

"Are you kidding? Your mom wouldn't have gone for it. It's okay. I made it." Emily looked over at the sofa. "They will, too."

"Yeah, they will. Hey, would you and Maribel be cool with Isabel and her sister staying for a few weeks in my room while I go out of town?"

Emily studied her with eyes that seldom had such a serious look. "Where are you going? San Francisco?"

"Yeah. Maybe."

"Which is it?"

"I'm still deciding."

"They're cool. So long as rent is paid, it's okay. Do what you gotta do. I'm sorry I didn't make it to the funeral. I'd used up all my sick days."

"It's okay. And thanks. I'll let you know what I decide." Jessie gave her a quick hug. "I think I need to sit outside for a while until the Tylenol kicks in."

She breathed in the damp night air as she made her way to the chairs in the garden. Shadows loomed large and the chilly stillness reminded her of the many nights Mario had taken her riding. She had a feeling there would always be something that reminded her of him no matter where she went or what she did. Just like her father. So why hide then? Which is what she'd be doing if she stayed here. Shouldn't she go and see what happened? Maybe if she talked to Phil, she'd be forced to decide one way or another.

She pressed his number and wasn't surprised when he answered sounding fully awake. "Where are you?"

"In bed. You?"

"I mean in San Francisco or home?"

"San Francisco is my home. I went home and now I'm back in Boulder. My mom's having health issues."

"Can you meet me before you leave?"

"Why? I didn't think you liked my company." He was teasing her. Or maybe not.

"To finish our conversation."

"I'm going to see a band at Ghost Hunters, a club in Denver tomorrow night before I catch a red-eye out. You know it?"

"Yeah, I've been there. At nine?"

"That'll work."

Crawling back into bed beside Sara, glad she didn't have to be alone, Jessie felt sleep finally come.

She couldn't say no to Nana's invitation to dinner the next day, so she put on her brave face and accepted the comfort her family tried to give. With her aunt and uncle and cousins it was easy enough to let the chatter and gossip flow around her without really participating. When Jessie excused herself to use the bathroom she found Nana waiting for her when she came out. No matter how much she tried to fool her mother, Jessie had never been able to get away with fooling Nana.

"What have you decided?" Nana put a hand on her shoulder to keep her from turning away.

Jessie saw understanding in Nana's eyes and sighed. "I ... don't know."

"After I heard the recording I was pretty sure Mario asked you to move there with him. But now things have changed, haven't they?"

Jessie leaned into Nana's arms. "What is the right thing to do? I wish somebody would just tell me."

"Only you know that," Nana whispered in her ear. "But if you do go and it doesn't turn out right, we'll still be here for you." Nana gave her a kiss on the cheek.

"If I go, Mom's gonna hate it. And me. And I'll hate myself for letting her down. College has been her dream for me."

"You underestimate your mother's love. If you go, I'll work on her and she'll come around."

"Really?"

"We want you to be happy, that's all."

"I know." Jessie moved away with one final squeeze. "I've gotta go meet Phil."

"You should talk to your mom after you decide. It'll be worse if you don't."

"I will. I promise. Say goodbye to everyone for me?"

"Of course."

The drive to Denver felt like the calm before the storm. As much as the quiet of the foothills called to her, so did the city lights sitting on the dark horizon. She got lucky and found a parking space without a problem. After paying the cover charge, it took a moment for her eyes to adjust to the dark interior of the club. She walked slowly, putting her ID back into her slim purse, and looked around at the changes. She hadn't been here in a while and new management had made improvements. Everything was black except for murals from ceiling to floor of ghostlike dancers on one wall and a single strip of its mirror image on the opposite wall. Jessie noticed a few draped alcoves with occupied booths as she passed into the central part of the club. The stage was empty, but set up for a band. The dance floor was half-full of young people moving slowly to piped-in music. The mirrors along one wall reflected her short black dress with its long sleeves and steep dip in the front and back as she scanned the crowd for Phil.

She got a bottle of water and found a stool so she could sit with her back against the wall. She felt a touch at her elbow.

"You do what I do." Phil's voice, as much as his words, made Jessie raise her brows.

"What's that?"

"Sit in the back with a view of the whole place."

Jessie shrugged. "I thought we were here to talk."

Phil looked at his watch. "The band starts in twenty. Plenty of time." He grabbed her hand and with it her attention.

Her insides trembled when he looked at her the way he did. This was going to be harder than she expected. If she said yes, would he think she'd decided to go because of him or for herself? Did it matter?

She looked away to regain some composure. Many of the women standing around were scoping Phil out, even though his attention was all on her. He was good looking, his casual silk shirt, nice pants and confident ease had captured their attention. Loneliness swept her up and held her in a tight grip.

"I thought if I agreed to see you and the moment came for me to decide, I'd know what the right answer was."

Phil smiled, probably the first she'd seen since he'd come back. "You know what I think you should do, but I can't make the decision for you."

She blew out the breath she'd been holding. "That seems to be the message I'm supposed to get tonight."

"Let's imagine you've just said yes." He studied her for a minute. "I never canceled the gigs I set up. Wanna do them?"

Jessie moved her bottle in a slow circle on the table. "Okay, as long as the band plays with me."

"I think they're up for it."

"I'd like to live in Mario's place if I can."

"Really? Caryn offered you her second bedroom."

"Tell her thanks, but I'd like to stay at Mario's if Mitch doesn't mind. Or his girlfriend." She took a sip of water. "Although I don't know how I'll pay rent. My grandmother might be able to help me out but I won't be able to touch the money my dad put away for me 'cause it has to be for college."

They watched the band come on stage and test the equipment. Phil turned Jessie's hand over, and began to lightly caress her fingertips with his. The gesture of intimacy startled her but she couldn't pull away.

"So how does that feel? What you just imagined - does it feel right?"

Yes. But she really didn't know if she could do it, trusted herself to do it right, without Mario. She hoped her eyes didn't show the bleakness she felt inside.

"You're trying too hard. I don't know, maybe I'm pushing you when you're not ready. It's just so obvious to me."

"My voice is untrained. I've never studied music. How do I know I'm any good?"

"It doesn't need much. You can study there too, if you want." He watched her intently. "Remember that conversation we had about Mario? New Year's Eve?"

Jessie nodded.

"You said there was something about him that drew the eye. Well, you've got it too." Jessie's heart stumbled at his words. It should be Mario standing here making deals with Phil, not her. She got off the stool and gently slid her hand from his. Sounds of guitars tuning blasted around them.

"You leaving? I'll walk you out."

"You'll lose the table," she warned.

He just smiled and followed. She stopped at the ladies' room and he waited. Outside, the night was thick with sounds of sirens and traffic and partygoers entering the club. They walked without speaking, tension between them. Her heels clicked on the sidewalk, just like they had the day on the stone floor in church.

She opened her car door and tossed her purse onto the passenger seat, the silence stretching. The tension in the air pulled tighter. She couldn't read his expression as he reached over and cupped his hands around her face.

"Phil..." she started to say.

"Shhh. Just let me breathe you in."

How was she supposed to respond when he said things like that? She held still and didn't pull back, allowing herself to take his warmth, knowing he was suffering too. But the longer they stood like that, the more she noticed. He vibrated with an energy she was desperate for, had been missing since the moment she'd learned of Mario's death.

And he was just as aroused as she was.

Then they were in the back seat of her car, she was on his lap, the windows were steaming up and she couldn't stop her hands or her mouth from devouring him. When she was out of breath she leaned back so he could lift her leg to straddle him. His hands kept up a dance upon her bare legs, his face intent.

This was such a bad idea.

But his hands felt so good and they knew just what to do. Her body was moving and she didn't think she could stop. She reached down and unfastened his pants.

His grip tightened, stopping her. Unspoken questions hovered in the air.

Without warning, the thick foliage of the maze and its music shimmered between them.

No, not now.

Uncaring what might happen, she reached through the branches, grabbed his shoulders in a grip so harsh he sucked in a breath. She was going to push the maze away through sheer force of will.

His ragged breath and the way his gaze pierced her, hacked away at the wall of hedges like a machete. "Where did you go just now, Jessie?"

"What do you mean?" Damn, it came at the worst possible moments.

"Explain it to me, Jess. Try me."

But she couldn't. It was too much to put into words.

The bass beat thumped out its rhythm from the direction of the club. "The band. Don't you have to go in?"

"No." He touched her cheeks, brushed at tears she couldn't stop from sliding down.

Jessie shuddered, flooded with guilt and want and need all mixed together. She'd lost control and now the confusing things she felt about Phil had become even worse. God, what a mess.

Abruptly she got off his lap and with barely controlled movements straightened her clothing. "You have a flight to catch." She opened the door and climbed out, waited for him to get himself together while she took some deep breaths.

"Jessie..." Phil shut the car door and turned to her but she was already in the driver's seat, starting the engine.

"Don't say anything. Please."

"Ignoring what just happened is not gonna help."

She let the car idle for a minute, then put it into drive. "When I decide I'll let you know."

"I think you already have." She heard exasperation. "But fine, take more time if you need to."

She took a different route home, one that took her through Golden and alongside the mountains as she headed back to Boulder. It was longer, but she needed the time to get things sorted out in her head. Meeting Phil had been a mistake, meeting him alone a disaster of gigantic proportions. She tried to think back to all the times senior year they'd hung out as Mario's best friend and girlfriend. She couldn't recall anything out of the ordinary. She was sure the whole electricity thing started that night at the club when she'd gone to the maze in the middle of the dance floor and Phil had later stepped in to help her.

By the time she pulled up to the house it was eleven-thirty and she knew when she went in there'd be five females for company. Thank God she wouldn't have to be alone, something she'd only recently begun to dread. Playing with her pendant as she walked up the drive, Jessie wished Brilliance weren't so silent.

Where was she when Jessie really needed her?

Twenty-Eight

Isabel

The reception was exactly what Isabel imagined after hearing all the student gossip about the previous year's event. A chamber group played in the corner of the hall and waiters hovered with trays of hors d'oeuvres. Most everyone was dressed in formal eveningwear. The winning paintings, sculptures and drawings were showcased around the large room.

She was so out of her element. This kind of fancy had never been her thing but she intended to enjoy every minute of it. With Maggie along as her guest, she didn't doubt they would. She watched her sister flirt with a tall blond at the drink table and envied her just a little how easily she hit it off with people.

Sara and Jessie had insisted on taking her shopping that morning. The long golden brown silk skirt and long-sleeved blouse kind of shimmered in the light and she actually felt comfortable in them. Maggie had put her hair up and applied a little makeup in the ladies restroom earlier. Isabel knew she looked better than good, and somehow that helped.

She wandered around, studying people and the art. A thrill went through her as she found "The Graces" displayed next to a blue ribbon. In a simple black mat and silver frame, with a spotlight shining down, it caught the eye. Just standing in front of it, watching other people's reactions to it, listening to their comments as they studied it, made her a little lightheaded. She almost jumped when there was a tap on her shoulder.   "Mr. and Mrs. Caldwell. What a surprise."

"Hello, Isabel, and congratulations." Sara's dad gave her a hug.

"You look wonderful, Isabel," Mrs. Caldwell bent over and kissed her cheek before turning to the pieces on the wall. "The art committee chose well. Your work is exceptional."

"Thank you." She looked at Sara's mother, the differences so apparent between mother and daughter in voice and manners. She'd only met the woman once. Usually whenever they were at Sara's house, she wasn't around. "I didn't realize you were going to be here."

"We've been sponsors for a number of years now," Mrs. Caldwell explained.

Isabel smiled and sipped a drink. She introduced Maggie to Sara's parents when she joined them a few minutes later and they chatted about the pieces they liked.

As the chamber music drifted around her, Isabel heard the talk float by, and the walls turned to stone. She stood alone and apart, watching and waiting. Far off she could make out the sound of rock crumbling. The scent of water and wet sand came to her. Then she was back in the hall and Maggie was looking at her strangely. Something made her turn sharply toward the entrance.

"What is it?" Mr. Caldwell asked. He turned and then smiled. "Oh, good. I was hoping she'd come." He nodded at the open doors.

Jessie and Sara walked in. When Sara spotted Isabel and Maggie with her parents, she hesitated, her smile fading before she followed Jessie through the crowd.

"Excuse me." Sara's mom turned and headed to the ladies room. Which was okay. She didn't think Sara wanted to talk to her mother anyway.

Jessie grasped Isabel's left hand, Sara her right, as they surveyed each other.

Jessie whistled lightly. "I knew that outfit would turn some heads tonight."

"It's perfect on you, Isa," Sara said, looking her up and down. "Sorry we're a little late. There was a car accident and by the time I got home from class I didn't have a lot of time to change."

"It's okay. Come on." Isabel pulled them along, signaling Maggie to join them. "Excuse us, Mr. Caldwell, but we have some catching up to do."

Jessie and Sara seemed as proud as she was at the sight of her drawing framed and hanging on the wall, since they took credit for getting her to enter the contest. After they finished wandering the room and examining the winning entries, her friend Sylvia and another art student and their guests joined them. Maggie had somehow saved a table with enough chairs in one corner of the room.

"Hey, Professor Dowling finally showed up," Sylvia said with a slight push on Isabel's arm.

"I'll introduce you and you can tell me what you think of him," Isabel whispered to Sara and Jessie as she rubbed one of her aching heels.

When she saw Dowling at the open doorway, her heart did a flip. Michael was with him. He was wearing a tux, like most of the men present, but her breath caught at the purely physical effect he had on her.

They hadn't talked about it but it didn't surprise her that he'd come. It's what he'd meant when he told her not to doubt him. She just didn't want any of the students to know she was dating Dowling's best friend. That would so not look good. Gossip would spread like fire, and she'd be the one to get burned.

They came into the room and paused to stop and talk with all the winners. Although Michael took part in the conversation, his attention was clearly in their direction.

"Isabel, you look even more stunning than your art piece tonight." Dowling commented when he approached their table.

She stood, and after a pause, found her voice. "Thank you, professor. It's a wonderful event."

She introduced Jessie, Sara and the others. They all shook his hand before Dowling introduced Michael. Mercifully, Jessie, Sara and Maggie, too, followed her lead without saying anything to indicate they'd already met. Isabel watched, a little wary. Michael's focus went to her sister, who smiled brilliantly at him. Maggie looked beautiful in a short red dress and much older than her eighteen years. Sara, dressed in an aqua-colored silk skirt and top, and Jessie in a black sleeveless cocktail dress and stiletto heels, gave him warm smiles, too.

"Isabel, would you mind? There are a few other people I want to introduce you to." Brian Dowling smiled with confidence. "Don't worry, we won't keep her long." He took Isabel's arm.

She walked, dazed, through the next thirty minutes and tried to remember the names of everyone she met. Two board trustees, members of the city's chamber of commerce and even a city councilwoman. A small group gathered in front of her drawing. She was aware of Michael's presence in the back listening to her talk about the inspiration for her drawing.

An hour later when the party wound down, Isabel walked with Jessie, Sara and Maggie out into a night that had turned windy with black rain clouds hovering overhead. She was immune to all of it. She could barely believe the night had been such a success as she listened to Maggie laughing with Sara and Jessie over a story the college president had told earlier. She should've been exhausted. Instead, she felt a mix of adrenaline, hope and fear.

"There was one point, early on in the evening, when I didn't think I could pull it off. But I did." She linked her arm through Maggie's and smiled. "I'm so glad you were here with me."

"This was so much fun. I can't wait to go to college," Maggie exclaimed.

"Where have you applied?" Sara asked.

"Stone, of course. And the two big state universities."

"She got early acceptance letters from both," Isabel told them, "but she's holding out for Stone."

"I wonder why you haven't heard yet." Sara pulled a shawl around her shoulders with a shiver.

"Isabel! Ladies!" Michael's voice called out as he came from a side entrance and joined them on the well-lit walkway. "May I walk you all to your cars?"

"Sure," Jessie answered, including him easily into their group. One night of pizza and he'd won them over. Or maybe it was the obvious way he took care with her. Of her. She still was having a hard time getting used to it.

Maggie chatted with him about how Boulder had changed and they debated the best coffee places. When they got to Jessie's car, Isabel turned and met his gaze.

But instead of asking her, he spoke to Jessie, Sara and Maggie. "I'd like to take Isabel home, if that's all right."

"Of course," Jessie answered with a laugh.

"See you at home later," Maggie said, getting in the back seat.

"Don't wait up," Isabel said, sternly. "You have another big day tomorrow."

"I don't think any of us will be up for long. Good night," Sara said and got in the front.

After they'd driven away, Michael held out his hand. Isabel couldn't explain her hesitation. They were almost the last to leave the reception, the parking lot was empty and there was no one around.

"Walk with me. My car's on the street."

Isabel gave in, slid her hand in his and fell into step beside him.

"You work tomorrow?"

"Nope. The final round of Maggie's cheerleading competition is upon us."

"You speak like you're a team, you and your sister."

Isabel realized he was right. "We are."

"You were a big success tonight." Michael took off his coat and put it over her shoulders. "Your drawing, your story, all of it."

"I was so afraid I wouldn't be able to find the right words to say."

"But you did. Everyone was quite taken with your vision of the statue."

The wind was dying down, a rustle through the trees the only sound.

She felt there had been enough talk about her, so shifted her gaze to him. "How was your day?"

He smiled. "Good. Full."

"Of what?"

"Meeting people, talking about projects."

The warmth of the Graces' gift against her skin dislodged something inside her. Then instead of sky, she saw stone, and the clouds became brilliantly painted scenes. She pulled herself back to him with difficulty. "The other night, Sara finally admitted to herself and to Jess and I that she's gay. But she was so afraid to say it. So we told her we were afraid of things, too."

"What did you say you were afraid of?"

Now that she'd begun the conversation she didn't know if she wanted to continue. She hated talking about feelings as much as she hated showing them.

"I'm not going to even try to guess," he added, "because you always surprise me."

That made her laugh. So it was easier to just say it and be done with it. "Having a future with you."

They kept on walking and Isabel breathed deeper with every step, letting his presence calm her. That was one of the reasons she'd been drawn to him from the very beginning. He never judged, always seemed to understand what she was going through.

"Are you ever afraid?" she asked.

"Yes."

"Of what?"

He sighed. "Of the same thing you are." His grip on her hand tightened. "But it's okay to be scared as long as we don't let it keep us from trying."

"I guess I'm still getting used to..." She stopped because she didn't know what to call it.

"Having others in your life who care about you and what you're doing?"

A sudden burst of wind shook the trees around them, carrying away stray leaves.

"What about your father?" he asked. "Your brothers and sisters?"

"They care. In their own way. But I don't remember ever feeling a sense of connection. Like I belonged in my own family. Except for Maggie." Isabel stopped, leaned over and slipped off one shoe, then the other.

"And now you've found friends who do," he added. "It was obvious tonight. You all made a formidable presence at that table."

Isabel smiled. He was right about Jessie and Sara. They were the ones who'd pushed her to show her work, to enter the contest.

"I can be, too, if you'll let me." At his car, he leaned against the passenger door and pulled her against him. "You've come to me when you've been upset and didn't know what to do. What about the good times, like tonight?"

"I knew you were coming with Dowling."

"I understand you're worried about how it might look, especially to the other students. But believe me when I say that your talent is obvious and whatever happens will be because of that, not because of my connection to Dowling."

Isabel figured if he said that a few more times she just might start to believe it. She felt her heart accelerate as she shifted closer so their bodies were aligned. "I feel like I'm about to jump off a cliff."

He held her gaze, and moved in. His kiss was sweet, familiar, and filled her, pushed her in ways she hadn't expected. Or imagined.

A throat cleared behind them.

She was so startled her first instinct was to pull quickly away. But Michael held her to a slow easing from him that locked their gazes for a moment before they turned. What a moment for Dowling to show up.

He was smiling. "We did drive here together, Michael. You should've told me you had other plans and I would've found a ride."

Isabel glanced at Michael's profile and saw him grinning, while at the same time she hoped her own face showed no signs of embarrassment.

Spearing her with his gaze, Dowling said, "I have some great news. You received a couple of offers on your winning piece. The highest from one of the college's trustees."

Isabel blinked, trying to catch up with the turn in conversation. Stunned, she thought about some of the people Dowling had introduced her to earlier, trying to imagine them displaying her drawing in their home. She couldn't. She didn't know where The Graces belonged. She'd never imagined letting any of her pieces go.

"That's wonderful," Michael was saying. "How much did Mrs. Thornton offer?"

"You were paying attention to all the introductions after all. Five hundred," Dowling replied.

"You've got to be kidding," Isabel blurted out.

Dowling raised a brow. "Don't you think it's worth it?"

"I don't know. I've never thought about putting a monetary value on my drawings. I draw for many reasons but money isn't one of them."

Michael held her against him but said nothing.

With a sweeping gesture toward the almost sleeping city, Dowling continued: "Anyone can create art. But you came into the program to be an artist. To make it your life, to make a living from it. Didn't you?"

Isabel stepped away from Michael, conscious of the cold of the sidewalk on her bare feet. She wasn't ready to sell her work. Was she? Suddenly faced with the decision, she discovered she was more attached to her drawings than she'd thought. Giving one as a gift was one thing, but taking money for one? Deep down she knew Dowling was right, yet was she ready to do it?

She could feel both men studying her every move, but wasn't going to be intimidated by it. She'd learned a few things growing up in a house full of boys. Raising her eyes, she squared her shoulders. "Honestly, I hadn't thought that far ahead. I guess I'll have to now."

Dowling crossed his arms and flicked a glance at Michael. "Well, it's time to take the next step. It will secure your place as a serious, mature artist in the community if you take Mrs. Thornton's offer."

When she didn't respond, he continued, "Look, Michael told me about your three-hour drawing spree the other night."

Michael didn't appear sorry even though he knew it was a sensitive subject with her. "I simply told him you'd done more drawings featuring the same statue in your winning piece. How many in total? Twelve?"

Isabel's heart thundered with the thought of something she hadn't considered. What would happen if Joy no longer came to her? No longer gifted her with this sight that allowed her to draw how she'd never drawn before? She fingered her pendant with something close to despair.

Dowling's voice sounded far off in the distance. "I'd like to see them. I'm sure Mrs. Thornton would, too. She reminisced about seeing the statue at Hearst Castle as a young woman for quite a while tonight."

Isabel rubbed her aching temples. Exhaustion was taking its toll. She took a step toward Michael and found herself at a hollow entrance of a giant cave. She knew it was hers by the distinct smell of musty water and the rough edges of stone in front of her. Frowning, she ran a hand over the cold rock that arched over her head and crumbled lightly beneath her fingers. A still pool lay beyond the path that led outside, its water less placid as it went farther out to sea. Green meadows stretched on either side of the water and the sky above was the palest cornflower blue she'd ever seen. Joy shone softly in resplendent gold where water and grass met.

This was so not happening to her, was it? In front of Dowling and Michael? It took her a moment of wishing it away and nothing changing to realize she couldn't do anything about it.

A quick peek inside the entrance showed the familiar wall of drawings that had crumbled the last time, now standing whole again. Beckoning her to come closer. She took a step. Images were appearing and disappearing, as the wall randomly lit up in different places. Turning to peer back outside she remembered Jessie's experience of the light and dark sides of her maze. Was the same thing happening here? To her right, the cave, to her left, Joy and beauty and open sky and land and water. Yet, wasn't there beauty in the cave, too?

Why had her two fragmentary worlds come together?

Back inside, the paints and brushes sat next to the wall swirling with color. The pictures were familiar, comfortable. Outside was the mystery of a beyond that she couldn't see.

Isabel had never asked for any of this to happen to her, it just had. Was the cave her past? Her solitary place where it was just her and her art? Yet, she'd started to make connections with others, hadn't she? The day she'd met Jessie and Sara was when all of these crazy experiences had begun. For each of them. And if it hadn't been for Jessie and Sara, she wouldn't have gone on the trip. They never would've seen the statue. She'd never have met Joy.

She scanned the short corridor that led to the art. It was dark and lifeless compared to the wall of light and color that lay within.

What was that at her feet? Something moved. Was moving. Growing, expanding. Thank God it wasn't insects or snakes, because she would've screamed.

It was the rock. Adding layer upon layer of itself from the floor up. And from the ceiling down. Taking minutes what should've taken thousands of years.

It was going to block the entrance, close her in.

Every curse word in Italian her brothers had taught her came to mind.

What was she going to do?

If she had to make a choice, she didn't want to stay in the cave. But her feet were rooted to the spot, unable to do what her heart wanted. Holding on to the stone sides of the opening as if she could keep it open by sheer force of will, she focused on the one who could help get her out.

All at once, sparkling in gold, Joy stood beside her. Moving past Isabel, she glided to one of the small pots, the one filled with Isabel's favorite color, a deep azure, and picked it up. Grasping Isabel, Joy pushed her through the narrow opening that was closing fast, out toward the grassy land and sapphire sea that waited beyond.

"What happened? She fainted?"

"I don't know. Isabel? Talk to me."

Male voices brought her back to the chilly air and the lean hard length of Michael's body, cradling hers, in the front passenger seat of his car.

His hand gentle, he pushed a strand of hair away from her face. "There she is," Michael said, as she opened her eyes.

She blinked a couple of times and struggled to sit. Michael loosened his hold but wouldn't let her get up completely. Dowling watched, leaning over the car door, concern on his face.

She glanced at Michael, discovered her breathing was steady, then focused on her professor. "Can you arrange a meeting with Mrs. Thornton. I'd like to talk with her before I sell her The Graces."

Twenty-Nine

Sara

The campus coffee shop mid-afternoon was almost empty. Two student workers behind the counter chatted as they cleaned, giving Sara no more notice than a glance. She headed for the back at a leisurely pace. She was the first one here, even though she was ten minutes late. Backpack on the floor, she settled into one of the armchairs and began to re-read her written version of Isabel's journey with Joy until Jessie and Isabel arrived a few minutes later.

"Hey there." Jessie slouched in the nearest chair and put her feet up on another.

Isabel carried three cups to the table, setting them down with practiced ease. "As if I haven't done enough of this today. Getting up was so hard this morning."

"You made enough noise to wake everyone," Jessie said.

"I tried to be quiet. Anyway, you won't have to worry about that much longer, will you?" Isabel sat down, opened the lid of one and dumped two packets of sugar in it.

"I'm still undecided about going." Jessie grabbed her coffee, adding cream and a bit of cinnamon.

Sara blew softly on her tea and watched Jessie with concern. She knew Jessie had already decided, so did Isabel. Why was it so hard for her to just admit it and go? Probably because it was going to be painful without Mario there. And who was she to talk? It had taken her years to admit to something she hadn't wanted to.

"Did you finish?" Isabel was eyeing the notebook on Sara's lap like it was chocolate cake and she wanted to devour it.

"Yeah. I guess you should read it first since you started this whole thing."

"Did not. It was Joy's doing." Isabel snatched the notebook and headed to the small sofa in the corner.

Sara tried to let the tea relax her, the soft hum of the workers chatting and the noise of a fan somewhere overhead, coming and going through her head. All the work due next week was crowding around in her brain, too. She was barely keeping up with her class load, which was a first. She wasn't one to procrastinate, but before there'd always been time to get things done. Now she understood why students struggled to finish a paper. There were distractions, and her life seemed full of them at the moment.

Sara dug into her purse and pulled out some lip gloss, applying it with two swift strokes. Looking at Jessie, she asked, "You making it to your classes?"

Jessie shook her head.

Sara slid her hand over Jessie's in a silent show of understanding. Still, she pushed herself to say what she'd been thinking. "I want to go back home and get some more of my clothes and things." She really couldn't live out of her duffle bag any longer.

"Of course. Don't worry, we'll find somewhere to put all your stuff. The front closet is big and we don't really use it."

Isabel was turning pages, a frown of concentration on her face.

"You read too slowly, Isa, c'mon, hurry up."

"Chill, would you." After a few seconds, Isabel held it out. "I'm done."

With a sigh, Jessie moved to the sofa next to her and Sara moved her stuff to a nearby chair and pulled it closer.

There were a few minutes of silence while Jessie read the story and Sara read a text from Leslie. They'd made plans to meet for dinner and movie next Friday night.

Jessie shut the journal. "It's great, Sara. You wove all those historical facts with what Isabel told you and made it come alive."

"Thanks. What'd you think, Isabel?"

"Better than I could've ever done."

Jessie slumped back onto the sofa. "I haven't seen the maze or Brilliance since the funeral. What's up with that?"

"It's only been a couple of weeks." Sara answered.

"What about you? Have you seen Bloom?"

Sara remembered how the aromas, the textures, the flavors at The Graces' dinner had heightened Sara's senses so that now every smell, every taste was larger than the previous one. But no, she hadn't seen Bloom either. "The chains come and go still. And so do the scents of different kinds of flowers. I hear Bloom's voice."

"Like when?" asked Isabel.

"At odd moments. Sometimes I smell lavender, or gardenia, or roses. Just briefly; there one second and gone the next. Half the time I think I'm imagining it."

Jessie raised her eyes to the ceiling in exasperation. "Well at least that's something. Tell us, Isabel. I know you've got something to say."

"I just think it's interesting how I dread it and you welcome it. Even after the scare in the car and night club and you fainting, you still want these things to continue."

A silence fell among them.

Her gaze distant, Jessie finally spoke in a whisper, as if she were talking to herself, just figuring it out.

"I was so bored, unhappy, trying to find my way, in what I see now was not the place for me." She shifted restlessly and looked from one to the other. "This is the right place for you two but not me."

"I think we all get that," Isabel said.

"So when the maze thing started and I met you, it was like something new came alive inside me, even though, yes, it was scary at times."

"You thrive on that sort of thing."

Jessie smiled at Sara. "Well, the maze kinda woke me up."

"So what you're saying is, you want answers. And you're not going to the maze or seeing Brilliance to get any," Isabel said, curling up into the corner of the couch.

Sara thought grief must be clouding Jessie's brain. "You say you haven't decided, Jess, but deep down, you have. It's what I've been trying to tell you. You want to go. You need to go."

"So just go, would you?" Isabel said lightly, trying for a smile.

Sara knew that was hard for Isabel to say. And they'd ganged up on Jessie enough. "All right, Isa, tell us the latest."

"It's about time," she said with a smile. "You know, I don't think that I'll be going back to the cave."

"Really? Why not?" Sara asked.

They listened to Isabel's story about the offer for her drawing, her reluctance to sell The Graces, how she'd stood at the entrance to the cave and how Joy led her out from it. Even Jessie was looking excited by the time she finished.

"You certainly hold out on exciting stuff longer than I ever could," Jessie exclaimed. "Five hundred is an awesome start, isn't it?"

"I'm having trouble believing it. I had to call Michael today on my break and ask if it was really true."

"Did he say anything more about you fainting?" Sara asked.

"Just that I was damn lucky he was standing right there to catch me."

Jessie cleared her throat. "In more ways than one."

That was so like the old Jessie it made Sara laugh in relief. Once she started so did the other two. It felt like forever since they'd laughed together.

"Oh, and on my way here I stopped to see Dowling who said Mrs. Thornton wants to see me tomorrow afternoon."

"Wow. You're really gonna do it. Good for you," Jessie gave Isabel a hug and started gathering up her things. "I'm going for a run. Need a ride, Isa?"

"Sure." Isabel got off the couch. "Where are you headed, Sara?"

"I really need to go home. Dad said I had some mail and stuff. The timings good 'cause they're having an associate of Mom's for drinks at five and I can sneak in and out without bothering anyone."

"That's probably better than trying to confront your mom like I did mine," Isabel agreed. "Nothing came of that."

"You're going to see her at some point," Jessie reminded Isabel. "Some family get-togethers and she'll thaw."

"You ready?" Isabel asked. At Jessie's nod, they slung their bags over their shoulders and made their way past the now-crowded tables.

Sara watched girls chatting and laughing nearby and finished her tea. She'd been trying not to think about her own family, focusing on Jessie and Isabel instead. Unlike Isabel, there were no family gatherings for Sara's mother to get used to things. And her situation was far different from Isabel's. Sara hadn't simply done something against her mother's wishes. It was a lot worse than that.

Her mother was ashamed of who she was.

She'd always been embarrassed by Sara's panic attacks and her daughter's need for therapy and medication, Sara knew. The only thing that kept Sara from feeling desperately hurt by it was her father's love and support. Dr. Bernstein had helped too.

But being gay wasn't something she could change with drugs or visits to a psychiatrist. It came down on her hard and heavy. The chains were there, too, in an instant, sleek and cool, adding to the feeling of restraint. Falling back on her old techniques, she did some deep breathing and visualizations for a couple of minutes until she could get up. Grabbing her bag and jacket, she headed out. She thought about calling Quinn just to say hi since they hadn't talked in a few days. And, well, because just the sound of his voice made her feel better.

But she didn't. Because she also thought it might make her cry.

When Sara got home, the house and yard were well-lit, a car she didn't recognize in the driveway. Perfect timing. She eased the back door open, listening carefully. The kitchen was clear. The mail sat in a pile on the counter next to the hors d'oeuvres tray Brenda had left ready and the liquor bottles for martinis. She sorted through the envelopes and grabbed what had her name on it. She moved quietly up the stairs, hearing her parents' voices in the living room. Once her door was closed, she left the lights off and collapsed on the bed.

Staring around in the dark she realized she missed her room. She longed for the place of delight it had been during her childhood and the quiet sanctuary it had become in the difficult times of her teenage years. But she wasn't either of those girls anymore. She needed something different now.

Tears rolled down her cheeks unchecked.

She smelled jasmine. It was sweet and strong, penetrating her battered senses. She touched her pendant. Bloom stood before her in a long flowing dress that reminded Sara of sky and ocean. When she sat down next to her the jasmine intensified. Their hands touched, palm to palm.

Eye to eye in the dark, the distant sounds of her parents' cocktail party under way, Bloom flicked her gaze to a small candle on her dresser, lighting it instantly. With one hand, Bloom took one of the buds she wore in her hair and tucked it behind Sara's ear.

Sara had to close her eyes for a minute. The allure of that gaze, the scent of blossoms was more than she could bear. She didn't deserve to have this happen to her, to know such beauty.

Without warning, the familiar metal chains suspended her above a bottomless space.

Sara turned side to side. Braved a glance beneath her and felt nausea come in waves. Vast and endless was the void she hung in.

Empty. Even the streaks of color that had been there before were gone.

She was alone.

Time ticked on, slower and slower until Sara thought she might scream. Yes, the chains were of her making. She got that. They were her fears, her anxiety, her nerves, keeping her wrapped up, solitary and needy.

But she didn't know how to make them go away and stay away for good.

Think, Sara, think.

All the little things she did to keep her panic attacks at bay she'd had to practice. Over and over again. What could she do to keep the chains away? They seemed to appear randomly. Well, that wasn't true she admitted. They mostly came when she encountered Leslie. When she was faced with a growing awareness of her sexuality. Just like her panic attacks in the past. The changes in her body and her feelings of attraction to other girls had terrified her.

The thought that she would be wrapped in chains forever struck terror in her heart.

Immediately the metal bindings tightened. The ones around her chest and arms pinched her sides, squeezing her, until she could only take in shallow breaths.

No, no, no, please.

She begged, although she didn't know who she was pleading with. The chains continued to restrict her, a little tighter with each passing minute.

Sara began to feel faint, her head dropping, blood draining into her face. Her vision faded in and out of focus. Slowly, colors penetrated the haze she seemed to be in. She realized then that Bloom sat in the middle of the chasm, smiling up at her. Her arms were spread wide, her flowing dress of multi-colored blossoms billowed around her, filling up the vacuum.

Thank you.

Sara watched Bloom's soft, warm, inviting arms get closer until she was within reach. Sara once thought she'd be broken if the chains unraveled and she fell. But she'd been wrong. All the panic, tears, and dread of the past seemed ancient and dim when Bloom was within reach.

A slender ivory finger traced the curve of Sara's cheek.

The chains slithered from her arms and legs like a snake releasing its prey.

Sara sunk into the comfort of soft flesh and silk petals. Then she touched the skin of her arms, smooth and sprinkled lightly with freckles, the imprint of chains swiftly fading. She breathed without struggle, and the calmness she felt wasn't only on the surface, it went as deep as her very soul. Something else was missing. Fear. Weary to the depths of her bones, she rested there, knowing that she was finally safe.

When she opened her eyes she was back in her room. Bloom set Sara on her feet, took her hand and led her to the closet door on which hung a full-length mirror.

"How did that get there?" Sara asked, surprised.

Bloom gently pushed Sara in front of it and settled both hands on top of her head. With an energy that felt almost alive, they began a slow descent over Sara's body.

Her eyes followed.

It was agonizing. And astonishing.

Her lips quivered. "This can't possibly be me."

When Bloom reached her ankles, she looked up at Sara and the bedroom disappeared. Sara was in a garden. A garden she'd seen and walked through. The garden at Hearst Castle.

It was dark on the hill, but Sara wasn't afraid. The air was warm, fragrant and fresh, the view evoking the same strong emotions as the first time she'd seen it. The porch lamp from Casa del Mar cast light on the red tile flagstones, the white marble bench, the Graces standing on their pedestal.

She turned her full attention to them and in a flash the reason for Bloom's earlier examination of her body became clear. From everything she'd read, this depiction of the three was considered by many throughout history to be the height of sensuality of the feminine body. Her own curves, her own fullness so resembled theirs that if she were to shed her clothes and join them she would fit right in.

Her inspection of the Graces became her own reflection once again in the mirror on her closet door. Her room was stifling in contrast to the clean air of La Cuesta Encantata.

She breathed deep anyway and gathered her courage. Knowing the chains would never return again, she shed her clothes piece by piece, her eyes never leaving the mirror. She allowed herself the privilege of a lover's hand as she got to know her body - no longer a stranger's.

Thirty

Jessie

The bright beam of the flashlight narrowed the path to what lay directly in front of them. Isabel kept it steady but Jessie was familiar with the uneven patches in the dirt road. The small animals skittering around in the dark had Sara clutching Isabel's arm while trying to carry the blankets. Jessie didn't know why her heart beat so fiercely, why her sense of sight and hearing grew with every rustle of pine and oak until they felt a part of her.

None of them spoke, preferring to breathe deeply of the night air. It was enough that they were together.

Jessie pushed away the thought that they might never do this again. She could hear Sara and Isabel's inhale and exhale sharpen as their steps up to the monument of rocks fell into sync with hers. Jessie began the ritual of setting up the small clearing. She put down the bag of Chinese take-out, grabbed the blanket Sara held and laid it in their usual spot. Isabel set the lantern at the edge, her slim fingers moving without hesitation. In jeans, a hoodie and Converse sneakers, Isabel appeared happier than Jessie ever remembered seeing her. One hand brushed back hair that had come loose from her ponytail and fallen into her face, as the other adjusted the wick.

Sara bent slowly to her knees, her black yoga sweats and zippered sweatshirt blending with the night. She placed a napkin and pair of chopsticks next to each paper plate with the same care one would set a table with fancy china.

Their movements were serene and graceful in the midnight blue of the evening mountain. Jessie took all of it in, her hunger clutching the image like a treasured prize.

Isabel set the lantern in the midst of all the little boxes, their flaps open, steam drifting up. The flame was central and steady, Jessie thought, like this place and the three of them. Jessie had seen the half dozen drawings Isabel had done of their special site, all dark shadows mixing faces and trees, rocks and river. Like tonight. Incredible, really, how Isabel could bring something alive on paper.

Jessie focused on the treetops where two birds calling to each other suddenly took flight. She shivered. Every movement felt weighted, gradually slowing the world to precise seconds. Her usual confidence wavered. It seemed to be happening a lot lately. The smell of fried rice brought her attention back. When she looked down, her plate was full. Digging deep to find some calm, she picked up her chopsticks. A few bites was all she could take.

They talked, tentative at first, before slipping into their easy rhythm. When Jessie raised the subject of their afternoon visit to Mrs. Thornton, Sara brought out three small bottles of champagne to toast Isabel's success.

"It's unbelievable how much money this woman has to spend on art," Isabel said, traces of awe in her voice.

"So you shouldn't feel guilty about the price you put on each piece," Jessie advised, taking a sip. The bubbly liquid burned her throat a little. Or was that the backed up tears that threatened to unleash? Why now when she needed to be strong?

Sara frowned. "What do you mean each piece?"

"She likes them all. She talked about doing a showing in her home of the whole series," Jessie answered.

"But that's wonderful!" Sara exclaimed. "Aren't you excited?"

Isabel's smile was wary. "Yeah. I guess I'm still trying to wrap my brain around it." She downed the rest of her glass and set it aside, reaching for the one bag they hadn't opened yet. "Time for dessert, don't you think?"

They cracked open fortune cookies and read them aloud.

"Love is for the lucky and the brave," Jessie's said. She didn't feel either, particularly.

"A truly rich life contains love and art in abundance." Isabel looked skeptical.

"That fits you perfectly, Isa."

"A little too much if you ask me. Read yours, Sara."

"Change is happening in your life, so go with the flow."

Jessie smiled, "Perfect advice for you Sara."

After packing up the leftovers, they lay back, side by side on the blanket, the black pool of sky and stars turning their voices to whispers.

"So what happened when you went home, Sara?" Isabel asked softly.

"How do you know something happened?"

"There's something different about you."

Sara smiled to herself. A difference inside and out. She told them about the chains, and the terror of being trapped in a void sent shivers all over Jessie's body. Isabel clutched Jessie's hand on the blanket, affected too by Sara's tale. She related how Bloom caught her when the chains disappeared and the electrifying touch Bloom had given her from head to toe.

"But then the most amazing thing happened. Bloom took me to Hearst Castle. I was there and I saw the statue again."

"Really?" Jessie exclaimed. "What did it feel like? The first time we saw them?"

"I realized looking around that the place may be beautiful, but they are more so. When Bloom comes to me she is ... illuminating. Isn't that true of your encounters with the Graces, too?"

Jessie turned to look at Sara, saw the tears, even though Sara's voice was even as she went on. "I saw them differently this time. I saw myself, my actual body in each of theirs. I saw how…beautiful I am."

Jessie handed over a napkin from their take out bag and Sara wiped her eyes with a smile.

"We've been trying to tell you that all along," Isabel said softly from Jessie's other side.

"I know, I know. I think between you two and Bloom, it finally got through."

They were quiet then, each lost in thought. Jessie remembered every visit with Brilliance. The warmth. The vitality she'd been drawn to. The things she'd felt and seen. She'd been the first to accept that these strange things happening to them were real. But she kept coming back to the same questions. Why them? Why that moment? Everything hinged on the statue. When she'd touched the figure in stone, at the same time Isabel and Sara had, they'd somehow connected with the goddesses themselves. But why would The Graces be living in the statue? Were they in other works of art, too?

"We still don't know why they chose us, how they come to us, and why they gave us these necklaces," Jessie said, breaking the silence.

Sara pushed up on one elbow, the darkness obscuring her expression. "Because we needed them."

"They seem to be helping you and Isa more than me."

"Maybe they helped the others Joy showed me that day," Isabel said thoughtfully.

"You brought the drawings?" Sara asked her.

"Yes. Why?"

"When I got out of the car I was going to leave my bag behind but somehow I knew I needed to bring my journal."

Isabel reached for her bag. "Same here. It was like my portfolio was shouting at me from the back seat. Weird, huh?"

"They're trying to tell us something. Again." Jessie said. She stretched her arms over her head, relieving the stiffness in her shoulders and sat up. "We're smart. We have to be able to figure it out."

"Come on, let's look," Sara encouraged.

Isabel opened her portfolio, took out the first drawing. Pulling the lamp closer, she studied it, her eyes grew distant as she relived what happened in that room. "I think it began here. This night. Something happened. At this moment."

Sara opened her journal and found the part Isabel had described about the artist and the statue. "I wrote, 'There lingered both sad resignation and a growing jubilation as the celebratory farewell toast was made by his friends,' because of the way you described it Isabel."

"That's it." Jessie tugged the paper from Isabel's hand and examined the face in the drawing. "You had a similar look this afternoon discussing the sale of your work, Isa."

Sara glanced up. "So somehow that night The Graces became part of the statue. We don't know why or how, though. Do you think the answers are here?" She gestured to the portfolio. "And that's why Joy took Isabel there?"

"That sounds right, Sara, so let's assume that's true." Jessie moved the lantern closer and flipped through the portfolio, pulling out the main scenes, leaving the rest. "Maybe more important is the journey they've been on inside the statue. Joy showed you all the statue's different homes."

They sat cross-legged, the drawings in sequence in front of them.

"Not just the homes," Sara said after a moment, "the people too." She examined the second one again. "Don't you think it's interesting that there's a book open on the Duchess' lap and a pen in her hand?"

"Maybe she journaled. Like you, Sara."

"I read the little that is known about her. Apparently, at first she had a strained relationship with her husband. Over the years that changed and they were reported to have been happy in the later years of their lives."

"Maybe when the statue was bought?" Jessie felt that same slowing of time she'd sensed when they'd first arrived. Pulling her golden ribbon free from her sweater, she caressed it lightly, sure they were on the right track. Hoping The Graces would appear.

"Why do you think they're in the statue?" Sara asked.

"That's only where we first encountered them. I just know I'd hate it. Being trapped like that," Isabel said.

Jessie straightened. "Of course." How had they not guessed it before? "They're trapped. Why else would they be there?" At the edges of her vision, lights flickered, momentarily distracting her.

Sara hummed low in her throat. "But how can they be trapped when they appear to us?"

Yes.

And as seemed to happen a lot lately, an overwhelming sadness threatened to smother Jessie. Grief at all she'd lost felt like an insidious companion. The flat engraved disk of Jessie's pendant flared with heat beneath her fingers. She dimly heard a voice calling her name as her world went completely dark for an instant.

She was alone.

Face down on a bed of grass.

Why did she end up in the maze when they were so close to figuring it out? Turning her head, she realized there was light, faint, but out of sight. Quickly she pushed herself up, leaves and earth clinging to her top and jeans, even her knee-high boots. Tall hedges stood sentinel on all sides, the branches thick and tightly entwined. She brushed herself off as she got her bearings.

This was the same corridor she'd come to before. The scent of trees and earth was the same, as were the look and feel of the hedges. Only the music was startlingly absent. She waited for a moment. Usually something happened without her having to take but a few steps. Not this time.

Only darkness was at the bend in one direction, so she went toward what appeared to be a light the other way. As soon as she turned the corner her breath caught in her throat and she stopped.

She stood next to her mother in the nightmare of her father's death. The sun was hot on the pavement and her mother was sobbing and pleading with her father not to die. The sounds of panic surrounded her, the police sirens getting louder, coming closer. She felt a hand at her back gently guiding her.

She whirled around, but there was nobody there.

Jessie took a final moment to look at the scene.

Her mother still had that dress in the back of her closet, she realized. Her father was looking at her with love in his eyes, knowing he wasn't going to make it. And she knew this was her second chance.

"Goodbye, Daddy," she whispered. "I love you."

She forced her feet to move, around another corner that took her farther into the depths of the labyrinth.

Mario lay on the wet ground next to a motorcycle overturned a foot away. Two people stood to the side, the man calling 911, the woman wiping tears from her face. Heart stumbling, Jessie knelt beside Mario. She took his hand and gently removed the leather glove so she could touch his skin. His hair was matted with blood and dirt. Pushing a lock of it back from his face, Jessie watched his lashes flutter open.

His mouth lifted slowly into a smile. "Sing for me."

But she had. At the studio, at his funeral. She almost said so but his eyes closed again.

"No, wait," she pleaded, gripping his hand tighter. She wanted to listen to him, she really did. "Don't go. I miss you. I need you."

Hands lifted her to her feet but she knew if she turned to look there would be no one there. His smile faded. Then he was gone, leaving behind wet grass and walls of shrubs.

The passage was getting slightly narrower. Jessie rubbed her eyes to still the tears and rubbed her arms for warmth before continuing. With one hand she touched the side of the maze in passing, while the other clutched her necklace. Ahead, there was a flash of a bare white shoulder and flowing emerald silk that vanished as the path veered sharply to the right.

Brilliance.

When she got to the bend, a loud creaking sound halted her progress. The path was a dead end. A terrible slashing from behind had her spinning. Vines and branches flew past as if pulled by a magnet to the other side. She ducked. One caught her on the shoulder knocking her to the ground.

Within minutes she was surrounded by thick branches and confined within their leaves.

Her labored gasps filled her ears, shock holding her immobile. She wanted to fight it, her first instinct to thrash her way out. But the sun medallion, still grasped in one hand, steadied her just enough that she fought the impulse.

She was curled on her side, with room to breathe. For the moment. Her shoulder ached from the blow and from lying on it. Jessie thought about Isabel and the cave wall closing in on her. Sara too, had faced the horror of the chains in an unending void. Just thinking of them helped.

Focus, Jessie.

She replayed her visits to the labyrinth from the first time until now. The music had started it. A song that reminded her of her dad. She'd chased after him but never caught him. Then Mario, too, had died and that's when she'd stopped hearing the song. Just moments ago she'd been given the chance to say a final farewell to them both. She realized that all through her grieving for her father and even in the short days since Mario's death, she'd never done that. Never put them to rest. But they had wanted her to sing. They believed in her. Why didn't she? She'd always thought she had confidence, except that she'd hidden her one true talent away for all those years. Now Phil was giving her the opportunity the two men in her life, each in his own way, had pushed her toward.

Did she dare take it?

How could she not?

"Jessie! Jessie!" Muted yet insistent voices penetrated the dense foliage.

"Sara? Isabel? Where are you?" Jessie's voice, hoarse at first, gained strength quickly as she realized she was no longer alone. "I can't get out. I'm trapped and the maze is so thick it's impossible to press through."

"We're here." Sara's voice called out.

"We need to find a way to get you out." Isabel's frustration was evident.

Jessie sighed at the sound of their voices so close. If they could just figure out what to do. "Are you two okay? Have you seen the Graces?" she asked.

Sara's laugh was light and quick. "We're fine. You need to get yourself out of there."

"We could try and help her, you know," Isabel's grumble came through loud and clear.

"Jessie, listen to me." Sara sounded suddenly very sure of herself. "I figured out how to get out of the chains with Bloom's help, and Isa got out of the cave with Joy's. You're smart. Figure it out."

"Imagine Brilliance there with you. She'll come," Isabel ordered.

God, she loved Sara and Isabel. She really did. It was obvious, and yet, she'd needed her friends to help her see it.

Everything around her flickered dark then bright, like a strobe light. The maze, the garden at the castle. Her alone, then with Isabel and Sara. She closed her eyes and pictured Brilliance. Remembered the feel of her warm skin, how it felt to walk hand-in-hand.

Heat filled her hand, radiated up her arm. Eyes flying open, Jessie found herself lying face to face next to the goddess. Who drew her up to her feet, the branches easing away in their wake.

When she pulled her eyes from the beauty of Brilliance's features, she noticed the labyrinth still surrounded them but at a respectable distance. Still, the only way Jessie could think of to get out was to make the final decision. Not the decision to go to San Francisco or stay in Boulder. But to sing or not to sing.

"If I decide not to sing, I will always be trapped in the maze," she said to Brilliance, who smiled serenely at her. "If I sing, I will be free." Jessie clasped the Grace's hand tighter. "I want to sing."

Nothing changed. She waited in hushed anticipation.

"I choose to sing!" she shouted.

Jessie tumbled into Sara's waiting arms, swiftly followed by Isabel's close embrace. Laughing, they hugged each other for long minutes until Jessie's trembling stopped and she was able to pull back and look at the familiar mountains around them, the dark night lit by the soft glow of a rising moon.

"The foothills never looked so good," Jessie said, and they laughed again.

"We heard you, you know. We'll hold you to it," Isabel warned.

"Look," Sara said, pointing behind Jessie.

Brilliance, Joy and Bloom held out their hands, beckoning them.

"I didn't think I'd see Joy again after she helped me the other night," said Isabel.

"I told you," Sara whispered. "They're breathtaking."

Jessie took a long look at Brilliance. At the striking beauty, the glorious curve of each feature. Her gaze settled on the eyes. So full and wise. Yet, heartbroken. Brimming with sorrow.

"Why do they look so sad?" she asked, noticing the same melancholy in Joy and Bloom.

"Why don't we find out what they want?" Isabel asked, acknowledging the outstretched arms.

Fingertips met, palms touched.

The air became warm, decidedly different from the thinness of the mile-high Rockies. A tangy sea breeze lifted the hair from their shoulders. They stood in the passageway between the house and the garden at Hearst Castle. Light from ground fixtures illuminated the flagstone pathway as the six of them walked to the statue in its alcove.

Jessie looked at the creation in stone and back to the Graces beside them in amazement.

"Perfect symmetry," said Isabel.

"It's incredible, isn't it?" Sara breathed softly.

In a blink, the Graces were gone and only the statue remained. Jessie reached for Isabel, who caught up Sara's hand.

"However they came to be inside the statue, I don't think they want to remain there." Jessie nodded to the work of marble.

"But what do we do?" asked Sara.

"How can we help?" Isabel stared at the figures.

"Get closer," Jessie suggested. "Maybe we just need to touch them like we did the first time."

They agreed to try on the count of three.

Nothing.

Think.

Jessie stepped away, Isabel and Sara followed without missing a beat.

"We have to stick together," Isabel said with a shake of her head. "Don't go off without us."

"Concentrate," Sara said. "There has to be something we can do." She paced a few steps then turned back.

Jessie pushed at the curls that kept blowing into her face, never taking her eyes off Sara or Isabel. "Mostly they've helped us, guided us."

Sara sucked in a breath sharply. "We were trapped, just like they are."

"They need to find their way, just like we found ours," Isabel said slowly.

Jessie was listening while part of her kept going back to what had happened before. Each time they appeared, it had been to help her or Sara or Isabel. Except when Joy had taken Isabel to their past.

"You've got your bag, Isabel," Jessie said, pointing to the strap across Isabel's body. "But not your portfolio."

"No, but I've got the drawings," she said, pulling her bag to the front and opening the flap. "When you disappeared on us, I gathered them up and stuffed them in here," she explained.

Isabel took out the first drawing of the three men.

Jessie grabbed Sara's arm and tugged at the purse she had slung over her shoulder. "Where's your journal?"

"Right here," Sara said, removing the small book with a flourish. "What are you thinking, Jessie?"

"These just might do the trick." Jessie towed Isabel and Sara back to the statue.

Isabel looked skeptical.

Sara's face lit up with excitement. "Three is a magical, mystical number. And look, three of them, three of us."

Jessie felt a flutter deep inside. "I just got one of those nervous feelings, like time is running out."

"So?" Isabel said impatiently. "Keep going, Sara."

"So, by my count, we've got three goddesses, three women and only two things: your drawings and my story."

The full force of their stares fell on her. The flutter had turned to a growing wave of fear and excitement. Drawing was Isabel's gift, writing was Sara's.

They all knew hers.

The Graces had the chance to be free. But it all depended on Isabel's, Sara's and her own willingness to act. To use their gifts. Isabel had done her part. Sara hers. Now it appeared, it was up to Jessie.

That panic she'd known as she'd faced the congregation at Mario's funeral came back to her.

"You can do it, Jess. We know you can."

Jessie shook her head trying to clear her mind. "This is what we'll do. Isabel, hold all the drawings in one hand. Got it? Good, stand here," she directed. "Sara, stand to her right with your journal." Jessie moved into place on Isabel's left.

303

"What are you going to sing?" Sara asked, the book secure in her hand.

"I don't know."

"You're gonna have to do what you did at the service." Isabel shifted, placing one hand on top of the drawings to keep them from being carried away in the wind. "C'mon. I think we've got to hurry."

"Concentrate on them. It'll come to you," Sara encouraged.

Jessie nodded. "Ready?" She trailed her fingers over the arm of the figure that was Brilliance, watching Isabel and Sara do the same to Joy and Bloom. Clouds were moving in quickly. The swaying trees cast dancing shadows all around them.

Quieting her mind, focusing on the gifts the Graces had given them, Jessie sang.

"Love shook my heart
like the wind on the mountain
rushing over the oak trees."

The words, ones she'd never thought or sung before, flowed from a place she couldn't name, didn't recognize. But there was a freedom in it and her heart took flight. With a voice that was clear, pure and bright, she gave the gift of herself in song.

A rumble rolled toward them on Jessie's final note. Under their feet the earth shook, and the air above roared in a tempest of thunder and lightning. For an instant the Graces appeared again next to the statue in a blinding light that was so intense and beautiful it hurt to look at it.

Then they vanished.

Red Rocks Park returned.

She held Isabel and Sara in a tight embrace, their breaths sharp like her own. Stillness clung to the night, marking it. They stood for a while like that until the serenity of the mountain air settled her shaking heart and trembling hands. She met Sara's eyes, then Isabel's.

"There are no words to describe that." Jessie thought it the most wondrous thing she would ever see.

"We did it, didn't we?" Sara still clutched the journal tightly like a talisman. "I don't think my legs will hold me up any longer." She sank to the blanket.

Jessie felt like she'd run for miles without stopping. She slid down beside Sara, pulling Isabel down with her.

Isabel was smiling as she smoothed out the edges of one of the pictures. "Did you see them at the end of the song? I have to try and draw them again."

"I think they'd like that. The ideal finale to all this." Jessie gestured to the drawings, journal, the three of them. "And Sara must write it."

"But there really is no end, is there?" Sara reached out and touched Jessie then Isabel where their necklaces lay. "We still have these. We still have each other."

Epilogue

The three sister goddesses stood ready and waiting. Candles were lit, the table overflowed with savory dishes on full platters, and music swirled around the room.

A bell chimed. The guests were arriving.

The youngest sister, Brilliance, smiled at the couple that entered. The handsome young man, whose name she remembered was Phil, set a bottle of wine on the table and helped Jessie take off her jacket. The goddess was pleased to see he had impeccable taste in drink and was courteous as well as good-looking. She observed Jessie with fondness, in her slim-fitting red dress and matching high heels. Gliding over, Brilliance brushed a hand over her siren's arm. Happiness radiated outward, encompassing the entire room.

The middle sister, Joy, watched with pleasure as her beloved artist Isabel, dressed in black pants and an emerald blouse, extended an embrace with genuine affection to both guests. Her man, Michael, attractive and good-hearted too, entered from the kitchen with long-stemmed glasses, offered his greetings and began to open the wine. Joy held her sisters' arms, content that at this gathering, there would be no work to do. They could relax and join in the celebration.

Bloom, the eldest, breathed a sigh of relief as the bell chimed again and the two women rushed to open the door. The third of their beloved threesome, Sara, stepped over the threshold, impeccably dressed in a wool pantsuit and high-heeled boots. She made some remark to the vibrant redhead who accompanied her and there was laughter and hugs all around.

The Graces listened in.

"You look fabulous," Jessie said.

"We all do," Sara replied with a smile.

"I meant happy, content." Jessie put one arm through Sara's and led her into the room. "Living with Leslie agrees with you."

Sara glanced back with a smile at her partner. Isabel was showing her the latest piece of art showcased on the living room wall.

Jessie handed Sara a glass and smiled as Phil passed her one. "Thanks. So, how long did it take her to do that one, Michael?" she asked.

"A few months. I surprised her by hanging it today. It looks great there, doesn't it?" "Absolutely," Phil said. "Sorry we missed your opening, Isabel. It just wasn't possible with Jessie's tour schedule."

"It's still at the gallery. You can go while you're here." Satisfaction and pride were evident in Michael's face as he watched Isabel point out some detail to Leslie.

Jessie sipped her wine and smiled as Phil eased his arm around her and pulled her close.

"Did you bring me the CD you promised?" Sara asked. When Jessie nodded, she added, "Did you sign it?"

Jessie laughed. "I will. Why don't you just download it?"

"I have. But I want something I can hold in my hand, show everyone. I'm making a collection of all our stuff. You know how I am." Sara sighed and took a drink of wine before continuing, "Leslie thinks I'm a little nuts that way."

"Do not," Leslie said, from across the room. "Hey, where's our drinks?"

Michael filled two more glasses and joined the group in front of Isabel's charcoal print.

In silence, everyone studied her most recent depiction of the statue in the garden. It reached from floor to ceiling in height. Shards of light, all jagged edges, broke apart the stone, shattered pieces everywhere.

"Jessie and I visited Hearst Castle a couple months ago," Phil commented. "After seeing all your drawings, Isabel, I had to check out the statue for myself."

"Oh, that's not even half of it. Wait 'til you read Sara's book. You'll never think of it the same again," Leslie sent a teasing smile in Sara's direction.

"We should have a toast," Phil suggested.

"Great idea," said Michael, lifting his glass. "How about to The Graces?"

"Oh, no, no," Isabel shook her head with a look for help in Jessie's direction.

"Isabel's right. Let's just celebrate us."

"Yes," Sara agreed, "to all of us."

At the clink of glasses, Brilliance, Joy and Bloom were reassured, watching with affection and pleasure, knowing their handiwork would continue to bear fruit.

Author's Notes

The Three Graces, *Euphrosyne, Aglaea and Thalia*, are as you've come to know them, Brilliance, Joy and Bloom. In Greek mythology they were the goddesses of beauty, delight, festivity, dance and song. They were attendants to Aphrodite and other deities and always depicted together since it was believed that true joy exists only in circles where an individual gives up the self to pleasure others.

The statue of the Three Graces that resides at Hearst Castle is a copy by an artist named Boyer, modeled after the original by Antonio Canova.

John Russell, the sixth Duke of Bedford, commissioned the second of Canova's Graces' statues after seeing Canova work on one for Napoleon's wife Josephine. It is interesting to note that Canova was responsible for the original design of the statue, but had assistants roughly block out the figures. He then completed the final carving himself to ensure the soft flesh of the figures and a harmonious relationship among the three. This statue is now jointly owned by the Victoria and Albert Museum and the National Galleries of Scotland.

All of my historical characters lived, including Canova's friend Falier, who was the son of Canova's patron. Canova did indeed have a half-brother with the surname Sartori.

Even though I have the Graces arriving at San Simeon in 1926, Norman Rotanzi didn't begin working at La Cuesta Encantata until 1934. He became head gardener in 1948 and worked there until his death in 1992. George Loorz was Superintendent of Construction from 1932 to 1941. Mr. Loorz considered the Hearst Castle project the most important of his career. After his death, his family found personal letters and saved memorabilia that detail the people and the time.

As one of the first women to break the barrier into the male-dominated world of architects, Julia Morgan was respected and admired for her commitment, her designs and her planning. However, her role at the Castle extended way beyond that to include all purchasing, hiring and firing, feeding and housing of workers, and caretaking of the art and land. She was an amazing woman.

My characters in the present day are fictional.

If you would like to read more interesting facts about the historical people and places in my novel, here are some starting points. Enjoy!

Loe, Nancy, *Hearst Castle: An Interpretive History of W.R. Hearst's San Simeon Estate*, Santa Barbara CA, Jane Freeburg Publisher, 1994.

http://www.vam.ac.uk/content/articles/t/the-three-graces/

http://articles.latimes.com/1985-01-27/realestate/re-9933_1_san-simeon

http://hearstcastle.org/history-behind-hearst-castle/archival-information/

http://www.getty.edu/art/gettyguide/artMakerDetails?maker=361

Meet The Author: Michele Wolfe

Michele Wolfe, a resident of sunny Southern California, has done extensive research on the statue of The Graces, the sculptor, and Hearst Castle. She is also an art appreciator and belongs to the Greater Los Angeles Writers' Society as well as a Santa Barbara writing group. During the day she is an English as a Second Language (ESL) instructor with 25 years experience teaching and exploring the written word. Along with The Three Graces, Michele has also written a short fiction piece about an immigrant family in LA.

WEBSITE/ FACEBOOK/ TWITTER

Made in the USA
San Bernardino, CA
25 June 2014